"Terrific . . . wonderfully entertaining . . . a literary delight. . . . There's a bit of John Updike's *Rabbit* trilogy in this charming narrative, just as there are traces of Richard Brautigan's *In Watermelon Sugar*. But mostly there's Peter Hedges, who grabs the reader early on with this tale. . . . The pace of the narrative sweeps the reader along to a most compelling and poignant conclusion. . . . Nuggets pop off the page with regularity and make this story come alive. . . . WHAT'S EATING GILBERT GRAPE has the feel of simplicity, but you know you're reading something complex and artistically crafted. The book has the air of whimsy, but will grab you with fierce credibility. Hedges is a young author to be reckoned with."

—Cedar Rapids Gazette

"Hedges writes with energy and wit . . . charged with sardonic intelligence."

—The Washington Post Book World

"A very funny, ultimately moving book. . . . Hedges gives us something rarely seen these days—small town Midwestern life. Not just characters but the context of little towns comes alive here. . . . But Hedges does more than give us a slice of this life; he takes a slap at it as well. Gilbert lets loose with biting observations. . . . The conclusion . . . leaves us both emotionally rewarded and well entertained. That's a rare combination. . . ."

—Winston-Salem Journal

"WHAT'S EATING GILBERT GRAPE is a story that outruns the covers of the book in which it is contained. Once you read this story, it will be with you forever—this place and these people will live in your heart and in the blood it pumps. I am utterly dumbfounded when a first novel of this quality comes along. I send Peter Hedges the ultimate compliment one writer can send another: I'll surely read the next thing you write."

—Harry Crews

WHAT'S EATING GILBERT GRAPE

Peter Hedges

Simon & Schuster Paperbacks
New York London Toronto Sydney

Simon & Schuster Paperbacks
Rockefeller Center
1230 Avenue of the Americas
New York, NY 10020

This Simon & Schuster paperback edition 2005

SIMON & SCHUSTER PAPERBACKS and colophon are registered trademarks of Simon & Schuster, Inc.

For information about special discounts for bulk purchases, please contact Simon & Schuster Special Sales at 1-800-456-6798 or business@simonandschuster.com.

Manufactured in the United States of America

20 19 18

Library of Congress Control Number: 94132330

ISBN-13: 978-0-671-73509-8
ISBN-10:   0-671-73509-8
ISBN-13: 978-0-671-03854-0 (Pbk)
ISBN-10:   0-671-03854-0 (Pbk)

The author gratefully acknowledges permission to reprint lyrics from the following:
        "Taking Care of Business" by Randy C. Bachman. © 1973 Top Soil Music. All Rights Reserved. Used by Permission.
        "Iowa Corn Song." Lyric by R. W. Lockard and George Hamilton. Music by Edward Riley and George Botsford. © 1921 Edwin H. Morris & Company, a Division of MPL Communications, Inc. © Renewed 1949 Edwin H. Morris & Company, a Division of MPL Communications, Inc. International Copyright Secured. All Rights Reserved.

for my mother
  who is not fat
and my father
  who is not dead

Part One

1

Standing with my brother Arnie on the edge of town has become a yearly ritual.

My brother Arnie is so excited because in minutes or hours or sometime today trucks upon trailers upon campers are going to drive into our home town of Endora, Iowa. One truck will carry the Octopus, another will carry the Tilt-A-Whirl with its blue and red cars, two trucks will bring the Ferris wheel, the games will be towed, and most important, the horses from the merry-go-round will arrive.

For Arnie, this is better than Christmas. This beats the tooth fairy and the Easter bunny: all those stupid figures that only kids and retarded adults seem to stomach. Arnie is a retard. He's about to turn eighteen and my family is planning an enormous party. Doctors said we'd be lucky if he lived to be ten. Ten came and went and now the doctors are saying, "Any time now, Arnie could go at any time." So every night my sisters and me, and my mom too, go to bed wondering if he will wake up in the morning. Some days you want him to live, some days you don't. At this particular moment, I've a good mind to push him in front of the oncoming traffic.

My oldest sister, Amy, has fixed us a picnic feast. In a thermos was a quart of black cherry Kool-Aid, all of which Arnie drank in such a hurry that above his top lip is a purplish mustache. One of the first things you should know about Arnie is that he always has traces of some food on his face–Kool-Aid or ketchup or toast crumbs. His face is a kind of bulletin board for the four major food groups.

Arnie is the gentlest guy, but he can surprise this brother. In the summertime, he catches grasshoppers and sticks them in this metal tab on the mailbox, holding them there, and then he brings down the metal flag, chopping off the grasshopper heads. He always giggles hysterically when he does this, having the time of his life. But last night, when we were sitting on the porch eating ice cream, a countless sea of grasshopper bodies from summers past must have appeared to him, because he started weeping and sobbing like the world had ended. He kept saying, "I killed 'em, I killed 'em." And me and Amy, we held him close, patted his back and told him it was okay.

Arnie cried for hours, cried himself to sleep. Makes this brother wonder what kind of a world it would be if all the surviving Nazis had such remorse. I wonder if it ever occurs to them what they did, and if it ever sinks in to a point that their bodies ache from the horrible mess they made. Or are they so smart that they can lie to us and to themselves? The beautiful thing about Arnie is that he's too stupid to lie. Or too smart.

I'm standing with binoculars, looking down Highway 13; there is no sign of our annual carnival. The kid is on his knees, his hands rummaging around in the picnic basket. Having already eaten both bags of potato chips, both peanut-butter-and-jelly sandwiches and both chocolate donuts, he locates a green apple and bites into it.

By trying to ignore Arnie's lip-smacking noises, I am attempting the impossible. You see, he chews as if he's just found his mouth and the sounds are that of good, sloppy sex. My brother's slurps and gulps make me want to procreate with an assortment of Endora's finest women.

It's the twenty-first of June, the first day of summer, the longest day of the year. It isn't even 7:00 A.M. yet and here I stand, little brother in tow. Somewhere some smart person still sleeps.

"Gilbert?"

"Yeah?"

Bread crust and peanut-butter chunks fall off Arnie's T-shirt as he stretches it down past his knees. "Gilbert?"

"What is it?"

"How many more miles?"

"I don't know."

"How many, how many more till the horses and stuff?"

"Three million."

"Oh, okay."

Arnie blows out his lips with a sound like a motorboat and he circles the picnic basket, drool flying everywhere. Finally, he sits down Indian style and starts quietly to count the miles.

I busy myself throwing gravel rocks at the Endora, Iowa, town sign. The sign is green with white printing and, except for a divot that I left last year at this time with my rock throwing, it is in excellent condition. It lists Endora's population at 1,091, which I know can't be right, because yesterday my second-grade teacher, Mrs. Brainer, choked on a chicken bone while sitting on her porch swing. A great loss is felt by no one.

Mrs. Brainer retired years ago. She lived half a block from the town square, so I'd see her pretty much every day, always smiling at me as if she expected me to forget all the pain she'd inflicted. I swear this woman smiled all the time. Once, as she was leaving the store, her sack of groceries ripped. Cans of peaches and fruit cock-tail dropped out onto the floor, cutting open her toes. My boss and I saw this happen. She pushed up a real big grin as the tears fell off her cheeks. I resacked her cans, but she couldn't stop smiling and crying, and her toes couldn't stop bleeding.

I'm told that when they found her on the porch, her hands were up around her throat, and there were red scratch marks on her neck, in her mouth, and pieces of flesh under her fingernails. I won-der if she was smiling then.

Anyway, they took her body to McBurney's Funeral Home in Motley. They'll be planting her tomorrow.

"Gilbert?"

"What?"

"Uhm."

"What?"

"Uhm. The horses, the rides, the horses are coming, right? Right?"

"Yes, Arnie."

Endora is where we are, and you need to know that describing this place is like dancing to no music. It's a town. Farmers. Town square. Old movie theater closed down so we have to drive sixteen miles to Motley to see movies. Probably half the town is over sixty-five, so you can imagine the raring place Endora is on weekend nights. There were twenty-three in my graduating class, and only four are left in town. Most went to Ames or Des Moines and the really ambitious made it over to Omaha. One of those left from my class is my buddy, Tucker. The other two are the Byers brothers, Tim and Tommy. They stayed in town because of a near fatal, crippling car accident, and they just kind of ride around the square racing in their electric wheelchairs. They are like the town mascots, and the best part is they are identical twins. Before the accident no one could tell them apart. But Tim's face was burned, and he's been given this piglike skin. They both were paralyzed but only Tommy lost his feet.

The other day in our weekly paper, the *Endora Express,* pigskin Tim pointed out the bright side in all of this. Now it is easy to tell which is which. After many years Tim and Tommy have finally found their own identities. That's a big thing in Endora these days. Identities. And the bright side. We got people here who've lost their farms to the bank, kids to wars, relatives to disease, and they will look you square in the eye and, with a half grin, they'll tell you the bright side.

The bright side for me is difficult on mornings like these. There's no escaping that I'm twenty-four years old, that I've been out of Iowa a whopping one whole time, that you could say about all I've done in my life to this point is baby-sit my retard brother, buy cigarettes for my mother, and sack groceries for the esteemed citizens of Endora.

"Gilbert?" says Arnie. He has frosting all around his mouth and a glob of jelly above his good eye.

"What, Arnie?"

"You sure they're coming? We've been standing such a *long* time."

"They'll be along any second." I take a napkin from the basket and spit in it.

"No!"

"Come here, Arnie."

"No!"

"Come here."

"Everybody's always wiping me!"

"Why do you think that is?"

"Because."

For Arnie, that is an answer.

I give up on spring cleaning his face and look down the road. The highway is empty.

Last year the big rides came pretty early. The trailers and the campers came later. Arnie is really only interested in the horses from the merry-go-round.

I say, "Hey, Arnie, there's still sleep in my eyes," but he isn't interested. He nibbles on his bottom lip; he's working on a thought.

My little brother is a somewhat round-looking kid with hair that old ladies always want to comb. He is a head shorter than me, with teeth that look confused. There's no hiding that he's retarded. You meet him and you figure it out right away.

"Gilbert! They're not coming!"

I tell him to stop shouting.

"They're not coming at all, Gilbert. The rides got in a big crash and all the workers hung themselves...."

"They will be here," I say.

"They *hung* themselves!"

"No, they didn't."

"You don't know! You don't know!"

"Not everybody hangs himself, Arnie."

He doesn't hear this because he reaches into the basket, stuffs the other green apple inside his shirt, and starts running back to town. I shout for him to stop. He doesn't, so I chase after him and grab his waist. I lift him in the air and the apple drops out onto the brown grass.

"Let me go. Let me go."

I carry him back to the picnic basket. He clings to me, his legs squeeze around my stomach, his fingers dig into my neck. "You're getting bigger. Did you know that?" He shakes his head, convinced I'm wrong. He's not any taller than last year, but he's rounder, puffier. If this keeps up, he'll soon be too big for me to pick up.

"You're still growing. You're getting harder and harder for me to carry. And you're getting so strong, too."

"Nope. It's you, Gilbert."

"It's not me. Believe me, Arnie Grape is getting bigger and stronger. I'm sure of it."

I set him down when I get to the picnic basket. I'm out of breath; beads of sweat have formed on my face.

Arnie says, "You're just getting little."

"You think?"

"I know. You're getting littler and littler. You're shrinking."

Stupid people often say the smartest things. Even Arnie knows that I'm in a rut.

Since I don't believe in wearing a watch, I can't tell the exact time-but this moment, the one when my goofy brother rips the bandage off my heart, is followed by a yelp. Arnie's yelp. He points east, and with the binoculars I locate a tiny dot moving our way. Several dots follow.

"Is it them? Is it them?"

"Yes," I say.

Arnie's jaw drops; he starts dancing.

"Here come the horsies. Here come the horsies!"

He begins howling and jumping up and down in circles; slobber sprays from his mouth. Arnie is entering heaven now. I stand there watching him watch as the rides grow. I just stand there hoping he won't sprout wings and fly away.

2

It's the same morning of the same day, and I'm asleep on the couch in the family room.

I'm truly savoring this period of rest, this catnap, when a rude smell comes dancing up my nose and starts screaming in my head. My eyes smack open. I look around, fuzzy at first, only to find my little sister sitting there in shorts and a halter top, painting her nails. The smell of that–Jesus.

My little sister's name is Ellen. She turned sixteen last month. She also just got her braces off, and for days now she's been walking around the house, running her tongue all over, going "Oo-ah"–like she can't believe the feel of teeth.

Ever since Ellen got her braces off she has been one big pain in the butt. And now with a sudden penchant for lip gloss and painting her toes red, she has bumped to the big time–becoming even more of an already impossible thing.

The smell of the polish forces me to rise up and look her in the eye. She stays fixed on the toe of the moment, so I say, "Little sister, must we?" She keeps painting, coating toe after toe. No response, no answer. So I say, "CAN'T THIS BE DONE SOMEWHERE ELSE?"

Without looking at me, my sister dishes this shit: "Gilbert, some of us are only sixteen. Some of us are trying to do something with our one chance at life. I am trying something new, a brand-new color is being applied, and I could use your support and your encouragement. When that is there I might consider moving, but you are my brother, and if you don't support these new steps, who will? Who will? Tell me, who will!"

She breathes a few times fast through her nose, making a whistly noise.

"I'm at such a difficult age. Girls my age bleed. We bleed every month and it's not like we did anything wrong. Just to be sitting there in church . . ."

"You don't go to church."

"Hypothetical, Gilbert."

"Don't use big words."

"Okay. I'm at work, mixing the toppings or making cones. And suddenly I feel it coming, and I didn't do anything. You are a guy. So you don't know how this feels. You should be understanding, and let me in peace do the one thing that brings me joy and a sense of completion. So thank you, Gilbert, thank you sooooo much!"

I stare at her trying to decide the most discreet way to murder. But she turns suddenly and stomps out of the family room leaving only the smell of her new toes. I decide to smother myself, as it is my most immediate option. Covering my face with an old orange sofa pillow, I begin the process. It gets to the interesting part where my lungs want air and my heart doesn't, when I feel this poking on my arm. This family. If it's Ellen, I'll smother her, first thing. And if it's Arnie, we'll have a pillow fight, laugh a bit, then I'll do the smothering.

But this time the voice is that of my big sister, Amy. She's whispering, "Gilbert, come here."

I don't move.

"Gilbert, please..."

I'm almost dead. Surely she can see this.

"Gilbert!"

I give in to the idea of air and say, "I'm busy" from underneath the pillow.

"You don't look busy."

Amy pries off the cushion and pulls it away from me. My eyes adjust to the sudden light. She's wearing a worried and concerned look. But what else is new? This look of terror is most often her face of choice, and I've grown fond of it. I find its predictability somehow comforting. It's only when Amy smiles that you know something is wrong.

Amy is the oldest of us Grape children. At thirty-four, she's ten years older than me. Most of the time she feels more like a mother than a sister. During the school year she works for the Clover Hills Elementary School in Motley. As assistant manager of the cafeteria, she serves the little ones green beans, frankfurters, and sugar cookies. She also works as a teacher's aide, spending her nights drawing elaborate smiley faces on the papers of those students who make no mistakes. Most important, though, is this—Amy doesn't work in the summers. Since, during the school year, our family finds a way to fall apart, she uses June, July, and August to put us back together.

"I'm sleeping," I say. "I'm *trying* to sleep."

Amy puts the pillow between her fleshy arm and her light blue Elvis T-shirt. She squints, her eyes searing into mine.

"Amy, please. God, if there's a God, please. I took the kid to wait for the rides. We got out there at four-thirty something. I need sleep. I work at ten. Please, Amy. Please! Don't stare at me like that!"

"You might think about Momma."

I want to say that I think about our mother all the time, that every move I make is made with her in mind, but before I can say anything, Amy grabs my wrist and jerks me up. "Ouch. I'm coming already."

Amy pulls me toward the dining room.

"This house stinks," I say. "The smell, God!"

Amy stops. We're standing in the kitchen, buried in several days worth of dirty dishes and numerous sacks of trash. She whispers, "What do you expect? No one helps around the house. Ellen is good for nothing, you're working all the time or never home. I can't do it all."

She takes a deep breath and then turns around in a circle like those fashion models do.

"Look at me. Look."

"Yeah?" I say.

"Don't you see?"

"New outfit? Uhm. I don't know. What do you want me to see?"

"I'm starting to get like Momma."

I lie and say, "You're not."

"My skin is rolling over my clothes. I can't fit into chairs so well."

"Momma's on a whole other level. You're nowhere near . . ."

"These are the early stages, Gilbert. What you see here is the early phase." Amy wipes her eyes with the backs of her hands and smiles.

Oh boy.

Okay.

It's time for you to know the rarely spoken truths about my mother, Bonnie Grape.

There is no nice way to break it to you. My mother is a porker. She started eating in excess the day our dad was found dead seventeen years ago. Since that day, she's been going at it nonstop, adding pound upon pound, year after year, until now we have a situation where no one knows her actual weight. No household scale goes high enough.

Momma has the first room at the top of the stairs, but she doesn't like climbing, or even walking for that matter. She sleeps all day in this blue padded chair and only wakes up for meals and many occasional cigarettes. She doesn't sleep at night but stays in the chair, chain-smoking and watching the TV. We splurged and bought her the kind of television with a remote control. When Momma walks, she holds on to things, she clings to counters and shelves. It will take her fifteen minutes to make it to the bathroom and get situated. She hates baths, and quite honestly, she's barely able to fit in the tub. Not a particularly happy lady, she does laugh when Arnie dances for her and is all smiles when one of us, usually me, brings her a carton of cigarettes. She smokes Kool.

It's been over three years since she stepped out of the house, and other than her children and a former friend here and there, no one in town has seen her. They talk about her, sure, but mostly in whispers. Only the water-meter man during his monthly checks has gotten a good peek at Momma. Dr. Harvey came by once when we thought she was having a heart attack. It was a false alarm, though. Apparently she swallowed wrong, or there was some kind of intestinal gas in her veins, something like that.

If you were to gripe to my mother about her weight, or express in any way any fear you have about her steady growth, she would say "Hey! I'm here! Alive! I didn't cop out like other people we know!"

I've tried to tell Momma that her eating is a suicide of sorts. But those words are never easy.

So.

Amy drags me through the kitchen. We stop short of the dining room where Momma sits snoring with her mouth wide open. Amy points to Momma's feet. They are swollen, very red and purple and dry, crackly. Her feet don't fit into shoes anymore.

"I've seen her feet before," I whisper.

She points again, mouthing these words: "*The floor.*"

I'm unable to believe what I see. The floor below Momma curves down like a contact lens. "Oh my God," I say.

"This is no longer a joking matter, Gilbert."

Once, after several beers, I suggested to a sloshed Amy that maybe Momma would fall through the floor and we'd be done with it. We laughed hard about it then.

"Something's gotta be done about this," Amy says, not laughing now.

Please realize that I'm no carpenter. I have no skill in home repair or craftsmanship. And with that in mind, notice how Amy's still got me in mind to fix the floor.

"Gotta do it without her knowing it," she adds in a hissed whisper.

Amy's right. If Momma knew she was slowly drilling a hole in her house, she would cry for days.

"I'll talk to Tucker."

Tucker is my best friend. He loves to build things—birdhouses, wooden ducks, and shelving for his beer-can collection.

"When will you talk to him?"

"Soon. Real soon, I promise."

"Today."

"I work today."

"This is urgent."

"I'm aware of this, Amy." I walk away, because her face is starting to contort into that weird shape again.

"Later today then. Okay, Gilbert? Gilbert, okay?"

I shout "OKAY!" and Momma wakes up with a snort.

"Morning, Momma," Amy says. "You want some breakfast?"

The next sequence of events define predictability. Momma will say, "Wouldn't you think?" Amy will ask, "What will it be today?" and Momma will order a stack of pancakes or a couple of waffles or French toast, half a pound of bacon, some eggs maybe, fried or scrambled, and lots of pepper. Pepper on everything. And Amy will make whatever Momma wants, and it will taste great, and Momma will clean her plate like a big girl.

Having lost what little appetite I had, I head for fresh air. As I swing open the screen door, Arnie dives into the evergreen bush next to the mailbox. He loves to hide, but only if you take the time to find him. And while I suspect that's true for most people, only a retard or a kid would admit it.

"I wonder where Arnie is," I say too loud. "Where could he be?"

Amy is at the front door and speaks through the screen. "Thanks for talking to Tucker."

I make a face, like it's no problem, point to the bush, and say, "Have you seen Arnie? I can't find him anywhere."

Amy is a pro at this game. "Gilbert, I thought Arnie was with you."

"Nope, not with me."

"Shoot, 'cause I was hoping he'd help me with breakfast."

"I've looked all over for him."

The evergreen bush is giggling.

"Momma's up and she's hungry. Guess I'll have to make those pancakes by myself!"

The garage door rises, and Ellen emerges wearing her candy-cane bikini. Her red toes and fingers match. She unfolds our only lawn chair and lies back to receive the morning sun. In an effort to include her in this, a family activity of the rarest kind, I say, "Ellen, have you seen your brother?"

She ignores me. I look to Amy. The bush is getting restless.

"Little sister, did you hear me? We can't find Arnie."

Ellen flips through *Cosmopolitan* magazine. She's still mad from this morning.

Amy says, "We're looking hard. Have you seen him?"

She pretends to read.

Amy hates not being answered. "Ellen, did you hear me?"

"He's in the bush!"

I will kill her.

"No, he isn't," Amy says. "Gilbert checked the bush."

"Yeah," I say.

"Gilbert is blind and a liar and quite, quite stupid!"

Arnie rises, oblivious, and shouts his traditional "Boo!" I make a big noise and fall to the ground. "You scared me, Arnie. Oh God, you scared me."

With a new batch of pine needles in his hair and a thick streak of dirt across his mouth, he laughs in a way that reminds us he's retarded.

Amy says, "Breakfast," and he runs into the house to watch her cook.

I walk to my pickup, climb in, and it starts up right away. My truck is a 1978 Ford: it's blue, and even though the bottom is rusting out, I know you'd want to go for a ride in it.

Before backing out of the drive, I study my little sister. Most people who sunbathe do so in their backyards; at least this is how most people sunbathe in Iowa. But Ellen will be the first to tell you that she is not most people. She knows that she is the prettiest girl in these parts. And that by strategically placing herself on our oil-stained driveway, she also knows that all day long cars and trucks and bicycles from all over the county will drive past and watch as she toasts her skin. Ellen likes an audience.

I've this dream of building Arnie a lemonade stand and setting him up in business. The kid would make a killing.

I honk my horn, even though it's a sound I can't stand. Ellen looks up, and in an attempt to make peace, I wave and shout, "Have a nice day!"

She says nothing, pushes out a fist with the back of her hand facing me, and her middle finger stretches toward the sun. It stands there like a candle.

She loves me—she just doesn't know it yet.

I wait for her finger to go away, and when it doesn't, I shift into drive and take my foot off the brake. My truck and I roll slowly toward her. She looks up confident that she'll win. The closer I get, the louder her laugh becomes. At three feet, I press on the horn, and she is up and off the lawn chair. Before she can pull it out of the way, I accelerate fast and drive over it, crush.

The chair is dead.

Ellen stands to the side, her face matching the red in her bikini, the red on her toes. She wants to cry, but it would mess up her makeup.

I was fine till the finger, I say to myself, as I shift to reverse. You don't flip off Gilbert Grape. Let that be known.

As Ellen struggles to bend the chair back into shape, I back out of the driveway. I see Arnie looking out the living-room window. He starts banging his forehead on the glass. He does this seven, eight times before Amy pulls him away.

3

In Endora, there are two grocery stores. Smack on the town square is Lamson Grocery, where I work, and on the edge of town, there is Food Land, where everyone else shops.

Food Land was built last October. Apparently, it's loaded full of every cereal imaginable and Italian sausage that hangs down. They say a smile can be found in every one of their fourteen aisles. They installed these electric doors that open when your foot hits the black rubber mat. Many would say that this is the greatest thing ever to happen in Endora. Also, they installed a stereo system that plays this dentistlike, elevator-like music, whatever you call it. The *Endora Express* reported at the time that this music was intended to calm the customer, to soothe. Please, spare us. Food Land is equipped with special cash registers that have conveyor belts, the kind of belt you see in Des Moines, the kind you never thought would make it to Endora.

Food Land had a kind of grand-opening celebration this past March. Amy made me drive Arnie and her. Having made up my mind never to set foot inside, I sat in my truck while Amy took the retard in for a look around. She said that when Arnie saw the beans and Pop-Tarts and peanut butter move along the belt for the first time, he started whooping and hollering.

I regret having to describe Food Land to you. I tried to avoid even mentioning that garbage dump, but there is no way around it—not if you are to fully understand Mr. Lamson and Lamson Grocery and why I, Gilbert Grape, can still be found there in his employ.

You won't find electric doors and conveyor belts and computerized cash registers at Lamson Grocery. The store is composed of only four aisles—each only twenty-one feet long. Lamson Grocery contains everything that a reasonable person requires. But if you need the trappings of technology to think you're getting a good bargain, then I guess you better mosey your brainless body down to Food Land.

We at Lamson Grocery price every product by hand. We talk to our customers, we greet them without faking a smile, we say your name. "Hello, Dan." "Hello, Carol." "Hi there, Marty, you need some help?" If a person wants to write us a check, we don't take down all kinds of information or make you prove that you're you. There's none of that crap. We say without saying it that your word is good. Then we sack up your groceries and carry them out to your car.

Perhaps it is this excess of integrity that keeps the crowds away from Lamson Grocery. Perhaps Mr. Lamson is like a constant reminder of our shortcomings. A man who works all day, every day and loves each apple he uncrates, who cherishes each can of soup–a man like that surely puts us all to shame.

I started working for Mr. Lamson on a part-time basis when I was fourteen, and since graduating from high school seven years ago, I've worked full-time.

It is a white building with gray steps, red trim, and a sincere sign that reads, "Lamson Grocery–Serving you since 1932."

I push open the door that says ENTER and see Mr. Lamson at the cash register. His wife of a thousand years is in the little closetlike cubicle that we use as our office, stacking pennies. The store is empty of customers. As I get my apron from off the hook, he says, "Good morning, Gilbert."

"Hi, boss." I poke my head in the cubicle and say, "Good morning, Mrs. Lamson." She looks up and smiles the nicest smile. I get the push broom from the back and start sweeping Aisle One.

Mr. Lamson moves toward me, his hands in his pockets. "Son, are you all right?"

"Uhm, yeah. Why?"

"You look like you aged ten years. Honey, look at Gilbert."

"I'm in the middle of counting."

"Is something wrong at home?"

There is always something wrong at home. "No, sir," I say.

Mrs. Lamson pokes her head out of the office. "Oh, he just looks tired. You just look tired, that's all."

"Is that what it is?"

"You're looking at me like I'm dying, please, I'm not dying. It was an early morning. I took Arnie out to see the carnival rides come in. I didn't get a whole lot of sleep."

"How do they look?"

"The rides? Okay, I guess. You know, same old rides."

Mr. Lamson nods as if he knows what I mean. He goes to the cash register, rings it open, and brings me a crisp five. "This will help."

"Huh?" I say.

"Arnie and the merry-go-round. This will get him a couple of rides, right?"

"Yes, sir," I say. "It will buy a bunch of tickets."

"Good." Mr. Lamson walks away.

There is nothing he wouldn't do for Arnie. I put the five in my back pocket and continue my sweep.

I'm whipping down Aisle Four, my rhythm really rolling, when I see two feet in ladies' shoes. A cloud of dust floats over these shoes, and I look up to find Mrs. Betty Carver standing before me dressed like a Sunday-school teacher. She sneezes.

"Gilbert."

"Hi," I say.

"Bless me."

"Huh?"

"You bless a person when they sneeze."

"Oh. Bless you."

"I can't reach the Quaker Oats. Could you for me?"

"Yes, ma'am."

She smiles when I say "ma'am." I notice my fingernails are dirty. I try to hide my hands.

The Quaker Oats are on the top shelf in Aisle Three, and I'm tall enough to reach. I hand her a box. Mr. Lamson comes around the corner and says, "Oh, Gilbert got that for you. Good."

Mrs. Betty Carver suddenly blurts out, "Is Gilbert a good employee?"

"Yes. The best I've ever had."

"He's reliable, I assume. Conscientious?"

18

"Yes. Very."

She follows him to the cash register. "I'm perplexed, then. Why is it, do you think, that he's not prompt with his insurance payments? For his truck. Why do you think that is?"

Mrs. Betty Carver is the wife of Ken Carver, the only insurance man left in Endora.

"I'm afraid you'll have to ask Gilbert that."

She turns to look at me.

"I'm sorry," I say. "I'll take care of it right away."

"Of course you will," Mr. Lamson says. "In fact, Gilbert, why don't you run on over there and set the matter straight right now?"

"No!" Mrs. Carver practically shouts. Then looking at me, and in this churchlike voice she says, "I believe an afternoon appointment would be better."

I look at my feet and say nothing.

Mrs. Betty Carver and the Quaker Oats are gone.

"That woman could have been a movie star," Mrs. Lamson says. "Don't you think, dear?"

"Prob'ly so," Mr. Lamson says, all the while looking at me. "You think she could have been a movie star, Gilbert, huh?"

I find the broom and go back to sweeping.

It's forty minutes later and there have been no customers since Mrs. Betty Carver. I'm in the back of the store. Mr. and Mrs. Lamson are up front. Opening a carton of eggs, I drop two of them on the floor. I break the shells of three more. I make a noise like I just fell. From the floor I start yelling, "Darn it. Man! I can't believe this!"

Mr. Lamson hurries down Aisle Three. "What is it? What's wrong?"

He sees the eggs. I sit there, my hands covering my face. "I can't believe this day. I'm sorry. I'm really sorry, boss. . . ."

"It's all right, son. You're having one heck of a day."

"Yes, sir."

"Listen. Clean up the mess, okay? Then take the rest of the day off."

"No, I can't do that."

"I insist."

"But . . ."

"Gilbert, I know when you need a day off."

I pick up the shell bits with my fingers and then mop up the rest–half impressed at my theatrics, half ashamed that I've deceived him. Never has a man been so good, so honest.

As I'm hanging up my apron, Mr. Lamson approaches. "Just a friendly reminder. I know that it isn't any of my business. . . ."

"The insurance?" I ask.

"Yes."

"I intend to take care of that today, sir."

"I knew you would. You're a good employee, son. You're the best I've ever had."

There was a time when I would have agreed with him.

I'm heading out the door when he says, "Gilbert, keep hanging in there."

I stop and look at him.

"Why do you think that you should keep hanging in there?"

Nothing will come out of my mouth. I'm stumped.

"Because . . ." Mr. Lamson pauses in that I'm-about-to-say-the-most-important-thing-ever way. "Because . . ."

"Yes," I say, trying to hurry him along.

"Because there will be wonderful surprises."

Taking a moment to soak that in, I then smile as if to say "I hope so" and proceed to leave by the wrong door.

I get in my truck and start it up.

Inside the store, the Mrs. brings her husband a clean rag and he begins polishing the cash register. They must sense me watching because they look my way and wave in unison.

I drive off.

I feel sorry for them, believing in me the way they do. I'm not the stock boy I once was. Plus, there's nothing worse than being told you're good when you know you're bad. For a moment, I even mourn for the eggs. Their sudden, tragic death at the hands of a deceptive employee. Life might be full of wonderful surprises as Mr. Lamson says. But more than that I believe Life is full of unfairness. I offer the fate of the eggs as proof of my point.

4

It isn't even eleven in the morning and already the day is boiling hot, the seat in my truck is on fire, and I'm sweaty wet. How I wish I were a fish.

I drive two blocks to that bastion of security and protection, Carver's Insurance. Housed in an old gas station that's been converted, Carver's Insurance is one of the many buildings in Endora that have been remodeled or made over—only Lamson Grocery has remained the same.

I pull into the gravel parking lot. Tears of sweat roll down the back of my legs as I climb out of my truck. I'm careful going inside because there's a bell above the door that smacks in your ear. Clink, clank, dong, bang.

Melanie, Mr. Carver's secretary, looks up, startled, as if she can't believe the sight of another human being. She puts the cap on her White-out and says, "Well, hello there, Gilbert Grape."

"Hi," I say.

Melanie wears her red hair in a beehive style that is completely out of date. She has a mole on her face that must weigh a pound and a half, but I guess she's nice enough. She's over forty but has always insisted that we call her by her first name. When I was in high school, she worked as the library monitor. She would let me sleep in the conference room. Once I saw her smoking, and something about her smoking disappointed me.

"Are you here to see Mr. Carver?"

He calls from the back, "Is that you, Gilbert? Melanie? Is that Gilbert Grape?"

"Yes. Hello," I say. "I think I'm late on my payment."

Melanie doesn't even check my file. "You are late, Gilbert. Write us a check for a hundred twenty-three dollars and forty-three cents, and then you can scoot on out of here." She closes the door to Mr. Carver's office. "But you're always late with your payments—why the sudden appearance of responsibility, why now?"

"Oh, I'm trying, you know, to better my life."

21

Melanie smiles. Bettering your life, getting a fresh start, the bright side. Spout these concepts daily and you will survive in Endora; you might even thrive.

"You don't need an appointment, am I right? You just need to pay up."

"No. Uhm, also I've some confusion regarding my whatever you call what insurance does for you."

"I think you're inquiring about your *benefits*."

"Yes, that's it."

"So am I hearing that you actually do need an appointment?"

I don't know what Melanie is hearing. I can hardly talk to that hairstyle of hers. I wish I had a can of paint and a pair of hedge clippers. Fortunately I rarely speak what I think.

"An appointment would be most opportune."

"Gilbert, what a fine vocabulary you have."

I want to explain that any flashes of intellect that spit through me are a tribute to the many study halls I spent sleeping in the library. "I only have you to thank for my vocabulary. I owe it all to you, Melanie."

"You charmer."

"No, I mean it."

"Well then, you exaggerate."

"No, I do not. All those study halls we shared. You were the finest study hall supervisor at the school. No question about it in my mind or in anyone else's."

"How kind of you to say that."

"Is it kind if it's the truth?"

"Oh, I don't know. Rest assured, I love working for Mr. Carver–I would never say otherwise–and I believe in Insurance. But, between you and me, I miss working at the high school."

"And the high school misses you, I'm sure."

"The high school is closed, Gilbert. How could it miss me?"

"It would if it could."

"I'm hard to anger, you know that, but I could bite off the heads of the people who made that decision to close our high school. Busing all those kids to Motley."

"Well, everyone's moving away."

"I know, but still."

"There were thirty-nine in my freshman class and only twenty-three were left when we graduated."

"You don't say. Well, we could talk all day, couldn't we? We have so much in common, don't you think?"

I don't know how to answer that without lying in the most blatant of ways. "So much in common, yes, come to think of it."

"I've always thought it a shame that we're not the same age. You older or me younger. We'd have made a lovely couple, don't you think? Really, it's quite a shame."

"A pity."

"Yes, pity is a good word."

I left this conversation hours ago, but somehow my mouth is still moving, words are still forming, and none have seemed to offend. Amazing, the mind. My mind, I mean. Not hers.

It's suddenly down to business for Melanie. Her voice becomes sharp and biting. "So you'd like to make an appointment to see Mr. Carver?"

"Yes, ma'am. Please."

"One moment." She stands, moves to his door, and taps ever so lightly. She gently pushes it open. I hear classical music playing from inside his office. It takes a few minutes but soon she's standing in the doorway, smiling as if she's the most wonderful news. "How fortunate. You can see Mr. Carver right now if you'd like."

Mr. Carver calls out, "It would be a treat to see you! Step on back and let's see what we can do."

"Thank you, Mr. Carver, but I'll have to come back later. Errands and all."

Mr. Carver says, "Oh," like he's about to cry, Melanie smiles, smacks her lips and says, "I know how that is. I run errands day in, day out. Sometimes I think it's all I do."

"Well..."

She opens his appointment calendar, which, for this particular Wednesday, the first day of summer, is completely blank. "Well, you have picked a marvelous day. Mr. Carver lunches at noon sharp. He's back at one sharp. At four o'clock, he and his wife are driving to Boone to make a surprise visit to their boys at church camp. So up until four, you have free rein."

"How does two sound?"

"Perfect. A perfect time for an appointment. If it suits you, that is."

"Yeah, fine."

"We'll see you at two o'clock sharp, then."

"Okay."

"Have a nice day. And hello to Amy, your family. Your mother. I haven't seen your mother in years. How is she?"

"Oh, you know..."

"No, I don't. It's been some time since I've..."

I say, "Big things are happening for her, big things." I'm backing up toward the door.

Melanie puts a finger over her mouth, signaling me to be quiet. Then she waves me over to her and whispers, "You haven't mentioned my new hairdo?"

"That's true."

"You like it, don't you?"

"Oh, it's you."

"You think?"

"It suits you perfectly."

Melanie stops for a moment. She shines—all four and a half feet of her. I don't know how I did it, but somehow I made this woman's day. "If I were any younger..."

Oh God. Here we go again. Leap for the door, Gilbert. "Bye now!" I open the door slowly but still the bell jingles and clinks.

5

I drive off with the windows rolled down. My hair is getting blown all over, scratching my eyes. My hair is so long that it's beginning to eat my head.

I pass Endora's Gorgeous, one of two beauty parlors in town, and suddenly the image of Melanie's bright red cotton-candy hairdo returns to haunt me. The way it stands straight up, it's like a new eraser on an old pencil. I try to picture her after a morning bath, her hair all wet and droopy. She looking in the mirror, trying to create the lie she tells herself to get up and get moving. I'll never know how she keeps such a positive point of view. If I were her, I think I'd cry all day, all night.

My truck's gas gauge says it all. I drive over to the other side of town and pull up at Dave Allen's station. Buying my gas from Dave is a pleasure because of his cord or tube or whatever you call the black thing that stretches across the station. It's supposed to go bing-bing or bong-bong or ding-ding when tires go over it. The one at Dave's stopped working several years ago, and he won't have it fixed because he feels as I do—that none of us need to be reminded we exist.

So I always drive there for my gas. No cord, no bing-bing, bong-bong, ding-ding. Bliss.

I pump in a few bucks' worth, buy an Orange Crush from the pop machine and a bag of Cheetos. I pay in exact change.

Dave says, "The carnival."

"Yep?"

"Real good for business, you know."

"Really?" I say.

"Some of the rides run on gasoline."

"They buy it from you, I hope."

"Yeah." Dave smiles. I've never seem him look so proud.

Driving out of town, I pass Chip Miles driving a tractor on his daddy's farm. I honk and Chip waves—all happy, I guess, that someone recognized him. Chip is a nice enough guy, strong in that I-throw-a-lot-of-hay way. He was a champion wrestler for the high school team in Motley. He graduated a few weeks back. The tragedy with Chip is that he never had a date the whole four years he went there. See, he's got one of his front teeth capped in silver and that just discourages any girl in these parts. When he talks, he barely moves his top lip. But if you catch him off guard, like I just did, he will open his mouth wide, yell "Hey!" and you'll get a glare from his tooth.

I've got time to kill before my insurance appointment, and I'm going to relax. I speed up to seventy, seventy-five miles an hour and head for my favorite county road.

The roads all around Endora are completely straight and flat and bland except for Highway 2, which I am presently on. This road curves, and there is a small bridge stretching across Skunk River, which is actually just a creek, but since it's officially named a river everyone thinks that's what it is.

It's eleven miles later and I'm at the county cemetery. I drive under the metal framelike gate thing. I turn off my truck and walk across the graves. I find my place and sit. I eat my Cheetos, drink my Orange Crush. I lie back and look at the sky. Every five minutes or so I hear a car or a semi drive past. I look at the clouds, which are not even clouds today—wisps of white, little streaks, strokes, that move, but not in any interesting way; even the clouds have their doubts.

I eat two Cheetos for every sip of soda and soon both are gone. I roll over on my stomach and try to picture what my father looks like now. His skin is surely gone, and his heart and brain and eyes have turned to whatever it is they turn to. Dust, maybe. I'm told hair is one of the last parts of you to decay. The bones most certainly are still there, still rotting.

There are two weeds to the left of his tombstone. I pull them out and throw them several feet onto somebody else.

My heart beating confirms I'm alive. Sitting in this particular cemetery on this particular day makes me feel special. Like I stand out.

I lie back and breathe myself to sleep.

The sound of a truck driving into the cemetery wakes me. It's two guys and a hydraulic shovel, and it appears they've come to dig a grave.

The sun has moved far across the sky. My skin feels all warm. I did the dumbest thing—falling asleep with no sunscreen lotion and no shade. I have cooked my skin and by tonight, I'll probably glow in the dark. I cross over to the grave diggers and say, "Hey, you know the time?"

"Four o'clock or thereabouts."

"Thanks."

Already feeling the burn of my skin, I quickly seek distraction. "So is this how they dig graves? I thought you'd use shovels."

"No, man, shovels went out years ago."

Suddenly I've this sincere interest in their process. "You dig a lot of graves?"

"Yeah. Me and my partner, we dig for all three cemeteries in this county."

"You wouldn't happen to know who you're digging this one for?"

"Yeah, we know. It's on the sheet."

The one who hasn't said anything looks at the sheet.

"I'm wondering," I say, "because a friend of mine died yesterday."

"Sorry about that, man."

"Well, that's the way it goes some days."

"Yeah, some days you die."

"Exactly," I say.

"Braider is her name."

"Brainer, that's her."

"This is your friend we're digging for?"

"Yeah."

I try to look sad and forlorn.

"You don't seem all that upset about it."

"No, I do my grieving, you know, in private."

"Sure, that's cool."

They've dug about three feet when I say, "You can't make that hole deep enough."

"Huh?"

"Oh, nothing. See ya."

As I walk away, the guy who has been silent mutters something to the other guy.

"Hey, buddy, hey you!"

"Yeah?"

"Uhm. My partner here wants to know something."

"Okay, shoot." I'm now about ten graves away from them.

"He's wondering if you're one of the Grapes! We're from

Motley, you know. And for a long time we've been hearing about this family. . . ."

It takes two tries to get my door shut. And with my truck kicking up a cloud of dust, I leave them wondering. I drive home. Of course I'm a Grape, I want to shout. I'm Gilbert Grape.

6

Driving fast back to town, I see Endora's water tower, silver with black lettering, looking like an old whistle or a cheap rocket. If it were a rocket I'd get in and blast off.

I speed past Chip Miles again. He waves, but this time I don't honk.

A quick check in my rearview mirror and it is confirmed. My skin is already a hot pink. It will be bright red by bedtime.

There is something in the middle of the road a few houses up from ours. Slowing down I hit the horn a few times. But "it" doesn't move.

I come to a stop, put my truck in park and walk up to it. I whisper, "Moooooovvvvvveeee." I make the I'm-about-to-spit sound. This something doesn't flinch. So I scream, "OH MY GOD! ARNIE IS DEAD!"

He smiles as if he likes the idea.

"I saw that," I say.

"Saw what?"

"That smile."

"But I'm dead, Gilbert. Jeez."

"You are not."

"Yes, I am!"

I start wailing and crying and moaning. I pound my chest. Of course it's all done in that pretend sort of way because Arnie is still very much alive. To a neighbor watching, my performance must be completely unbelievable. I don't cry. I just never do. And no one expects me to. I want to scream. At least something is going on here! At least we have some brotherly action here! If you'd open your eyes and look out your window, you'd see some Life happening! But I keep the screaming inside me, lift Arnie up with one arm under his shoulders and the other under his knees. His head drops back; he's dead again. I lay him in the bed of my pickup and pull into the driveway.

Arnie jumps out and runs into the house, letting the screen door slam. It's a miracle that he's lived this long. He'll be turning eighteen on July 16, a little less than one month from today. Who would have thought? The party to end all parties is being planned. For the members of my family, especially my mother, Arnie's eighteenth birthday will be the biggest day ever. More treasured than Thanksgiving, with more presents than Christmas, Arnie's birthday will also unfortunately bring the return of the other Grapes.

My mother is a woman of few words. The words used are choice, and you can break her conversation categories into three sections.

The first and most frequent is: "Where's my food?" Or: "What's for dinner?" Or: "I don't smell anything cooking, do you?" Food.

The second goes something like this: "Get me my cigarettes." "Who took my cigarettes?" "Matches! Matches, anybody!" Smoking.

The third category is always repeated in the same word order. She speaks it at least once a day. This is Momma at her most poignant. Her words are these: "I don't ask for much. Just let me see my boy turn eighteen. That's not too much to ask, is it?" At my father's funeral I saw Momma write something down on a paper napkin. I'm not sure but I think it was those words.

I open the door and go in the house. I see Arnie under Momma's table, his arms wrapped around her feet. She's saying, ". . . turn eighteen. That's not too much to ask, is it?"

"Hi, Momma," I say.

She lights a cigarette. Her blue lips take a long drag. She smiles, not because of me but rather because of the boy at her feet and the cigarette in her mouth. "Gilbert, you hungry?"

All of a sudden I see Momma and Arnie disappear through the floor. When I cross to the hole they made, I see that they kept falling and this wind blows and they went through the center of the earth and out the other side, which is probably Vietnam or something, and they keep going, surely, toward the sun and when Momma and Arnie hit the sun, the sun grows too bright and hot and the earth melts into nothingness.

Fortunately, this is just my imagination.

I glance at the floor below Momma. The saglike curve is bigger than it was this morning. I go into the kitchen where Amy is baking a couple of meat loaves. "Smells good," I say.

"You think?"

"Yep."

Amy would like it if I gave her a hug when I came in from work. But Gilbert Grape is not the hugging type.

"I called you to bring home some potatoes for dinner. Mr. Lamson said you'd . . ." Amy stops when she looks up and sees my skin.

"Gilbert, my God."

"Yeah, ouch, huh? The sun was something today. . . ."

Amy turns back to the oven, shaking her head.

"Mr. Lamson gave me the day off."

"We need the money. You can't just go take off the day to work on your tan. . . ." She takes a toothpick and sticks it in a meat loaf.

"It was just one of those days. . . ."

She burns two fingers on the second meat loaf pan. "Ow. Darn it! Darn it!" Amy isn't the swearing type. She runs cold water over her hand. I take the pot holders and lift out the second meat loaf.

"You okay?"

"Of course."

I lie and say, "Looks really good."

"Oh, and Melanie called. Seems you missed some appointment with Mr. Carver. . . ."

"Oh, crap." I completely forgot about my appointment.

"She wasn't happy with this. . . ."

"I'll reschedule...."

"She said that you better hope Mr. Carver can fit you in."

In the dining room Momma has given Arnie the controls to the TV and he's pushing the buttons fast.

"So I guess I know why you took the day off from work. At least I hope this was the reason. Is he going to help us? Say that he will."

"Who?"

"Tucker."

"Sure, sure. Of course."

"So you talked to him."

"Uhm."

"That's the reason you took the day off. To work on the floor situation."

"Yes?"

"You say that like a question. Are you asking me or telling me?"

"Tucker will be glad to help."

Amy doesn't know whether to believe me or not. She turns off the water and dries her hands on her apron. She half smiles, lifts her foot and stomps suddenly.

"Ants," she says. "There are ants everywhere in this house."

"At least something likes us."

"Cute, Gilbert."

"If Ellen would do the dishes..."

Washing dishes is Ellen's job, mine is laundry, and Amy does everything else.

"Oh, and that was a real clever thing you did this morning. That was Dad's lawn chair, you know."

"Yeah, I know."

"It was his favorite lawn chair."

"Well..."

"And Ellen went off all morning."

"I'm sure she did."

"Please. Please stop inciting her." Amy is using some of her I'm-a-teacher's-aide big words. "I told her I want this resolved today. I want this family cooperating. We don't have to love each other but we have to get along. Are you listening?"

31

"Yes."

"You've got to do your part. You're older than she is...."

When Amy finishes today's lecture, she points to a pink envelope that has been taped to the refrigerator. In purple is a giant "G."
I take it into the downstairs bathroom, sit down on the toilet, and
begin to read.

> "Dear Brother,
> I am sorry.
> I say that even though I'm not.
> Things are happening in me that I can't explain.
> Things that a guy can't understand.
> Your Sister."

There is a water spot at the bottom of the page. Ellen has circled
it with a turquoise marker and written "One of many tears you
caused."

I slowly crumple up the note, drop it in the toilet, and flush.

Amy has split one of the meat loaves in two. One half goes to
Arnie, one half goes to me. The other meat loaf is on Momma's
plate and she's fast at work. She takes a bite, changes the TV channel, then takes another bite.

"You eating, Amy?"

"No. Starting a diet," she whispers. "Tooooo-day."

"Oh. You should eat something."

"Look at me, Gilbert."

Good point.

If Amy's so worried about the floor, why did she bake Momma
an entire meat loaf? I better not ask. Instead, I grab a fork out of
the drawer only to find that it has a piece of cereal crusted on one
of its prongs. The next fork has this line of grease or oil or butter
or something. I pull out fork after fork, and all of them are grungy
or dirty or whatever. So I take the meat loaf in my fingers and eat
like an animal. At least I know where my hands have been, I'm
thinking, when Amy comes into the kitchen.

"Jesus, Amy, these forks." My mouth is full of meat loaf. "Have
you seen these forks?"

Amy didn't get a word. "Swallow before talking."

"These forks—cleaned lovingly by my premenstrual sister, whom I love and like and cherish..." I pause to push a chunk of meat out from between my teeth. "These forks prove..."

Amy is smiling. She loves to see me upset. It proves to her, I guess, that this brother has feelings.

"These forks prove..."

"What do they prove?"

"THE EXISTENCE OF SATAN!"

Momma drops her silverware. "Amy?"

"Yes, Momma."

"Tell him this is my house. Tell him we don't have any shouting during dinner. Tell him that."

"He knows, Momma. Gilbert didn't mean to raise his voice."

The hell I didn't.

"Have him get his momma some cigarettes."

Amy moves toward the dining room and says, "You've still got an entire pack left."

"But after that! WHAT AM I GONNA SMOKE AFTER THAT?"

Amy takes a ten-dollar bill from the Folger's coffee can on top of the refrigerator and hands it to me. "Get her some cigarettes. And please speak with Tucker. Don't tell me you have when you haven't, okay? And pick up Ellen from work at nine. She likes it when you pick her up. It would mean something."

"Sure, Amy. I'll do it all."

"Good. I knew I could count on you."

It's nights like these that I have to get out of my house. I drive around town and dream about going places. I dream about the kind of families I watched on TV as a kid. I dream about pretty people and fast cars, and I dream I'm still me but my family is someone else. I dream I'm still me.

7

Tucker says, "Did you hear? Did you hear?"

"Hear what?"

"They're finally building..." Tucker has to stop because a bug gets in his mouth.

"Finally building what?"

"A Burger Barn." He looks at me like he expects me to start dancing around the room.

I say, "Yeah, so?"

"Don't you see what this means? Don't you see the uh...uh..."

"The implications."

"Yeah, that's the word. Burger Barn is just a first step. Someday we'll have a Pizza Hut, a Kentucky Fried Chicken. Maybe a Taco Bell. I'm gonna get me a job. Wear one of those uniforms."

"Neato," I say.

"Gilbert, I hate you. All day I've been waiting to tell you this and now you stand there like a telephone pole."

"You got any beer?"

"Does Tucker have beer? Tucker has Canadian beer."

"Yeah, so?"

"Canadian beer uses a certain kind of water."

"Big deal."

"It is a big deal, Gilbert. It's not every beer that uses this special Canadian water."

He tosses me two cans and I start drinking.

Tucker lives in a converted garage behind his parents' house. He has a little refrigerator and a hot plate that is more for show than anything because he eats every meal with his parents. He and his dad did all the work on the garage conversion, and while it's not very impressive-looking, his garage/bedroom/apartment is functional. They cut a hole in the garage door and put in this stained glass window of a horse. Other than that, the place is dusty and dark, very Tucker. They installed track lighting to illuminate his

34

beer-can collection which totals over nine hundred cans. You go to his place and it smells like you're in a bar. A bar without women, though, because Tucker never dates.

I'm finishing can number one when he says, "I guess it's that special Canadian water."

"Nope."

"It's the water—admit it."

I'd rather be wrong than concede that Tucker was right. I never let him win, either, and if he were ever about to, I'd have no choice but to change the rules.

"Anyway, about the Burger Barn. You know, they bring in a team of experts and they build the whole thing, start to finish, in less than thirty days. I drove out there today. They're putting it up right next to Food Land. They've leveled the ground and it will be open, get this—by the middle of July."

Tucker is on a roll. It usually takes two beers for him to like himself but tonight he only needs half a can.

"I mean," he continues, "just this morning I wake up, I look around my room, and I see achievements. I see that I have a life. Some people don't have what I have, right? I've got my own place. Certain skills, you know?"

I nod, but my mind is elsewhere.

"So I couldn't get out of bed today. I couldn't even move! Does that ever happen to you? Tell me it does. Well, I get up finally and go to my truck . . ."

Tucker got his pickup the week after I got mine. He bought his brand-new. He never had to spend a penny because his dad took out a loan to pay for it. It has remained in mint condition because Tucker covers it every night with a black tarp.

". . . and my truck starts right up—engine humming nice—and I drive to Food Land to get some donuts . . ."

Lamson Grocery has superb donuts, I want to say. I make a fist to punch him in the arm but I stop when I see his eyes watering.

". . . and my life suddenly wasn't what I wanted, you know? I'm thinking 'Is this it?' You know? Have I reached my uhm . . ."

"Potential."

"Potential, yeah."

Those can't be tears forming. Surely a gnat or a dust ball got in his eye.

"I hope I haven't, because why get up? Why wake up? You know? So I see the sign announcing the arrival of the Burger Barn and ... I don't know how else to say it ... but it was like suddenly my life made uhm ... uhm ... made ..."

"Sense."

"Yeah. And well ..." Tucker wipes his eyes. Those are tears and I suddenly feel sick. "I knew then that this was supposed to ... uhm ... happen. I had hit bottom and now I was on the way back up."

Tucker stops talking and waits for a response. I open the second can of beer and begin to chug it.

"Aren't you happy for me? Aren't you happy for me? Aren't you happy for me?"

I can answer him now that the second beer is inside me. "Tucker?" I say. "I'm happy for you."

He smiles. He can't tell when I'm lying. He takes the empty can from my hand, rinses it out in his little sink, and dries it with a towel. He turns on his track lighting and, without much ceremony, puts the can in its new home next to the others. "Whew. It's been a big day. I need to wind down. Pro wrestling comes on in a couple of minutes. You're welcome to stay and watch."

"No thanks on the wrestling, buddy."

He moves his beanbag chair to the center of the room, turns on his TV, and as he sits, the chair makes that bean bag sound. "Okay," he says, "well, see you, then."

"Tucker, I got a favor to ask."

"I knew it. The minute you said 'buddy' I knew it. It's not a good day for favors, okay? Oh man, I'm tired!"

"But ..."

"I just told you my day. It's been unbelievable. I can't absorb any more...."

"It's Momma."

"What?"

I repeat that it's Momma and Tucker is suddenly interested. He loves my mother maybe more than his own.

"Is she sick? Is she okay?"

"Well, Tucker, you're one of the few who has seen Momma these last few years."

"Yeah. And it means a lot to me."

"You know that she's about the biggest thing around."

"I was at the state fair and I saw this guy that was a little bigger...."

"Yeah, but..."

"I'm just saying that she's not the biggest I've ever seen. That's all I'm saying."

I tell him about the floor and how it sags.

He says, "Your momma isn't that big."

"Afraid so."

"No way possible."

"You've got to see it to believe it."

"I'll come over tomorrow."

I stand and walk to his TV. I block the screen with my body and turn it off with the back of my hand. "Momma needs you tonight."

We head home, stopping to pick up a carton of cigarettes at ENDora OF THE LINE, the stupidest name for a store ever. I walk in, and Maggie or Josh or whoever's working just grabs a carton of Kool and rings it up before I'm even at the cash register. This is the one advantage in having a mother so set in her ways.

Inside the house, we find Momma and Amy watching "The New Dating Game" and Arnie asleep on the floor.

"Tucker and I are gonna play some cards," I say, handing Amy the carton of Kool. "Or throw some darts."

"Careful with the darts," Amy says.

Tucker waves and says, "Hey, Mrs. Grape."

Having just picked bachelor number two, Momma stays fixed on the TV. She doesn't acknowledge Tucker, and there's no thank you for the cigarettes. She says a person shows their gratitude by action, not by words. So I guess that means she thanks me by smoking every cigarette in every pack.

Downstairs, Tucker's mouth is open. He's in shock. The sagging floor looks even worse from below. Taking out his tape measure, he says, "We got to act fast. These beams could snap at any time." He wants to talk to Momma. "To see if she'd consider moving to another part of the house for a while."

"She won't move," I say. "And anyway, if she knew she was cutting a hole through her floor, she would lose it big time. Especially since she's drilling right directly above where my dad hung himself."

"What?" All of a sudden Tucker gets this squeamish look on his face. "Right here, right here is where they found your dad?"

"Yep. He was hanging from that support right there. A puddle of piss was below him and there was vomit all across here." I point to the washer and dryer. "He was found swinging. His body still kind of warm. But it was too late."

Tucker is confused, so I explain that when a person dies often their bowels let go for the last time. "You dump in your pants and piss down your legs. If you're hanging."

He says he doesn't see how I can be so cold about it.

I say that if you live with something long enough, it becomes normal. "Besides, my getting all teary isn't gonna change anything. It's done, he did it, and what's foremost is that Momma's gonna fall through the floor if we don't do something fast."

Tucker estimates that she'll fall through by the beginning of next week. "There's even a chance she could go tonight." With that, he grabs my arms and pulls me out of the way.

I say, "What are you doing?"

"She might go right now."

Upstairs, we're heading outside to my truck.

Amy says, "Pretty fast cards."

I say something about not being in the mood for playing games, and then I wink at Amy, trying to hint that we're working on the floor situation. My guess is that she didn't get my signal, because she says, "Remember to pick up Ellen."

"Yeah, yeah, yeah," I say.

"Bye, Mrs. Grape," Tucker calls out.

Momma doesn't move. It occurs to me that maybe Tucker loves my mother because she has no interest in him.

* * *

We're getting into my truck, when I hear Arnie scream. I run back to the house, certain that Momma just fell to Hell. I throw open the door and find Amy hugging Arnie, who woke from a bad dream. "Everything's fine, Gilbert. You go on with Tucker. Go have a fine time," she says with a wink.

I guess she got my earlier point.

8

It will take great planning to save your mother. No floor is made to withstand such... such..."

"I know, buddy, I know. But if anyone can do it..."

"Thanks. Means a lot coming from you."

I pull up at Tucker's. He jumps out while my truck is still moving, calls out, "I'll get right to work!" and sprints inside to begin drawing up his plans.

My sister Ellen works at the Dairy Dream. Some dream. They've got cones, colored sodas, candy bars, sprinkles, nuts, malts, shakes and one of those real dippy, sissy, piss-me-off bells that tinks or clanks or chimes when a person enters.

Before you enter the Dream, look in and study whatever girl is working. Make sure she doesn't see you and then observe how she is hating her job. She wants to be in some fast car, you see, or home doing her nails—anywhere but in the Dream. Then push in the door, she'll hear the bell, and this smile will snap on like a zipper unzipped. Or like God will take her face and turn it inside out. All of a sudden she'll be smiling like some beauty queen and so friendly and so interested and so happy. This is some shit, huh?

When I pull up at the Dairy Dream, I notice three girls. Two of them are chubby and plain and they are walking toward the Dream. They look familiar. The third girl doesn't. She is straddling a boys' bike, standing motionless, staring at something. The third girl my eyes can't deny.

She has black hair, thick and full. It drapes her shoulders. She has legs. Oh my. From where I'm sitting, she is not to be believed. She is the moon.

I put my truck in park, turn off the engine, take the headlights out, and roll down the window—all in slow motion. I breathe with great difficulty. Certain that I must be imagining this, I look around to see if this is Life that is happening. This is my truck. These are my hands. That's my little sister scraping the insides of the fudge machine. Yes, this is Life.

The other two girls go inside to order, but the one I'm aching for doesn't move. The bell clinks or clanks or dings, and one of them holds the door, thinking the girl on the bike is coming in. She's staring at something on the dirty white stucco wall of the Dream, however, and waves them off with a "No, thanks."

Now, Gilbert, get out of your truck now.

I remember my beer breath and find some Bazooka in my glove compartment and chew rapidly. I close my truck door slowly; my heart is pounding now, firing blood bullets. Minutes ago I was calm, a walking coma practically, and now, in seconds, I'm so glad to be alive. And so scared.

She's looking at some insects or maybe a spider. I move closer, trying to look at what she's looking at and trying not to look at her. I get close enough to smell her hair and make out the slope of her nose, the shape of her pillowlike lips. The round black glasses. The creamy skin, perfect skin.

I have seen God and he is this girl.

I better say something fast. My mouth is drying out. As I step up behind her, she says, "Praying mantis. The male is sneaking up on the female. He wants to mate. If he's not careful, she'll turn around and bite off his head. His instinct will keep on mating. But when the rest of him is done, she'll eat what's left. That's how praying mantises mate. Interesting, huh? My name is Becky."

She turns, pulls down her glasses, and looks at me.

"Uh," is all I can say.

"I'm from Ann Arbor. My grandma lives here and I'm only here for that reason. My grandma's old, her hair is blue, and she'll die soon. Want to smoke?"

"No, thanks. I'm trying to quit."

"Really. Why?"

"Makes my skin gross? My teeth gross?"

"If you think it does, then I guess it does." She puts a cigarette between her perfect lips. "Smoking makes me feel alive. Helps me get through it. You know, the bullshit?"

I nod because I'll agree with anything she says. She lights her cigarette, looking like a magazine ad.

"You like me, don't you?"

"Yes."

"You think I'm beautiful."

I fight nodding but lose.

"I might be now, but one day I'll have blue hair and blotched skin and plastic teeth and maybe one breast left. If the thought of that appeals to you, then we might talk about hanging out. But if you're into the surface thing, the beauty thing, then I might just have to turn around, snap off your head, and eat you."

I laugh but don't know why. This Becky girl doesn't even crack a smile. She goes inside and when that piss of a bell clinks or chimes, I fall back on the stucco of the Dairy Dream. I'm thinking, was the wind just knocked out of me or what?

It's then when I hear a soft crunch, a chomping of sorts. Turning, I see that the female mantis has caught the male, and his head has been snapped off. She is munching, he is squirming, and I run to my truck and drive out of there fast. She expected me to follow her. I guess I told her.

As I pull out, I see Ellen pressing her face against the take-out window. Oh God, I left Ellen. I've got to go back.

Oh God.

9

"What about the third girl, who came in after them...?"

"I don't know who you're talking about."

"She... she... come on... you saw her!"

Ellen turns on my radio and says for me to speed up.

"Her eyes. She's got these eyes. Dark brown. And her hair is uhm and her nose... slopes...."

"What was she wearing?"

"I don't know that. I'm no fashion expert."

"Then I can't help you out."

"You just served her! She..."

Ellen lets out this high-pitched giggle and it pierces the night air. I check to see if her door is locked. It isn't, and a big part of me wants to reach over, open the door, and shove her out onto the street.

Instead I say, "Thanks a million, Ellen."

"Why yes, brother dear, and a big thank-you for this morning."

"You're welcome."

Did I do something this morning? It seems so long ago—like 1983.

"It was perfect tanning weather," Ellen continues with her eyes closed. "Thank you for ruining my morning...."

Oh. The lawn chair. "Well, what is family for."

Her sound changes to a gentle, kind of throaty just-had-sex voice. "I've never known what you have against me, really, except maybe the regret that you are my brother, and being my brother just means that you can't date me. You can't kiss me or ever know me in a sexual way. Could that be what's keeping you in Endora?"

I won't honor that with an answer.

"We all expect the floor to be fixed. After all, you are the man in the family."

"What does that mean?"

"Men fix things."

"What?"

"Women cook things. Men fix things."

"Oh."

"This is the way in America. Men have their thing and we women have our thing but you, Gilbert, you will have NO-thing if you don't fix the floor."

I drive faster.

"Ellen, we're home."

She opens the passenger door. The overhead light kicks on and she sees my sunburn for the first time.

"Oh, rub it in, why don't you!"

"What?"

"You can have sun. But not me. Real fair. Fine!" She stomps into the house.

I'll sit for a bit.

From my truck I can see Amy and Momma are watching TV. There are no lights on in the house except for the flicker from the screen. Upstairs, the light comes on in Ellen's room. She starts to take off her white polyester Dairy Dream top. She doesn't pull down her shade and part of her probably wants me to watch. I don't. Instead, I study our house. It is big and sort of white. The roof needs replacement shingles, all the floors are sagging, and the porch is on a slant. The outside and inside both beg for a paint job. My father built this house with his own hands the year he married my mother, in honor of their nuptials. No wonder it all droops.

I'm walking to the porch, when Ellen lifts her window to ask if I want to see the tragic remains of the lawn chair. "No interest in dead things," I say as I go in the front door.

"So that's why you've no interest in yourself." Ellen thinks I heard her say that but I didn't.

Inside, the TV is on a commercial break, but it's commercials that Amy and my mother like best on television. I head back to the kitchen but don't know why, so I turn around and move fast toward the stairs hoping to make it up to my room without any familial contact. But I come across Arnie asleep in the coat closet with a ring of chocolate around his lips. Instead of waking him, I struggle to scoop him up in my arms. The kid is getting porky and lifting him pinches my sunburned arms.

Up we go.

My foot pushes open the door to his bedroom. He has bunk beds and sleeps on the top because he believes that's where heaven is. There was a time when we shared this room. But I got my own when one of the other Grapes moved out. Arnie's room is full of toys. There's a path that winds and curves to his bunk. Amy makes his bed every morning.

I set him on the bottom bunk, yank back the sheet up top, pull off his shoes and socks, and begin to lift him, when a giggling starts. I pretend to ignore it, because that's the way Arnie wants it. But he says, "I wasn't sleeping. I fooled you." I tuck him in. "I fooled you!" he shouts.

I turn the light out on him, not saying a thing. I go downstairs to say goodnight. Ellen is in the kitchen stirring her yogurt with a plastic spoon. Even she can't eat off the dishes she rarely cleans.

I go in the living room, where Amy is using the remote control to change between Channel 5 and Channel 8. Momma is mumbling, "...let me see my boy turn eighteen. That's not too much to ..."

"No, Momma," Amy says.

"Let me finish what I'm saying."

"Sorry."

Momma stops, her big tongue pushes out of her mouth like on those "National Geographic" specials when a whale rises out of the water for air. "Now I forgot what I was saying." She looks up and seeing me, her eyes bulge for a second, her head snaps back, and then her face softens. "Jesus!"

"What?"

"Gilbert, my God. For a second..."

"What is it?" Amy says as she turns the TV to mute.

"For a second I thought you were Albert. I almost called you Albert. I almost did that."

"It's okay, Momma," Amy says. "Gilbert kind of looks like Daddy."

"Kind of? He's the spitting image."

I shouldn't have come down to say goodnight. Whatever possessed me?

Momma's lips stretch out as she sticks the next cigarette between her teeth. Her big fingers are eager to light a match. She can't get one going, so she tries a second. Amy reaches her ever-growing hands in to help, but Momma clutches the matches, hacks out a laugh, and stomps both feet on the floor. The table jiggles, a picture falls.

"Don't stomp like that!" I shout.

Momma stops. She puts out her unlit cigarette, glares at me, and takes a new one from the pack.

"Is this my house, Gilbert?"

I nod.

"I believe it to be. Amy? Is this my house?"

"Yes, Momma."

"Ellen? Come here, honey."

Ellen appears with her yogurt. "Yeah?"

"This is your mother's house, is it not?"

"It's *our* house."

"But I'm the mother, right?" They nod. "Amy–Ellen–girls–tell me it's okay for me to stomp in my house." Momma talks with the cigarette in her mouth. It waves up and down. "Tell me that I can do whatever I want in *my* house. And why is that? Why do you think I can do whatever . . ."

"Because it's your house," they both say fast.

Momma looks at me.

I say, "Sorry, I'm sorry," as I move to the stairs.

"Your father always said that. Sorry. I used to think 'sorry' was his middle name. And you can see where 'sorry' got him!"

I want to scream, Momma, stomp all night. Punch yourself right through the floor. Instead, I simply say, "Good night," and climb the stairs two at a time.

The mute is taken off the TV and the sound of studio audience applause for some talk show can be heard. In the bathroom mirror, I study my face. The burned skin, the almost purple redness of it. I squirt some skin cream into my hands and cover my face, hoping it will cool me down. My cheeks and nose and chin are slippery now. The sound of applause from the TV grows, and I take a bow.

10

Arnie is in bed, Ellen is playing records in her room, and down-stairs Amy is setting out the assortment of snacks and little cakes for Momma to nibble on during the night. I'm sitting on the upstairs toilet with the lid down, talking on the phone.

"What, Tucker, what?"

"Gilbert. It's grim."

"What is?"

"The floor."

I don't know what to say.

"It's all changing," Tucker says. "Your mother is like twice the size of when I last saw her."

"I know."

"She's like a balloon. I swear."

"I know this, Tucker. Don't you think I know this?"

Suddenly there comes this violence at the bathroom door. "Gilbert? Gilbert!"

The return of Ellen.

"Open up, please. Hurry!"

"Go downstairs."

"What I need isn't downstairs!"

Even Tucker is startled by the screaming. "Who is that yelling?"

"My little piss of a sister."

"Which reminds me. You ever gonna set me up on a date? Get me a date." Tucker has wanted to date Ellen since she was nine. For years, when I've needed something, I've bribed him with the promise that one day he could take her out.

"Gilbert. Please open the door. You don't understand. It has to do with hygiene!" Ellen screams at the top of the stairs, "Amy! Amy!" She pounds on the door, she kicks at it. She is quite loud.

So I go, "And you want to date this girl? This noise? My sister is all noise."

He listens, but it will have no impact.

Arnie is screaming now, too. So much for him all tucked in bed.

46

"Girls my age! We . . . bleed!"

I reach under the sink. I locate the blue-and-pink box, lift out one of those tubes wrapped in white, and slowly push it under the bathroom door. Ellen makes it disappear fast and runs off. All she had to do was ask.

"About the floor, Tucker. You got any ideas?"

"I got a plan. But I'm scared. For your mother. For your house. For you."

"Yeah, well, we can only do so much."

I hear the pitter-patter, titter-tatter of Arnie's fingers on the bathroom door. "One second, Tucker." I open it, let him in, and shut the door, locking it fast. Arnie smiles like he's just been made a member of a secret club.

I say, "You were saying?"

Tucker continues. "I've designed what I think to be the only possible solution that can save her."

"Okay, great."

"Tomorrow we'll get the wood."

"Fine."

"It's gonna cost."

"We'll pay you whatever it takes."

"Oh, I don't want any money. The materials are what's gonna cost. My services are donated."

Arnie pulls at my T-shirt. I shove his hand away. He pushes down the toilet handle and the bathroom fills with that flush sound. Tucker says, "You taking a dump?"

"No."

"Liar. I heard the flush. You were taking a dump."

"But I . . ."

"I just wish you'd admit it. We got to be honest with each other."

"But . . ."

"I heard the flush, Gilbert. You can't fool Tucker Van Dyke."

"See ya tomorrow, Tucker." I hang up.

Arnie taps me on the arm. "Gilbert? Hey . . . ?"

"What, buddy?"

"Can't sleep."

"You got to."

"But I can't."

"Tomorrow is a big day. We're going to ride the horses tomorrow."

"Lots of times, right?"

"Yep."

"Uhm. Maybe we could go now and ride 'em. Ride 'em now."

"The horses are sleeping, buddy. Like you should be."

"Oh."

"You know they gave me the day off from work tomorrow."

"Oh."

"You know why? Because Mr. Lamson wants you to have a good time. He even chipped in for some tickets."

"All 'cause of the horsies?"

"Yep."

He turns and heads for bed.

"Good night, Arnie."

"Good-bye."

"Good *night,* Arnie. It's not good-bye. It's good *night.*"

"Yeah."

"Good-bye is for when you're going away." He mixes those words up. "And you're not going anywhere."

"Yeah."

He walks down the hall. I watch his wide feet and his messy hair. He farts. I'll wait for the smell to clear.

Last Christmas I made him a sign that says "Arnie's Place" on it with my woodworking kit. I nailed it to his door so he'd know which room was his.

I check on him—he's lying in bed pressing his feet to the ceiling. I turn his light out.

"Good night," he says from the dark.

"That's right, buddy. Good night."

It's later. I'm not getting any sleep because Arnie's bapping his head to a steady beat. If you wake him to explain that it's bad for him, he'll nod like he agrees. Then, though, within the hour (I promise) you'll begin to hear the pulse or punch or pound of his head into the bed, and you realize that what you tried to teach him has not and cannot be learned. So. You want to die. No, I mean, you don't even want to go through the hassle of dying. You wish you didn't exist. If only you could disappear.

I don't have a clock in my room, so I can't tell you the exact time. But it must be the middle of the night. My sunburn has made my arms and face dry out. I'm longer than my bed, so my feet hang over the edge. I lie on top of the sheets in my underwear. The night is dry and hot. The farmers are worried about the weather these days. There has been no rain in weeks. My boss, Mr. Lamson, says it's what we've done to this planet. He says that it's the car fumes and air conditioners in buildings and the chopping down of some rain forest.

I've often thought that my dad killed himself because he could see the future. They say he was the most hopeful man ever. He was apparently a constant supporter, compliment giver, and always had a kind word for everyone. I was seven when he hung himself, and I don't remember all that much, and anything I did remember, I've managed to forget.

Amy says you could count on him to smile even after the hardest, longest of days.

Him hanging in the basement had the same kind of impact in our town as President Kennedy's death. That's what Amy told me once.

In the last two weeks at least five people have called me "Al." I always say that I'm *Gil*bert Grape, not *Al*bert, but people believe what they want to believe. They stare and gawk at me like I'm some freak of genetics. "Okay," I want to scream, "so I look like him—that doesn't make me him."

The only pictures of my father are kept in a shoe box under Amy's bed. The shoe box is surrounded by her overflow of Elvis books and lesser Elvis memorabilia. The pictures of him are kept hidden like they're some awful secret.

Downstairs, Momma changes the channels. She likes the TV loud, and it can be heard all hours of the day. A person adjusts to it or they don't.

I sit up on my bed. There are no posters or pictures anywhere. I believe in bare walls. I check outside for the moon, but there isn't one tonight.

* * *

49

I'm asleep now, dreaming.

Arnie takes me to a restaurant. I notice he's much bigger than me and really confident-looking. I say, "But, Arnie, you're retarded," and he says, "No, I'm smart like Einstein." He smiles, and his teeth are perfectly straight and very white. I say, "What is going on?" He says, "Gilbert, here is a hamburger. Eat it. It is good. Mom ate it. She started crying it was so tasty. Everybody—look over there." And I turn to see my entire family at a long table. They all wave and wipe at the hamburger juice on their chins. All of them have been crying. "But I'm not hungry," I explain. "Eat the burger. It's what you need." He holds my arms down. Then that girl from the Dairy Dream, that Becky girl, materializes. She holds a giant burger and moves it slowly toward me, saying, "It is so tasty," and I realize she's seducing me. She says, "You'll love it, you'll want to never stop chewing." I whisper, "I believe you." I open my mouth to bite. "And best of all, Gilbert Grape, it will make you cry." "No!" I shout. "NNNNNOOOOOOO!"

The light snaps on in my room.

"Gilbert?"

My face is scrunched, fighting the light. I've covered my eyes. "What?"

"You were yelling in your sleep again," Amy says.

"Was I?"

"Yes."

"Ha. Funny."

"You okay?"

"I'm okay."

She turns off the light and says, "You must have been having a bad dream."

"Huh?"

"A bad dream. You were having a bad dream."

"Oh," I say. "Is that what I'm having?"

Part Two

11

It's the same horse every year. The big white one. Arnie is on his twenty-second consecutive ride.

The merry-go-round guy walks across the ride, gliding between horses, and steps off to where I'm standing. He looks off at the other rides when he talks to me. "Your friend on the horse..."

"My brother, you mean."

"Your brother uh has to uh move. Other people want that horse. See, buddy, the white horse is the most uh popular."

I look around. "That may well be, but nobody is waiting on line."

"That's not my point."

I look at this greaseball with his chipped teeth and his frequent tattoos and wonder if he's ever had a point. "So what are you saying?" I ask.

"My uh point is that other people should have the chance at least. They got to have the opportunity."

Tucker appears out of nowhere carrying a big pink cloud of cotton candy. "Gilbert, they just asked me to be in the dunk tank." He tears off a hunk of the candy and waves it my way.

"No, thanks."

"I just happened to have my swimsuit on underneath my jeans. What luck, huh? And guess what? This year they have a microphone so I can heckle people. They throw the baseball, hit the red dot, and Tucker is dunked. Take this." He forces the cotton candy on me and half jogs to the tank.

Turning back to the carnival guy, I say, "My brother is awful fond of that horse."

"But the rules..."

"He waits every year for this day. Pretty much, it's all he has to look forward to."

Arnie circles by and shoots an imaginary gun, shouting "You're dead, Gilbert. You're dead!"

"Look at him," I say. The carnival guy does. "See the odd shape of his head?" He nods. "My brother...well, he was bright like you...smart like you...until last summer when he was thrown from a horse...and kicked repeatedly in the head...by a *white* horse...and uhm that's why his head is warped. My brother riding your ride is a triumph over his fear. And you, without knowing it, have given him a great gift today. You have given him a reason to live. To recover. To go on."

I offer the guy some of the candy, but he shakes his head, having lost any appetite.

"But we better take the horse from him, because it's not fair to all the other children...who should be showing up any minute now. That wouldn't be fair to them, and since when was life fair? And as soon as this ride stops, I'll take my brother off. Rest assured."

"Oh, man," the carnie says. "Don't. Oh, man. Christ, he should be riding for free."

"But that wouldn't be fair...."

"Forget fair, you know what I mean? This kid, your brother, man oh man. He rides for free. I just decided that. He always gets the white horse, too. Always." The carnie wipes his eyes and composes himself.

We watch as Arnie circles around again. He hits his horse to go faster.

"I'm Gilbert Grape," I say. "And that's my brother Arnie."

"I'm Les," the carnie says, preparing to go back to the controls to stop the ride.

"Here," I say, offering the cotton candy.

"No, I couldn't," Les says.

"Please. For me."

He takes it.

Seven free rides later I move toward Arnie. "Hey, buddy. You tired of going in circles?"

"Nope."

"I'm getting dizzy just watching you. Let's take a break, huh?"

"Nope."

"Hey, let's say we go up in the air. Let's go up."

"Nope."

I try to pull him off his horse, but he won't budge. Les is watching this and he says, "What's the problem?"

"I need a break from all this going in circles," I say. "I got to go up. Rise above this. You understand?"

"Totally."

"So that's the problem."

"Hey, I got an idea," Les calls out, taking a ticket from a kid, "I'll watch him for you. He's A-OK right here with me."

I give him the thumbs up and step off the ride as it starts up. My walking away goes unnoticed by the retard. Free at last, I say to myself. *poor Gilbert*

Making my way through the carnival, I pass the Tilt-A-Whirl, the Octopus, the games, and the Bingo tent. Pretty much every person I see I know. They say "Hi" and I say "Hi." I pass the tank where Tucker is heckling anyone who passes. He's still dry—and not because people are missing but because no one has tried. He sees me and starts to call out, "GILLLLBEEERRRT GGRRR . . . !" I move out of range fast.

I walk to a booth and pay the seventy-five cents for a ticket in exact change. I turn to find a beehive hairdo blocking my view. I look down. Her mole has expanded since yesterday, and I say, "Hi, Melanie."

"You're avoiding me, aren't you?"

"No. Never."

"You were just looking at me from the merry-go-round."

"Was I?"

"Yes. Didn't you see me waving at you? Flagging you down?"

I must have mistaken her head for cotton candy. "No, I didn't see you."

"Well, you were looking right at me. Got a little sun, I see. You feeling bad about missing yesterday's appointment?"

"Should I feel bad?"

"Yes! It's rude and unadultlike to miss an appointment. No call. No apology even."

"I'm sorry."

"Don't apologize to me. It's not me who you were scheduled to see."

I sigh and grab my head. All I want is to ride the Ferris wheel. Somebody or something, please lift me up and out of here.

"Would you like to reschedule? Gilbert?"

"Yes. Tomorrow."

"He picks up his boys at church camp late in the afternoon tomorrow. It's a very hectic day. He's an incredibly busy man. But show up at your regular time, two P.M. He'll get to you when he can."

"Fine, great, yes, looking forward to it."

"Don't forget." Melanie brushes one forefinger over another as if to scold me, smiles like all is forgiven, and sways off, her designer jeans too tight, her hair too big, too bright.

"Here's my ticket." A bald carnie with a Hitler mustache signals for me to sit, the protective bar is secured, he shifts a lever-back and up I go. Each time I descend, this tingly, whooshy feeling washes through my balls. So I think naughty things on this wheel tonight. Sex things.

As I spin, I close my eyes. I picture places far away from Endora, places where no one knows my name.

I must go up and around ten, fifteen times with my eyes closed. When I come to a stop at the very top, I open them and look out. The sun is down. The lights from the rides make this night colorful. From up here I can see our tired house, my old school, and the Dairy Dream. Far away I can even make out the glow from the Food Land parking lot. Peering over the side I see below me a little boy and his mom being helped off the ride. The carnie picks up a bucket of water and splashes it across their seat. One of them must have thrown up. I check around me for any vomit remnants, but fortunately this car or basket or whatever it's called is as spotless as these rides ever get. Stuck up here for the time being, I continue my look around. I notice a rip in the merry-go-round's tent roof. Les should be told about this. At the dunk tank, Tucker is still dry and no one is throwing. There's a long line for the Tilt-A-Whirl, but that's always the case. Some kids are playing the balloon game and the basketball toss and the cranes.

I'm checking on the status of the puke cleanup when I see a bicycle coast past, a boys' bike, with a certain girl on it. She wears a white T-shirt and blue jeans and her black hair blows like a horse's mane. The wheel starts up with a sudden jolt. I follow the girl as she coasts past the games, past the kiddie cars. As I go by the operator

I say, "I'm ready to get out now," but he waves like I paid him a com-pliment or something. She zips over to the Octopus and passes the Scrambler, the popcorn booth and the Pillow House. "Let me off! Let me off!" I scream, trying to remain nonchalant but failing. The carnie rubs the tip of his nose with a knuckle and spits.

I'm at the bottom and going back up. The girl is pedaling toward the Ferris wheel. She stops and studies it. When I come down in front, I'm all set to wave some gesture, but she's gone.

She's gone.

It's another five minutes before I'm finally let off.

I thank the operator for a "marvelous" ride and under my breath utter, "You asshole." The girl from Michigan has left the grounds, I can feel it. I check all over anyway. There is no sign of her. No bike tracks, even.

"Thanks for watching him," I say, pointing to the rip in the tent. Les nods like he knows. "Okay, Arnie, time to let the horse rest."

"But my horse isn't tired...."

"Arnie!"

"But...but...!"

"Say goodnight."

Arnie gives his horse a hug and starts to kiss its nose.

"Arnie, no!"

I take him by the hand and pull him off the ride.

We're walking out after buying him some taffy when I hear amplified: "GILBERT GRAPE IS A RAISIN! GILBERT GRAPE IS A RAISIN!"

It's Tucker and still no one has nailed him. I flip him the bird from about seventy-five yards.

"REAL TOUGH, YOU RAISIN YOU! REAL TOUGH OF YOU!"

Arnie is running around wondering where the sound is coming from, people are looking at me, and in hopes that the Becky girl might be watching from some hiding place, I walk real cool-like toward Tucker. Arnie tags along.

"OH, HERE COMES MR. TOUGH! OOOOOO–I'M SCARED!"

It's three balls for a dollar and I pay five bucks' worth, giving me fifteen throws. The first six throws miss. A crowd is gathering. No sign of the girl yet. Tucker talks faster and faster; he's getting meaner and meaner. The seventh ball I throw right at him. The chicken-wire screen protects him, but it feels good to have scared him. The people watching are getting loud, half of them want Tucker wet, the other half don't. Balls eight through eleven aren't even close. Ball twelve hits dead on, but Tucker doesn't drop.

"YOU GOT TO THROW IT HARDER, YOU WIMP! YOU GIMP!"

This has become an exercise in humiliation. Everybody is laughing and I'm suddenly angry. Tucker is having a field day with my name and the length of my hair and the rust on my truck. Normally I could ignore it, but not in this situation, not today, not now. Ball thirteen slips out of my hand. I bend down to pick it up, when Arnie ducks under the sawhorse divider and runs straight at the bar. Tucker sees this, but before he can stand up, Arnie pushes the red bull's-eye, the tractor tire seat drops, and Tucker falls in the water. The people cheer.

Victory, Arnie Grape style.

I reward my retard brother with a celebratory malt at the Dairy Dream. We drive home. He goes to bed early because the "horsies" wore him out. I lie in my bed, horny as all get-out, and think about the girl from Michigan. I picture it all perfectly. After I relieve myself, I clean up, using an old sock.

12

It's the next morning, and I'm back at work, describing Arnie's carnival experience. Mr. Lamson laughs so hard he cries. "That brother of yours—a good boy," he says.

I'm sweeping Aisle Four when Mrs. Betty Carver comes around the corner carrying a box of brown sugar.

"Gilbert?"

"Yes, Mrs. Carver, I know, Mrs. Carver. I've made an appointment for two P.M. today!" I say this loud because I know Mr. Lamson is listening. He walks up behind her, looking puzzled.

"I missed my appointment–I'm sorry–I'll do it today. Really sorry, Mrs. Carver!"

She holds out the box of brown sugar and says, "How much?"

"Huh?"

"There's no price on the box. How much?"

"Oh."

Mr. Lamson says, "The sticker must have fallen off, because Gilbert doesn't miss a box."

"I'm not here to scold or condemn," she says. "I'm only here for the sugar."

Mr. Lamson takes the box and they go to ring it up. As she walks out the door, she looks back my way and I shake my head.

"Don't worry, boss, I'll be using my lunch hour to go to my appointment."

"Of course, son."

"I messed up on Wednesday, sir, and now it's getting way out of hand."

"Life's like that." *The affair*

It's my lunch hour. The clock on the outside of the Endora Savings and Loan blinks out 1:55, then 97 degrees, 1:55, 97 degrees, 1:56. I drive by the insurance office and see Mr. Carver's car. I keep on driving, though, down Elm Street and two miles out the south end of town. I turn left at Potter's bridge, make a right at the shingled mailbox and do it all in record time. I pull into the driveway of a two-story farmhouse with green shutters. The door to the red brick garage opens–eager to swallow my truck and me. I pull into the garage. Using my fingers like a comb, I try to make my hair nice. She is watching me from the side porch, looking lovely, holding the controls for the garage. She pushes the button and the door begins to close. I have to crouch to get out in time.

"Your hair looks fine," she says, turning and going back inside.

I smile, but my thoughts are "Here we go again." We're in the house fast. All these precautions seem absurd now, but when we began all those years ago, it was the only way. When the Carvers moved to the country, I thought the need for secrecy would lessen. But Mrs. Betty Carver respects tradition, and this, I'm afraid, is ours.

She has changed to work-around-the-house clothes. Her hair looks as if she took a brush and unbrushed it. Her lips are made up bright red. She smells like expensive soap and her teeth are shiny white. She does not in any way look like her name. It's not her fault that she was born in a time when people believed in names like Wanda, Dottie, and Betty. She's more of a Vanessa or Paulina.

"You got dough and stuff on your fingers," I say.

"I'm making cookies." She washes her hands, then dries them off with a flower-patterned towel. She takes out a food timer and sets it for eighteen minutes.

I say, "Cookies take that long?"

"This isn't for cookies. You know that."

"I know. Isn't eighteen minutes an odd time, though?"

"I like odd times." Mrs. Betty Carver has never looked so ready. It's been a while since our last uhm whatever you want to call what we're about to do here.

"What kind you making?"

"Oatmeal."

"Oh," I say. That explains the Quaker Oats from Wednesday and the brown sugar from this morning.

"I was a good actress today, wasn't I? And Wednesday, too. Really believable. They don't suspect a thing. Nobody does. Nobody ever will."

I tell her that she should have given me more notice.

"Wednesday. I was expecting you Wednesday."

The timer ticks.

I start to say "I'm here now, aren't I?" when Betty, who-doesn't-look-like-a-Betty Carver, wife of the only remaining insurance man in Endora, mother of two little snotty boys, Todd and Doug, covers my mouth with her now clean, soap-smelling hands. Talking is not the idea of this.

She points to a slip of paper on the counter. As I dial the number written down, she unhooks the barrette in her hair. She unbuttons her shirt. She takes it off. She lifts my T-shirt and kisses my stomach—leaving the red shape of her lips like a scar.

"I'm dialing," I say, hoping she'll wait till I'm done.

She unzips my pants. Kissing my tummy, she licks lower. I dialed wrong, I think. I hang up and she giggles. I dial again as she pulls down my underwear.

"The phone is ringing," I say. But there is no stopping Mrs. Betty Carver. She holds me in her hand. She puts me in her mouth.

"Carver's Insurance, good afternoon."

"Melanie, yes uhm...this is Gilbert Grape...two sharp, I know...I'm going to be late...I've been held up...."

Mrs. Betty Carver is moving her mouth slow and soft.

"Gilbert, I should have known." Melanie is mad at me, I can hear it. "Well, when might Mr. Carver expect you?"

"Soon, very soon."

"How soon? We run a tight ship here. I need a specific time. I'm very disappointed in you."

"You're not the only one."

Mrs. Betty Carver is bobbing up and down now, her hair all in her face.

Melanie says, "This a repeat of Wednesday? This your pattern? Mr. Carver has family obligations later today, you know? So?"

I make an "Oh God" sound—Mrs. Betty Carver just hit the spot.

"No, not God, Gilbert—you. You have to make up your mind. I'm waiting."

"It might take longer than I think."

"Gilbert, come on!"

"Okay, okay. Eighteen minutes!"

"Good boy, Gilbert. We'll expect you at two twenty-four sharp then."

Mrs. Betty Carver is working harder than ever, making slurpy noises. Her lipstick is smeared all over me, I bet. I put my free hand on top of her head and wish that the mouth on me was not hers but rather the mouth of that Michigan girl, that Becky from Ann

Arbor, the people eater. Melanie is droning on about my responsibilities and I'm about to hang up when Mrs. Betty Carver's teeth get a piece of me.

"Ow!" I say.

Melanie asks, "Is something the matter?"

"No. Nothing is wrong."

"Is it a family matter?"

"Is what?"

"Is what's keeping you a family matter? Everything okay at home?"

Mrs. Betty Carver takes me out of her mouth and checks to see if I'm cut. She whispers, "You're okay–no blood," and she puts me in her again.

"Melanie, I'm okay. I've got to go."

"But if I can give Mr. Carver a reason, he would be most pleased. He always appreciates a reason."

"Tell him it's all my fault."

I hang up.

Mrs. Betty Carver looks up and with apologetic eyes says, "I'll be gentler." She starts in again.

"Please stop."

"Sometimes it takes longer, that's all."

"Stop."

"Is it me? Tell me what I'm doing wrong. Tell me."

"It's not you."

"Give me a little more time, you'll see." She wets her hand by spitting in it and she is about to start up when I firmly say "Stop!" Her hands move to her side and she stays on her knees. I kneel down and wipe the hair out of her face. Her lipstick is gone.

"It's not you," I say.

The timer says eight minutes. She slumps over on the floor. This will be all for today, I guess. I lean over and kiss her forehead. She wants a hug, but it's hard for me to when all my thoughts are of the new girl.

She whispers, "Do I make you happy?"

I shrug like "Yes, you do, kind of."

* * *

We hold an awkward hug for the remaining eight minutes, and when the buzzer goes off she bursts into tears.

"I gotta go."

"I know."

"Please stop crying."

"I will."

"Your husband will be home soon."

"I'll stop."

As I'm leaving, she whispers, "I hope I make you happy. I want to make somebody happy. Just once. Somebody happy just once."

The screen door shuts. Mrs. Betty Carver fights to wave as I drive off.

I wonder if I'll remember her fondly when I'm eighty. I think so. I'll probably consider her one of the best things that ever happened to me. I'll probably want these days back.

13

"Gilbert, good to see you. Good to see your face." Mr. Carver looks mad as he waves me into his office. He signals me to have a seat in one of the two brown leather chairs that face his desk. He does this in a manner that makes me wonder if at one time he directed traffic.

I say, "Your hand gestures are really something, Mr. Carver."

"You think?"

"I know, sir."

"Well, I love the human hand. There's nothing I admire more." He holds his hands out and moves his fingers in all directions. This goes on until Mr. Carver is chuckling and chortling at the sight of this. "When Betty and I lived in Boone, before the boys were born—you, of all people, will find this interesting—there was a boy, a prodigy. This kid was eight or nine years old. He was Chinese or

Japanese or whatever it is that you are when you can play the piano really well. This boy was a genius and he had *white* parents. He had been *adopted*. And these parents insured this boy's hands for *half a million dollars*. Can you imagine?"

He looks at me for a response, and all I want to do is apologize.

"Isn't that a splendid example of the possibility of the human hand? And is it not remarkable what some people will insure? Proof that it's important to protect that which is special! Jesus, I feel necessary. Would you like to feel necessary, Gilbert? Have you ever thought about a career in insurance? I could get you started. You could kiss those grocery bags good-bye."

"Uh," is all I can say.

"It's good work. I have a house and two kids. We have two kids. Two boys, even. We are buying a trampoline. You'll have to come over and try it out. We ordered it for the Fourth of July. My boys wanted a swimming pool and even though I can't provide that, I can come through with a trampoline. I mean, I'm not a doctor, for Christ's sake–Dr. Harvey could provide a pool. At my house, a trampoline will have to do."

As Mr. Carver drones on about how this new trampoline is much easier to insure than a swimming pool and any other topics that leap into his great, cavernous mind, I just stare at him. Might he be what I'm becoming?

Behind his desk, hanging in a brown wooden frame, is a recent Carver family picture. Each Christmas season the Endora Savings and Loan offers its customers a family portrait. We haven't had one taken in years, due in large part to Momma's inflation and, I guess, because we think that families are what other people have.

In the picture, Mr. Carver sits with his teeth exposed, a boy on each side. The boys curl their lips, forcing out smiles. Mrs. Betty Carver stands behind them, her face expressionless, her eyes sad.

I want to take him by his shirt collar and say, "Do you ever look into your wife's eyes, you asshole?" but I don't. He talks on and on. The phone rings and he stops mid-sentence. He says, "One second, Gilbert," leans back in his chair, and closes his eyes. He waits as Melanie answers it out front. The phone ringing must be such a rare occurrence that he has no choice but to savor it.

Melanie's fake fingernails drum lightly on the office door. "Mr. Carver?"

"I'm talking with Gilbert. You know that."

"I know, sir."

"It better be important."

"It's your wife."

"Tell her I'm in a conference...."

"It sounds important."

"Okay. Okay. Gilbert, one moment, is that all right?"

I shrug like "no problem," but inside I think "oh shit."

He picks up. "Yes, Betty. What is it?"

I look around like I'm not listening.

"Uh-huh. Uh-huh. Calm down. Calm down!" He swivels his chair so as to face away from me. "No. Yes, I'm in a conference. With Gilbert Grape, yes." Mr. Carver pauses and, without turning back to look at me, says, "Gilbert, my wife wants to know how you are?"

"I'm uhm fine."

"He's fine. Uh-huh. What has Gilbert got to do with this?" There is another silence. "Honey, don't start crying again. Please. Talk to me."

Mr. Carver's voice is barely audible now. The back of his neck is turning red.

"Of course I'm disappointed. Of course I'm sad."

He is drenched in sweat. A strong man, surely he could pull off my arms with relative ease.

"Well, my concern is the boys. What are we going to tell the boys? They are the reason for all of this. The boys are who I'm thinking about. That just won't be the same. Calm down, Betty, or I'm coming home. That's it. I'm coming home. Right now. We can't do this over the phone." He hangs up and sits there motionless. Oh God. With his feet he kicks his chair around. Mr. Ken Carver stares at me with a smile like the one in the picture. "Something has come up. You will excuse me."

He moves out of the office fast—I stand and follow in a daze. Melanie is saying something about rescheduling, but I don't hear her. I open the door to leave and the bell rings or dongs. The heat outside slaps me confirming that this is no nightmare.

"Gilbert," Mr. Carver says, standing next to his Ford Fairmont. "Would you drive me home?"

I stop and stand there, hesitating to answer. My heart starts racing. I feel sweat forming.

"I'm in no state to drive," he says, smiling like I have no choice.

"But..."

"If it wasn't an emergency..."

We climb into my truck and he looks for the seat belt. "I took them out," I explain. "They always got in the way."

He takes a moment to lecture me about the safety risk. "If you don't have them put back in, we'll have to raise your rates."

"Okay," I say, "I'll put them back in."

We're on the highway with the windows rolled down. Mr. Carver starts speaking, or shouting, rather. She told him about us. He knows. I know that he knows.

"Women, Gilbert. I'm married to a woman." He pauses here for effect. What effect exactly I do not know. "And God knows I love her–God knows it. And we have two boys, but you knew that. And Todd and Doug–they are at church camp and they miss their parents, their house, and I thought when we picked them up, you know, today–this afternoon–I thought we'd bring them a reminder. Something that states our love without saying it. So my wife–God love her–this afternoon something happened to my wife–do you know what...?"

"Uhm."

"You'll never guess."

I almost say "Don't be so sure," but this isn't the time for clever-ness. "What happened to your wife?" I ask.

"Well, my wife sets out to make a batch of cookies for my boys. It seems to me these cookies were the perfect gift. How many mothers make cookies for their kids? Not many these days. There was a time when all mothers did was make cookies. I am married to an exceptional woman. But sometimes, Gilbert, sometimes I wish I was somebody else's husband because sometimes..." He takes a breath, pressing his lips together, making them disappear. Then he continues, "My wife..."

Oh God. Here we go.

"My wife. Burns. A batch of cookies. It is no big deal. A

disappointment for the boys, sure. But it is no big deal! Now she is crying like her life is destroyed, crying over a bad batch of cookies. Sometimes, I tell you, honestly, sometimes I want to put her head in the oven and turn on the gas."

Mr. Carver suddenly pushes at his forehead with the palm of his left hand. "Oh God. I can't believe I just said that. Can you? I did not mean that about the oven. I can't believe I just said that."

I pull into their driveway. Through a window, I can see Mrs. Betty Carver sitting with her head down on the kitchen table.

"I think what you mean, Mr. Carver, is that sometimes she gets on your nerves."

"Yes. That's what I mean."

Whew. Breathe, Gilbert, breathe easy.

There's a silence while he licks the sweat off his top lip. "Oh, Gilbert?"

"Yes, sir?"

"Remember–the trampoline. On the Fourth. We'd love to have you come try out our trampoline." He climbs out of my truck. His baggy, sweaty body walks to the house. He goes inside without turning back to me. I'm glad he didn't thank me for the ride.

I'm halfway home when I pull off onto the shoulder of Highway 13. I put my truck in park and leave the engine running. I let go of the steering wheel. I hold my hands in front of me. I'll sit here as long as it takes for them to stop shaking.

14

It's Monday. It's the morning, and Arnie's flailing both arms as the merry-go-round horses are being driven out of town. The other rides pass by us, too, and my brother, all smiles, waves as each driver gives a toot or a honk or a beep. As the one carrying the Silver

Scrambler drives off, I say, "Arnie, that's it. That's all she wrote." He stands watching, leaning forward and squinting. He always waits until whatever he has been watching is completely gone.

"This year's carnival was one of the best, don't you think, buddy? Huh? Don't you think?"

"Some parts were."

"What parts weren't?"

"Uhm. You know what was bad, Gilbert—you know what was bad?"

"No."

"The horses..."

"The merry-go-round?"

"Yeah, the horses were mean this year. They spit on me."

"No."

"Yes."

"Where? I don't see any spit."

"It dried up."

"Those were fiberglass horses, Arnie."

"Still. Ouch, they were meanies. They were biting me, ouch."

I stop, because I'm not going to engage in this kind of conversation at this particular moment in my life.

A '73 Dodge Coronet passes us with a bunch of kids in back. Arnie waves and I look for a trace of that black-haired girl from Michigan. Ever since she sank her teeth in me at the Dairy Dream, I've watched for her to see what she'll look like in daylight. She must have freckles or speckles or a gap in her teeth, surely something that will make forgetting her possible. Other than her brief appearance at the carnival Friday night, this Becky creature has been invisible.

I start walking home. Arnie trails after.

"Gilbert, I'm not lying."

"Huh?"

" 'Bout the horsies. I'm no liar on this. It was..."

"What was?"

"The horses was..."

"Were."

"Was a phen. Phenah. Phenah-ha. Uhm."

"The word is phenomena."

"I know, Gilbert. Jeez."

Arnie tries to stick one of his short, stubby fingers through one of my belt loops. He pokes me repeatedly. I normally don't mind this, but today it's like a reminder of all that I loathe about my life, and I snap, "Stop it!"

He pulls his finger out and steps away fast. He looks at his shoes. A pickup truck speeds by carrying people we don't know. This time he doesn't wave.

"Truck is just like mine, buddy. Look."

Arnie stays staring at his feet. One little snap from me somehow ruins his life. It's as if the last four days of constant carnival rides, of buying him whatever candy and popcorn he wanted, of standing there watching him go around on the merry-go-round fifty-four times in a row—it's as if none of it ever happened. You just wish he'd remember some of the good times.

Having pushed out his bottom lip, he's holding his breath, which is making his face turn beet red. In a minute his brain will probably hemorrhage, he'll die, and since I don't want the guilt of that, I say his name as nice as I know how.

The kid doesn't answer. He just scrunches his face tighter, his skin is more purplish now, and he's clenching his fingers into white-knuckled fists. A red truck whizzes past heading for town, but he still won't wave.

"That was your favorite color," I say.

His entire body is starting to convulse; veins are jumping out on his neck; a road map pops up around his eyes.

"Arnie, guess what you are? Guess." I wait a second. "You're a phen. A phenah. Uhm. I can't say it. You're a phenomha. What is the word? Maybe I can't say it, Arnie. But it's what you are. Phenon. A phenom?"

Suddenly eager to know what he is, Arnie stops his seizure.

"Help me out, buddy."

"Sure, Gilbert."

I'm saying "Phenom" over and over and he's making *fffff* sounds, and this goes on for some time. "Maybe I can't say the word, but I know it's what you are."

"I know it's what I am too, Gilbert."

I conveniently suggest that we head home and ask Amy.

"She works at a school, Gilbert."

"That's right. If she doesn't know, then no one does."

"Right, Gilbert." He takes my hand and we begin to walk home. He likes to say my name when he talks to me. I've always thought it was his way of proving to himself that he knows something.

Walking down Vine Street, we go past the Methodist church that sponsored the carnival. Arnie slows down. Sensing that he's about to run over and stand where the rides used to be, I say, "I got it. I got it, Arnie."

"What what what what!" he says, fast and loud.

"You, buddy, are a phenomenon."

"Yes!" he sings.

"Race you home." And before Arnie has a chance to go to the church grounds, I'm off and running. He chases after me.

My usual procedure when racing him is to get out in front by a house or two, let him catch up with me, and then, at the last possible moment, let him win by mere inches. But today I want to remind him who's boss.

So I run fast for me. When I get to our driveway, I jump up and down like some sporting champion. I look back to cheer him on only to find that he's quit the race, turned around and is heading toward the church grounds.

With Arnie, even when you win, you lose.

I've not even reached our screen door when Amy calls out from the kitchen, "Where's Arnie?"

Notice how it's never "How are you, Gilbert? You're looking good, Gilbert. Combed your hair, did you, Gilbert?" But it's always been this way; it's been this way for years.

I explain that we had a great time and that, for me, watching the rides leave town was almost as exciting as watching them come into town. "Arnie and I learned a new word today," I say, "but he had his heart set on some private time with the church grounds, so he's there, and I'm here, and no way in hell am I going back after him."

She starts to protest.

"Amy, who has spent the last four days entirely with the runt?"

"He's not a runt!" She takes a deep breath. "But I know what you mean. I appreciate it. You've been a big help." Then she yells, "Ellen. Ellen!"

The little one appears at the top of the stairs, looks at Amy, and says, "Just know one thing. I am watching this great movie, and don't ask me the name of it because I don't know the name, but it's in black and white, and it is good. Of course I'll do what you ask. Just know that the movie is great. Be aware of the sacrifice I'm making."

"Forget it," Amy says. "I'll do it."

I glare at Ellen. But since she hasn't looked at me in ages, she doesn't notice.

"I don't mind doing it–whatever *it* is...."

I pantomime breaking her neck. This, too, has no audience.

"Just so you know that I'm suffering."

For Amy, the thought of anyone suffering, even Ellen, is unbearable. So she goes into the kitchen, changes her sandals for tennis shoes, and walks toward the front door.

The puberty girl screams, "I'll do it!"

Amy stops and says, "Momma's sleeping," as if it were some new occurrence. "Get back to your movie. Hurry up, you're missing it."

"The movie isn't all that good, even though the lead actress looks just like me. So, in truth, my not watching the movie is not the sacrifice that it seemed." She smiles like there was never a problem. Her smile makes you think for a moment that there aren't any problems, that all is smooth, that Ellen Grape possesses humanity, and before Amy can say anything, Ellen hops down the stairs and shoots out the front door.

It's over a minute before she's back in the house. She walks past me to the kitchen, where Amy is looking up a recipe.

"Amy?"

"Yeah."

"Uhm."

"What, Ellen?"

"What was it you wanted me to do?"

15

Momma snores from her chair as Amy clears away the breakfast dishes. I drown my cereal with milk and stir it with the least dirty spoon I can find. I'm lifting the first spoonful when Tucker's truck motors into our drive. Amy looks up, relieved.

"It's just the wood," I say. "It's still gonna take days to assemble everything."

"I know."

"I don't think you do." I stand up and move down the hallway.

Amy follows. "I understand that this takes time. Just so we're doing something. Just so we're trying to make our mother's life better."

It is arguable as to whether installing an entire network of support beams and boards will have anything to do with making her life better. She might live longer. But since when were longer and better the same thing?

Tucker is kind of tiptoeing toward our house with his red toolbox. I shout through the door screen, "Tucker, she won't wake up!"

"You never know, though," he whispers back.

"She won't! She never does after breakfast!"

It takes him an eternity to make it across our yard. Finally Tucker and his tools are safely in the house.

It was last Wednesday that Tucker appraised the floor situation. He ordered the wood on Thursday and we picked it up Friday. Saturday was spent carefully measuring and cutting it in his dad's workshop. Yesterday he drilled holes in the boards so today we can assemble support beams with long screws and bolts. This way there will be no hammering in the basement, no loud noises. This way Momma will never know.

Working fast, we make three trips down to the basement; half of the wood is on the floor. We're downstairs, panting and sweating. Tucker says, "Gilbert?"

"Yeah."

He smiles for the first time in four days. "This is going to work." I don't know if he's ever been so proud of anything. He's starting to sport a new image—one of adequacy.

"Great," I say.

There's a glorious silence while he struggles to think of a new topic of conversation. He checks one of the boards. "This is warped."

"It doesn't matter."

"It matters to me."

"No one is going to come down here. This is not for show-and-tell. This is purely a functional project we're engaged in here."

"I know this. Don't you think I know this?"

I rub my nose with the palm of my hand because hearing this guy talk makes me want to sneeze him into oblivion.

"I'm a believer in the very best for the very best people. Your mother is one of the best people."

I want to say that my mother is a cow. But instead I say, "We should finish, because I work at noon."

"Oh. Are you rubbing that in?"

"Rubbing what in?"

"That you have a job and I don't."

"No. Not rubbing in anything. Merely saying that I have to work today. So let's hurry."

"I'm planning to get a *real* job."

"Yeah, I know you are."

"The Burger Barn could benefit from people like me. I'd like to be an assistant manager. Give me a title, give me power."

I say, "Let's get going," when Amy flicks the basement light off and on fast.

Tucker gets twitchy. "What's going on up there? What's going on?"

The basement goes from light to dark to light.

"She's awake."

"Who is?"

"The beached whale."

"Gilbert."

"We've got to wait."

I lie down and close my eyes. "Hopefully, Momma won't look outside and see all the wood left in your truck."

Tucker paces about. "If you'd just tell her—if you'd just be honest with her..."

"No."

"But isn't honesty the best..."

"Sorry, Tucker."

"But..."

"This is the way it's got to be."

The only sounds upstairs are that of the TV changing channels and Amy's muffled voice.

"Oh, Gilbert, man oh man. Have I got some news or what? I was going to call you."

"Yeah?"

He kneels beside me. "I drove out this morning to the Future Site of the Burger Barn, you know?"

"Don't tell me they've already started building it."

"Yes! But there is something else that I saw...."

I say to Tucker that I don't care about the Burger Barn. "I will never eat there," I say.

"This isn't about the Burger...."

"Tucker, just thinking about this gives me reason to die. So will you please shut up!"

At this point, a creaking and cracking noise starts moving our way. Tucker stands, he's suddenly nervous. "Holy Jesus. Holy God. What is going on up there?"

I explain that Momma's heading for the bathroom.

"No way." He looks up and starts to hyperventilate. We stare at the basement ceiling. Each step Momma takes makes cracks in the paint. "It's like she's drawing a road map."

"Jesus," Tucker says, holding his arms above his head to protect himself from the falling plaster.

It takes Momma many minutes to get to the bathroom. The creaking stops as she gets situated. Amy turns on Ellen's stereo with Elvis's *Aloha from Hawaii* album and his version of "Suspicious Minds."

"That's our signal," I say. We sprint up the stairs and grab all the remaining wood.

It takes three more trips to get all of it downstairs. As Tucker and I shoot out of the house, Amy turns off Elvis. We get in our respective trucks. Standing in the doorway, Amy starts to give us the thumbs up but turns away suddenly. Momma must have flushed.

Our trucks race up the street. We turn left on Vine and pass the Methodist church. I slow down when I see Ellen dragging Arnie by the ankles. The retard is on the ground, clawing at clumps of dry grass, effectively slowing Ellen down. She grabs his hair and pulls up hard. I hit my brakes, jump out of my truck. "Stop it! Stop it!" She lets go of his hair, brushes her bangs out of her face, and smiles in her this-didn't-just-happen way.

Whoa

"You little bitch," I shout, crossing the street.

Arnie curls up into a little ball. Ellen starts to cry. "What am I supposed to do? He won't come home! I've tried everything! Candy! Bribery! Sexual favors! Nothing will get him home and I've uhm I've uhm . . ."

"You've uhm what?"

"You know—things to do."

"You hit him again . . ."

"He's been eating the leftover bits of popcorn. It's all muddy and dirty. . . ."

"You hit him again and I'll . . ."

Ellen holds her face in such a way as to make certain I see her tears.

As a brother and as a Grape, I put up with a lot. My sisters, my mother, this town. I will endure anything. But one thing I will not allow. *No one hurts Arnie.*

I will kill for that kid.

"I wasn't hitting him exactly. . . ."

"You pull his hair or touch him even. I swear I'll kick your ass."

"Aren't you the tough one?"

The retard is crawling back across the field like an army man. I walk over, lie down next to him, and say, "I've gotta go to work. Somebody has got to be at home protecting Momma and Amy.

75

Even Ellen. Will you be their protector? Will you be their guard? I'm counting on you, buddy."

He lies there motionless as he thinks hard; then he nods without looking at me. He stands, gives me a salute, and starts toward our house. Ellen says nothing and follows. Hold his hand or give him a squeeze or something, I want to say. I'm tempted to throw a rock, when she turns and mouths, "Thank you."

They walk home, never touching.

As I go to my truck, I call over to Tucker who has been a spectator to all of this. "And you want to date that monster?"

"I did want to. Not anymore."

Happy days are here. "How great. You've finally seen the light. You finally got my point." Suddenly this is shaping up to be a breakthrough day for Tucker.

"Let me clarify," he says.

I walk right up to his truck. I've been waiting years for some clarity from this guy.

"Your sister is a kind of Miss Iowa material. Sexy, appealing, corn-fed look. Okay? She's still incredible by every uhm stretch of uhm whatever it is that stretches."

"Your imagination."

"Yeah, right."

"For the record–I don't agree."

"I know. Hey, do we uhm have to discuss this in the middle of the road?"

"Think so. This could be the happiest day of my life."

"Okay. You see, I was trying to tell you this earlier. This morning, when I was at the Future Site of..."

"Yeah, I know where you were."

"I saw this girl. On a bike. Jesus, Gilbert. It was religious."

"What?"

"Well, you've never seen a girl like the one I saw this morning."

"You saw a girl?"

"Not 'a' girl, Gilbert. 'The' girl. The 'ultimate' girl."

"Does she have black hair?"

"That's all I'm gonna say."

"Is she about this tall?"

He shrugs.

"Do you know her name?" In desperation I add, "She's a friend of mine."

Tucker throws back his head and laughs like some sea creature. "Yeah, right–a friend of yours?" He cackles and giggles and rips out of there.

I jump for my truck. It takes a few tries before starting. He is long gone. I accelerate fast, chasing after him.

16

Tucker's truck is at the Ramp Cafe. I pull in and park between it and the McBurney's Funeral Home hearse. Beverly, the waitress, is taking Tucker's order when I get inside. She sees me, fakes a smile, and goes back to the chef, who also happens to be her father, Earl Ramp. Beverly never writes down her orders; she has this incredible memory. She can't seem to forget the numerous cruel things I did to her in grade school. She was one of those tall, bony girls that made a guy feel like a nothing. She also has a cherry-red birthmark on her neck the size of a small Frisbee. One day, when I was in fourth grade and she was in sixth, I wet a paper towel and gave it to her to wash it off. Everybody found it pretty funny except Beverly. She's never had a sense of humor.

[handwritten margin note: not nice in grade school]

Tucker is sitting with Robert McBurney, Jr., son of Robert Sr., and heir to the finest mortuary in the county. McBurney's Funeral Home is located in Motley. They do all the major burials in these parts. They do cremations, too. Bobby, as his intimate friends call him, has been away guest teaching at funeral school and has recently come back and is working hard. He is dressed in a funeral-black suit with a white handkerchief sticking up, his red hair immaculate, his face dotted with pink freckles.

"Bobby–welcome back."

He looks up. "Oh, thanks, Gilbert. How've you been?"

We talk small for a while. Tucker's pancakes come. Bobby is eating eggs, and Beverly forgets to take my order. "Beverly?" I ask.

"What?"

"I'm feeling a little famished. Could I get a slice of toast? Butter, grape jelly. The works." Beverly walks by without acknowledging my order and under her breath says, "Get it yourself, you fruit." I want to say, "Fruit is what is on your neck," but what would be the point?

Tucker pours his syrup and says, "So you saw her, too, Bobby?"

"Why do you think I'm over here?"

"I was wondering..."

"The talk in Motley is only about this girl."

Tucker says, "Not only is she gorgeous and beautiful, she's not bad-looking either." Tucker was born backward.

Bobby says, "I haven't seen her yet. But I've heard plenty."

"So," Tucker continues, "you drove over here to find her?"

"No, not exactly." Bobby licks the leftover egg off his fork. "Nobody's dying these days, and when it's slow Dad sends me into other towns to drive the hearse around—get some free publicity. Remind people of the McBurney option."

I say, "You're the only funeral home we got around here."

"True, Gilbert, but even then you have to remind people that you exist. People forget McBurney's Funeral Home. They begin to take us for granted."

"I know what you mean, Bobby," I say.

"Well," Tucker starts to say. He's about to put an entire pancake into his mouth. "We're preventing you from some business, I'm afraid." Bobby looks confused. Tucker stuffs his face but somehow manages to keep talking. "Gilbert's momma. We're fixing the floor so she..." Under the table my shoe finds his shin. He stops.

Bobby's interest is piqued. He says, "Go on."

"No," Tucker says. "It's rude." He tries to swallow. "You know, talking with my mouth open?"

Bobby is adamant. "Please don't go preventing my family from doing business. You know, as Americans we have a duty to die."

Thinking quickly, I say, "You guys buried Mrs. Brainer, didn't you?"

"Oh yes. We do pretty much all the schoolteachers."

Tucker stops. "Mrs. Brainer? She . . . ?"

I say, "Come on, you knew that she died."

"No, I didn't!"

"Well, she's very dead, Tucker, and the McBurney Funeral Home planted her deep, didn't you?" Bobby nods. "Tucker and me had Mrs. Brainer in the second grade."

"She must have been a great teacher," Bobby surmises.

"Why's that?"

"Big funeral. Many of her former students were there."

Tucker, starting to choke up, says, "I would've been there. I didn't know she died. Damn."

"Lots of people, huh?"

"More flowers, too, than I remember in a long time. Apparently she was a real happy lady."

Tucker says, "She had a smile for every student, every day."

I change the subject by asking Bobby what the procedure is when a person dies. He explains that he and his dad will drive to get the body. They bring it back to the funeral home. And while the family picks out a casket from their "impressive" selection room, the body is taken downstairs and embalmed. A process that sounds a lot like pickling to me. The dead person is stripped. I ask him what it is like to see someone he might have known, naked.

"Seeing them, you know, one day walking the streets—waving to their friends—and then, the next day, lying on the slab. It's harsh. It's fun, too. You live life differently when your primary contact is with the dead."

"You ever, you know . . . ?" Tucker is trying to articulate one of his obscure thoughts. "You ever uhm . . . ?"

"What?" Bobby is patient.

"You know, fool around with one of the bodies?"

"No!"

"You ever think about fooling around?"

I go, "Tucker, please."

"The worst we do—and I tell you guys this in confidence—the worst we do is take the ugly people—you know, the grotesque ones, and make jokes about them. Harmless jokes, though. I mean, after all, the people are dead. They don't hear us. My dad and me—we make some great jokes. We'll just look at their naked bodies and laugh and laugh. But it doesn't hurt anyone. No one even knows we do it."

"Now me and Gilbert know."

"Yeah, but who are you guys?" Bobby sets down his fork, having cleaned his plate. He wipes his mouth with his silk handkerchief.

Tucker says, "You ever worry that the dead are watching, though? You know, from up above somewhere."

"No."

Tucker says, "Oh." There's a lull while he ponders this. Maybe he'll be quiet for a while.

I ask, "What jokes did you make about Mrs. Brainer?"

"None. She had this smile on her face that made her so endearing. The most endearing dead person I ever remember. My dad thought so, too."

"She was a great teacher," Tucker pipes up.

"I guess so, because you hardly ever see flowers like the ones she got. Students from Chicago and Minneapolis even. Most impressive was a Dick and Jane reader series arrangement sent from Des Moines. Lance Dodge the newscaster sent them."

"NO WAY!" Tucker is in shock.

"I'm not lying. The arrangement must have cost three hundred dollars."

"Lance Dodge was in Gilbert's and my class," Tucker says in hopes that this will impress.

"Really?"

I nod.

"Gilbert and me have known him since like we were two."

"He moved here when we were seven," I say.

"Lance is you guys' age?"

I nod.

"I thought he was older. He's done so much for a young guy."

I don't nod. "We all had Mrs. Brainer."

"Well, people were mighty impressed with the floral display he sent. He must be quite a guy."

Finally my toast arrives, cold and with no jelly on the side. Beverly continues to seek her revenge.

Out of nowhere Tucker begins this giggling/laughing/hacking attack that he can't stop. "Oh God. Remember. Oh my God. No wonder he sent those flowers."

Bobby is turning pale. Apparently he's never suffered through a Tucker laughing spell.

"Second grade–Jesus!"

"Breathe, Tucker," I say, imploring him to slow down.

"How could I have forgotten?"

Bobby encourages Tucker by saying repeatedly, "What happened? What happened?"

"It was before afternoon recess. I look over and Lance Dodge is sitting in a puddle of his own piss. It had run out his pants, down his chair. Remember how she made him clean it up in front of everybody and he started crying? He was such a pussy, Lance was. Gilbert–remember that?"

I shove the small plate of toast crusts at Tucker. Then I slide out of the booth and stand.

"Gilbert? Hey! Where you going?"

I leave the Ramp Cafe and drive home.

Ellen is sunbathing on the front lawn on the nicest towel we own. She says nothing to me and I'm in the house fast. I run the water faucet in the kitchen sink and fill a half-gallon jug and proceed to chug every drop of water. The phone rings. Amy calls to me, "It's Tucker!"

"Tell him I'm not here."

I put my mouth up to the faucet and gulp down as much as I can. My stomach is stretched full with water. Amy comes into the kitchen as I turn the faucet off.

"He was calling about toast. Apparently you forgot to pay for some toast."

I take a paper towel and dry my mouth.

"Aren't you supposed to be working?"

"At twelve."

"Oh."

I ask what time it is while I'm heading for the front door.

"Eleven thirty-fiveish."

"Great! Bye, Amy."

Ellen is rubbing lotion on her stomach as I shift my truck into reverse. Arnie has climbed the willow tree out back and is shaking a branch as if to wave. I wave back and drive away.

I pull into the parking lot of my old school. It is red brick, and the windows have been boarded up since it closed seven years ago. I went there for thirteen years. The summer after I graduated they closed it down due to declining enrollment. There are those who think the building should be torn down—as it has no apparent use. They'll never do it, though. Too many memories for too many people.

I sit in my truck and remember going there. I look at the rusty playground equipment. The slides and swings are smaller now. I listen for the sounds of kids playing at recess, but there is only quiet. I lift my T-shirt and wipe the sweat off my face. Minutes pass.

When I spin out of the parking lot, my truck kicks up gravel. I hit Highway 2, the curvy, twisting highway, going twenty-two miles over the speed limit. I'm at the county cemetery in no time. I park to the far side. I walk to a certain grave where the dirt is brown and freshly dug. There is no tombstone yet—just a slip of paper, a tag, that identifies the deceased. My father had the same type of tag seventeen years ago. I guess dying never changes. An old woman is over near where Dad is buried, so I face away from her. My desire is not to offend the innocent. I am ready. I unzip my pants and proceed to pee all over Mrs. Brainer's grave.

No way!

I speed back to town with my radio blaring. I sing along to a song by one of those whatever-happened-to-them? groups—Bachman-Turner Overdrive.

> *"Takin' care of business*
> *every day*
> *Takin' care of business*
> *And workin' overtime"*

Back at the Ramp Cafe, the McBurney Funeral Home hearse is driving off with Tucker's truck set to follow. I pull in behind him, blocking his exit.

Tucker is out fast, shouting, "I hate you, Gilbert. I hate you! I'm telling a story, a funny, funny story and you just leave like that! You don't even pay your bill! I mean, some friend you are. Embarrassing me like that. I have pride, you know that? Huh? Did you know that!"

I let him go on for some time about how I don't deserve his friendship. He sounds like a bad boy scout. Finally I say, "Hey, dummy."

"I'm not the dummy! You are the dummy, Gilbert."

"It wasn't Lance Dodge who peed his pants."

"Yes, it was. I was there."

"No, dummy. It was me."

I rolled up my window.

Tucker says, "You? No way. No way!... uhm ... oh boy."

I shift to reverse and begin to back out.

"Oh yeah." Tucker remembers now. He's frantically trying to apologize as I drive away.

If it were possible, I wouldn't talk to Tucker for a week. I deserve better friends.

The Ramp Cafe is in the distance now and I'm alone with my thoughts. My only regret is that I didn't pee on Mrs. Brainer while she was alive.

17

A case could be made that Gilbert Grape became the thinker, the dreamer that he is while stocking the many cans and bags and food items for the people of this town.

Over the years my technique has become so automatic, so natural, that I don't need to think about what I'm doing. No, my thoughts wander off wherever they want. I'm usually not in the same place mentally that I appear to be physically. Either I'm in Des Moines at Merle Hay Mall or driving across the desert or standing on an Omaha rooftop waiting for a tornado to come ripping. Know this—I am rarely in this store or in this town in my thoughts.

I'm pricing the breakfast cereals when Mr. Lamson comes up behind me. "Wonderful surprises are in store for us all, Gilbert."

Startled, I almost drop the Wheaties I'm holding. I manage a "Huh? What?"

"Surprised you, did I?"

"Yes, sir."

"So you see my point."

I nod.

"I knew you would."

For years Mr. Lamson has taken great joy in surprising me. He's hidden under the counter, behind the dog food, and once he almost froze to death in the freezer waiting for me to open it so he could yell "Surprise." When I finally did, his eyebrows had begun to frost and his lips had turned blue.

I whisper under my breath, "Wonderful surprises—I'm waiting."

Mr. Lamson sees my mouth move. "What was that?"

"Nothing, sir."

Mrs. Lamson, who is in the little office cubicle waiting for money to count, calls out. "Dad, do they got some special going on at Food Land?"

"Not that I know of. Gilbert, anything going on at Food Land?"

"Oh, I'm not the one to ask. Never shopped there. Never will. Would rather die."

"You do not mean that."

"Sir," I say, "I'm afraid that I do. I go to a store for food. Not for . . ."

"They must have something going," Mrs. Lamson chimes in, walking all over my words and not seeming to mind. "Because nobody is here."

I can't bring myself to tell them what Tucker told me the other day. It seems that Food Land installed an aquariumlike tank where they keep crabs or octopus or lobsters with their arms or claws or whatever taped shut. People crowd around; kids make faces at the creatures—glad, I guess, that they're not the ones trapped inside.

I look up at the Wonder Bread clock. The forty-seven minutes I've worked today feel like forty-seven days.

"Gilbert, you sure you don't know something we don't know?"

"Honey," Mr. Lamson says, "I'm sure Gilbert would fill us in if he knew something was up over there. Wouldn't you?" Mr. Lamson smiles his yellow-toothed grin and glides down Aisle Two.

Mrs. Lamson starts singing the "Iowa Corn Song."

> *"Ioway, Ioway*
> *State of all the land*
> *Joy on ev'ry hand*
> *We're from Ioway, Ioway*
> *That's where the tall corn grows."*

I feel a tap on my back. It's Mr. Lamson—he's circled around and his eyes look misty. "If only there was another woman like her. If there were two of her, you could have one," he says.

Oh wow!

Finally, for the first time in weeks, I'm able to say something and mean it. "You don't know how much I would like that, Mr. Lamson."

"Oh, I know, son. Believe me, I know."

The singing stops. "What are you boys talking about?" she calls back. "You're not poking fun at my music?"

"Never!" Mr. Lamson says.

"No, ma'am."

"Then how come no applause?"

So me and the boss clap. He yells out a bravo and I toss a dime.

Outside, the Carver family station wagon drives by with the boys in back. Mrs. Betty Carver half waves. I turn away hoping she didn't see me see her.

I uncrate a box of assorted Campbell's soups. I stamp on the purple prices and sort them into flavors or types or whatever. And as I stack the cans, the image of that station wagon of hers stalled on Highway 13 flashes. I pulled over and helped her. I was almost seventeen and it was an easy fix, her car, and she seemed surprised that I could fix things, and I was surprised that a woman who'd seemed so uninteresting to me before could suddenly become so interesting. She complimented me on my skill and I replied–innocently, I might add–that I had always been pretty good with my hands. She said I was "adept," and I said I didn't know what that meant, and she said I should look it up in the dictionary, and I said I'm not interested in looking up things, that if you have to look it up then what is the point, and she said that she would be happy to teach me.

"Gilbert?"

Mr. Lamson is standing next to me. I listen without looking. My sights are on the soup cans.

"Between you and me . . . ?"

"Yes, sir?"

"Man to man?"

Sensing his concern, I stop with the cans and turn his way. I look him in the eye and almost succeed in ignoring the Band-Aid that holds his broken glasses together.

"It's those goddamned lobster tanks, isn't it?"

"I think so, sir." How did he know that I knew?

"Crap."

"Sir, it's just a fad. How long can lobsters in a tank be interesting? Flash and pizzazz and neon are but passing fancies. There will be a resurgence of simple dignity."

"You think?"

"Yes, sir. You and your way. It–we will prevail."

"You sound any more hopeful, Gilbert, I'll begin to think I'm talking to the ghost of your father."

I want to say, "I've never missed having a father, because of you," but I stay quiet.

He whispers back to me, "Let's keep those lobster tanks between us. It would break Mother's heart."

"I won't say a thing."

It's later now and I've moved on to the coffee cans. As I zip along, I review the sequence of Mrs. Betty Carver in my life.

It was the summer after I graduated high school. The Carver family was in the checkout line and the boys were just babies. Mr.

86

Carver was saying something to his wife about not buying candy. "Candy is bad for your teeth and why would you want to damage your wonderful teeth?" I was doing something, listening rather than working, and Mr. Lamson was ringing up their purchases. I was back by the metal stockroom door that swings, and Mrs. Carver walked right up to me, holding her newborn baby in one arm and a pound of bacon in the other. She said, "Gilbert?" I said, "May I help you, ma'am?" She spoke softly because there were other shoppers. "Forget it," she said. "No, what?" I said. Her baby was dribbling on her nice breasts. I remember her words exactly. "Gilbert, will you come..." She swallowed. Her voice was shaky. "Ken works most days and I can drop the boys off at a sitter. Will you come see me some time?" Mr. Carver called from the cash register. "You coming, honey?" She said, "Just a second," and continued whispering to me. "Come by Tuesday. I know that's your day off. Can I expect you?" I remember wondering how she knew when my day off was and why she was looking at me in this new way, this eager way. All of a sudden I said, "Yes," without thinking. She looked deep into my eyes, deeper than anyone ever had, to see if I was telling the truth. "I hope you'll be there," she said. Mr. Carver called again, "Honey, what are you doing?" While holding the drooling child, she exchanged one package of bacon for another and said loudly, "I'm looking for some better bacon!" The cash register was still ringing when Mr. Carver, who always speaks louder than he needs, said, "What's wrong with what we've already got?"

only a boy

I've finished pricing the coffee. I move on to the pickles. "Aren't pickle prices higher than this?"

"Maybe at Food Land, Gilbert. Not here. We've always had a reasonable deal on pickles."

That is an understatement.

I'm fast at pricing foods. I do the work that three or four of those high school puberty types do at the Food Land. This is not bragging. This is fact.

I stamp the first of several pickle jars and remember that Tuesday in June. It was seven years ago. I showered twice. We hid my truck in their garage and I sat in Mr. Carver's chair. She brought out lemonade and cookies. She said nothing the entire time I sat there. I said "Thank you" when I left. She smiled as if to say "You're welcome" but there were no words. This went on for six or seven Tuesdays. It was August before I walked in and took her head in my hands and kissed her. Her mouth tasted like coffee. September came and my classmates went to college. I stayed and studied Mrs. Carver.

"The pickles are done, what's next?" The kneeling has made my legs stiff, so I stand and shake them out. The purple ink from the stamper is all over my hands. "Mr. Lamson, did you hear me? Boss?"

He's ringing up a purchase at the cash register, so no answer comes from him. "What's next?" I call out. "I'm on a roll." Walking briskly down Aisle Three, I get a whiff of a certain perfume. My walking slows. I peek through the potato-chip rack. I see the hands of a girl getting change. The hands lift a large watermelon. Don't let those hands be hers. I quietly move two bags of chips to get a better look. I see hair, black and full, shiny and clean. I see skin, such beautiful skin. A nose with a slope, yes. My heart is racing. I make a quick check for some flaw or mole or harelip. I haven't had a good look at her teeth yet. Surely there has to be some imperfection.

Mr. Lamson says something about this particular watermelon being about a fifteen- to twenty-pound piece of fruit. He asks how she intends to get it home.

"Bicycle."

Mr. Lamson calls out my name.

I usually beam with pride when my name is shouted across a room—but today, at this moment, I wish my name were Roy or Dale. Maybe Chadwick.

"Gilbert! Gilbert!"

"He's behind the chips."

I step out quick and stand there certain that my fly is open or my hair is all matted and gross. How did she know where I was?

"Delivery, Gilbert. Would you be so kind?"

"Huh? What?"

"Delivery, son."

"Yes," I say, as if I have a choice.

The Becky girl turns. She seems totally unimpressed. She's wearing one of those flower-patterned summer dresses, green and white. The kind of summer dress that my grandma would like her granddaughter to be wearing; the kind of dress Gilbert would like to help her hike up.

"Son, get moving."

"Huh?" I stand there numb.

"Help the young lady already."

"Yes. Yessir. Help."

18

She holds the door for me. I wish she wouldn't. I place the watermelon on the passenger seat. Without looking at her I say, "You can ride in back."

"I have a bike."

"The bike will fit in back, too," I say without turning around.

"I prefer to pedal," she says. She hops on her ten-speed and starts down Main Street. She cuts across the empty lot next to Carver's Insurance. I follow, going slow, careful not to let the melon sitting next to me fall to the floor.

She pedals up the path to the water tower. My truck can't go there so I wait for her to make a move. She's a good distance from me; she faces my way and waits. So I wait. She'll stay there all day, undoubtedly, so I get out of my truck and begin to walk toward her, cradling the melon. I'm about halfway there when she starts toward me. I expect her to stop but she zips past, almost knocking me over, and cuts back across the empty lot. She shoots across Main Street.

Me and the melon are back in the truck driving to find her, when I see the McBurney Funeral Home hearse make a U-turn. I pull up next to Bobby at the stoplight, one of three in Endora. He rolls down his passenger window.

"Did you see her? Did you see her!" he shouts.

"Afraid so," I say.

The light stays red for an eternity.

"Bobby, how old are you!"

"Twenty-nine!"

"Aren't we a little too old for this kind of thing?"

He looks at me, his red hair windblown. He presses his lips together, squeezes the steering wheel like a race car driver and calls out, "We're never too old to feel *alive!*"

The light clicks to green, and Bobby and the hearse peel out.

I make a slow right turn onto Elm. I've lost track of her but no way am I joining some search party. I drive past the Dairy Dream and remember that fateful night when I met the viper there. At the Church of Christ parking lot, I drive in a slow circle and see no sign. There's no trace of her in the field where the carnival was. A couple of Pastor Swanson's kids are picking up what's left of the popcorn boxes and candy wrappers and ticket stubs. I head down Third Street to the Endora town pool. Four kids splash each other while Carla Ramp, sister of waitress Beverly and daughter of Earl and Candy, watches from the lifeguard chair. I've always said that I would rather drown than be revived mouth-to-mouth by Carla Ramp. She makes her sister Beverly seem beautiful. She has swimmer's hair, yellow and starchy, and her nose is covered with that annoying white stuff to protect against sunburn. My burn, incidentally, is fading fast; my arms are beginning to peel. I pass Mrs. Brainer's house, which already has a FOR SALE sign posted out front. Her porch swing hangs triumphant.

The girl has vanished and part of me couldn't be happier.

I'm considering my options regarding the watermelon when thirst becomes a factor. I head to ENDora OF THE LINE for an Orange Crush. I lock the doors to my truck for reasons that disappoint me. I'm worried that someone might kidnap the melon. How sad that I would even care.

Donna is at the cash register. She was in the same class with my older brother, who I should never have mentioned.

Anyway, I'm about four steps from Donna and the door, when that girl and her bike coast across the parking lot. She rides with no hands. I stand there motionless as she disappears down the block. I feel like I'm thirteen again.

The McBurney Funeral Home hearse followed by Tucker's truck pulls into the parking lot. The boys leap out of their respective vehicles and say, "Gilbert, Gilbert, Gilbert!"

"I know my name. Christ, you guys."

So they start in about this girl, and I am losing interest by the second. The more they talk, the more convinced I become that there's something wrong with her. —→ Becky

"Have you seen her teeth?" I interrupt.

"No."

"Uhm. Not really. But surely..."

"You don't know," I say. "She could have those black, blotched teeth. Or maybe she's got one of those hairy faces or maybe..."

"You've got a point."

"Yes, he does."

"Of course I do. And furthermore, don't we, as citizens of this town, have more useful and important things to be doing with our time? I think we do."

I drive away as they stand there pondering my words. My gas gauge is on "E" so me and the melon are forced to drive to the closest station, which is Standard Oil. Dave Allen's is on the other side of town, so no luck in terms of the cord or hose or whatever it's called. I sing real loud as I go over the black tube thing but the bing-bing or dong-dong still makes it to my ears. Buck Staples is working today. He's a year younger than me but he was held back twice, once in fourth grade, once in sixth. One could argue that he wasn't held back enough.

Buck says, "Hey, Gilbert."

"Hey, Buck."

I'm putting gas in. He kicks some gravel and says, "Wow."

"Wow what?"

"Uhm. I don't know. Just wow."

"Oh, wait," I say. I finish with the gas, open the passenger side of my truck, lift up the watermelon, and say, "You any use for this?"

Buck shakes his head.

"Damn."

"But uh I swallowed a couple of watermelon seeds once. Ugh."

I say, "Oh."

I'm checking my oil when I hear that clicky-ticky sound of a bike come coasting up.

"Gilbert?"

"What?" I unhook the bar that keeps my hood raised and let the whole thing drop. It makes a "WHAM" sound. I turn toward you-know-who.

"Your name is Gilbert. I didn't forget. But then again, who could?" She puts some stray hairs back behind her ears.

"Who could what?" I say. I'd be lying if I said I didn't want this girl in a reproductive way.

"Forget a name like Gilbert." She chews on a knuckle.

"You get germs that way."

"What way?"

"Chewing on your hand. Licking your fingers."

"Oh well," she says, continuing to chew.

I'd also be lying if I said that this girl appealed to me as a person. Quite honestly, she's the weirdest thing in these parts.

I pay Buck the $13.52 in exact change. He asks how my truck is running, and I say, "Like a kitten," and he kiddingly goes, "Meow." Let me say that this was the first interesting thing I've ever seen Buck do.

Outside Becky stands between my truck and me with the bike between her legs. She rolls the front tire over the black cord thing and bing-bing and ding-dong and binga-dinga ring out and I want to scream. Turning to Buck, I try to say with my eyes that what is happening here is not my fault. But Buck is standing up, staring at her, gnawing on his tongue. He likes the noise.

Becky moves the bike slightly from side to side up underneath her. I shake my head and climb into my truck. I turn on the radio, kick into gear, but as I pull out, she pedals out in front of me. I hit the horn long, and she holds up a finger like she's saying "One minute," so I shift into park. She coasts to my window and says, "Just one more thing."

"Yeah?"

"It's the insides of a watermelon that are best. Maybe if you expressed an interest in getting to know my insides." She giggles like those girls on "The Dating Game," her head cocks back, and she laughs with her mouth wide open. I move close to her and look quick in her mouth. Her teeth are shiny and straight, pure white. Perfect. Damn. So I reach across my truck, open the passenger door, and roll the watermelon off the seat. It kind of bounces over to the gas pump. I drive off. I look in the rearview mirror and see her standing there. No more giggle, no more laugh. The watermelon at her feet.

Perfect.

19

Thanks for doing that, Gilbert."

"Sure thing, boss."

"It's that extra-special care we take of our customers . . ."

"My feeling exactly," I say. The less said about the melon, the better. I put on my apron, clip on my name tag.

"Your sister was by," Mr. Lamson says.

"Amy, I hope."

"Yes. And she brought you this." He gives me a white envelope and I notice the confidence of his hands, his gold wedding band secure. I want to say, "Mr. Lamson, you and your wife are the only known proof that marriage is a reasonable life option," but instead I just say, "Thanks."

"You know, Arnie stayed in the car while your sister came inside. I told Amy that he could pick out any gum or candy bar he liked for free. She went out and told him but he ducked below the dashboard."

"Arnie's not your normal guy," I say.

"It used to be he'd come here and follow you around at work. He'd cry when it was closing time. Remember that honorary name tag we made for him?"

I nod. Mr. Lamson has always gone out of his way for Arnie. Free candy, store tours, pennies for the gum-ball machine.

"Did I do something?" Mr. Lamson asks. "Did I hurt his feelings in some way?"

"No, sir. Not you."

"He won't even come into our store, for Christ's sake."

"I know. But, boss, it's not you," I whisper. "It's those electric doors at the ... uhm ... other establishment. The conveyor belts, too."

"Nooo." Part of Mr. Lamson just died.

"But fortunately he's been banned from their store."

"What!"

"Well, not banned actually. They want him to be supervised from now on. Last Saturday he pocketed about three dollars' worth of candy. Amy tried to explain that he's used to getting it for free."

"Arnie always gets free candy...."

"I know, sir."

"He's always welcome here! Hell, I'll put his picture right up there, right next to Lance!"

A color 8 by 10 photo of Lance Dodge, autographed, hangs framed next to the Wonder Bread clock. Lance is enshrined in many of the stores and shops in Endora. He smiles with teeth that aren't as nice as Becky's.

"Your brother has free rein! He can dig the prizes out of whatever cereal! You tell him!"

"He knows. It's just his particular interest in those electric doors, the conveyor belts. And now—with the lobster tank."

"Fine. It's fine. Whatever the boy wants." Mr. Lamson moves out of view. He's gone into the stockroom for some time alone. My boss can deal with the declining business, the almost total absence of customers, and the rejection of the masses. But it's Arnie's refusal of free candy that has wounded him. When my boss is in pain, he goes to the stockroom. When he aches, he does so quietly.

* * *

Inside Amy's envelope is the grocery list for the next few days. It is two and a half pages long. She writes:

I've reduced the list to the necessary items. The coffee can had only thirty-six dollars and something cents. Here's thirty. Do you think he'll credit the rest till we have more money? Be charming. If anyone can do it, you can. I love you and will make you fried chicken soon for dinner. Oh, get an extra jar of peanut butter. That's all Arnie's interested in eating these days. Thanks, little brother. Love, Amy. P.S. *Blue Hawaii* is on TV tonight. It's one of his best movies. You want to watch?

I look over the shopping list. You'd think we had an army or a football team living at our house. Five loaves of bread, countless bags of potato chips, cases of diet ginger ale, mayonnaise, tubs and tubs of butter–the list is endless. She didn't have the strength to ask me to my face. I've worked for years for this stellar husband-and-wife team and I've never had to beg for charity for me or my family. But since our combined incomes cannot keep up with our increased appetites, I have no real choice in the matter.

It takes until six-fifteen for me to muster up enough courage. Mr. Lamson is sweeping under the cash register and the store is empty.

"Boss?" I say, walking up to him.

"Yes." He stops sweeping and says, "What is it, son?"

"Uhm."

"Is everything all right?"

"Amy dropped by a grocery list."

"Well, we're stocked to the brim. We're only out of canned peaches and pears. So–go to it." He smiles, happy that his food will soon be ours.

I can only look at my feet. "It seems that with uhm Ellen getting her braces off and uhm some emergency construction work that we have to do on the house and uhm . . . she only gave me thirty dollars. . . ."

"I'm ashamed you'd even ask. You can credit whatever you like. And, Gilbert, you'll pay us when you can. I know that."

"Yes, sir."

"Is that all, son?"

I nod.

"Get shopping, then." Mr. Lamson walks away whistling.

I get a cart and systematically start checking off each item and it's an hour and three cartfuls later when I finish. Mr. Lamson rings it all up and it comes to twenty-three grocery sacks worth $314.32 total.

I start to say, "I'm sorry," when he says, "No need to be."

It takes an eternity for me to secure all the bags in back of my truck. As I'm squeezing a sack of eggs and milk into place, the Carver family station wagon pulls into the parking lot. Mrs. Carver rolls down her window, turns her headlights off, but keeps the engine running. This will be one of those talk-fast meetings.

"Hi," she says.

"Hi," I say.

I go about my work.

"Guess what Thursday is?" she says fast.

I shrug and place another sack.

"A certain anniversary. Seven years. It will have been seven years since your first . . . visit."

"You don't say," I say slowly.

"Ken has many appointments Thursday. I can drop the boys off at the pool. How about an anniversary picnic?"

"Uhm," I say. I stop and look at her. I'm sweating from all the groceries.

"I'll make all your favorites," she says, talking even faster now.

"It's a little hard for me to think about food right now. I haven't got much of an appetite." I point to all the sacks but she doesn't seem to get the correlation.

She only seems to notice me. Suddenly her lips scrunch together. "What's the matter, honey?"

My back hunches up when she says "honey." For seven years I've been her honey, her secret, her little toy. I've never even gone on a date. It's only been Mrs. Betty Carver. These secret meetings—enough.

"What is it?"

I turn and look at her. She sees the coldness in my eyes.

"Oh, just like that," she says. "Is it that easy for you?"

"It's not easy—no."

The last bag is in place. I turn the lights out at Lamson Grocery and lock the door. I walk toward her and it starts pouring out. "Why'd you choose me? Huh? You could have had anybody. You could have had Lance Dodge! But you chose me. Even now there are any number of young guys in this town who would love to uhm learn from you. Good-looking guys. Muscular guys. Farm-boy types. Why the hell you chose me I'll never know!"

"I'm choosing to ignore this outburst. You've had a long day."

I kick a tire.

"Picnic. Our spot. Thursday is our anniversary. You're there or you're not."

I don't answer.

"Yes. I could have had others. But I chose you."

"Why? Why did you do that? Huh?"

"Because."

"Go on. Say it."

"Because I knew you'd never leave your family. I knew you'd never leave Endora."

I stare at my truck. The back window is dirty.

"Picnic, Gilbert. Our spot. Thursday. I do hope you'll be there." She stops her speed talking and in an almost different voice says, "Or is this how you say good-bye?"

I look at my tennis shoes. I need a new pair.

She says, "I can say good-bye, too. I can."

"Listen," I say. "The milk is getting warm. I got ice cream that's melting."

"Huh?"

"The groceries." I don't look in her eyes.

She shifts into reverse and whispers, "Good-bye."

"That must make you really happy to say that!" I shout.

"No. I'm so far from being happy!"

"You're smiling, though!"

"That's how it is sometimes, huh? Funny."

She backs out of the parking lot and starts to drive away. I wave for her to stop. She rolls down her window. "What is it?"

"Your headlights."

Her face stays fixed on me as her left hand reaches to the knob and her lights flick on. I stand there until her car is out of view.

I guess I'm supposed to feel sad. Or at least feel.

I look at all the groceries and an image of starving children comes to me. Their bony bodies, puffy stomachs, and the dry breasts of their mothers. Something is not right about all this food going to my house. Something is wrong inside me, I start to think, but I change the subject. I drive home and sing along with the radio.

Her words "I knew you'd never leave Endora" keep echoing in my head. I'll show them, I think to myself, I'll show them all. Endora's middle stoplight turns from green to yellow to red. I pull to a stop. And I wait. I've enough gas to make it to Illinois or Kentucky, and I've enough food in my truck for a lifetime. I could start fresh.

The stoplight turns green. This is my chance. But I turn at the top of my street and flash my brights. The retard is standing on the curb, waiting for my signal. He runs to the house, convinced it's me. Before I'm even in our driveway, Amy and Ellen are out the front door.

"Thank you," Amy says as she grabs two sacks.

"Yeah, thanks," Ellen says.

I load Arnie up with the breakfast cereals. "Go to it, kid."

Amy is back for her second load. She's moving fast and puffing. "Ellen just broke a nail."

"Oh," I said. Am I to grieve over this? I want to ask.

"Momma is getting punchy. She wants to eat. Did you get the potato chips?"

"Yes."

"Six bags, I hope."

"Whatever's on the list. I got what's on the list."

"See, though, I wrote five–then I wrote six over ..."

"I don't know. Amy–just take the groceries."

Arnie runs back out and says "Peanut butter" ten times fast.

"Yes, Arnie, I got you peanut butter."

"Chunky, chunky, chunky, chunky, chunky?"

"Yes, chunky."

He falls down next to the mailbox. He's about to orgasm. Ellen emerges with a fresh Band-Aid where her nail used to be. "You get me my yogurt?"

"Yes."

"You have a use, after all," she says, lifting up the smallest, lightest bag she can find.

All the sacks are inside, and while Amy and Ellen are in the kitchen putting everything away, Arnie marches up and down the front hall stomping on little black ants. Momma is asking for tonight's dinner menu and Amy says something about chicken pot pie. Momma goes, "Hoooowwwwww nice!"

Amy approaches me, a jar of mayonnaise in each hand, and whispers, "We've got to meet for a bit later, okay?" I'm about to say "I'm busy" when she squeezes my arm and says, "It concerns Arnie's party." She smiles as if she expects me to say "Yippee."

"Okay. I'll be at the meeting."

She says, "Good."

"But," I continue, "my appetite was lost somewhere along the way, so no dinner for me, okay?"

"Gilbert..."

"I gotta pee."

I'm about to shut the downstairs bathroom door when Amy shoves her way in. Because of her increasing size there is barely room for the two of us. I sit on the sink as she says, "Is it the money? Is it because you had to ask for credit? Is that it?"

"I don't know anymore."

"Sorry about the money. We'll have it soon. I know it was hard for you to ask. You don't know what it means to be able to buy on credit like this."

I say, "It's no big deal," when in truth it is a big deal. I'm about to scream that maybe she should budget our money better when she says: "Both of them are late with their checks."

I shrug like "It's not my problem."

"What can I do when both of them are late?"

"I really have to pee, okay?"

Amy says, "Don't let me get in the way of nature," as she shoves her way through the bathroom door.

So. It's time that you know.

There are other Grapes. One sister, one brother.

The sister is Janice. She is three years older than me. We send her to this amazing college, she majors in psychology, and what do you think she does now? What do you think she does that utilizes her immense and profound talents? She is an airline stewardess. Do you believe this? It is the truth. Janice is ideal stewardess material because she has a fake face. She's perfected the kind of phoniness that gives the majority of people comfort. The smile full of teeth that makes Joe businessman breathe easy because Joe businessman knows that even though life is hard at least he's not a stewardess. This makes him feel better about who he is; helps him justify the drinking without ice cubes, the taking of liquor straight.

Janice visits every so often. She lives in Chicago and flies out of O'Hare airport. She says that while O'Hare airport isn't the prettiest or the cleanest, it has the most character. In terms of what, I ask her—airports? It's hard for me to describe what it is that stewardesses do. I've ignored Janice every time she's tried to explain her work. And I've never flown in a plane because I don't believe in the idea of flight. So.

Five years older than Janice, eight years older than me is my brother Larry. Each month he sends a substantial check with no letter or note and no return address on the envelope. Janice sends two smaller checks each month, so along with Amy's work at the elementary school and my grocery income, we're able to get by. Larry must be very successful in a money sort of way. He returns only once a year and it's always on the same day—Arnie's birthday. He'll arrive sometime in the early morning bearing gifts, like Santa, and on the same day, before the stroke of midnight, like Cinderella, he leaves. He does this every year; his annual arrival and departure are like clockwork.

Get a couple of beers in Amy and she'll tell you Larry stories. For instance, the first time he wiped out on his bike, his skin was ripped off his face, dangling like strips of bacon, his knuckles all opened up with bone sticking out—you or me, we'd be screaming and crying, sobbing. Not Larry. He walked into the house, blood dripping everywhere, with no expression on his face.

When he found Dad hanging in the basement, as Amy tells it, he walked nonchalantly up the stairs and dialed the phone in front of Momma and Amy, who were baking bread. He told the operator to send an ambulance. "My dad has hung himself."

Janice says that there are deep, psychological reasons why Larry will only return home once a year. As a self-proclaimed expert in psychology and the only Grape to hold a college degree. Janice says that none of us will ever understand the impact that finding Dad hanging had on him. She says that just because he didn't scream and cry and freak out doesn't mean he wasn't affected. On the contrary, she says, the wounds are so deep, too deep for a layman's comprehension.

All I know is that Arnie's big eighteenth birthday is going to be something else. And if Momma hasn't fallen through the floor and if Arnie hasn't died in his sleep and if Ellen isn't pregnant and if the other Grapes haven't gone further off the edge, maybe, maybe we'll be okay.

I wash my face in the bathroom sink. I look in the mirror. I've these lines around my cheeks from pretending to smile too much, little webs around my eyes. Early signs of aging.

I dry my face using my T-shirt. I flash on this afternoon and my talk with Mrs. Betty Carver. Her saying "I knew you'd never leave Endora" returns to haunt me. "I knew you'd never leave." I lean over the sink, form a ball of spit with my lips, and let it drop.

20

A velvet painting of Elvis playing a white guitar hangs above Amy's headboard. Countless posters of "the King" plaster the other walls in her room. Each picture is of him when he was young and thin. The pudgy, piglet look that he got later in life is not documented here. Amy's stereo is an old model. Our father bought it for her when she started seventh grade. The system has speakers that have been pencil-poked by Arnie. She has a collection upward of thirty Elvis albums and a purple container thing which holds all sorts of his 45s, including an original of "Love Me Tender." Also hanging on the wall, in a shiny gold frame, is the *Des Moines Register* headline announcing Elvis's death. The newspaper has faded to yellow.

Unable to stomach any more of this Elvis museum, I flip off the light switch, fall back on her bed, and wait in the dark. My sister is thirty-four but her room is thirteen.

Downstairs the TV is going strong and dishes are being stacked in the sink. There is no sound of washing or rinsing or scrubbing, though, because Ellen now claims that, due to the emergence of a new, rare rash on her hands, she can no longer put her hands under water.

I lie on Amy's bed, wondering what a guy like Elvis had over a guy like me.

I remember the day he died. Amy was asleep on the orange sofa in the family room. We woke her with the news. She sat there making Janice repeat it like ten times. She wouldn't believe us, so I got this pink transistor radio and spun through the channels. She thought it was a coincidence that three stations had Elvis songs playing. Then some DJ said that he'd had a heart attack. Amy made her way upstairs and closed her bedroom door.

That night we made Amy's favorite dinner. This was when Momma still did the cooking, when she baked and fried and sautéed, when she still appeared in public. Arnie helped me take up the food—fried chicken with cole slaw. We set it outside her door and knocked, but she wouldn't eat. Elvis was blaring on her record player; song after song could be heard through the cracks in the floor. You could hear it down the street.

This whole bit about Elvis is to tell you my big sister didn't bounce back that night. In some ways, you could say she's never recovered. One thing is certain—she hasn't forgotten him. One glance at these walls and you'll see what I mean.

The door to her room opens, the light flicks on and Amy says, "There you are. We've been looking for you."

"I'm where I said I'd be."

"Aren't you hungry?"

I say nothing.

"You all right, Gilbert?"

"I've been better."

"We've all been better. What does that mean?"

I go on to explain how, from my perspective, we're eating too much as a family. "There are starving people, Amy, and we're eating like . . ."

Amy, not hearing me, calls, "Ellen!" and goes down the hall into the bathroom. Ellen appears with a pad of rainbow paper and a package of colored markers. She'll be taking notes, making lists, etc. She ran for Student Council secretary last year and won, of course. Her motto was "Ellen Grape–Food for Thought."

"Gilbert," Ellen says, "I hope this is a productive meeting." She pulls a tube or whatever out of her pocket and begins to spread this oil or grease or goop on her lips.

"Jesus, what's with your mouth?" I say.

"Lip gloss."

I grunt my disgusted sound.

"What's wrong with lip gloss? Everybody's wearing it."

"Everybody?"

"Yes." Ellen presses her lips together.

"Arnie wears it? And Momma? And the Byers twins? And Lance Dodge? No, no, no. Don't think so."

"You know what I mean."

"I know what you *said*. You said everybody. You said wrong."

"It's a figure of speech."

"Don't figure with speech. Speak with speech!"

"What's up your butt?" she asks.

She's just a braceless teenager, I remind myself, as Amy opens the door. "Stop it, you two."

I fake a smile as if to say "Whatever you say, Amy." Ellen says nothing, uncaps the lip-gloss tube thing and proceeds to paint a second coat.

"We haven't got much time," Amy says.

"Sure we do," I say. "His birthday isn't for a month."

"Twenty days," Ellen pipes up. "If you had bothered to look at the calendar I gave you, big brother, you'd know the time con-straint we're operating under."

I can't look at her. The glare is too great. "I don't have that cal-endar, little sister, anymore...."

"Well, your tough luck then."

"Arnie used it for toilet paper."

Amy knocks her knuckles like a gavel on her white dresser drawers. Ellen and I fall silent as the meeting has been called to order. "We don't have much time tonight," she says.

"This isn't due to a certain Elvis movie?" I ask.

Amy nods. "It's his best movie. If it wasn't his best..."

Nobody objects. Amy is always putting others first and she deserves her Elvis fix.

So I sit back and listen to my sisters voice their ideas. Amy says, "Should we go with a lasagna-spaghetti-like dish, hot dogs and hamburgers, or simple sloppy joes?"

I shrug.

Ellen graces us with these words: "Arnie has always seemed like a hot-dog kind of kid, but he is turning eighteen. And as you know, eighteen is the year that signifies adulthood. A plate of pasta might give Arnie a bit more permission to act his age."

Amy listens like a good older sister. She nods and smiles, while I consider laughing out loud. I want to say, "Arnie is a retard, dummy. Feed him anything and he'll still have half of whatever meal on his face, he'll still be climbing the water tower every other day, and he'll act like he's six till the day he dies." But I say nothing.

Amy must sense that I'm about to rip into Ellen because her hand squeezes my knee.

I seek a constructive route. "Which food is easier?"

Ellen sighs as if my question were the rudest one imaginable.

"I'm only saying that we shouldn't kill ourselves over this...."

Ellen blurts out, "Easier is not the issue."

Sensing yet another argument, Amy raises both hands and whis-pers, "Please, you two. Stop it. We all want this day to be special. It is a kind of culmination of all that our family is."

If Amy only knew the truth of that statement.

*   *   *

104

As the drone of the plan-making continues, my mind drifts away to everything female. The women in Gilbert Grape's life are too bizarre to believe. His whalelike mother, his oldest sister the Elvis worshiper, his little toothpick sister with her tennis-ball breasts, and Mrs. Betty Carver, his teacher, his whore. And now, the creature from Michigan, a veritable cannibal with pillowlike lips. Becky and her watermelon—this girl might be the weirdest yet.

"We can serve the food outside...."

"But if it rains ..."

"We'll serve it inside...."

"Of course, sure. What was I thinking?"

"How long till *Blue Hawaii*?" I ask.

Amy brightens up, checks her digital clock, and says, "Twenty-four minutes."

"Good," Ellen says. "Then we'll have time to go over games and party activities."

"Whew," I sigh. "I was worried we wouldn't get to that." Amy and Ellen both nod and smile. They must think I meant that.

Ellen opens a small purple notepad. "Jeff Lammer's mother's uncle loves to give hay-rack rides on Halloween."

"We know," I say.

"But only on Halloween," Amy says.

"I know. But, Jeff likes me. He wants me. Badly. And if you guys are in agreement, I'll get him to get his mother to get her uncle to do a hay-rack ride on Arnie's birthday. It's not a problem." Ellen smiles. Her eyes dart back and forth between Amy and me, looking for some sign that she has impressed us.

"What do you think about the hay-rack idea, Gilbert?" Amy asks.

"Not much."

Ellen pouts.

"Me either." Amy continues, "I'm leaning more to activities that take place around the house."

"Well, if you don't like that idea, if you can dismiss my well-thought-out plans so easily, I have no choice but to throw away my notes and sketches. Clearly the work I've done has not been appreciated. Clearly you both can plan a better party."

"Ellen, please," Amy says in a panic. "We love your ideas. We love the time and energy and care you're giving. We're grateful for all your work. Aren't we?"

I just sit there.

"Aren't we happy with what Ellen has done, Gilbert? Gilbert?"

"He doesn't want to answer your question, Amy."

"Oh, I do. Very much I do, but..." I fall silent. Ellen starts to gather her things, when a *meow* sound pierces the air. "Did you hear that?" I ask. Another *meow* sounds. "Right there. Did anybody hear that?" The noise comes from outside of Amy's bedroom door. "I heard a cat!" I practically shout. "Amy, did you...?"

"Yes!" she says.

"I hope it's a friendly cat! Are you a friendly cat?"

During this exchange Ellen takes out her lip gloss and coats her mouth a third time.

"Hello, kitty! Are you friendly or are you mean?" The "cat" answers back with a meowlike "Yes."

Amy asks, "Yes, are you friendly or yes, are you mean?" No noise comes in response. The cat must be confused.

"I hope the cat is friendly, Amy! Don't you?"

The cat barks once, twice.

"The cat is being silly," I say.

"The cat is talented," Amy says.

"The cat is stupid!" Ellen screams. "The cat is retarded!"

I tackle Ellen on the bed, my hands cover her mouth. My palms get gooey from her greasy, oily lips. She claws me, her red nails scratch my neck and pinch my arms. Arnie pushes open the door and runs into the room. He leaps into Amy's arms. They watch as Ellen and I wrestle. He whoops and hollers. "I fooled you, didn't I? Didn't I!"

"Yes, Arnie." Amy is looking at me like she wishes I were dead.

"No way is Ellen going to get away with calling him names," I want to say. I stop the attack and roll off. She slaps me twice, but I don't do anything except close my eyes with each impact. Arnie imitates Ellen by hitting Amy about the head until she stops him. Ellen covers up her notes and papers so Arnie can't see them, even though he can't read. "The party is supposed to be a surprise," she says.

The phone rings.

Ellen and I both say, "I got it," and race to the phone, which sits on the bookcase full of Nancy Drews in the hall. Ellen beats me to the phone–I don't know how–and when she answers she says, "It's me, hi!" as if she knows the phone is for her.

Who am I kidding though? The phone is always for Ellen.

But this time she listens for a second, drops the receiver, and walks away. She goes into her pink-and-white bedroom and closes her door.

I pick up the phone.

"Hello?" I say. "Who's this?" I hear this hiccup come from the other end. "Hey, Tucker."

"How'd you know it was me? I didn't say (hiccup) nothing yet."

"Somehow I just knew."

"Oh." (Hiccup.) "Gilbert, you need to know that a miracle has happened. In our town. In this state. Your buddy Tucker has had one hell of a day."

Amy must be tickling Arnie, because he's giggling loud. Ellen is in her room probably braiding her pubic hair, and downstairs, every five or so seconds, the channel changes as Momma looks for suitable family entertainment.

"You got a moment?"

I don't answer. No answer to Tucker means "Yes."

"So Bobby McBurney had to go because somebody died in Motley. He drives out of ENDora OF THE LINE. I head back home thinking the day has been a total bust, when I see that girl, walking her bike, struggling with a watermelon. I pull up next to her and ask if she'd like a ride."

"Did you drop her off?"

"Yeah, but wait till you hear."

"Where does she live?"

"I'll get to it."

"Where does she live?"

"Let me finish!"

"Tell me!"

"I'll get to it!" He shouts this so loud that I hold the receiver a foot out from my ear. I wait until he's quiet. When I bring the phone back, a scream comes from downstairs. Momma's scream. "AMY! ELLEN! ARNIE! COME HERE! COME HERE!"

"Gotta go," I say to Tucker, slamming the phone down. Amy is out of her room fast; Arnie follows; Ellen, too. I would have been the first downstairs but I jam my big toe on Arnie's Tonka cement mixer. I hop down the stairs, holding my foot. When I get to the bottom, I find Momma pointing in silence at the TV. Amy and Ellen stand around her watching, and Arnie puts his face right up to the screen.

"Sit back, Arnie," Amy says. "Sitting so close is bad for your eye."

"What is it?" I ask.

Momma says, "SHHHHHH!"

Amy turns to me and whispers, "It's a special report...."

Momma again, like a sea wind, "SSSSSHHHHHH!"

Lance Dodge is on TV. He is in a light blue shirt and a red tie with white dots. He looks like a subtle flag. He is reporting live in front of a suburban house. A large crowd stands behind a yellow-taped line. Police are milling behind him.

"Thank you, Rick," Lance says. "A shocking, sordid tale. A family. Three daughters, two successful, hard-working parents, and a demented lonely son. Today, everything cracked for Timothy Guinee. It appears that he came home after a week in Lincoln visiting some of his college friends. He bought a gun somewhere along the way, loaded it, and waited until dinnertime. While his family was eating dinner he proceeded to shoot them dead. Victims include his parents, Richard and Pam, his sisters, Brenda, Jennifer, and Tina, and their pet dog."

"Can you believe it?" Amy says.

"Lance is soooo cute," Ellen says.

"His head is soooo big," Arnie says, trying to touch him through the TV.

Lance interviews a few of the shocked neighbors. They express their dismay, their horror. "Such a lovely family, such good people."

Amy says, "Why does it always happen to the good people?"

Lance speaks with the police chief. Everyone is shaken. Lance turns to the camera and says, "Rick, it's impossible to describe the feeling here. The shock. I'm Lance Dodge in West Des Moines, reporting live." He shakes his head as the announcer says, "This has been a special report. More at ten. Now back to our regularly scheduled programming."

Momma turns the TV to mute. There's a short silence where none of us know what to say.

I look around the room at my sisters and mother and retard brother. I see the sagging floor, the wilting house. I smell the garbage in the kitchen, feel the dirt and dust in the carpet, the mildew of my clothes, and I understand wanting to erase this place, erase these people.

Momma's doughy head begins to shake, her fat hands make fists and she shouts, "Popcorn!"

"Yes, Momma."

Amy goes to the kitchen. She pours the kernels into a pan and it sounds like little bullets. Arnie tries to stand on his head, while Ellen goes off for some time about the beauty, the humanness of Lance Dodge. Only Momma senses whatever is going on in me. "Gilbert, why would he do that? Why would a boy kill his family?"

"Because. Because he ..."

"Because he hated them?"

"Not hate. Because he thought ..."

"He must have hated them. Didn't he know he had other options?"

"I don't know, Momma."

"He could have left by the same door your daddy did, couldn't he? Not that I advocate that option, God knows. He also could have just walked out the door, walked away from it."

"Yes, but ..."

"Yes but what?"

"Maybe he didn't feel that he could leave them."

"Well, he could've."

"Maybe he felt that they couldn't manage without him. That he was integral to their uhm ..."

"To their what?" Momma lights a cigarette.

"To their survival."

Momma laughs like "how absurd." She hits the mute button and the sound returns to our TV. Ellen has gone upstairs to gab on the phone. Arnie waits with Amy for the popcorn to start popping. Momma changes channels, and I stand motionless.

21

G ilbert, don't go."

"Who said I was going anywhere?"

"I can tell, Arnie can tell. You're gonna go." The bubbles from the bubble bath are in his hair and cover his face. "You're goin' down to Elvis. And just when we're starting to have fun. Just when." He holds his head under the water and stays down longer than ever before. When he pops up, his mouth sucks in air and he says, "This is better than Elvis."

"That's right."

"Yeah, the girls are watching Elvis. Ugh."

I'm sitting on the linoleum floor outside the tub. Every few min-utes Arnie turns on the hot water to warm it back up. Tonight his entire collection of bath toys are floating in the water–the plastic speedboat, the sponge basketball set, his water goggles, which he never wears.

"Gilbert."

"Yeah?"

"I hate Elvis. I *hate* him."

"You don't hate anybody. You don't like him is what you mean to say."

"Nope."

"You shouldn't hate anybody."

Arnie shakes his head in disagreement.

"What did Elvis ever do to you? Huh? You can't hate somebody who never hurt you."

Arnie points to where his left eye used to be.

"Wow. Arnie. You remember that?"
He nods.

The day Elvis died was the same day that Arnie lost his left eye. It wasn't like he misplaced it or anything. Momma was worried about Amy, who'd been locked for hours in her room, grieving and crying. So she sent my older brother, Larry, who was twenty, out for beer. Then, Janice, who was fifteen at the time, and Amy, who was twenty-two, and Larry spent the evening in the attic getting drunk. They played those annoying early Elvis songs and danced and made much too much noise. Meanwhile Ellen, Arnie, me, and Momma watched TV downstairs. Mamma sent Arnie up to borrow some cigarettes. The dart board was on the back of the attic door. Arnie opened it just as my older brother was throwing, and the dart stuck in Arnie's eye, and Janice screamed out, "Bull's-eye!" They were so drunk they found it funny.

"It hit right here and it hurt. It hurrrrtttt."
"I bet it did."
"Ow. Ow."
"It doesn't hurt anymore, though, does it?"
"No."
Arnie's eye was a goner and for a while he wore a patch that did not in any way make him look like a pirate.

"They flashed the light the whole way," he says.
Momma arranged for an ambulance to drive her and Arnie to Iowa City, where there are specialists in that kind of thing. His proudest moment is that the ambulance driver flashed the light the entire length of the trip. They didn't use the siren, Arnie told me once, not until he begged them. He said that people are nice to a one-eyed kid.

The bubbles in Arnie's bath are almost gone. I notice his stomach—how his belly is growing. The flab is beginning to roll over like ripples in a lake.

"I was gone a long time," Arnie says.
He was there for about a week, which was way too long. I always thought he was pretty stupid and worthless, but I didn't realize he was about the best thing going—till he lost his eye.

When he came back, I remember telling him that it looked good as new. I said something to the effect that glass eyes are as good as real ones. Arnie told me that the eye was plastic, really, and that he wished it wasn't plastic but rather a rubbery kind of superball-like thing so he could take it out and bounce it. "Oh well," I remember saying, and Arnie said, "Oh well."

He stands up in the tub and demands a towel. I give him his, the one with a purple dinosaur on it, and he dries his hair. He climbs into his Superman pajamas. The red cape Velcros on the back, and before he can soar toward his bunk, I take a washcloth and say, "Close your eyes." I try to wipe the remaining peanut butter off his chin. I press too hard and he tries to bite my hand. I say, "Stop that," but he keeps trying to bite.

Arnie flies downstairs and I hear Amy say, "Don't block the TV," and Momma says, "You know what, Arnie? I don't ask much. I just want to see you turn eighteen. Is that too much to ask?"

He won't be answering that question. He's never had the remotest interest in answers.

I dry my hands off on a small towel. I head toward my room and lie down on my bed. Restless, I stand, go to my window and look out over our backyard. Since there's been no rain, I haven't had to mow in weeks. The bright side. Tonight there are crickets, the sound of neighbor kids playing hide and seek, and the beginnings of a new moon. In the middle of my backyard, a tiny light appears. How odd. The light glows for a second, fades out, then another light appears. My first thought is firefly. But this light starts out like a match, burning for a few seconds and then goes out. I press my face up to my window screen. I see the shape of a person dressed in black. I turn off the light in my room. This eerie sequence of match lit, match glow, match out continues. I creep down the stairs as Elvis sings "I Can't Help Falling in Love with You." I go out the door to the garage, find a flashlight in the dark, and slip into our backyard.

"Hello?" I say. "Who's there?" There is no sound. I walk the yard using the flashlight as my eyes. I go to where the light was glowing and look for used matches. No trace of anything. I cover the yard quick with the flashlight. Perhaps I was hallucinating. I turn off the flashlight and sit on the swing.

Larry hung the swing years ago. He used to push me real high.

The night is so humid that my hair is beginning to curl. I wind myself up and let myself spin. The faster I turn, the louder I laugh. The spinning slows. I look at my house. As houses go—ours tries hard. I put my hands up under my T-shirt. I lightly run my fingers over my nipples. I lean back, my eyes close. I get a tingle. Even Beverly (with the birthmark) Ramp would do right now. I hear a giggle.

I open my eyes and look around. "I heard that," I say.

I move over to where the tetherball set used to be. I listen but the only sound is crickets. Going toward our house, I almost bump into our peeling red picnic table. I look up and see a warm, glowy light coming from the giant tractor tire that serves as Arnie's sand-box.

Something very strange is happening in my backyard tonight.

I walk toward the sandbox.

Looking over the tire, I see a candle. Below the candle, a paper plate with a white plastic fork. On the plate, a slice of watermelon being devoured by an army of black ants. In the sand, written with a girl's cursive, is this message:

It's the insides that count.

Part Three

22

S o I was driving along, you know, thinking."

"Good for you."

"And," Tucker continues, "I was wondering about those Burger Barn applications..."

It's the next morning. Tucker and I have been installing the wood support beams in the basement. He's been speaking nonstop since arriving with his red toolbox.

"...and how I might be able to get my hands on one of them. So I'm driving to the construction site when I see that girl walking. And get this! She was carrying this uhm oh God, it's uhm an uh..."

"Watermelon."

"Yes! And I pulled up to offer her..."

"Tucker, please, I've heard the story."

"No, you hung up on me is what you did. You didn't even begin to hear..."

"Let's talk about the girl later."

"You're hanging up on me again, aren't you? That's what you're doing right now."

"How can I hang up on you when we're in the same room?" This seems to stump Tucker. "We're supposed to be fixing the floor." I say, "We're trying to save the walrus upstairs."

Tucker covers his ears. "Jesus! Don't talk about your mother that way! Your mother is a great woman."

I sit and clean the dirt from under my pinky finger.

"You're cruel!" he shouts.

I want to say that to keep Momma from falling through is ~wow~ what's cruel. Let her die if that's what she wants. At least my father could make up his mind.

"I'm gonna forget," Tucker says, "that we've even had this discussion. Because? For me, things are looking up. Finally there's been sunlight in my life. This girl rode in my truck! Sat on my seat cushions! I wanted to go up and down every street, honking at every house so the people in this town would see me and this girl together...."

I find a bolt for the lower board while Tucker stops talking for a moment to tighten the C clamp that will secure the critical top section. This divine silence will more than likely be brief.

Part of me wants to tell Tucker that I know the creature. I want him to know that she's taken a bite out of me, too. I'm tempted to show him the slice of watermelon. For now, though, it remains hidden in a Ziploc bag under my bed. Last night I used our hose to wash the ants off. I dried the melon with my T-shirt. Using the same stick she did, I wrote "Eat me" in the sand over and over until her evil message about insides counting could not be made out.

Ellen comes down the stairs smelling of suntan lotion. She carries two paper plates with ham sandwiches and potato chips and pickle on the side. "Food by Amy," she says as she drops the plates on a bench in the corner. She rubs the back of her neck and half studies the boards and braces that will try to support Momma.

"What do you think?" I ask, hoping that she'll send a compliment Tucker's way and silence the Becky tirade.

"Hmmmm," she purrs.

"Is that all? Hmmmm? Is that all you have to say?"

"No."

Tucker, up near the ceiling, straddling two lower boards, looks at Ellen, expectant.

Ellen speaks. "She's not what you guys think. She's not so pretty really. That's what Randi Stockdale from Motley says. She says that if the Miss Iowa pageant were held tomorrow, this 'girl' wouldn't make quarterfinals even. And Randi would know, wouldn't she? Yes, I think so. I urge you to spread the word, okay? She's not so cute. Really, she's not." Ellen walks back to the washer and dryer. She finds her Dairy Dream uniform in a laundry basket and as she walks past us, she says, "There are pretty girls right here in Endora. Right under your noses." She carries her uniform upstairs, holding it like it's a baby.

"You hungry?" I say.

Tucker looks at me and says, "How'd she know?"

"You can have my sandwich. I won't be eating."

"Sure." Tucker dives for the food. "Gilbert, your sister like just read our minds. Does this not amaze you?"

"No."

"We were talking about the new girl and then she like appeared and somehow knew..."

"Tucker," I interrupt, "she was standing at the top of the stairs listening to us for the past ten minutes."

"Yeah? How do you know?"

"I could smell her."

"Oh."

He begins to inhale both sandwiches. For a little guy he's got quite an appetite. With his mouth full, he garbles, "You lie. You didn't know she was listening."

"I can smell her lotion. I'm not kidding. Like right now, she's listening right now."

"I wasn't listening to you guys!" Ellen shouts down.

Tucker looks confused. I simply laugh.

It's an hour later and we're still tightening and screwing and bolting.

"How much longer, you think?" I ask.

"Depends."

"Depends on what?"

"On how easily you satisfy."

"Oh, I satisfy very easily," I say.

"I know. That's why you live as you do."

I'd be eternally grateful to my mother if she could fall through these support boards right now and crush Tucker in the process.

"Your hair is getting stringy, Gilbert. The way you neglect the washing of your truck. Those rare times when you speak the words 'Thank you.' All of this points to my uhm..."

"Conclusion."

"Conclusion, yes, that you're not interested in being complete, being..."

"Thorough."

"Huh?"

"The word is thorough."

"I know! See, you don't let me finish. . . ."

The phone rings upstairs. Please be for me.

"Hold it, Tucker—hold that thought."

I can hear Amy walking toward the basement door. She opens it and calls down, "Gilbert."

"Don't lose that thought, Tucker."

Upstairs Amy stands with a bowl of cookie batter in her arms. She says, "That was Sheriff Farrell on the phone. Arnie's climbed the water tower."

I say, "I'll get him," because I'm always the one to get him. But before I start out, two of my fingers slip into the batter and I get a mouthful. Amy slaps my hand but I get it behind my teeth and smile.

I'm going to let the screen door slam loudly so as to communicate to the women in my family that I am fed up with being the one who always has to get Arnie down from the water tower. I send the door flying, and as I bounce outside, I hear Amy say, "Don't let the door . . ." but it slams before she can say "slam."

23

It started last summer. Arnie found out he could scale the water tower and so now he does it every chance he gets.

When I arrive there, I find a small crowd staring up in awe. Arnie is hanging off the railing, dangling by his arms. Sheriff Farrell says, "You better get him, son. No way am I going up there." I scream "Arnie!" and as he shakes his feet, one of his shoes falls to the ground. The water tower is tall and if he falls, then no more Arnie. I climb up the metal ladder on the side fast. The kid is giggling, having the time of his life. He's never shown off like this before. It must be because the police lights are flashing.

*   *   *

I get up to him.

"Gilbert, they're watching Arnie. They're watching Arnie."

I say, "Course they are," as I pull him to safety.

We climb down.

We're halfway to the ground and I'm already out of breath; my jeans are full of sweat, and the crowd, for whatever reason, won't go away.

Sheriff Farrell waits, holding the shoe. When we touch down, I take it and put it on Arnie's foot and tie the laces in a square knot.

I say, "It's okay now. I'll get him home. It won't happen again."

"Son, we hear this every time. And then a couple of days later here we are again." Sheriff Farrell has a toothpick in his mouth and never has a toothpick looked so menacing.

"I know, but this time I'm sure was the last time. Wasn't it, buddy?" Arnie stares at his feet, his bottom lip pushed out. "Wasn't it!" I squeeze his arm hard. Arnie doesn't budge.

"This is the ninth or tenth time. I got to take him in. You understand."

"What?"

"We'll take him to the station. We'll fingerprint him. Lock him up for a bit. We told you, we told your sister the next time this happened, we'd have no choice. This is the next time, so don't act surprised that this is happening."

Blood rushes to my face; my heart races. I say, "Oh, come on."

"I'm sorry, son."

I whisper, "But he's retarded."

Sheriff Farrell says, "Seems pretty clever to me," as he moves the toothpick from side to side.

So Arnie, my retard brother, who cries because he killed a grasshopper, is taken in the police car and driven off to jail. As they put him in the back, I hear him say, "Be sure to flash the lights and play the siren. Okay?" Arnie waves to the crowd like he's in a parade, the car drives off. But there is no siren or lights. No hoopla.

The people watching are whispering to themselves and two young girls are laughing. They are Tom Keith's little sisters, and the sight of them in their pink dresses and plastic barrettes pisses me off. I flip them the bird. Some mother says, "Real good example you're setting, Gilbert Grape." I don't respond to supermom. I just get in my truck and hurry on home.

As I'm pulling out, I see the Becky girl standing there in a pair of white shorts and halter top. She's with an old lady who must be her grandma. She's holding a peach. She takes a bite and half smiles. I spin out of there and race home. I just flipped off two ten-year-olds, I think to myself. Surely that looked real impressive to Becky. Oh, fuck her. She eats people.

At home Amy stands waiting on the porch. When she asks, "Where's Arnie?" I start laughing and not because it's funny. I say, "They took him to jail." Amy can't believe it, and then, from inside the house, we hear, "They did what?"

Amy says, "Nothing, Momma."

"I thought she was asleep," I whisper.

"I heard you," Momma says. "What did they do to Arnie?"

Amy and I look at each other. "We've got to tell her," Amy says.

So we do, and when Momma hears, she hits her fist on the table, spilling the milk from her Cheerios. "Get my coat."

I look at Amy with a face of "What did she just say?" We plead with her to stay home, but she won't hear of it. "Maybe you should . . ."

"Get my coat!"

Amy gets Momma's black coat, which looks more like a pup tent. Working fast on the shoe problem, I come up with a solution. I dig my winter boots out of the hall closet. Momma stuffs her feet in them. She's ready for snow.

Amy says, "You'd think the police would have something better to do than pick on some poor boy who likes to climb water towers."

Momma doesn't say a word. Her face has turned bright red—she is practically growling.

I bolt down the stairs and explain to Tucker that Momma is on the warpath. I urge him to work quickly. "Maybe you can finish by the time we get back."

"Maybe," Tucker says.

The creaks and plaster cracking indicate that Momma has begun her journey across the living room to the front door.

I'm up the stairs fast.

Outside I clean out all the wrappers and cups and papers from the floor and dash of Amy's Nova. I jam the front seat back as far as possible. Momma oozes out of the house. Amy follows. I hold open the passenger door like a chauffeur as Momma squeezes in. It must be ninety-five degrees out and Momma is dressed for winter. I'm wanting to ask her if she realizes how long it's been since her last "public" appearance, but I say nothing. Amy climbs in back and I'm set to drive. With Momma in the car we all tilt to the right. I look back at Amy and try to say with my eyes that I don't know if the car can make it. Amy looks back and with her eyes says, I know what you mean. Momma demands her cigarettes so I run back inside and bring three packs. It could be a long day.

The county jail is in Motley. It's a twenty-minute drive in ideal circumstances but with the added baggage, the trip could take thirty-five, forty minutes.

We're driving through town to get to Highway 13, when Momma says, "Get Ellen." I say, "She's working," and Amy says that we can handle this alone, but Momma won't hear of it. She repeats, "Get Ellen," and when Momma repeats, you can bet it's done.

We lurch on toward the Dairy Dream.

Ellen is giving change to two little boys with ice cream cones when she turns and sees us pulling into the gravel parking lot. Her mouth drops open and anyone can see the blood leave her face. I get out of the car and approach the take-out window.

"Come on," I say.

She says, "What happened?" and I say it's Arnie and that he's all right but that she's got to come with me because Momma wants her in the car.

Ellen is working this particular day with a certain Cindy Mansfield who is not only a born-again Christian but, at seventeen years of age, also the assistant manager. She has hopes of owning the Dairy Dream someday. As Ellen walks out and the bell makes its noise, Cindy asks in a panic, "Did anybody die?" I want to say, My sincerest hope is that you, Cindy, might die within the day. Instead I say, "No one died. Not yet."

So most of the Grape family is driving down the highway. Amy has moved behind Momma. Ellen sits behind me looking like a nurse in her white polyester outfit. She tries to check her makeup in the rearview mirror. Amy presses the tips of her fingers together and smiles, a sure sign that she's worried. I roll down the window a crack because, quite honestly, Momma hasn't bathed in some time and the smell is too much.

Amy says, "Gilbert, the radio."

Momma grunts something.

I spin the dial, checking stations when I come across Elvis singing "In the Ghetto."

"Turn that up," Amy asks. I do. She mouths the words and I'm grateful she doesn't sing.

No one is talking, and after the song it's the news—Momma moves her hand in a turn-off motion. The inside of our car is silent now. Amy says that a person can take only so much news and that she hopes Arnie is okay. She quickly adds, "Of course he's okay. They're probably just trying to teach him a lesson."

Ellen, having recently completed her lip-gloss touch-up and eye-shadow check, says, "Would someone be so kind as to inform me of what is going on here, what has happened to our Arnie?" Sometimes I wonder who taught Ellen how to talk. Where she gets off sounding like some big-city girl is beyond me. She is from Endora, I want to remind her. She's not royalty, for Christ's sake. She's a Grape.

I condense the sequence of events and recount them for the little princess. Amy adds comments and Momma just sighs and moans during the bad parts.

Motley, Iowa, is the county seat. It is a town of over five thousand and is loaded with fast-food establishments, a dis-cotheque/bowling alley, and two movie theaters. The police office/county jail is smack downtown and the only parking spot I can find is across the street. I'm hoping Momma will wait in the car, but when she throws open her door, all hope dies. As she struggles to her feet, the passing shoppers and the kids on bikes all stop and stare. A dog barks. A dog runs away. Momma stands her ground though, her black coat and my winter boots there to support. The girls and I walk toward the station. Traffic slows. Motley is silenced. It takes five minutes for Momma to make it across the street.

County Sheriff Jerry Farrell had, or so the story goes, proposed to Momma the same summer my father did. And after Daddy killed himself, Officer Farrell would patrol by our house and wave to us kids. At one of Larry's Little League games, you might look over and see him in uniform, sitting on the hood of his police car by left field, cheering my brother on. The one time Larry got a hit, Officer Farrell flashed the police lights. You can bet that Arnie squealed. Officer Farrell was so in love with my mother.

They haven't seen each other in years.

When I open the police-station door for Momma, a bell rings or dings and she squeezes through. I watch as Sheriff Farrell looks up from his desk and the expression on his face turns to one of sudden death. His eyes are stuck open; it's like they've filled with milk.

Momma says, "I've come for my son."

The radio dispatcher stops in mid-sentence, two secretaries look up, mouths drop open, and a young officer stares at Sheriff Farrell with a look that says "What do I do?"

While looking at his black shoes, the sheriff says, "You'll need to fill these papers out."

"No. I don't fill out papers."

"Police procedure requires..."

"No, Jerry. Give me my boy."

"But, Bonnie..."

"My boy. I want my boy."

Sheriff Farrell looks at the young officer who disappears down the hall fast. In a matter of seconds Arnie rounds the corner. The young officer says he's free to go.

As we're leaving and the bell is tingling or dingling, I look back and see Sheriff Farrell slumped in his chair, not able, I guess, to digest the sight of Momma. I shut the glass door hard, making the bell chime out in hopes that it might snap the sheriff out of it. He doesn't even twitch.

We're driving back home. Arnie sits in the middle, sandwiched between Momma and me. Amy and Ellen are in back. I have the gas to the floor but the car can't break 40 mph. There is no radio. Momma is holding on to Arnie so tight that his face is turning blue. Imagine a harmonica and that is the noise Momma's making. I've always thought she sounded like a harmonica when she cries.

In my rearview I see Amy fighting a smile. She looks around at all of us, happy, for once, that we appear to be a family. "We're hardly a family," I want to say. Cars and trucks are having trouble passing so I turn on the hazard lights and drive close to the shoulder.

The Endora water tower is in the distance.

Momma's holding on to Arnie so hard you can see her finger imprints forming on his left arm. She's dropping so many tears into his hair that a person might think Arnie had gone swimming.

We drop Ellen off at the Dairy Dream and then drive home. Amy fries up some pork chops for dinner. I set the table as Arnie clings to Momma's feet.

24

My mother has become Endora's own Loch Ness Monster. It seems those who saw my mother told those who didn't and each day since everybody hopes for a glimpse. The sudden run on camera film at ENDora OF THE LINE is due solely to a desire of many to be the first to document the new and improved Bonnie Grape.

Within hours after she freed Arnie from the county jail, the Town Council went behind closed doors to try and decide what to do. Yesterday morning a basket of diet books, wrapped like baby Moses, appeared on our doorstep, signed, "The City of Endora– With Love." I told Amy to show Momma the books, but she said she didn't dare. Instead, she hid them in her room, behind her Elvis records. Elvis certainly could have benefited by anything dietary–a shame about Elvis.

The Elks Lodge, made up of aging men with hairy noses and fleshy ears, passed a hat at their weekly meeting. A whopping seventy-two dollars and something cents was contributed. This is an astronomical figure, considering most of the Elks are farmers, and for them, with the absence of rain, these look to be tough economic times. Many of the men–Harley Barrows, Milo Stevens, Johnny Titman, Jerry Gaps–had a love thing for my mother when they were younger. They often ask about her. Each will tell, if asked, his particular version of how my mother broke his heart. Milo Stevens said, "Your mother, Gilbert, broke us open the way a hailstorm will shatter glass." Filby Baxter told me, "Bonnie Watts was the eighth wonder of the world." He whispered that in the store to me once while his wife was buying paper plates. The seventy-two dollars and something cents appeared mysteriously in a white envelope with BONNIE spelled out in block printing. Inside along with the cash was the name and number of a dietitian in Motley. Amy returned the cash to them with a note which read, "Thanks but no thanks."

I do not mind the Elks Lodge doing as they have done. It's purely a natural desire on their part to recapture their lost whatever it is they've lost that propels them to help in the reduction of my mother. Maybe if she gets thin, they'll get young.

And I have no anger at the countless women who, since the sighting of my mother, have gathered in clusters at Barb's Beauty Shop and Endora's Gorgeous, the town's two rival beauty parlors, and gloated and sung about how Bonnie Grape is no longer the beauty she once was.

Amy and her watery eyes spoke to me yesterday afternoon as I was washing my truck. "The women in this town are laughing at our mother." Amy said it in such a way that she expected me to be upset. I said, "It doesn't bother me." She threw her hands in the air and stormed back inside.

My mother spent several years deciding who she would marry. All of the men in town hoped for her hand and she kept her preference a secret for so long that when she finally chose Albert Lawrence Grape, the other men scrambled for their second, third, and sometimes fifth or sixth choices. Nobody likes to feel like a consolation prize.

Momma has, by tripling in size, given the other ladies in town the sense that justice has been served.

I spent one fun hour yesterday outlining the best idea I've ever had. I decided to commission Tucker to pain a giant sign that said "BONNIE THE BIGGEST!" I'd rent billboard space for several miles on Highway 13 & I-35 heralding the most amazing family in these parts. I'd post signs like "DISCOVER THE GRAPES," "WATCH ARNIE DANCE," "ELLEN GRAPE, TASTY AND GOOD." Amy would run a concession stand serving popcorn and lemonade; Ellen would convert her pink-and-blue bedroom into a kissing booth; Arnie would sit in a chair and look at people and they could guess which eye was glass; Janice would lead a carefully scripted tour of the house while revealing pertinent historical tidbits. She'd wear a uniform and smile her stewardess smile, gesturing in that stewardess way. In the basement, I could hang the stuffed version of my father. Larry would stand there, frozen like, staring up at my dad, exactly the way he did the day it happened. The tour would culminate with a viewing of my mother. The people would all write down their prediction of her weight. I'd wake her up and she'd struggle to stand, the customers would applaud, she'd step onto a scale, her weight would appear on a digital readout. Whoever was the closest would win a prize of some kind.

In that brief hour, I saw a family business that would rival any other. I pictured this struggling town experiencing a financial rebirth; people from all over driving to see us. Here was an idea that would allow us to work together, celebrate our past, and share it with the world. I explained it all to Arnie and he loved the idea.

At dinner last night, when Arnie was gargling his Kool-Aid and

Momma was screaming, "I WOULD RATHER EAT CIGA-RETTES THAN THIS STEW," I burst out laughing. Amy looked cross at me; Ellen almost stuck a fork into my hand. How could I tell them what I had spent the afternoon picturing?

Okay, anyway, I've survived and there's a certain dignity in surviving. Currently I keep on going by indulging in frequent fantasies of the girl from Michigan. Her black hair, her skin, her smell all haunt me. But it's her eyes that look through me, that seem to know my every secret. The last time I saw her was at the water tower as they were taking Arnie off to jail. She's waiting for me to make the next move, but I can't top her watermelon-in-the-sandbox routine. So I'll wait. I'm older than she is and this means that I'm to act more mature, be more patient. I'll starve her out.

It's almost lunchtime–Thursday, June 29–seventeen days till Arnie's party. I'm at work. Mr. Lamson is in a particularly sporty mood today. He's been moving and spinning up Aisle Two with the mop. I finally ask, "Why so happy?"

He says, "Sometimes it occurs to a person all the blessings of this life." His optimism is so overflowing that on this particular morning I begin to enjoy rearranging the dry dog-food section.

Minutes go by. The dog food has never looked more appealing. I smell like Purina Puppy Chow now. Mr. Lamson is whistling a tune I don't recognize, when Mrs. Rex Mefford steps out from behind the bread rack and says, "Gilbert, come here."

"I'm uhm uh busy. . . ."

Mrs. Rex Mefford smiles that I-know-you're-afraid-of-me-Gilbert-Grape smile and I've this sudden urge to tape her mouth shut. Mrs. Rex Mefford is a staunch member of the Baptist church and every year she makes the butter cow Endora sends to the state fair.

"I need you for just a second."

"Mr. Lamson would be glad to help. . . ."

"It concerns the eggs. Gilbert, you're to help us customers."

So I follow Mrs. Mefford and her perfume that smells like a certain laundry detergent. She wears a puke-green polyester dress with black shoes and a plastic hat on her head in case it rains. It hasn't rained in weeks, though, and I can't decide if she wears it to keep others hopeful or if she wears it just in case.

I study her. She must be almost sixty. Her hair is dyed brown and it's been curled into these little curls. It has that helmet look hair often has in this town. The kind of hair that can withstand any weather, the kind that stays facing front when a person looks from side to side.

I follow her past the milk, past the cheese, to the egg section. She lifts up a carton and pops up the Styrofoam lid. "These eggs are broken. Cracked."

"Yes, ma'am. That happens sometimes."

"Does it?"

"Yes, it's the unfortunate part of being an egg."

I dig lower, hoping to find a carton with only unbroken eggs.

"You know, Gilbert, eggs are like people."

Oh boy, oh no. I start to move away. She grabs my arm. This woman is strong.

A couple of kids have entered the store and are buying candy from Mr. Lamson. I want to scream, Rape!

"We're all little broken eggs till we turn to Christ."

I say, "You will let go of my arm. You will let go of my arm."

She does. I back away—smacking into the canned fruits and vegetables. She smiles. "Gilbert, turn to God. Turn away from false idols, prophets. God loves you. He always has."

"Well, tell him thanks anyway."

At this point, Mrs. Rex Mefford goes off, speaking as if what she says is memorized, planned, as I dig frantically for some better eggs. Her words are not her own. I listen, trying to appear open, and when I think she's finished, I say, "Here are some fine eggs. Some fine Christian eggs. Perfect. White. Round. Shells intact."

She stops smiling.

"Take, eat," I say. "Eat your eggs."

Mrs. Rex Mefford, her face all aworry, her eyes darting about, takes in a simple breath as her lips form a frozen line. "God forgives you your sins."

I say right back, "And I forgive him his."

She backs up slowly, almost forgetting to pay for the eggs.

As soon as she is gone, a sudden fear washes over me. I sense that a holy war, of sorts, has been declared; a war that many in my family might not be able to win. Mrs. Rex Mefford could be just the beginning.

I hang up my apron and run my fingers through my stringy hair. "Mr. Lamson, I'll be back after lunch."

I climb in my truck and drive home fast. It occurs to me that Endora's countless churchgoing, Jesus-loving Christians might be plotting to bring the Grape family back to God.

Understand that my father was the soloist in the choir of the Endora Lutheran church for many years. And while he was the worst singer ever, he was the only one with sufficient courage to go it alone. When he tied the knot in his neck it came as quite a shock. Dad hung himself on a Tuesday and was buried on that Thursday, and by Sunday, pregnant Momma, Amy, Larry, Janice, me, and a baby Arnie were back in church, sitting in the front row. Fortunately or unfortunately, the Bible reading that particular week included a small reference to how suicide is a sure ticket to hell. Those in the pews who minutes earlier had taken tremendous heart when we showed up for church were dumbfounded when Momma stood up and led us all down the center aisle. Pastor Oswald stopped reading, some church ladies whispered while Mr. Kinzer, the biggest and most sincere usher, tried to block Momma's exit with an I-love-Jesus smile and one of those wicker baskets used to collect offerings. Momma stopped and with her swollen, Ellen-filled stomach sticking out, spoke to Mr. Kinzer in a voice loud enough that even the organist, Mrs. Staples, could hear. Momma said, "God's made it clear about my Albert. I trust that I'm being as clear toward God." She pushed open the door–all eight months pregnant of her–and Amy followed holding a crying Arnie. Then Larry, Janice–then me.

So we stopped going to church. Sunday mornings became our only genuinely happy time. While other kids were kneeling and praying and singing praises and not knowing what any of it meant, we would still be in our pajamas, throwing food at each other, and laughing at the preachers on TV.

25

When I stopped by the house to see if Jesus or his friends had paid a visit, I found Arnie in quite a state. While running around barefoot, he had stepped on a dead bee. His foot swelled up and he was screaming. As I was holding him down to stop the squirming, Amy was putting on this mixture of baking soda and warm water–this paste–which is designed to help the sting go away. Arnie just kept saying, "But I didn't do anything. I didn't do anything." I spent upward of twenty minutes trying to convince him that it wasn't anything he did wrong that caused him to get stung. I tried to point out that sometimes people get bit or hit for no reason whatsoever. This concept didn't get through to my little brother. The only comfort he seemed to find was that the bee was already dead. Arnie said, "If I'd killed him, oh boy, oh boy..." It's true. If Arnie had caused the death of a bee, the whole chopping off grasshopper heads issue would have come surging up and he'd have fallen apart.

So I park off the highway and hike the hundred or so yards to where Mrs. Betty Carver should be waiting. I see her under a giant oak tree that bends toward Skunk River which, as I told you, is barely even a creek. The first words out of me are, "It's because of Arnie and a dead bee that I'm late."

She looks up and listens in a friendly way. When I take a moment to breathe, she says, "Happy Anniversary."

"I stopped by my house for a second and, of course, there was this crisis...."

"It's all right, Gilbert. Happy Anniversary."

"Yeah, but..."

"I expected you to be late."

This throws me. "You did? Why's that?"

"You didn't want to come."

I'm tired of people knowing my innermost thoughts. I feign shock at her accusation.

132

"It's okay. I don't know if I'd want to come see me either."

I can't take much talk like this so I lean over and kiss her on the cheek. I couldn't make it to the lips.

Mrs. Betty Carver has prepared a picnic lunch complete with the red-and-white checkered spread or blanket or whatever it's called, a large container of fried chicken, and containers with cookies, candies, and lemonade. There's even a bottle of wine, cole slaw and, of course, potato salad.

"Wow." I stare at the food. "You've got everything."

Mrs. Betty Carver tucks a napkin in my shirt and lifts the lid allowing me a quick peek and then she closes the Tupperware container fast. The chicken has a crunchy yet moist texture. I want that chicken in my mouth right now.

"I heard about your mother going to Motley."

"Yeah, you and the world."

"I admire her. She loves you kids."

I hold my stomach and make a sound like I'm starving. Mrs. Betty Carver stops, and deep in her eyes I see her disappointment. I see her wishing I would grow up. She sets the biggest chicken leg on my red, white, and blue paper plate. I hold my first bite in my mouth as some juice or grease runs down my chin. She moves to kiss it or lick it off me but my napkin beats her to it. Mrs. Betty Carver turns away as if it were no big deal. She wants to kiss.

I say, "This is perhaps the best chicken ever."

She is filling my plate with cole slaw and potato salad. Her hands, I see, are much older than her face. The fingers are wrinkly, the skin around her fingernails is dry and peeling. Her nails are short—and not because they've been kept that way by clippers. It's as if they've been eaten.

She covers her hands by sitting on them. She must have felt the judgment of my eyes.

I say, "Your wedding ring."

"What about it?" she says, pouring the lemonade.

"It looks expensive."

"It was."

"You and Mr. Carver were happy once, right? I mean, there were good times."

Mrs. Betty Carver doesn't answer. She wears a white summer dress. Her hands begin to creep out from under her. They fidget with a napkin.

I'm on my second piece of chicken now. A wing.

"You love chicken, don't you?"

"Yes."

"Chicken is your favorite."

"Yep."

"I love making a person's favorite food." She takes two rubber bands out of her picnic basket and puts her hair in pigtails. "And I made some cookies. Chocolate chip cookies."

I smile because I'm supposed to, adding the obligatory "Great," all the while wondering if she burned them.

I keep eating and she lies back and looks at the clouds and I keep saying "Hmmmm. This is good. Oh my God. This is great chicken. What cole slaw. Amazing potato salad." I feel like a food whore. But while she might not be getting everything she wants, at least she's getting something. My love of her chicken is more love than her pathetic husband ever gives her.

"That looks like a boat."

"What does?"

"Those clouds. See, there's the mast and the sail."

"I don't see it," I say.

Mrs. Betty Carver has put her hands in the two big pockets that hang on her white dress. "How old are you now?"

"I'm twenty-four."

"That makes me . . . oh, can you believe it?"

In the clouds, Mrs. Betty Carver sees a dinosaur, Santa's beard, a candlestick, and me. "That's you, Gilbert. You're the big cloud."

"That doesn't look like me."

"But it's your spirit."

"Hey—you going to eat any of this chicken?"

"It's for you. Everything there is for you."

I put the remaining four pieces on my plate.

"See that little cloud," she says. "The one moving the fastest?"

"Where?"

"The little tiny one—it's darker than the others."

"Yes—okay. I see it. Hey, will you give my sister your recipe for this chicken?"

"That little cloud is me. Did you notice how it was chasing the big cloud?"

"Not really."

"I didn't think you noticed. The little cloud was racing after the big cloud when it suddenly stopped."

"The wind died down."

"Exactly."

"So? I mean, they're just clouds, right?"

"Forget it."

Wait a minute, I'm thinking, was this another one of those conversations where what is meant and what is being said are not the same thing?

"You don't get it, do you?" Mrs. Betty Carver stands suddenly and walks to the footbridge that crosses Skunk River. When she reaches the middle of it, she drops into the water. Her arms flail—she coughs and chokes.

"I know you can swim!" I shout. "I'm not going to save you. I'm not going to!"

Mrs. Betty Carver goes under the water. I look for air bubbles. I stroll to the edge of the bridge but when there's no sign of her, I shout, "I don't believe this!" I pull off my shirt and kick off my shoes. I prepare to dive in when she rises out of the water. She stands where it must be only three feet deep. She is muddy and dripping and I see her bra through her wet dress.

"Not funny," I say. "Not funny at all."

"I'm not so old, you know. I'm not so stodgy. Jump in. Swim with me."

I shake my head.

"You're the one who isn't flexible anymore. You're the one who's . . ."

I've picked up my shirt. I put on my tennis shoes without tying them.

"You were going to save me, weren't you?" Mrs. Betty Carver bobs up and down in the water and watches as I back away.

"Thank you for the meal," I say.

"If you walk away, we're done. We're finished."

The last piece of chicken–a wing–has a nice piece of meat left on it. I'm about to reach for it when I think again. See this as leaving practice, Gilbert.

So I walk away without looking back, leaving Mrs. Betty Carver in the water, leaving the chicken wing with its last bite of meat.

26

I'm in the basement, sorting laundry, when I see for the first time the intricacy of Tucker's floor-support design. Clean white boards everywhere–smartly installed and securely fastened. The network of beams seems capable of keeping Momma afloat, even though we all know it's merely a temporary solution.

The phone rings.

Tucker has been in hiding since he finished. I know he's mad at me because he's gone twenty-four hours without calling.

The phone rings again.

I'll give him a call later to congratulate him. He has outdone himself.

The phone rings again and again.

"Gilbert isn't going to get it!" I shout. No one answers it. The ting-a-ling or the bing-bing has me throwing dirty clothes everywhere. I stomp up the stairs, screaming, "I love this family!" I yank at the kitchen phone. "Gilbert here!"

"May I speak with Amy?"

"Amy?" I call out. Momma's snoring drowns out my voice. "Amy!" Looking out into the backyard, I see that she's preparing the grill for hamburgers. Lifting a window, I shout, "Phone's for you!"

"Who is it?"

"I don't know. You ask them!"

"Find out, please. My hands are all dirty from the grill."

"Who's calling?"

"Don't insult me like that," the voice says.

I stop. Was I just insulting?

"You know who this is."

"No, I don't think I do."

"Great, fine. Thanks, Gilbert Grape."

"Oh. You sound different on the phone."

"It's that new girl, isn't it? The one from Michigan that everyone's talking about. She's the reason, isn't she?"

"I'm sorry," I say.

"No, you're not."

I listen to the phone static, not knowing what to say.

"I'm calling for Amy."

"Oh." I put my face to the window screen and yell, "Amy, it's Mrs. Carver!"

In the house, Amy raises her right shoulder, sandwiching the phone to her ear.

"Hello, Betty. Yes? Uh-huh. Well, how thoughtful of you. Let me get a pencil." As the conversation continues, I realize Mrs. Carver has called to give Amy her chicken recipe. When Amy hangs up, she says to herself, "Now wasn't that the nicest thing." If my sister only knew.

I go back to the basement.

As I pour bleach into a load of whites, I wish I could get clean from my days with Mrs. Carver. I wish I could wash it all away so that my first kiss would be Becky.

A colored load is in the dryer and I check to make sure the heat is on high. Then I climb through the network of boards and beams that support Momma. On one of the boards, written by Tucker in blue ink is this: "Because I love Bonnie Grape."

I climb the basement stairs, which creak and cry. Momma has stopped snoring. The evening news is on. I will get out of the house before any special report by Lance Dodge, I decide. I approach Amy at the grill and say, "I'm not in the burger mood tonight."

"Why?"

"I'm just not."

"Ellen's working, so it's just Arnie and Momma and me."

"I know."

"Gilbert, stay and eat. I hate it when you're not home for dinner."

"I gotta sort some things out. It's been one of those days."

"Every day lately has been one of those days."

"Yep."

I move to kiss her forehead, when she says, "They're burning down the school."

"What?"

"Burning down the school. Saturday. Two days from now."

"Noooo," I say.

"Don't seem so shocked, Gilbert. We always knew one day they would." Amy is all excited. "A schedule of activities surrounding the burning can be found in this week's edition of the *Endora Express*."

"Activities?"

Amy describes the events as scheduled. I am speechless and stand there in a daze.

"So are you gonna take Arnie to watch or am I? I need to know so I can plan the meals and coordinate getting Janice from the airport. She's landing in Des Moines Saturday morning. Let me know which you'd rather do."

I shrug.

"The fire will be something else."

I say nothing and walk immediately to my truck.

Arnie is sitting in the driver's seat. I signal "get out." He won't, so I pull him by his feet and leave him ripping the brown grass out of our lawn in dry clumps. "Stop digging!" I shout. He doesn't.

I drive away.

Tucker's mother, Ruth Ann, who has gold hair and a lazy eye, tells me where to find Tucker. She asks, "How's everything at home?"

I say, "My mother's fine, thank you."

"Is there anything we can do?"

"We're fine," I say.

Her eyes light up suddenly and she says, "You going to watch them burn down...?"

I cut her off with a "See ya" and climb in my truck.

*   *   *

I find Tucker parked across from "The Future Site of the Burger Barn." I pull up next to him. Dressed in a T-shirt that has a big beer-can design on it, he is listening to some heavy-metal music. He looks over at me and, with no expression of surprise or happiness, he turns back and watches with envy as the construction workers pack up their tools and load up for the day.

I move from my truck to his. He doesn't turn down the music. He squeezes the steering wheel, his eyes are mad and he won't look my way. I reach to turn down the sound, but his hand stops mine.

"Thank you!" I shout.

He doesn't hear me. He waves to a worker who doesn't wave back.

"THANK YOU!"

He heard me this time but pretends he doesn't. I lunge for the dial on his tape deck, the volume goes down and I speak like an auctioneer. "Thankyouforfixingthefloor. Youdidagreatjobthank-you. Itmeanssomuchtomyfamilyandtome. Sothanks!"

Tucker fights a smile.

"I know. I took you for granted. And I'm sorry, buddy."

He flinches on the word "buddy." I was premature in the use of that word.

"You think it's that easy? You just say the words and I forget the hours of unappreciation? You think I just erase my uhm pain so simply, with such uhm simplicity?"

I suggest that might be best.

Tucker goes, "Humpf."

We sit in silence for minutes that feel like funerals.

Across the street, the remaining workers drive out for the day. Tucker honks. I cover my ears, and the workers don't notice us. "They're good guys," he says.

"Yeah?"

"Real serious. Real pros."

"Oh."

Tucker opens his door as he is going in for a closer look. I follow.

"They poured the foundation Monday. I missed it because I was doing your floor."

"Thanks again for doing that, by the way," I say.

He squints his eyes like he can't believe the nerve of me. He continues, "They're ready for the frame and they'll have the roof up by Saturday. Now this whole thing is a first-class operation."

"Yeah, I see that."

"This Burger Barn will be a perfect replica of the original in Boone. You know there are over fifteen Burger Barns in the Iowa-Nebraska-Missouri area. It's a growing and prosperous company. And the whole idea that each Burger Barn is identical to the others makes me ... makes me ..."

"Well, it's impressive. It's reassuring."

"Yes. A guy walks into a Burger Barn and he knows what to expect. He knows what he can count on. And that's the problem with this world. A guy just doesn't know what to expect anymore." We walk to where I surmise the back of the restaurant will be. "We know, for example, that this is where the french fries will be cooked. Here will be the burger rack. And the milk-shake machine will be placed approximately here." Tucker talks on and on about various details and how the Barn will be the new Endora hot spot and how he intends to be at the center of said heat.

I interrupt with the news that they're burning down the school Saturday.

Tucker stops. He says, "I know this, Gilbert. They're making a whole deal out of it. Fire trucks from Motley even."

I look at him. I'm getting all emotional about this for no explainable reason. I say with a shaky voice, "They're making it into a celebration. Can you believe it?"

"I can't be expending energy for old, tired buildings. My focus is on the future. The Burger Barn future. Are you trying to upset me? Are you trying to ruin my day? 'Cause it won't work."

And I consider this man my best friend.

I cross the empty highway to my truck and sit on the hot hood. Tucker takes his time inspecting the grounds. He walks among the construction like he's Neil I'm-the-coolest-astronaut Armstrong bouncing on the moon for the first time. A few semis whoosh past, a car without a muffler. He heads to his truck, smiling, but still not trusting me.

"See ya, Gilbert."

"Hey, uhm..."

He stops. He knows I want something.

"This," I continue, "is really something." I point to the construction site. "It really is exciting for you, isn't it? You've been waiting a long time for the right thing and, Tucker, any idiot can see that this is the right thing. I mean, wow. In a matter of weeks, there will be customers and you'll be serving them...and it's...for *me,* it's great...to...see you...you know..."

Tucker says nothing as I run out of bullshit. I feel rotten for being so fake.

Finally he speaks. "She's not what you think."

"Huh, what?"

"I know it for a fact. I asked her out, okay? And she said 'No.' Which is okay, okay? But. Then she said, 'A bird doesn't mate with a fish.' "

Ouch, I say to myself.

"Who, Gilbert—who do you think is the fish in this situation? Who is the fish?"

I shrug. "Tucker, the girl is clearly stupid and you deserve better."

"Don't you think I know that now?"

"You deserve better. *You* do."

He looks at me long and hard. He knows I'm homing in on her. "Gilbert?"

"Yeah, buddy?"

"She stays at the old Lally place." Tucker's voice cracks. His eyes fill with water.

"Huh?"

"The old Lally place!"

"Uhm."

"Do I need to say it again, Gilbert? Am I not being clear enough?!"

"You're being clear, yes."

"And you're welcome."

My "thank you" follows, but already he's started up his truck. He leans over, rolls down his window, and shouts, "You're making a big mistake!"

The old Lally place is on the north end of town, eight or so houses from the water tower, five streets from the town square. The house is small, one story, covered with that metal siding people seem to be buying and loving these days.

I drive past and don't see Becky's bike out front. I drive past three times. No one seems to be home and the yard looks in bad shape. On my fourth and final pass, an old woman is standing on the porch waving for me to stop. I do.

She says, "So you're Gilbert Grape!"

I hesitate, amazed that such a strong, booming voice can come from such a scrawny, bony woman.

"I'm the grandmother!"

I remember her from the water-tower incident. She was standing next to Becky. "Oh, hello."

"Breakfast is at eight tomorrow!"

"Excuse me?"

"Breakfast. Eight o'clock. May we expect you?"

I nod without thought.

"Tomorrow morning, then, Gilbert Grape. Looking forward to it!"

27

I've been up since five-thirty, shaved twice, even though my face is still mainly fuzz. I combed my hair several times, trying my standard part on the side, a more daring part in the middle, and a low part, identical to the one I had as a kid. I settle for the hair that I'm used to. I washed my body in the shower extra long, and the skin of my legs and my arms itches from the dryness. In an effort to smell nice, I left a layer of soap on my skin that makes me feel like I'm covered in plastic. I brushed, flossed, and with my fingers scraped away at some of the yellow at the base of my bigger teeth.

I borrowed Amy's watch. It reads forty seconds until eight when my truck and I pull up in front of the old Lally place.

I sneeze twice when Becky's grandma opens the door.

"Good morning, Mr. Grape." She lets me into her house, which is full of little trinkets and rocks and tiny antiques. She says, "Have a seat," as she moves into the kitchen.

I sit on an old blue-and-white sofa with the softest cushions. I study the tiny living room. There is an upright piano with lace thingies on the back and little figurines of deer and sheep and dogs. On a bookcase, there are pictures. Becky as a baby. Becky in second grade. Becky in fifth. Becky in a pink dance outfit with a baton. Becky with her parents, who are plain and ordinary. In every picture, her eyes are piercing and she seems otherworldly.

The house has that bacon-for-breakfast smell. I lean over the sofa and peek into the kitchen. The table is set. A pitcher of fresh orange juice sits on the table next to a napkin holder that looks like a rooster. The silence of no TV in the house is a shock to my ears.

Minutes pass and I'm called to breakfast. I sit where she tells me. She pours me juice.

"Coffee?"

"Yes, ma'am." She pours it and I look at the brown spots on her hands.

She smiles. "Scrambled eggs all right?"

"Yes, ma'am."

She cracks the eggs and drops the shells in the sink. Then she disappears down the hall for a moment. Back at the stove, she stirs the eggs with a fork. They are ready fast. I'm also served bacon and wheat toast, which I cover lightly with strawberry jelly.

I'm about to take my first bite when Becky emerges in shorts and a T-shirt, those little kernels of sleep still stuck in her eyes, her hair all puffy and wild, and when she looks at me, squinting from the light, I realize she just woke up. She sees my combed hair and

my striped shirt, and she laughs silently and sighs, "Oh, Gilbert."
Moving past me, she goes into the bathroom, more minutes pass,
and finally there's a flush. She emerges, her hair still uncombed, her
eyes still sleepy.

"Doesn't Gilbert look nice, Becky?"

"No."

"Becky!"

"Yes, of course he looks nice. But I prefer him, Grandma, when
he's sloppy and caught off guard."

She pours herself a cup of coffee. Her grandma must have
scrambled a dozen eggs–all of which are for me–and, with the
pound of bacon on my plate and the many slices of toast, I find it
hard to take any bites at all.

"Becky doesn't eat breakfast, Gilbert. And, of course, it's my
favorite meal of the day. So I'm grateful that you came
because ... well, just because ..."

"I'm usually not a breakfast person myself," I say.

"Really? Are you not hungry?"

"Oh, I'm hungry. It's that my family has this thing with food."

"Your mother, I hear ..."

"Yes," I say, cutting the grandmother off. I chew on the eggs.

"Grandma, you know what I think?"

The grandmother stops and looks at Becky.

"I think Gilbert's trying to make a good impression."

I want to scream "OF COURSE I AM!" Instead, I wipe my face
with my napkin and shrug like "Well, maybe."

"Becky, dear, it's natural to want to make a good impression. It's
flattering that a young man would think so highly of us that he'd
want to impress."

Becky chugs her coffee, scoots out her chair, goes down the hall
to what must be her room, grabs her cigarettes, and goes out onto
their porch. I can't see her but I smell her smoke. *She's making*

I clean my plate. The first time in years. ← *him normal (again*

The grandmother tells me how she lived here thirty-five years
ago and how she wanted to come back here and live out her days.
"Endora, like all things, has changed." She remembers my father
and mother. They were newly married then, but she didn't know

them well. She tells me that her daughter and son-in-law thought a summer here would do Becky some good. She wonders if I think it will rain soon. I say that it better because the farmers are about to lose their crops. I tell her about my family and how my little brother's birthday is coming up and how we're planning a big reunion/party. "How sweet," she says, and I think to myself that it will be anything but sweet. We talk about her history, and I find out that Becky's parents are getting a divorce, an idea that Becky suggested, and then the grandmother says, "You know, Gilbert, Becky just turned fifteen."

"Uhm. Oh."

"Gilbert, she's still a young girl in many respects."

"Age isn't an issue."

"But fifteen is fifteen."

"Yes, ma'am." I want to say how I know a certain wife of a certain insurance man who, in her late thirties, is more of a young girl than Becky.

"I trust that you will treat her with respect and not pressure her to do what she is not ready to do."

I must be shaking my head, agreeing with her, because she is smiling. My thoughts race inside. Fifteen. Jesus, Gilbert, you're a joke.

Suddenly I need to use the bathroom. Instead of standing and peeing, I sit on the toilet seat. I do this because I know Becky was sitting naked and peeing minutes earlier. This might be as close to her as I'll ever get.

After breakfast, I thank the grandmother. She says that she's glad we've reached an understanding.

"Yes, ma'am," I say. I leave the house. Becky doesn't even wave good-bye. I'm about to get in my truck, when she says, "You want to go for a walk?"

"Uhm. Whatever."

Becky steps into her tennis shoes, and we start walking. We've gone about six houses when she says, "Gilbert."

I go, "Yep?"

"Age is a funny thing. It's deceptive."

"Yeah?"

"You're older than me in terms of time. But in terms of other things ..."

"Careful."

"In terms of other things, you're not so old."

We walk down other streets and I hear more of the same. Eventually I ask if we can change the subject and Becky does.

"A friend of yours ... black hair, a funny nose ... a short guy ..."

"Tucker?"

"He asked me out."

"I know. He told me."

"Is he upset with me?"

I shrug and say, "Disappointed is probably the best word for it." Actually, destroyed is the only word to describe how Tucker is feeling.

"Your friend is so far away from himself."

"You think?"

"Yes, I do."

We walk on. Becky rubs the sleep from her eyes. It falls to the ground and a part of me wants to collect it and save it, like the watermelon seeds from the other night.

Yesterday morning, a strange smell had pervaded my room and I traced the smell to the slice of watermelon I had put in a Baggie and slid under my bed. The slice had begun to spoil and turn green. Covering my nose, I extracted the seeds, which now sit in a paper cup by my headboard, and dumped the moldy leftovers in the garbage disposal.

Becky stretches to the sky. Her arms reach so far up that her stomach, pale and smooth, is revealed. She breathes out, her arms drop to her sides and her shirt returns to normal.

"My grandmother likes you."

"I'm glad." I smile a bit; we walk on.

"But she likes everybody."

28

As we walk down South Main to the square, cars slow and people peek out their windows. I look at the swirly candy-cane device in front of Lloyd's Barbershop. It spins upward. Lloyd is looking out the window, cutting Buddy Miles's hair. A man in his early fifties with waxy hair and a hook nose, Lloyd is one of the many entranced with Becky. So many people are staring that I feel like a Kennedy or like Elvis or, to a lesser degree, like how Lance Dodge must feel in those Des Moines shopping malls.

he's ok with being seen w/her

Becky's shirt is soft, fuzzy, and her nipples can be seen when a breeze passes.

As we walk slowly, my left hand brushes then bumps her right hand with the hope that she'll take it. "Sorry," I say, as if it were an accident.

"Are you?"

"I am. I hate it when people bump me."

"Please don't lie."

"But I'm not ..."

She puts her soft, smooth hand on my mouth, my words stop, and she looks into my eyes. I bring my lids down in an attempt to hide. She walks on. My eyes remain closed. Hopefully she'll tell me to come along, but she says nothing. I feel her getting farther and farther away so I open my eyes and follow.

When I catch up with her, she says, "Your mother was so courageous the other day."

I can't help but laugh.

"You think I'm joking, Gilbert?"

"I don't know what I think. Courageous isn't the first word that comes to mind."

"What comes to mind?"

"Oh ... I guess ... how ... my mother ... has ... *grown*." I am on my knees now, this laughter won't stop. Becky watches me and waits. Eventually I compose myself, I stand and put on a serious face. I point toward the Dairy Dream.

Arriving there, I tap on the take-out window. Ellen looks up from the magazine she's reading and seeing me, looks back at the magazine. I tap louder, but she won't open the window to take my order. I try to get Cindy Mansfield's attention, but she's in back on the phone—most certainly talking to her mother, Carmen, who is half owner of the Dream. Cindy doesn't see me.

The door opens and the bell tings and tangs. Ellen looks up, thinking it's me, only to find Becky standing there. She quickly shuts her magazine, stands, fixes any stray hairs and somehow knocks over a box of sugar cones. Becky orders for the both of us. Ellen's hands shake and she giggles almost nonstop as she spoons the sprinkles on a vanilla cone.

As Cindy talks on the phone, she studies Becky with condemning, judgmental eyes. Finished with the cone, Ellen fills up a large cup with Orange Crush. Becky waits patiently, treating Ellen as an equal. Cindy hangs up and slides open the window.

"You're invited, too, Gilbert."

"To what?"

"We're having this wonderful teen retreat/Bible study/picnic on the Fourth. Ellen is coming. I told her she could bring you."

"No, thanks."

"A great time will be had by . . ."

"I'm sure."

The bell sounds as Becky comes outside to me. She hands me my drink. I take a sip. My face is sweaty; it is very hot outside. I press my face close to Cindy, not because I want to be close to her, but so the air-conditioned air from inside can bathe my face. Ellen has returned to her magazine. She struggles to look unaffected by Becky's appearance. Cindy says a bunch of things about the "retreat" which I don't hear because I'm busy speculating on the number of coats of makeup that she has applied. The more Christian you are in this town, the more makeup you wear. I've always thought that it's because if you were to die suddenly, you'd look better for God.

"Cindy, I'd like you to meet my friend. This is . . ."

"Oh, hello."

"Hey, Ellen!" I call back to her. "I'd like you to meet . . ."

"I'm in the middle of an article . . ."

"I want you to meet someone."

"In a minute."

Becky pulls at my shirt for us to go. I look at her, she stands with her feet crossed and the cone pressed to her mouth.

"Bye, Cindy," I say.

"So you coming to our Bible study? Huh?"

Walking backward, I shrug like "We'll see, but doubtful."

We walk away. I ask if the cone is her breakfast. She says nothing. When she finishes, she takes a sip of my drink and says, "That wasn't nice."

"What?"

"You know."

I look at Becky like "What on earth are you talking about?"

"Gilbert, please. All the girls in this town think of me as some threat, some rival, which I'm not. Your sister needs to feel beautiful and special. I'm happy for her to feel that way." She walks on. "I know you've been hurt. But I don't want to be part of your cruelty."

We walk on in silence.

It takes fifteen minutes for me to admit my mistake. "Sorry," I say.

We're on North Main by the time I finish my drink. I say, "One second," to Becky and jog over to Carver's Insurance to throw away my cup. Mr. Carver's Ford Fairmont is out front, but a sign on the door says "Closed." How odd. I hear a noise inside and press my face to the office window. The shade isn't all the way down and I look through a crack. I hear a woman's moan, a man's groan. I press closer to see better. Melanie's desk light is on. Melanie is lying on her back, on top of her desk, her skirt hiked up. Mr. Carver is standing, his pants dropped, his back to me. He's ramming hard and her body jiggles with each thrust.

Becky says, "What are you looking at?"

I lift my arm like "Shhhh."

She starts to walk my way to see for herself.

At that moment, Melanie throws her head back, and lets out a deep moan. Her hair falls from her head, and it dangles by a bobby pin or two. It's a wig. Christ. Melanie wears a wig.

Mr. Carver is plunging deeper and deeper and the slap of that gets louder.

Becky touches my shoulder. I jump. She says, "What is it?"

"I'm just seeing if anybody's here. You know, to throw away my cup. Let's go." I leave my cup on the hood of Mr. Carver's car.

The next several minutes, Becky is talking about her house back in Ann Arbor, her friends, her parents and how they're professors at the university. I don't hear much of it, though, because my thoughts are totally on what I just witnessed.

"What was going on in there?" she asks. "Tell me the truth."

So I do. I describe what I saw. She asks if I'm all right. I just say I'm fine and that I'd really like to keep on walking.

Becky says, "Okay," like it's no problem. For her, true feelings never seem to be a problem.

As we walk on, the haunting image of Mr. Carver, Melanie, and her wig clogs my thoughts.

"Is something the matter, Gilbert?"

"Oh, nothing."

"What is it?"

"It's just that Mr. Carver has a wife. I feel bad for her, that's all."

"That's sweet of you to care so much for another person's feelings."

Funny—I don't feel sweet.

We walk up and down practically every street in Endora. At the self-serve V-shaped car wash, I put in three quarters and Becky stands there while I spray her with water. Her T-shirt gets wet and sticks to her chest. I dig my fingers into the backs of my legs to keep from ripping off her shirt. She sprays me with water, too, and we end up cleaner than any car.

After the washing, we sit on the wet pavement to dry out in the sun. She asks about my previous girlfriends and I say that there has been only one and that it's long in the past and that I don't want to talk about it.

"Sounds like you regret it."

"Yep."

Becky says, "I never want to regret. 'Regret' is the ugliest word."

To me, the ugliest words are "family," "Endora," "Jesus Christ." So I say, "I don't have a problem with 'regret.' "

Becky stretches out, her eyes closed. I sit Indian style, looking down at her smooth skin, her angel face. She breathes in and out slowly. Her eyes are closed while mine remain open and stay fixed on her.

The cement under us is no longer wet. We've been baking in the sun for over an hour and Becky hasn't said a word.

She stands up suddenly, stretches her arms above her head. She feels that her shirt is almost dry. I cup my hands in front of me in an effort to hide my erection.

"I want to walk."

"Okay," I say, sitting there a moment, hoping my bulge will go away.

"Your nose is turning pink, Gilbert Grape."

"Oh well."

Tucker drives past in his truck. He sees us first. I wave—he doesn't even honk.

We're walking in silence when suddenly Becky sprints ahead. I notice how smooth she runs, how it's as if she's floating. She skips a bit, picks a dandelion and puts it behind her ear. I keep her in sight—walking at a steady pace—refusing to speed up, unable to slow down.

29

That's my old school!" I call out.

Becky is walking toward the old building with its red brick and green tin roof. I have to run to catch up. "Pretty ugly building, huh?"

"I like it."

"You didn't have to go there for thirteen years."

Becky moves toward a window and looks through the dusty glass. Many of the windows are broken, and for the most part, the school has been boarded up since it closed seven years ago, the summer I graduated.

"They're burning it down tomorrow," I say.

"I heard."

"Practice for the Volunteer Fire Department. Can you imagine?"

"It's the most interesting building in this whole town. So it gets burned down. Some justice." This is the first time Becky has sounded anything like angry.

"Well, we live in a time of Burger Barns."

"Very true, Gilbert. How old is this building?"

"Nineteen hundred something."

She moves to another window.

"My sister says they're anticipating quite a crowd."

"Crowd?"

"Yes, hundreds of people are expected. The Methodist Church is selling popcorn. Mayor Gaps is going to start the fire."

"How morbid."

"Welcome to Endora."

I go on to explain that I'd rather pick up my sister in Des Moines tomorrow than be around Endora to smell the burning and listen to the cheering masses. "They're making a celebration out of it."

Becky looks in a second window, a third.

"That was the fifth-grade room," I say.

She lifts up a window and tries to climb in.

wow

"What are you doing?"

"Good-byes are important. You've got to learn to say good-bye."

"To a building?"

It's the middle of the day and Becky has disappeared into my old school, the day before its death. I have no choice but to follow. "I haven't been in here in years," I say, pulling myself through the now open window. I scratch my stomach on the bricks. Inside, I lift my T-shirt and show her my scrape in hopes that she'll kiss it to make it feel better.

"Ouch," she says.

"Yes," I say, trying to look as if I were in pain.

She turns away from me, no kiss. She crosses to the wall and says, "So this was fifth grade?"

"Yep."

She runs her nails lightly down the dusty blackboard. My hands are on my ears and I shout, "Don't!" I see her laugh. "Not funny," I say.

She walks out into the hall, which is dark and hot. She opens the doors to other rooms—she looks in where the old library was, where Melanie and her red hair would stamp everyone's books.

"So this was it?"

"Yep, you're seeing where my entire education took place."

She looks at me. "Are you saying that you've stopped learning?"

"Something like that." I laugh. Becky doesn't.

I show her where my locker was for grades seven through twelve. "Lance Dodge was six lockers down," I say. Becky doesn't seem too impressed. "Lance often would call out to me. He'd say 'Hey, Grape. How'd you do on the quiz? How'd you do on the Iowa Basic skills test? How'd you . . . ?' " I look to Becky, but she's writing on an empty, dusty trophy case.

"What are you writing?"

She steps away from the trophy case and I walk to it. Written in the dust are these words:

HELPING GILBERT SAY GOOD-BYE

We walk toward where the gymnasium/stage/cafeteria used to be. This part of the building is higher than the other part and the light pours through windows that have been broken. Several golf balls lie on the tile floor—they were the glass breakers, I decide. The basketball hoops have been removed, the championship banners and fold-up tables, too.

"One time, Lance Dodge stood up on the stage area. . . ."

"Gilbert, I don't care about Lance Dodge."

"Yeah, but it's a good story."

"I don't care about him. He's nothing to me."

Becky hands me a piece of chalk she must have found in one of the rooms. "I want you to do something." Her voice is suddenly sexy, suddenly very much the sound I've been waiting for. "Will you do it?"

"Sure," I whisper, thinking maybe this is our moment.

She tells me to go into each room and write "Good-bye" on the chalk board. Write "Thank you" or "Miss you" or whatever. I start to object but she says, "You'll be glad you did."

I climb the back stairs and start with my twelfth-grade room where Mr. Reichen taught. He was a toad. I look around the room, the green paint has peeled and even the light fixtures have been removed. I write, "So long, Seniors. Gilbert was the last one out." In the junior room, I draw a picture of Tucker farting, which he was always known to do. I write, "Gilbert was here." The sophomore room gets an elaborate "G" which I fill in, the freshman room gets a simple "Thanks." I do eighth grade down to kindergarten and only skip one room.

I find Becky dancing in the gym/stage/cafeteria and say "I'm all done." She stops moving, her face and arms are sweaty, her hair has started to curl. She shakes her head and her sweat splatters my face. I would like to catch some of it on my tongue but I'm too late.

"Can we go now?"

Becky smiles, and we walk out and down the cobwebbed, dirty hall. If this whole experience was supposed to move me or touch me in some way, it didn't.

The school is empty and echoey. I'll be glad to be out in the sun, walking across the brown grass.

I say, "Apparently, they've got to be careful with the fire because the ground is so dry that the grass could catch on fire. They're taking precautions...."

Becky stops. "You forgot this room," she says. She is standing in front of my second-grade classroom. The room where Mrs. Brainer taught.

"No, I didn't."

She opens the door. The blackboard is blank.

"Let's go, okay?" I say.

"Come to terms with it."

"With what?"

She walks into the room.

"I suddenly feel sick," I say.

"I bet."

I look at Becky. "How do you know about this room?"

She looks at me and my eyes find my feet. My shoes are a size twelve. In second grade my feet weren't so big. "It was a long time ago," I say.

"Tell me about it."

"No."

"Please," she says, taking my hand in hers.

I can't refuse her. I approach the chalk board which is the length of one of the walls. I wait for Becky to leave the room. I start writing. Half in cursive, half in block print. This is what I write:

Mrs. Brainer had a rule cause of Lance Dodge. Rule was—If you have to go to bathroom before break time you forfeit recess rights. So. 10/13/1973. Amy = Senior, Student Council Secy. Larry = 10th grade, Janice = 5th. I was in this room. 2nd grade. Second chair, fourth row. Tucker in front of me, L. Dodge to my left. I had uneasy feeling about my Dad. Had to get home. Wanted to get home. Momma was in Motley with Arnie for tests. Found out he was retarded that August. I had a sick feeling. That morning my dad had been in good spirits. He had been all smiley and picked me up by my ears. Larry said on way to school that Dad was happy. I had this sick feeling and made plans to run home during recess. But I had to pee so I squeezed my legs so hard. It was 8 minutes till recess when I wet my pants. L. Dodge told Mrs. Brainer. I cleaned it up while others went outside. Autopsy determined that about same time my Dad was hanging him-self, I was peeing in my seat. Ha. Ha ha ha he he he he ha ha ha. He ha.

I drop the chalk on the floor and it breaks in two.

I leave by the fifth-grade window as Becky reads what I wrote. I wait by where the slide used to be. I sit on the cement and pull at the weeds that have grown through the cracks. My hand is sore from writing. I covered the entire board.

Becky climbs out the window and walks my way. I don't look at her. She offers no hug, no consoling.

"They say you cried so hard. They say you were sitting in the biggest puddle ever seen and you were howling."

I say nothing.

"People remember this sound coming out of you. Like a dying animal. People remember it, Gilbert. You could hear it throughout the whole school. Is that correct?"

I shrug. Becky sounds like a detective.

"And Mrs. Brainer made you stay after school, right?"

I nod.

"And when you got home, what did you find?"

I look away from her.

"They were taking your father out of the house. Is that right?"

I don't move my head. I stand and rub the pebbles off my legs. They've left an imprint.

"No one saw you upset at the funeral. No one saw you cry."

I look at her.

"You're proud of that."

I say nothing, but I am. She stares at me. I close my eyes tight and begin to laugh. A jiggly laugh, high-pitched, my face scrunched.

"Gilbert."

I laugh. Oh, I laugh and laugh.

"Gilbert."

More laughter. The uncomfortable kind.

"Nobody can remember the last time you cried...."

With that, I start off running.

"Gilbert, wait."

I don't even look back. I run fast as I can. I cut through yards, hop the Hoys' fence. I run across Main Street, past Lamson Grocery, the Ramp Cafe. I cut through the Meffords' backyard and tip over their birdbath.

At home, I run upstairs and shut the door to my room. I wipe the sweat off my legs, my arms—I dry off my face by dunking my head into my pillow.

Later, I refuse dinner. As night falls, I keep watch at my window. I've shoved my dresser drawers in front of my door.

It is night now and I keep my door blockaded. I look out my window for a glowing match, a flaming watermelon, a sign from her, a surrender flag.

No sign comes and I fall asleep.

30

It's Saturday, July 1–fifteen days till the retard's birthday–it's seven-forty-something in the morning, and I'm on my way to pick up my stewardess/psychologist sister from the Des Moines Municipal Airport.

I'm maybe a mile out of town when I decide to drive past my old school one last time. I thought yesterday's good-bye was final, but I've this urge for one last look.

As I do a U-turn on Highway 13, my tires screech.

I'm a block away when I see that clusters of people have already gathered to watch. The burning won't start until ten and already there must be fifty people. I feel sick to my stomach, hang another U-turn, and head out of town.

I'm making great time when I need to stop and stretch my legs a bit. I pull off at a Burger Barn on the outskirts of Ames. The outside is a kind of simulated barn, with a black, red, and white sign that lights up at night. I walk in and look around. The food has a paper smell about it, the orange and blue colors inside make me dizzy, and a boy with braces stands waiting–he's practically dying to take my order. It occurs to me that this is what Tucker wants to be. The boy snaps at me to order and since he's left his microphone on, it's echoing throughout the store. "Sir, may I take your order? You, sir, your order!"

I walk out of the store in a daze–a young couple with their

pudgy baby in a stroller enter as I'm leaving–and I say, "They're burning down the wrong building."

It isn't until I'm in my truck that I realize that those people had no idea what I was talking about. My paranoia grows so great that for the next several miles, I check my mirror for the flashing lights of a police car. Maybe the couple reported that a young, unshaven, dirtily dressed man with arsonist tendencies was seen leaving the Burger Barn.

I drive for miles and no siren, no lights, no arrest.

I'm an hour early, so I cruise around downtown Des Moines. I see the giant buildings, the enormous car dealerships and hospitals the size of what I believe Moscow to be. I see the Equitable building, which at one time was the tallest in all of Iowa. My father, brother Larry, and I would take trips to Des Moines and Dad would always explain how it was the tallest building and somehow I always felt special when looking with them at the tallest.

I see the capitol with its giant gold dome and its four smaller green domes.

It is so hot that no people are outside. In downtown Des Moines, the surprising place that it is, a walkway has been built from building to building. This way a shopper or businessman won't have to go outside. I pass under one of those passageways and, through the tinted glass, I see people moving along. So–inside, where there's air-conditioning, they all mill about but outside, where I am presently, the streets of Des Moines are mine.

I pass a big, fairly new theater called the Civic Center, where important people perform. In a cement park across the street is this giant sculpture. It is a giant umbrella frame lying on its side. It's green. Stand under it, during a rainstorm, you'll still get wet–that's why it's art.

At the airport, Janice is waiting behind one of those electric doors, still dressed in her polyester stewardess blue. I pull up. She looks disappointed. "Thought Amy was..."

"Nope," I say. I put her blue luggage in the back of the truck.

"Couldn't you have driven the Nova?" Janice hates my truck. She has an aversion to trucks, seeing as she lost her virginity sev-eral times in pickups identical to mine.

I'm about to say "You wanna walk?" when Janice gives me this much-too-fake hug. Her arms about break my neck, but the rest of her stays two feet away.

"You look good!" she says.

Of course, I didn't shower this morning, I didn't shave, and I'm wearing the dirtiest clothes I could find. No sane person would say I look good, unless they lie.

My sister Janice would like to be as pretty as Ellen and she'd like to be as loyal as Amy, but she sits in the middle of all things. This is why she tries so hard, this is why our trip back will feel like an eternity.

"Can't believe you'd come get me. To what do I owe this honor?"

I'm about to tell her the truth: the town is burning down our old school and all, but before I can say anything, she says, "You proba-bly want to borrow some money."

"No!"

"Oooo–do not get hostile with me, young man. Your hostility is your own and I refuse to take responsibility for it."

I say nothing. My thoughts race. Yes, I could do with some money. A thousand dollars would get me started in Des Moines–a new life, a new name. But I'll never ask Janice.

Pulling in to get gas, we go over the black cord of a Des Moines gas station. The bing-bing, bong-bong becomes BING-BING, BONG-BONG. I'd swear it's in stereo. I hit the brakes and cover my ears. Janice looks at me as if I'm nuts. But this is how she always looks at me. She gives the station boy the most colorful of her many credit cards and then carries a garment bag into the ladies' room on the side of the station. As Janice walks away, the oily sta-tion boy looks at Janice's butt, studies it, and dreams. I fill the tank. Minutes pass and Janice emerges dressed in one of her many coun-try-and-western outfits. Her boots are lizard or rattlesnake or armadillo. She carries a black cowboy hat.

"There, that's better."

Says who?

She lays the garment bag in back and climbs in the truck, all the time aware that a group of men watch her from inside the station. I screw on the gas cap while the boy brings the credit card on one of those portable credit card thingies for her to sign. He gets close and almost gags from the copious amounts of perfume and hair spray that she has applied. Janice signs her name in that elegant fashion of hers, she makes the "J" really big, and instead of dotting the "i" in her name, she makes a tiny heart.

As we drive, I fill in Janice on family matters. I preface each update with "Your retard brother," "Your walrus mother," "Your ever adolescent little sister."

"Stop it. They're your family, too."

"Nope. Don't think so."

In disgust, she opens her blue purse and pulls out a long, skinny brown cigarette.

"You find everything about me pretty much repulsive?"

"Pretty much," I say.

You don't light a brown cigarette and then ask Gilbert Grape for an opinion.

We drive many miles in silence.

"Arnie's still alive?"

"Yes," I say.

"Good."

My sister is digging for conversation material. It takes a few seconds for me to register the nature of her question and I say, "Oh my God. I forgot. He did die."

"When?"

"About a month ago."

"How was the funeral?"

"Lovely."

"Many people?"

"The whole town."

Whenever we imagine Arnie's funeral, we picture tons of people. I get this clear image of me helping to carry Arnie's coffin, when

Janice launches into a tirade about how we must prepare for the inevitable. She explains what I already know, that our little brother has lived way longer than anybody expected.

"I know."

"We'd be fooling ourselves if we thought..."

"I know."

In the air, I'm sure Janice is the best stewardess going, but on the ground, her brain latches onto her body and the psychologist we hoped she'd never be surges forth. She explains why Momma is so fat. "Wouldn't you eat if you were her? Wouldn't you hate living in the house where your husband died?" She provides insights into Amy and how she'll never have a man because she puts the family first. This, too, can be explained because she's the oldest, the "man" in the family, in a certain sense. Larry's behavior is the easiest to understand. "The house is hell for Larry. It was Larry who found Daddy. The house brings all that back. Move to another house and I bet you'd see Larry all the time. Ellen never had a father and she's seeking in all the boys she dates the father she never had. Arnie is retarded and that's reason enough for why he does as he does."

wow

"That leaves you and me, Janice. How do you explain you and me?"

"Amy didn't leave, so I did. Larry and I are the breadwinners."

"I work...."

"The *major* breadwinners and that's all right. It's the part that makes us happiest. Keeping you all supported. It keeps us close."

I want to tell Janice that because she sent her last check late, we had to go on credit with Mr. Lamson.

"You're the only one, Gilbert, who defies a kind of definition or comprehension. I mean, one doesn't know what you want. You don't travel, you don't read, you don't expand yourself. I arrange for you to fly to Chicago, but you won't get on a plane. You play it safe in all things and I've never known if it's because you're scared or if it's because you're just lazy. Of course, I love you and don't in any way mean to hurt you. You need to examine your life on a deeper, more honest level. Quite simply—you don't know what you want and it shows. You're a scared little boy."

I look at my sister smoking her brown cigarette, her cowboy

boots resting on the dash, her makeup melting like chocolate in the heat–I look at her and consider the source.

Janice blows her brown smoke in my direction and a sudden urge to be anywhere but in this car with this particular sister hits. When the speedometer reaches 80, Janice begins to giggle. When it hits 90, she can no longer laugh. At 100 mph, she says "Not funny" three times. At 110, she digs for her seat belt and finds that it's gone. She screams, holds onto her cowboy hat and claws my arm until the skin breaks and I bleed.

One wonders who's scared now.

wow petty

31

We pull into the drive in time for dinner. Janice jumps out before I even get the truck in park, grabs her bags, and goes upstairs. Amy meets me at the door, sees me holding my bloody arm, and asks, "Did you two fight?"

"Why would you even think such a thing? We had a marvelous time."

I get Arnie to help bandage my arm. I've never been so proud of a wound. I hope it leaves a scar.

As we eat, Janice has lengthy conversations with Amy and Arnie and tosses comments across the kitchen into the dining room, where Momma occasionally grunts or moans in agreement. Janice is a big-city girl, so this gives her the right to tell us all about the "real" world. Amy is worried that the spaghetti isn't done enough and Arnie is much more interested in getting a noodle from between his teeth. I have a great time agreeing with Janice. I keep saying "I know" to whatever she says and she does an amazing job ignoring me. Janice is real top-notch about denying what's most obvious. I keep saying, "I know, I know." Amy presses her foot on top of mine to get me to stop it.

"Ouch, Amy, you're pressing on my foot."

Amy pulls it off and looks at her beans. Arnie looks up and stares at Janice, squints as if he's looking at something particular about her. He moves his face toward hers, so close that he's about six inches away and this makes Janice even more self-conscious and she says, "What is it, Arnie?" and he says, "Nothin'," and returns to his potatoes and beans.

After Momma falls back into a loud sleep, we move to the porch for a dessert of Popsicles and fudge bars. Ellen returns from work, and her reunion with Janice, as usual, is teary and screamy. They jump up and down like those little gymnast girls do at the Olympics.

Amy spoons out a plate of leftovers from the refrigerator. Ellen asks Janice hundreds of questions. Amy brings Ellen her plate, and she forgets to say thank you. The "girls" move upstairs. Their laughter and giggles grow even louder now. I'm convinced it's because they're mocking me and Amy's certain they're poking fun at her.

Amy and I sit on the porch swing watching Arnie attempting somersaults in the front yard.

"So how was today?" I ask.

"Arnie loved it. There must have been a thousand people there."

"Oh God."

"The fire got so hot and I had this rush of memories. I thought of walking to school. All of us walking to school. Funny."

"Not really."

"You know what I mean."

"Yeah."

"They let Arnie sit in one of the fire trucks. He wore a hat and everything."

"That's nice."

"He kept asking for matches on the way home and I said, 'No, matches are bad.' After lunch, he dumped out the junk drawer on the kitchen floor, and I said, 'Arnie, what are you doing?' and he said, 'Matches.' But you know how it is when he gets something into his head..."

Upstairs this summer's hit song plays on Ellen's cassette deck. Their girlie screams accompany it.

"They're having fun," Amy says.

Arnie unearths a big rock and runs around the yard with it, threatening insects and shrubbery.

"Arnie!"

He stops and turns, his lips and chin covered with brown from the fudge bar.

"Arnie, what are matches?" I ask, my voice firm.

He smiles.

"What are they?"

He shakes his head.

"Put down the rock and come here. Put it down."

He drops it. Amy flinches because the rock just misses his bare feet. Arnie runs to us, his drool splashing the porch floor. "Matches are . . ." he says, searching for the words.

"Matches are what, Arnie? Are what?"

Amy adds, "You know what matches are."

We wait a minute while Arnie slaps his head.

I say, "Matches are *bad.*"

"I know that, I know that."

"Say it with me."

And he does.

The screen door swings open—Janice says, "Tah-dah," and Ellen steps out wearing one of Janice's stewardess outfits. The blue dress fits tight across her breasts. Her hair is pinned up and she wears a stewardess hat.

Ellen turns like a runway model and Amy claps and I say, "Whoop-de-doo."

Ellen calls to Arnie and says, "Hey, Arnie, look!"

He turns and says, "Yeah, so?" Then he lifts up his rock and disappears around the side of the house. He has the right idea.

Amy says, "You look great."

I quickly pray for those two to go back upstairs when Janice puts a fist to her mouth, like a microphone, and speaks the following: "Good evening, ladies and gentlemen. We'd like to welcome you to flight 161. Nonstop from Des Moines to Chicago's O'Hare International Airport. For your flying safety, please direct your attention to one of our flight attendants who will go over safety procedures." Janice points to Ellen, who stands waiting, beaming and nervous. "In the seat pocket behind you, you will locate a . . ."

This continues as Janice describes the safety features of our plane/porch and Ellen points to where oxygen masks would be. She pantomimes the "correct" seat-belt procedure and in the "unlikely event of a water landing" we learn that our supposed seat cushions will act as life preservers. Amy watches politely as my hands grip my head.

They finish with a flourish and I stand to go to the bathroom.

I sit on the toilet much longer than I need to. When I come out, I find Janice sitting in my spot on the porch swing. Walking back and forth, Ellen asks if she can keep the uniform on for a few hours. "To get used to the feel of it."

"Practice makes . . ."

"I know," Ellen says. She throws her arms in the air, gyrates in a these-clothes-are-the-greatest way.

I stare at Janice, who stretches out in my seat. I hate it when someone takes my place. Janice lights another brown cigarette and I consider pulling her up by her frosted hair when the phone rings.

"Gilbert Grape," I say, happy to have been sprung from the activities outside.

"It's me," she says.

"Oh. Hello," I say. There's a long silence where I don't know what to say. I start doodling on an old newspaper.

Becky speaks cheerily. "It's no big deal, Gilbert—I just wanted you to know I'm going away. See my parents. Meeting up in Minneapolis. Just wanted you to know so when you came looking for me . . ."

I start to say, "Who says I'm going to come looking . . ."

She laughs. "Whatever. Just wanted you to know."

"Okay," I say. "Now I know."

"Bye, then." The phone clicks.

Weird call, weird girl. Come looking for her? Please. Gilbert Grape may be many things to many people but he's not desperate.

* * *

Later I walk to my old school. I walk the way I did all those years. Left at the mailbox at the top of the street, cut through the Pfeiffers' yard, past Tucker's house, under the water tower, down Vine, and left on Third Street.

It is gone. My school. The ground is charred, with chunks of brick lying about, bits of popcorn, too. An orange ribbon, stapled to wooden stakes, surrounds the barren site.

My school is gone.

Part Four

32

Becky has been gone for three days. Don't think for a moment I've missed her.

Lately my time has either been spent working at Lamson's grocery or in long, intense meetings solidifying the plans for Arnie's party. Janice and Ellen do most of the talking, Amy adds her wisdom. I was required to sit in and listen to these planning sessions. For the record, every suggestion I made was distorted or twisted or ignored. But as they would cackle on about what the "theme" colors should be, I was able to drift off and picture my life after Endora.

I liked what I saw.

Today is the Fourth of July. Twelve days and counting.

I'm standing outside the Dairy Dream, at my usual spot. Lori Kickbush, the girl working, is wearing blue lipstick and red-and-white eye shadow. She slides open the take-out window and I cover my eyes from the glare. She says, "You seen him? Huh? You seen him yet?"

"No." My retinas have been seared. I will be blind by tomorrow.

"He's over at Lloyd's right now and Lloyd is cutting his hair."

"Lloyd always cuts his hair." Where has this girl been? I say, "Lloyd is like a father to him." I order four soft drinks and a cup of ice water.

"Well, did you try to look in?"

"No," I say, as if her question is the stupidest ever.

"Well, the shade is down and people are gathered all around."

"Whoop-de-doo."

"I think it's great he came back for this. You know, there wouldn't be a parade if it weren't for him. He's gonna ride in the basket part of the fire truck. With his mother."

"No," I say.

"Yes, Gilbert Grape. Oh, man. He's the coolest. Lance Dodge is the coolest."

"You think so, huh?"

"I'm surprised he could find the time. That just shows what kind of a person he is."

"We were in the same class...."

"No way."

"No, we were. We used to talk a lot. About everything."

"What's he like? My mother and me both have huge crushes on him. Oh my God. I didn't know you knew him. I would have been much nicer to you over the last few years if I had known."

"He's Lance—what else can I say?"

The bell dings or dongs or whatever the stupid sound is and one of the two Little League teams in town crowds inside. They're dressed in their blue-and-white uniforms and they are noisy. Their coach is a guy, Mike Clary, who was a year behind me in school. He is one of many who have known Janice in the biblical sense. He sees me through the glass. We both nod like we give a small shit about each other. Lori gives me a cardboard-cup holder for the water and the soft drinks and also an employee discount because of sister Ellen.

I push my way through the crowd. The town is packed with cars and people from faraway towns like Paxton and Andlan Center who have come to town to watch Endora's first Fourth of July parade since 1959. Motley usually has the county parade. But since the end of May, when it was announced that Lance Dodge would be spending the Fourth with his mother in Endora, Mayor Gaps has been pushing for this year's parade. It's considered a great coup for the city fathers and a potential boon to our small businesses. Food Land, of course, remains open, but Mr. Lamson, who could make a tremendous profit today, closed up because "Americans don't work on America's birthday."

I push through the crowd, most faces I don't even recognize, and get to the girls. Janice takes her drink and Arnie's. Ellen asks for a straw and follows after Janice. Only Amy says "Thanks." We watch Janice, in the distance, adjust Arnie's hat while Ellen holds all three of their drinks.

"You did great, Amy. His costume looks great."

"You think?" Amy says.

"Yep. No doubt."

"You think he could win? It would mean a lot to him to win."

"I don't know about winning," I say. "But I do know that I like his costume."

The paper said something about boys and girls, ages five to twelve, coming dressed in costumes depicting something to do with our nation's birthday. Of course, the paper should have read, "Boys and Girls from ages five to twelve and Arnie Grape" but the Arnie part is assumed. And while I know there are mothers and fathers who think it unfair that Arnie be allowed to compete, they would never say it or try to have him disqualified. The citizens of Endora keep their rage and disgust quiet; their smiles and friendly nods are like fabric softeners for the face.

Amy and I scout the competition. There are about nine Uncle Sam costumes–all of which look awful. I see a George and Martha Washington that isn't bad except there are no powdered wigs. The only real competition is a girl with tremendous breasts. She looks about twenty. She has these antique glasses, a giant needle and yarn for thread, and a huge flag wrapped tightly around her chest.

"Betsy Ross is pretty good," I say to Amy.

"Yeah, but in no way is that girl twelve."

"Arnie is seventeen, so . . ." I say.

"I know," Amy says, "but Arnie is special." Special–the nice way of saying it.

Across the street comes an Abraham Lincoln.

"Hey," Amy says, "are those the Carver boys?"

"Looks like it."

"Great idea," Amy says.

"Yeah, but the execution of it . . ."

Abraham Lincoln towers over the other contestants. Todd, the bigger of the two Carver boys, must be on bottom and Doug rides on his shoulders. It looks like Mrs. Betty Carver just took one of her husband's suits, taped together a hat of black construction paper, and that was that.

"It's a horrible costume, Amy."

"But a great idea."

Mr. Carver follows after the boys–two fancy cameras hang on his neck. Mrs. Betty Carver trails along.

"Yeah, it's a pretty bad costume," Amy finally admits.

Mr. Carver screams at his boys to smile, even though the bottom boy can't be seen. After he takes their picture, Amy calls out, "Thanks for the chicken recipe!"

Mrs. Carver turns to us and shrugs like it's no big deal. She looks at me and says with her eyes, "Free me."

A voice on a bullhorn calls for all the contestants to line up. Janice and Ellen escort Arnie to his spot. In public, they love Arnie in the most visible of ways. You'd think he was the most important thing in their lives by the way they carry on and fuss over him. They are great girls when they have an audience.

The parade begins.

Mayor Jerry Gaps rides by in a convertible. His wife is Barbara of Barb's Beauty Shop. They smile and wave. Barbara Gaps is her own bad advertisement.

Chip Miles and his brothers drive by in minitractors doing figure 8's. Chip keeps his lips pressed together. That silver tooth stays hidden.

"Good for you, Chip!" I shout.

The costumes come into view.

"All of the Uncle Sams cancel each other out," I say.

"Good thing we didn't make Arnie an Uncle Sam."

Three chubby girls have tried to capture that image of the one with the pipe, one with the flag, those injured war soldiers. They do not succeed in creating much.

"We forgot the camera!" Janice screams from the other side of the street.

"Crap," Amy says under her breath. "Momma wanted pictures. We always forget the camera."

"Oh well," I say, imagining Momma at home, eating in her sleep.

A sea of Uncle Sams march past. The Carver boys are getting tired and we all watch as Abe wobbles along. "There are five more blocks. There's no way those boys are going to make it," I tell Amy.

Arnie is in sight now—easy to spot, too, because he's twice the size of the other kids. He's dressed as Washington Crossing the Delaware. Amy sewed the costume. She worked on it for weeks and designed the cardboard boat that I built in an afternoon. The boat hangs from Arnie's shoulders by elastic straps that give the illusion that he's actually floating. Janice spent yesterday afternoon coaching Arnie, rehearsing his movements. He walks with his right hand above his forehead, and all modesty aside, he looks great. The people are cheering politely for the other kids, but when they see Washington Crossing the Delaware, they start yelling, "Go, Arnie!" "All right, Arnie!" I scream, "That's my brother!" and he turns to where Amy and me are standing. But in turning, Arnie decks one of the little Uncle Sams without knowing it. When he hears the little girl scream, he turns to help her up. When he does this, though, the back of his boat smacks into George and Martha Washington. They fall over and George starts crying. Arnie decks a couple more kids before the parents push through the crowd to rescue their fallen children.

Amy shouts, "You can't turn, Arnie. DO NOT TURN!" He looks confused. He stops and starts to hold his breath. The others in the costume parade, the wounded, have moved on. Arnie looks to us for help.

"Walk. Keep walking!" I shout.

He stands frozen. The Lions Club tractor, the other parade vehicles, and the fire truck carrying Lance Dodge are brought to a stop.

"KEEP MOVING THAT WAY." I point where he should walk. "YOU CAN DO IT!"

A bright light hits Arnie. It's the news camera that has been filming Lance's homecoming. In seconds I'm out on the street with him, blocking the camera.

"I didn't mean to knock 'em down. I didn't mean to."

"I know." I gesture for the cameraman to look elsewhere for his news.

"Gilbert..."

"Let's keep walking."

"But I didn't mean..."

"Let's talk as we walk."

We're moving now. He's holding on to my hand. People in the crowd shout "Go, Arnie" and "Looking good, Arnie." Bobby McBurney, off to one side and dressed in his funeral black, says, "Arnie for president!" Tucker, standing next to him, says, "Gilbert for first lady!" I'm about to flip Tucker off when I remember this is a family parade.

Once we catch up with the others, I send Arnie on alone. As I make my way to the side, I hear him say to the other kids, "Sorry! Sooorrrrry!"

I see Abe Lincoln's legs walking next to his chest and head, his arms dragging on the cement. Mr. Carver walks alongside the boys, shouting with disappointment. "Abe didn't give up until he was dead! You don't give up till you're dead, boys. Boys!"

I back up into the crowd as the fire truck gets close. Lance Dodge is waving his bleached hand. He has got the best smile, the straightest teeth. And his mother, in the fire basket with him, is glowing as if this is the best day of her life.

I'm standing among a noisy group who reach their arms out frantically, begging for his attention. Cameras flash, old ladies orgasm as the truck passes. Lance gives a general I-love-you-all-deeply wave. I'm kind of nonchalant in my response, giving the cool, I-could-care-less wave. Having been his classmate, I expect him to at least acknowledge my presence. But he looks right at me, I swear it, and waves to me as if I were one of the masses.

Amy catches up to me and says, "Doesn't he look good?"

"Who?"

"Lance."

"He certainly thinks so."

The parade is over and Amy has gone off to keep Arnie from further destruction.

"The kid is a definite winner," Bobby McBurney says, pushing through the crowd.

"And Bobby knows about such things," Tucker adds, popping up, his face all sweaty.

"Yeah, I'm pretty good at costume contests."

"Pretty good—you only won like five Halloween prizes."

"Six. But when your old man's a mortician, you've got a certain kind of inside track on Halloween."

In a simple ceremony, Lance is given the key to the city. It looks more like a big fork to me. He holds it up over his head, like a race-car driver. His mother supplies him with Kleenex so he can wipe his eyes. "Thank you. Thank you, people of Endora. I never ever would have dreamed this."

Neither would I.

It's time for the costume parade, and the contestants line up to file by the judges. Lance sits in the middle of the table with a judge on either side. One of them is a prime mover in the Endora social scene and a devout Christian. Her name is unimportant and her face a visual sin. The other judge is Melanie, red-haired Melanie, Melanie with the big mole, Mr. Carver's Melanie.

An aging stereo system blares "The Battle Hymn of the Republic" as the contestants march past. As Arnie floats by the judges, the others keep their distance; one mother holds back her son.

The judges have reached their decision. Before they announce the "results," the mayor tells us that all of the costumes were great, that "all the kids are winners."

If that is the case, then please tell me why we even bother having prizes and ribbons. If everyone is a winner, then what is the point? I will tell you what the point is—and I will tell you because I think you might be able to understand. The point is that the man making the announcement, the mayor of this town, Jerry Gaps, is lying. Not all of the costumes were good. Most, in fact, look like putridity, if that's a word. We should be embarrassed by our attempt at patriotism. My brother's costume is the exception. He looks like an American. In fact, he behaves like one. When he tried to pick up the first kid he knocked down, he smashed into several others, it snowballed, chaos ensued. My brother very much resembled America today in pretty much all things.

Amy puts her hand in mine and squeezes. "It would mean a lot to Arnie to win."

"Yeah, I know."

"He didn't mean to knock down those kids. I hope they know that."

"They know."

Lance gets up to the microphone. The people cheer and cheer. "Thank you." There is piercing feedback from the sound system. Even machines can tell a phony. People cover their ears, babies cry. "Test. Test." Lance taps the microphone. He waits till he gets the signal to go ahead. He is so nonchalant about it. I have to admire his confidence. "The awards are as follows. Third prize is a free meal for one at the Burger Barn." At this point, Lance launches into an advertisement for our new fast-food restaurant. I should have known that we'd get a commercial of some sort.

The grand opening will be Friday, July 14, and it's the talk of the town. "Second prize is this plaque *and* a free meal for *two* at the..." Lance pauses for effect and the kids, and Tucker, say, "Burger Barn." Lance smiles, proud of the crowd for joining in like that. "And first prize is this trophy and a party for twelve at...?" The entire crowd, except for me, shouts, "THE BURGER BARN!" Adults clap, the kids jump up and down.

"A trophy would mean a lot to Arnie."

"I know." I want to tell Amy that she, too, deserves a trophy for all she gives.

Third place goes to George and Martha Washington. Second place goes to Betsy Ross. They get their certificates, Betsy Ross gets a plaque.

"Gilbert, we're in the clear."

"Yes, we are," I say. I focus in on Arnie, who stands in the middle of the other kids. I can't wait to see his face.

"Wish we had a camera," Amy says, about to burst.

Lance clears his throat and reads from his paper.

"First prize, for best costume based on an American theme, goes to... DOUG AND TODD CARVER for..."

"Bullshit!" Amy screams.

The other kids applaud politely as the parents whisper among themselves. Amy covers her face. Arnie doesn't seem to mind. As far as he's concerned, he's always been a winner.

I look around and see Mrs. Carver. She has put on a pair of dark sunglasses. Surely she knows her kids don't deserve that trophy.

"One of the judges is Mr. Carver's secretary!" I shout out.

A parent of one of the Uncle Sams says, "That's unfair."

Another parent yells, "Those boys should have been disqualified!"

Amy mutters, "We were robbed. We were robbed."

The people begin to separate and go their own way when Lance says, "Excuse me. Excuse me. One more thing."

Someone shut that fake up, I think to myself.

"As grand marshal of this parade, I have one more thing to say." I wish I had a gun.

"It is rare in this world that a person gets the kind of opportunity and privilege to do as I have done."

Yawn. Cough. Yawn. Yawn.

"Rarely do I see such courage, such quality, such dignity as I have seen today. There is an award I'd like to give. The Lance Dodge 'You'll be the next president of the United States' award and I am proud to give this award to the one, the only–Arnie Grape!"

Arnie looks around. Was that his name that he just heard?

"Arnie, come up here, buddy! Come on up!"

The other kids push Arnie to the stage. He and his boat ascend the platform. Lance shakes his hand. A couple of cameras flash. I don't believe this. Amy, in shock, says to me, "I wish Momma could see this."

The people clap politely. Lance raises Arnie's arm in the air, and I see Arnie mouth the word, "Ouch."

33

Janice and Ellen took the next president to the Dairy Dream for a victory malt. Amy and I are walking home and she is looking down.

"Amy, what's wrong?"

She stops, she considers her words carefully. "How is his birthday going to top this?"

I try to explain that Arnie's birthday will be different, not better or worse. "Different."

She sighs. "There's this pressure building, Gilbert. It's one thing to have Janice back and for Arnie to win some parade contest. But on his birthday, we'll have Larry, too. And Momma. And she has these giant expectations. I don't know what to do about her. She's eating in five days what she used to eat in seven. The supports under the floor won't last forever. I feel this pressure in my head, this pain in my head, and it's constant. It doesn't go away. Feel my shoulders."

I put my hands on her and feel dozens of bumps and tension spots. They feel like sharp rocks. "Wow."

"I can't last much longer. This movie on TV, the ground opened up and swallowed people. I keep waiting for the ground to open up and swallow me."

I massage her back. "Sure, of course."

Amy looks down. Cars pass and honk, little kids run around throwing a plastic beach ball that has a map of the world on it. We just stand there as Amy's oily tears collect on the sidewalk. She uses my shirt to wipe her face, sniffs up the runniness in her nose, and says, happily, "You deserve someone, Gilbert. Someone special."

We walk on. "No," I say.

"Yes—oh yes. Because, Gilbert, you've made sacrifices. And I'm grateful to you. You've always been there and you deserve someone." She talks on about what a good brother and fine person I am. I notice her mouth is about as gentle as they come, and her face, while beginning to puff out, has the kindest quality. My sister is not an ugly woman. I don't know if there's a better person around.

Amy had a boyfriend for a summer about three years back. He was a trucker and they met in the Ramp Cafe by chance one June day. He had lips like Elvis and wore long Elvis sideburns, even though his hair was strawberry blond. He didn't go by his real name, which only Amy knew. He went by Muffy. Every weekend for about three months he would drive up to our house and sound his horn. He treated all of us well. He became best buddies with Arnie and me and he always brought a special gift to Momma. It would either be a pretty rock that he'd find on the side of the road or 3-D postcards of cactus or whatever. Momma loved to look up from whatever food she was eating, her mouth still full, and say, "Muffy, you're the kind of man for me." He'd blush and go, "Aw, Mrs. Grape."

He and Amy held hands and I know they kissed a little. But it didn't go much further than that. He always slept on the sofa in the family room and would often wear these old pajamas of my dad's. Ellen and I placed bets on when they would marry. But one night, the last weekend that August, Amy was making a big end-of-summer barbecue. She went around the corner of the house and happened on Muffy who was locked in a kiss with Janice. Needless to say, Muffy was gone within minutes. He didn't even say good-bye to Momma, and you can imagine how upset she got. No one told Momma the real reason he disappeared. Amy said nothing, went straight to her room and played "Don't Be Cruel" over and over.

Amy and I are halfway down Elm Street when Mr. and Mrs. Lamson pull up in their 1970 Dodge Dart. Mrs. Lamson rolls down her window and says, with her red lips and light blue hair, "What a day, huh?"

Amy, her eyes all bloodshot, says, "Wasn't that the most wonderful thing?"

Mr. Lamson says, "You don't have days like that too often."

"True, boss," I say.

"You tell your brother how proud we are. You tell him."

"Yes, sir."

He calls out, "Wonderful surprises, Gilbert," as they drive away.

Later, the three girls and I try to recount the parade for Momma. We're all talking at once, each of us vying for our mother's ears and eyes.

"You're pulling my leg," Momma says.

We all cry "We're not," "It happened," "Seriously, Momma!"

She says, "Pictures. Let me see the pictures!"

Amy says that we forgot the camera. Momma throws a tantrum. Arnie crawls under her table. She shakes the table and scrunches her fleshy face. "I WANTED PICTURES!"

Momma ate double the number of hot dogs at dinner. I only had a few potato chips, as my appetite was lost due to her rantings about the lack of family photojournalism.

After dinner, we had our final planning session with Janice–this meeting was a review of sorts. Then Ellen got a call from Cindy Mansfield reminding her of the Fourth of July "I'm Born in the USA and I'm Born Again" get together. Cindy was there to pick her up within minutes. Then Amy drove Janice to the airport, with Arnie sitting in the back. After that, Tucker and Bobby McBurney stopped by wondering if I wanted to do something later. "I'm baby-sitting my mother," I told them, and they sighed, "Too bad," and drove off.

Momma licked her plate so clean I almost forgot to stack it in the sink. She fell asleep immediately after eating. I stared at her–unable to accept that at one time I was growing inside her. I was once just a couple of cells. My father and my mother were naked and something had to be satisfactory about it, because he came inside her and she got pregnant. She, like me, was once a baby in her mother's stomach and so on and so forth and so it goes. So it goes.

The TV was blaring, Momma was deeply asleep, making this sonorous kind of booming snore, her nostrils expanding and shrinking, her mouth open like an oven.

I devised a test.

I turned off the TV and instantly the snoring stopped. She began to move. When I felt her eyes about to open, I turned the TV back on and back to sleep she went. Then I'd turn it off and on–sometimes for a millisecond–and she never failed me. Each time it was off, she'd move and mutter–each time it was on, she'd sleep.

By the time the headlights from Amy's Nova turned into our driveway, my suspicion had been confirmed. <u>My mother has a more intimate, connected relationship with this television than she has ever had with me.</u>

First in the house is Amy, and she carries bags and paper cups that scream of fast food. She calls out the screen door, "Arnie, come on in, okay?"

"Hey," I say. "Did Janice's plane crash?"

"No, why?"

I snap my fingers and go, "Damn."

"Gilbert, you don't mean that." Holding the screen door open, Amy turns on the porch light and calls to the retard one more time, "Get in here now." He comes barreling up the steps, his face splattered with mustard, ketchup, and dirt. On top of his warped head is a cardboard fold-up Burger Barn hat.

"Amy, you didn't."

"It's what he wanted. Isn't that right, Arnie?"

"Burger Barn is the best."

I explain, in the clearest way I can, that Burger Barn is not the best. "It's an insult to your uniqueness, Arnie, your individuality. There's only one Arnie Grape, right?"

"Right."

"Well, there are hundreds of Burger Barns and they are ..."

"The best!"

Amy looks at me like I won't win this one. She's right, I won't.

In the kitchen, among the dishes that have fossilized and the trash that has crystallized, I ask Amy why she let Ellen go to this Born Again thing.

"Ellen needs to get out."

"And I don't? And you don't?"

"That new girl has changed her." Even Amy has heard of Becky, Becky who I do not miss. "She's not the beauty queen anymore. ..."

"Sure, she is. That new girl is nothing, believe me."

"The phone doesn't ring for her like it used to."

"Thank God."

181

"Yes, it's great for you and me. But for a girl whose worth is determined by the number of calls she gets ..."

"You sound like Janice."

"Well, Janice and I talked."

I beg Amy to consider that Janice understands absolutely nothing about any of us or this house, that sending her to college was our biggest collective mistake. I resent how she'll fly in when it's convenient, provide her less than perceptive opinions, and then always leave us with the work.

"Janice is your sister."

"No fault of mine."

"You must love her."

"No."

"I love her."

"The bitch kissed Muffy. How can you ...?"

Amy's left hand flies across my face. The slap sound doesn't wake my mother, and I hold my cheek, my tongue rummaging to see if any teeth are now loose.

"Thanks," is all I can say.

After a considered silence, she says, "I love her so much that I pity her." She has yet to get over Muffy.

"That hurt," I say, my head dizzy.

"Good."

Amy does the dishes while I sack up the endless bags of trash. I carry them out to the garage and a gang of flies attacks me. Later, I get our biggest swatter, turn on the garage light and chase down fly after fly, trapping them against the walls, in the corner where the lawn mower and rakes are, and proceed to annihilate them.

Back in the house, Amy fills the largest bowl she can find with a mountain of Neapolitan ice cream. "Good night," she says. Her solace is an entire half gallon and memories of happier times.

I run Arnie's bath water, get the bubbles big and plentiful, and dump in all his toys. Arnie is happy in the water and when the phone rings, I leave him splashing.

34

Hi, Tucker."
"Bobby's on the phone, too. Think of this as a conference call."
"Hi, Bobby."

Talking fast, Tucker says, "We're on our way over. . . ."

"Arnie's in the bath. I'm going to sleep. We're going to sleep here."

"Yeah, but . . ."

Bobby interrupts. "Gilbert, we just need to bounce some ideas off you."

So while Arnie swims in the tub and Momma sleeps with her TV and Amy makes love to her ice cream, I stand waiting at the edge of our driveway. The headlights that appear at the top of the street are from the McBurney Funeral Home hearse.

"Get in. Get in," Tucker yells.

I climb in back and kneel where the coffins usually ride.

"I brought some dandy beer," Tucker says.

Bobby launches into a speech about how it's not so easy for Tucker and him to get girls. They have turned to me, hoping for some support, some ideas, seeing as I'm thought to be something of a sexual god. "We're at a point of desperation."

I hear their schemes, each more tasteless, more stupid than the previous one. All of their ideas are unrepeatable.

Somehow we end up at Tucker's place, sitting around with a six-pack of obscure Australian beer. They're still talking over each other, on top of each other, and so much of what they say defies belief. They finish with a flourish and then say, in unison, "We welcome your input."

"Guys," I say. "Guys."

"Admit it, Gilbert. We have killer ideas."

"Guys."

"What? What what what?" barks Bobby.

"I'm . . . uhm . . . floored."

They take my statement as a compliment. Gilbert is speechless, Gilbert is in awe. But over time they begin to get the picture of my true feelings.

"Okay, maybe these are not the best ideas. But do you see what we're trying to do? We're trying..."

"I get what you're trying to do. It is very clear what you're *trying* to do."

Tucker snaps, "But you won't help? You won't advise?"

I look at them both. I say, "You guys think I'm something I'm not."

"Right. Who in town got the girl? Who in town is going out and presumably fucking the best girl ever? Who?"

I try to explain that they've got it all wrong. "I wouldn't even touch that creature...."

Tucker covers his ears. "Please, Gilbert. We're not stupid." He uncovers them and continues. "You don't want to help us and that hurts. It hurts me."

Bobby adds, "It doesn't hurt me, really. It disappoints."

I dig deep and start talking. I explain how each of them is enough. "That if a girl can't see you for what you are, then that girl doesn't deserve you. She isn't worthy of your time or your dick."

The boys laugh when I say the word "dick." I chose that word because I knew it would lighten the air. They've been deprived for so long, I say to myself, that their bodies have begun to eat their brains.

I end with a simple plea. "Before you guys do anything. Consult me. Check with me. I need to put some thought into your ideas and let's see how we can best move forward." I sound like a politician, a bad one, but my speech works.

Bobby nods and Tucker says, "It's a deal."

We all shake hands and Tucker says, "I knew Gilbert would be helpful. I knew we could count on you, buddy."

"Listen, guys, I got to get home."

They drive me home and I almost laugh and cry at the same time.

"Night, guys." I shut the hearse door, and my two sorry friends drive off in the McBurney hearse. Ellen's light is on in her room, she's home. The others are fast asleep.

In the house the blue light from the television flickers its changing light on Momma. The shadows highlight her thick, fleshy brow and drooping jowls. Her gray hair is wild, wirelike. She ends up not looking like my mother at all, but rather some kind of monster or extraterrestrial.

Tonight, for reasons unknown to me, I wander through the living room and move close to my mother, her smell ancient and distinct, her body settled like clay. Momma is listening to "The Star-Spangled Banner" on the TV. She has turned up the volume.

> *"And the rockets' red glare,*
> *the bombs bursting in air*
> *gave proof through the night . . ."*

In the dim, flickering light, I see that Momma has put one of her bloated hands over her heart. I know better than to speak during our national anthem. On the TV an American flag blows in the wind, and marines or soldiers or whatever stand in salute. An announcer says that Channel 5 is going off the air and the sound turns to static. Momma turns the TV to mute but leaves the blank, snowy picture on.

"Gilbert."

"Yes, Momma?"

"Sure was nice of Lance Dodge."

I don't say anything.

She reaches below the table, lifts up a bag of potato chips that must have been resting against her feet, and gently tears open the top. She sets the bag down and for the next several minutes, while I sit on a stool in the corner, she eats the chips, handful after handful. The chips vanish fast, Momma crumples the bag and smacks her lips. I don't look at her, my eyes stay fixed on the TV static.

"The next president of the United States?" she says. "He has got to be out of his mind." Momma laughs, clearly so proud of Arnie, so grateful that Lance could be so kind. "Just want to see that boy turn eighteen, that's all I ask."

I nod like I know what she means. I sit there saying nothing while she unwraps a box of Hostess cupcakes.

Working at the store, I think to myself, I bring the food home, I do the shopping and get whatever Amy asks for, I beg for credit from Mr. Lamson and each time Momma eats, I know that I'm an accomplice to the crime.

She grunts. I turn to her and see that she's pinched off a part of one of the black-and-white cakes and is extending it my way. I shake my head like "No, thanks." She opens her mouth, almost happy that I refused, and inhales the fingerful with a sound resembling our vacuum.

Five cupcakes later and Momma's still going strong. What keeps me here, I decide, is the odd hope that if I sit here long enough, breathing her smell and looking at her enormous head, *maybe* I can learn to love her.

She goes for the final cupcake in the box and I stand up, wiping my mouth while wanting to wipe hers. This sitting in silence and listening to her noisy mouth has been a virtual bust.

"Momma, you should get some sleep."

"What?"

"Get some sleep. Close your eyes and sleep."

"Huh?"

"Sleep. Rest. You deserve to rest."

"Gilbert. You ever seen a robber here? Has a killer ever gotten in here? To the best of your knowledge?"

"No, Momma."

"Why do you think that might be?"

The light from the television keeps on flickering.

"I don't know, Momma."

"Don't shake your head like that. Makes you look like your father."

"You were saying?"

"Yes, I was. I was saying that nobody has broken in here because I stand watch. They will have to get by me before they can get to you. I dare someone to try and get by me."

She's right. No way is any criminal or killer even going to think about coming into our house as long as she sits in her chair. Momma is our sentinel.

"There are entire families where an intruder, a night stalker, just wanders by. Picks out a house. Stakes it out. Enters with rope and guns, proceeds to tie down all the family members and shoots each and every one. I'll be goddamned if I'm going to let some mystery person enter my house and in a single night kill all that I've created."

She takes the last cigarette from her current pack and lights it.

"One day you might understand what it means to create. To know the feeling of looking in a person's eyes and know that you are the reason for those eyes." Momma thinks for a second. "I'm going to say something I know I'm not supposed to say. I see you and I know that I'm a god. Or a goddess. Godlike! And this house is my kingdom. Yes, Gilbert. This chair is my throne. And you, Gilbert, are my knight in shimmering armor."

"Shining, I think, Momma, is what you mean."

"No, I know what I mean. You don't shine, Gilbert. You shimmer. You hear? You shimmer! Now good night."

"What?"

"Good night." She blows smoke my way, it clouds around my face and I'm able to fight coughing until I make it to my room. Up there, alone, I cough until my stomach hurts and my throat feels torn.

35

I wake up early because I need to pee. I'm about to flush when I hear some sloshing come from the bathtub. Through the glass shower door, I see the shape of a person. Sliding it open, I see him there. Arnie. His boats and plastic fish are floating–the bubble bath has long since disappeared–his eyes are bulging out and he can't move. The retard fell asleep and spent the night in the tub. His fingers and his feet have all shriveled up, raisinlike, and he'll undoubtedly think it's permanent. Being in the water is hard enough, but the thought of being in it all night just must destroy him. I help the poor guy out of the water. I take his dinosaur towel and begin to dry him off.

"It's okay, Arnie. It's okay."

He's quivering and shaking. He doesn't utter a sound. And as I'm drying the water out of his ears, a different kind of water fills his eyes.

"It's okay."

At breakfast he ignores his toast. I shake on even more cinna-mon sugar, but still he won't eat. Amy, who is scrambling eggs, looks at me, concerned. I shrug. Then I make what I think to be an incredibly insightful analogy about how food is like gas and that "if you, Arnie, were a car you would be stalled in the driveway. Arnie needs gas." This has no impact. He sits with his face scrunched and his back rounded like a rock, staring at the waves in his fingers. "Arnie, they'll go away." He shakes his head. "They will. I promise that your wrinkly fingers will go away."

Amy says, "Gilbert knows about these things. You can trust Gilbert."

There is nothing more depressing than toast that no one eats. So, in a last-ditch attempt, I say, "Arnie, think how the toast must feel. I mean, if you were this toast, how would it feel to be unwanted, unloved?" He usually has sympathy for such things. But not today.

So I reach to throw the toast in the trash, when his arms and hands extend like springs and grab both slices. He scrunches each slice into a little ball and throws one at Amy, one at me, yelling, "I coulda drownded! I coulda drownded!" Then he runs out of the kitchen, out of the house.

Amy looks at me, I look at her. Usually one of us checks on him in bed and, for whatever reasons, we both forgot. But it was me who left him in the tub.

Ellen strolls into the kitchen and Amy says, "Could you go get Arnie?"

"Be glad to. And then what? What comes after that? What will be next?"

"Get Arnie, please."

"It's a good thing I'm here, isn't it? Good thing that someone does the dirty work around here. What would you people do without me?"

I say, "Be happier."

She doesn't hear this because she dramatically hits the kitchen closet door, lets out a sigh that sounds like a winter wind, stops off at the bathroom for a makeup check, and finally after all that, stomps outside. She screams "Arnie! ARNIE!"

In a minute she's back, saying, "Our Arnie has disappeared and no mortal can save him and maybe if we raised him differently, if we taught him to . . ."

Amy takes the eggs she has been scrambling and dumps them in the trash. She uses a paper towel to wipe her mouth and she leaves the kitchen.

Ellen says, "What about my eggs?" as Amy opens the back door. Amy says nothing as the screen door crinks shut. She goes out to the backyard and sits at our once red, now very weathered, picnic table.

Ellen whispers, "This family," as if she deserves better. She looks on the shelf where we keep cereals and there are three boxes of Momma's cereal. "Oh, great, only Cheerios. What a day this is shaping up to be. I shouldn't have even woken up."

I want to say maybe you shouldn't have even been born, Ellen. But I know that living is no one person's fault. There are those who say that we choose to be born, that we make out some request and it is granted, that we're put on this planet because we want to be alive. I think not. It's the luck of the draw. Some people have to live while others get to sit this living thing out.

"Gilbert?"

Some days I hate all those who know my name.

"Gilbert?" Ellen says again and again, speaking it nine times before getting to the point. Nine is nothing, fourteen is her record.

"Get to the point, Ellen," I say.

"Look at me."

"I know what you look like," I say, looking out the back window where Amy still sits at the picnic table.

"Gilbert? Look at me. Gilbert?" There she goes again, saying my name in that way.

I snap and turn. "WHAT DO YOU WANT!"

Ellen half smiles, she is startled by my tone but happy for the eye contact. She flutters her eyes and whispers, "Jesus and I both love you."

This I did not expect. Before I can think of what to say back, she takes a large bowl and pours it full of Cheerios and along with a big salad spoon and a half gallon of milk, she carries it to Momma in the dining room.

"Ellen, how nice of you. You love your mother, don't you, Ellen?"

"Yes, Momma, I do. And so does Jesus."

I hear a spoon hit the wall. Momma has thrown it at Ellen. Momma has missed.

I look out the window and see from the shape of Amy's back that she's in about the same condition as our lawn furniture. You can tell the idyllic nature of a family by the upkeep of its picnic table. Ours is its own indictment. We are splintered and peeling. We rot.

Out the back door and across our yard, I'm standing a good five feet from her. "I'll go find the kid, okay?" Amy doesn't say anything, but I can tell that my doing this has shifted her feelings. For her, the saddest times are those when she feels that she's fighting the war alone. I walk around the house to my truck, not explaining that Ellen might be born again. She'll find that out soon enough.

As I start up my truck, I wonder if Amy tries to forget about Muffy as often as I try to forget Becky.

The retard is nowhere to be found, so when I get to work, I call home to tell Amy.

"Did you check the water tower?"

"He wasn't there. But don't worry–he'll show up."

"Darn it," Amy says. "We're going to have to go through this water thing again."

"No, he's bigger now, he'll be fine. He'll take a bath tonight or I'll take him swimming. It'll be fine, Amy."

"I can't go through the water thing again."

I hang up when we finish our talk. As I struggle with my apron–

it won't stay tied in back—Mr. Lamson calls out, "Is everything all right?"

"Everything is great," I say. He walks back into his office cubicle and I mutter to myself. "Everything is peachy. I've got a mother who would eat her arm if she had enough barbecue sauce, a dork-ass older brother and a wicked sister who got out of this town, a little bitch of a sister who very likely made love to Jesus last night, an ever-fattening older sister who deserves a decent man, and a retard brother who, we have reason to believe, has gone into hiding and is once again terrified of water."

"What are you saying, Gilbert?" Mr. Lamson has poked his head out the office door.

"Nothing, sir."

"I heard you, though. You were saying something. Gilbert, you know you can talk to me."

"I was just talking about how you're right, Mr. Lamson. Life."

He looks puzzled.

"Life is full of surprises. Just the darndest, most nifty surprises. That's all I was saying."

"That a boy, son. That's the way to look at it."

36

I've filled the mop bucket with hot water and detergent. Staring down at the warm suds, I think of Arnie, convinced that the key is to get him in the bathtub pronto. As I push the gray bucket to Aisle Four, I check the floor for dust balls. I dunk the mop, press out the excess, and slap it on the linoleum tiles.

"Gilbert Grape!" a booming voice says.

I don't look up because I'm afraid to gaze at the source of such a sound.

"It's good to see Gilbert Grape!"

"Yes," Mr. Lamson agrees. "Look who's stopped by for a visit."
I can't look up.

"Gilbert, you can stop your mopping. Look who's here."

The mop goes in the bucket, I dry my hands on my apron and glance up to see if it's true.

The sun glares through the store window. Showered in a golden-yellow light, wearing a sport coat and a blue tie, nice pressed slacks with clean white tennis shoes, a red carnation pinned to his lapel, hair immaculate, and with a smile that rivals those found in beauty pageants is that one-of-a-kind freak of nature, Mr. Lance Dodge.

"Hi," I say, trying not to seem surprised.

"And a dandy hello to you, too," Lance replies with one of those hearty male chuckles used to dispel tension. "He's not happy to see me, Mr. Lamson."

"Sure he is."

"No sirree. Gilbert always was his own kind of guy."

"Still, he's happy you came by. Aren't you, Gilbert?"

I nod because Mr. Lamson wants me to.

A pack of Endora's children run across the parking lot in search of the town hero. There are at least fifteen of them and they're laughing and screaming and screeching as if Lance were one of the Beatles.

Realizing the kids are coming his way, Lance has a sudden change from confidence to panic. "Oh Christ," he cries. This leaves me with a smile. "Is there somewhere I can hide?" he asks, clawing Mr. Lamson's shoulder.

"Here–back here," I volunteer, guiding Lance toward the stock-room, where he hides.

The kids enter the store, all of them shouting at the same volume, "Where is he? Where is he? Mr. Lamson? Is he here? We want to meet him! We've GOT to meet him!"

The kids pull and tug at his apron, they jump up and down like popcorn. Mr. Lamson wants to protect Lance's privacy, but he's also incapable of deception–I've never known him to lie. Taking in a deep breath, he says, "Lance Dodge is an old friend of Lamson grocery. I can remember when . . ."

"Where is he? We know that he's here! His mother told us!" The kids start searching the aisles. I stand by the stockroom door, appearing to be reorganizing the dog food but serving more of a guard/protector function. This situation will soon be unmanageable.

"All right, kids, kids!"

They stop for a moment.

"A person of Lance's status has a lot of pressures. A lot of demands are made of him."

"Where is he? Where is he!"

"LANCE MUST BE RESPECTED!"

"He's in the back, I bet," a scrawny boy suggests.

"Okay, yes, but you must respect..."

The kids surge toward where I'm standing. They see me and stop for a time. Drooling and eager, they are the wolves—Lance is the deer. I sense the inevitability of it, and as I step out of their way, they rush past. Mr. Lamson throws his arms in the air.

"What could I do?" I ask.

"I know."

I'm thinking Lance should be an easy catch when I hear a pounding on the front door. It's the hero with his hair everywhere. Out of breath, he throws open the door and shouts, "Get me outta here!"

Mr. Lamson waves for me to help Lance. Taking my keys out and leaving my apron on, I sprint the thirty feet to my truck. Lance hides in the bed of it as the kids come around from the back of the store. He stays hidden as I slowly drive away.

When I've gone a few blocks and no kids are in sight, I roll down my window and shout, "We're in the clear!" Lance climbs up front and we cruise the streets.

"Thank you. My God, thank you."

"No problem," I say.

He's breathing like he's about to die. "It is so hot. Damn heat."

"I know."

"Whew."

He has these beads of sweat on his top lip. The same kind of sweat he would get during recess in grade school.

"Where can I take you?"

He stops for a second. He suddenly looks depressed. "Uhm. Dammit."

"Can I drop you off at your house?"

"No. NO!"

"OK."

"My mother has invited all the women in town over for a luncheon in my honor. I couldn't take it. I had to get out. I swear to God, she invited the entire female population of Endora."

None of the Grape women were invited, I want to say. But it is commonplace at the important social functions to leave any and all Grapes off the guest list.

"You got a minute, Gilbert?"

"Uhm. I'm supposed to be working. . . ."

"Let me buy you a burger. How's that sound?"

Lance Dodge, the most famous citizen in this county, wants to buy me, Gilbert Grape, a hamburger. If I were any less a man, I would probably pinch myself, convinced this was a dream.

Beverly with the birthmark is our waitress, and I ask for the corner booth in an attempt to give Lance some privacy.

"Can we sit here?" Lance asks, referring to the center, most visible table.

"Everyone will see you here," I start to say, taking my apron off and holding it on my lap.

"Oh well. That comes with being, you know . . ."

"A celebrity?"

"A newsman."

Lance sits facing the window, more aware of those who might pass by outside than he's aware of me. A part of him wants to flee the hungry crowds, but a larger part must love the attention and still worry that one day it will all be gone. Lance asks for a menu and two glasses of water for himself, three ice cubes in each glass. As Beverly listens, without thinking she covers her cherry-red birthmark with her left hand. She must feel that Lance shouldn't have to see such a thing.

From the back, Ed Ramp, wearing a chef's hat, peeks out of the kitchen and nods in disbelief.

We order. I go for a simple cheeseburger, fries, and a Coke.

Lance orders a strawberry milk shake, thick, with no whipped cream, the cherry on the side.

The milk shake is there in minutes. My burger, fries, and Coke take an eternity. Lance downs his shake in two long sips and when my food arrives, he takes the biggest french fry, dips it in the ketchup I just pounded out, and says, "Just one." He takes a bite. "Do you mind?"

"No."

I should thank Lance for giving Arnie the next-president award. But I make a point to not say thanks. Maybe he'll respect me more if I don't appreciate him. So I eat. And as I do, the most famous person I know sits across from me, eyeing my food.

"You like Endora, huh?"

I shrug.

"Obviously, you're still here. Every day that I've been in Des Moines doing my thing—you, Gilbert, you've been back here. In the seven years since high school, I've seen and done much. All you've done is Endora. Funny—how two lives can be so different."

"Funny," I say.

Lance stops, takes a fry, dips it in ketchup, holds it like a cigarette for a moment, and then eats it. "But that's what makes horse races. And America great. Where else could two guys from the same town become such different people? What a world."

"Yes."

Lance stops talking at this point. He eats french fry after french fry and he tries my burger, too. I push my plate closer to him. I guess this is what famous is. Eating other people's food.

I feel strange sitting with him, like I'm being watched. I hear the sounds of people and I turn to see that a small group of townies has gathered outside the cafe. They are talking among themselves, but with their periodic glances our way, it's clear that they're monitoring Lance and his every bite.

I go to shut the curtain.

"What are you doing, Gilbert?"

"Isn't the sun in your eyes?" I ask.

"No!" he says, his mouth full of my food.

"I thought I'd close..."

"Christ, no. God, no!"

"Okay." So I sit and he eats more. Beverly brings him an extra order of fries, covering her neck with one hand and setting the plate down with the other. "On the house," she says.

Lance has the ketchup in his hand, ready to eat, when I say, "My mother thinks you're terrific."

Lance looks up, stares at the awe-struck adults outside, and says, "I'm very popular with mothers."

"I know."

"What about the young people?" he asks. "What do they think?"

"Well, my sisters and my brother think you're tops."

"Really."

"My little brother—you know—the retard. He worships..."

Lance goes, "You mean the next president of the United States?"

I stare at him, feigning puzzlement, as if I've no idea what he's talking about.

Lance is looking everywhere but at me. "But most importantly, what does Gilbert Grape think of me? Huh?"

I stare at him and try to lie. After a considered silence, I say, "I think..."

"Yes?"

"I think you're..."

Lance looks up at the window and his eyes suddenly bulge a bit. The door swings open and I see that he's enamored. "Oh Christ," he whispers. "Oh my God."

I'm about to say "What?" when I smell that smell. It's her. I hear her walk our way. She snaps her fingers, practically shouting, "You're uhm...uh...you're uhm..."

Lance smiles, unfazed that she can't remember his name.

"You are that guy that uhm...oh boy...oh boy oh boy oh boy..."

Lance is gesturing for me to get up so that she can sit in my seat. I stand and back away. She is really snapping her fingers now, struggling to get his name, slapping the palm of her hand on her forehead, blushing and excited. This is not the Becky I know.

"Yes, it's me," Lance finally says.

She breathes in deeply. "I thought so."

Lance points to my old chair, giving her permission to sit.

"Would you excuse me one moment?" she asks.

Lance goes, "Why of course."

"Stay right here," Becky says, backing up to the door.

Lance smiles. "I'll be waiting." He looks my way, gives a look like this happens all the time. He sits back down slowly, adjusts his underwear, puts his elbows on the table, and chuckles.

Opening the cafe door, Becky whistles loud. "Hey, kids! He's over here!"

Lance freezes. His thoughts are "Did she just do what I think she did?" He looks to me. I shrug. Hearing the approaching mob, he is up like a shot. He ducks out the back through the kitchen as the mass of kids hits the door running. Ed Ramp blocks their way with a broom. The kids—who now must number close to fifty—turn and tear out, splitting into two groups instinctively—half going to the left, the other half to the right. Lance is on his own now.

Trailing behind the group is Arnie, running to keep up. He can't decide which group to go with, and I'm out of the cafe and grabbing him before he sees me. "Arnie," I go.

He looks at me, surprised that someone knows him. He studies me for a moment. It's as if he doesn't remember who I am. Then he smiles. Then he looks scared and shouts, "No water, Gilbert. No water!"

"Shhhhh," I say. A loud squeal is heard, Lance has been sighted and the kids are in hot pursuit. Hearing their yells, Arnie starts to go, but I get behind him and give him a bear hug. He struggles and he is strong. "No, Arnie. Amy wants you home."

Suddenly he stops his struggling. I'm thinking, This was easy, when I see Becky standing fifteen yards away, straddling her bike, looking our way.

I had forgotten about Becky.

Arnie walks slowly to her. He shakes his head slightly. He puts his hand up to touch her.

"Don't," I say.

Becky takes his hand and puts it on her forehead. She lets him touch her face, her mouth. He does what I've only dreamed of doing. He is quiet and reverent because even a retard knows that this girl is special.

I say, "Let's go, buddy."

She says, "When he's finished."

As he continues his exploration, I look back at the cafe. I catch Beverly watching us—she pulls the curtain closed.

I encourage Arnie to finish up so we can get on our way. I move to my truck, sit in it. Arnie's hands are moving all over now, touching her waist, her neck, one hand rests for a time on her breast. I honk my horn. His hand stays there. I guess she allows it because it's not sexual, Arnie's touch, it's curious. Still, though, I've no choice but to honk my horn long and loud.

Finally he finishes and runs to my truck, his head down and the sweetest smile on his face. He climbs up. We both look at Becky. He waves. I shift to reverse.

I guess I should thank her. I roll down my window before pulling out of the parking lot. I stick my head out to speak. But before I can, she says, "Don't mention it."

"No. Thank..." I stop. Something is wrong with this picture. I hit the gas pedal and drive Arnie home.

37

It's the next morning, July 6. It's only been twenty-four hours since Arnie spent the night in the tub and already his refusal to bathe is visually obvious. His face is colored with numerous stains and smudges. An anonymous call came minutes ago wondering if we could do with some soap. Amy got angry and I laughed. I say let him turn to dirt if it's what he wants.

But I have the day off, and I'm behind the bushes in our front yard, down on my knees, trying to get the hose on the outside faucet, thinking if I can get Arnie to run through the sprinkler, some of the dirt and gunk will wash from his body. I can't get the faucet hooked, though, and the evergreen needles from the bushes are pricking at my bare legs. I hear a car horn and, fearing that it will be Tucker or Bobby McBurney, I slowly rise from behind the bush. The boys have been calling incessantly, begging for me to meet with them, hoping that I'll give them girl pointers and woman tips.

My head is visible now—and to my surprise, I find Mr. Carver in his wife's station wagon, rolling down his window in a panic, shouting, "Gilbert! Gilbert Grape!"

The moment has finally come. Mrs. Carver has told him everything and he has come to remove my genitalia with a hacksaw.

"What? Hello?" I say.

"Oh, Gilbert, I'm glad you're here. Oh boy—thank God." Mr. Carver looks all over heated, his cheeks all red like winter time.

"Can I get you some lemonade or something, Mr. Carver?"

"No. Get in the car. You got a minute?"

"Uhm. Not really."

"Fifteen minutes, twenty at the most. I'll drive you back right away. Please. Just this once." The man is desperate and even though a ride in his car might mean my life, I get in.

Before we drive off I tell Amy that something has come up and that I'll be back soon and for her not to worry about Arnie. "I'll get him clean."

"You have ten days," she says as I get in Mr. Carver's car.

We're heading across town, our seat belts fastened, my knees jammed up to my chin because Mr. Carver drives with the front seat pushed all the way up. "Unbelievable."

"What is, sir?"

"You call me 'sir.' I am grateful for that. I appreciate that. I wish you were my son, Gilbert. You know how to make a man proud." He pauses. His hands tremble on the steering wheel. "I sure appreciate your doing this for me, Gilbert. You're swell."

"Gee, thanks." I sneak looks around the car, searching for a rifle or a handgun that he might use to off me. But Mr. Carver and I are guilty of the same crime. I saw him and Melanie together. Surely we can talk things out before he does something drastic.

"A man tries in this world. A man tries to do some good. Bring a certain dignity to this planet which it is clearly lacking. You try–through example–to touch those you can. And when you've done all that you're capable of and you still come up short–oh so short–it is a time of great sadness."

"Sure," I say. "Or at least I'd think."

"So they wanted a swimming pool. This was evident when we had our Memorial Day family chat. I heard them out–then I explained carefully. I took a pad of paper and broke down the costs and demonstrated in a methodical, somewhat impressive fashion how a swimming pool was not practical at this time. You'd think that that would be the end of that."

"You'd think."

"No. Not with my boys."

At this point, he pulls his car over into the ENDora OF THE LINE parking lot. "I need a minute to cool off. Is this all right?"

Well, what am I going to say? So I nod "it's fine" and I look at him like I care.

"It is so nice of you to care, Gilbert."

To which I reply–and where these words came from I'll never know–"Mr. Carver, you and your insurance have always been there for me."

"What a nice thing to say."

"Well . . ."

"I love my boys. I work hard. As hard as I can. For my boys."

Suddenly I remember the image of Melanie lying back on her desk, her skirt hiked up, her wig dangling down, and Mr. Carver thrusting into her, the crowded veins on his forehead, his eyes bulging out. I wonder if that's what Mr. Carver means by working hard.

"I sacrifice. I had all this planned to coincide with our nation's birthday on the Fourth, but wouldn't you know that the warehouse in Des Moines made a mistake and sent it to Mason City and that these last two days have been hell. We had to put a tracer on it."

"On what?"

"Come on! Don't you remember? Gilbert, I'm disappointed." I

can only conclude that Mr. Carver is a man easily let down. "Surely you remember my invitation to be one of the first to try out our new trampoline."

"Oh sure. Yes. What was I thinking?"

He starts up the station wagon and we're back on our way. When we pull into the Carver driveway, he says. "This whole situation has left me virtually paralyzed."

We walk around the side of the house. Mr. Carver holds open the white picket gate and I walk through. In the backyard, sitting dead center behind the house, is a brand-new trampoline. The frame is a dark blue, the springs silver and shiny, and the tramp part is impressive and black.

"What do you think?"

"Uhm. Wow," I say.

"BETTY! SEND OUT THE BOYS!"

I look back to the house, all the curtains and shades are drawn. The back door cracks open and I see Mrs. Carver's hand hold the door for Todd and Doug. They march out, their faces staring down at their feet. They wear their swimsuits.

"Todd, Doug—come over here."

The boys scuffle over and as they get close, Mr. Carver says, "Watch Gilbert."

"Watch Gilbert what?" I say.

Mr. Carver holds up a finger, the same finger that I saw diddling Melanie, and shushes me. He crouches down to the boys' eye level, in an effort I suppose to be intimate, but he looks stupid, uncomfortable. "Watch how much fun Gilbert has. Watch him." Mr. Carver pats the trampoline, signaling me to climb up. I start to when he says, "Gilbert, your shoes." I slip them off. "Watch him go up and down. Up and down. And study his face, too. You'll see how much fun this can be."

I begin my bounce but the boys don't look up.

"Jump higher."

I go as high as I can. The boys are still staring at their feet. "LOOK AT GILBERT. LOOK AT HOW MUCH FUN HE'S HAVING! LOOK AT HIM! HE'S HAVING A BALL! AREN'T YOU, GILBERT?"

"Yes."

"WHAT WAS THAT?"

"Yes! YES, I'm having A BALL!"

"So there, boys–so there!"

They still won't look, so I start hooting and hollering and not because I'm enjoying myself. I do this because I want to get it over with and get home. Part of me feels I owe him–that this is partial repayment for his wife.

I'm exuding the most positive outlook ever, making the big bounces, but the boys still won't look up. Suddenly Mr. Carver pulls Todd by the hair and grabs Doug by the arm. "Look, god-dammit. LOOK!" Todd sends kicks and punches toward his dad. Doug breaks free and runs howling inside to his mother. Mr. Carver proceeds to lift Todd and toss him through the air. He hits the ground with a thud.

"Stop it. Stop it!" I shout.

Todd runs inside, apparently not hurt and looking more in shock than anything.

I'm off the trampoline.

Mr. Carver is silent, on his knees. He slowly stands, brushes off his pants, turns to me and bares his teeth. "It's good to see you, Gilbert. Really, it's been a treat."

He walks back to his house, his chest in the air, a look of pride on his face, as if this all went as planned.

I put on my shoes and leave out the back gate. I see Mrs. Carver looking at me out the kitchen window. Our eyes meet for a moment–then I turn away.

As I leave the Carver property, I mutter to myself, "You don't hit people. A guy just shouldn't hit people."

I begin the two-mile walk home.

I write this note to Mr. Carver in my mind which concludes with a thought that goes something like this: At least some fathers have the courage to not live this life.

38

I'm walking down the side of Highway 13, when Chip Miles pulls over in his jeep. He gives me a ride home.

"Thanks, Chip."

"Anytime."

I almost say, "Too bad about your silver tooth," but I don't. With a polite "So long," I shut the door and we continue to fake being friends.

Standing on the porch is Arnie with the newest in dirt and food stains on his face. He holds a small box wrapped in brown paper and twine. The package is addressed to me.

"Can I open it? Can I open it?"

I tell him, "Dig in." He pulls at it, tearing at the paper on the edges. He gets frustrated, lifts the box over his head and is about to throw it to the ground.

"Arnie, no!"

He stops, scrunches his mouth to his eyes like he wants to erase his face. Amy appears with scissors. The retard and I cut the twine, he pulls away the paper fast and lifts the lid on the box. Amy watches. Our family loves a present.

Inside are hundreds of Styrofoam peanuts. Under them Arnie finds and lifts out a big black-and-white photo in a shiny gold frame. The face in the picture is fake, the teeth plastic, the hair sprayed stiff. Written in red marker is "Gilbert, thanks for lunch."

"Llllaaaaaaaannnnnccccccceeeeeee!" goes Arnie, taking the photo and running out of the house, presumably to show everyone in town the picture of his new best friend.

"That was for you," Amy says. "Nice of you to let Arnie have it."

"Good thing he can't read," I say.

"Yeah. Good thing."

Later I'm in my room, on my bed, my underwear down around my knees, looking at myself. I remember back before pubic hair, back when life was to be anticipated. Now, with a world full of Lance Dodge fans, I find it difficult to decipher the purpose of things. He is as phoney as you can be and everyone wants him, everyone wants to be him, or to know him, touch him. What about touching me?

I drop a wad of spit into my hand, preparing to treat myself. Suddenly my door pushes open, Ellen—all in a tizzy—shouts, "I have urgent news!"

I pull over a sheet, quickly covering myself. "The word is KNOCK!"

Ignoring me she asks, "You know Mr. Carver?"

"No."

"Yes, you do."

"Okay, what about him? What about him, what about him?"

"Something happened."

"What?"

"Maybe he won a prize or something. Maybe it's a coma or that he died. But something big has happened."

"What happened?"

"I don't know what happened, but something did and I don't know!" Ellen has grown frustrated. "Am I a news bureau or something?"

Amy calls the Carvers', but the phone is busy. I drive past. There are many cars out front, and people are pouring into their house. Someone in town will know, so I drive back to the square. I find Arnie trying to stick Lance's picture down the barrel of Endora's own replica of a Civil War cannon. I honk and he runs over.

"Hey, Gilbert. Hey."

"You want a ride?"

"Yep." Arnie goes to climb in the back of the truck.

"No, sit up here with me, okay?"

"But I don't wanna."

"I know you don't wanna, but you have to because something happened to Mr. Carver and we've got to find out what it was."

"I know what happened."

"Yeah, right. I'm not driving till you sit with me."

Arnie climbs up front, clutching the picture.

"Yeah, I know." He keeps saying this over and over. "I know. Oh boy, I know."

"Okay, buddy, tell me what happened."

He bites his lip.

"Tell me what happened."

Arnie falls silent. He slips a hand down his pants and starts scratching his butt, his groin. He scrapes at an arm.

"If you'd just take a bath, you wouldn't itch anymore."

"No!"

"Okay, I'm just saying . . ."

"NO! NO NO NO!"

I pull up to a stop at Endora's middle stoplight. I see Tim and Tommy Byers driving their wheelchairs. They are racing and pigskin Tim is winning.

"You can't make me clean!" Arnie shouts, opening the door and climbing out of my truck. I watch as my filthy brother runs off between two houses.

There's a tapping on my door, so I roll down my window and stick my head out–pigskin Tim is looking up at me while Tommy is on the other side of the road, snapping his fingers for pigskin Tim to come along. Tim says, "Did you hear?" He says it in such a way that I can't tell if it's good news or bad. "Carver, the insurance guy?"

"Yes?"

"The jerk that totally botched up our benefits? Fortunately for us, you know, our mom knew someone in Des Moines."

"What happened to him?"

"He's dead."

The laugh that shoots out of me is not because I find this funny. My laugh is the "holy shit" kind. Tim says that he laughed when he found out, too.

"I don't feel so bad, then," I say.

"He drowned. Something about a heart attack, too, but I don't know about that. Best part is? It happened in one of those plastic pools that are only ten, twelve inches deep." Tim hits the black stick on his wheelchair to reverse, smiles as much as the pigskin allows, says, "See you later," and the twins motor off together.

At home, I tell Amy who wakes up Momma, who says, "You know you've been around too long when the young people start dying." Ellen pipes up, a spoonful of yogurt having lathered her tongue, "He was forty something," and Momma says, "Yes, exactly."

Tucker calls to say that Bobby McBurney said they sent Mr. Carver for an autopsy. Foul play is suspected. "They think maybe it was murder."

"Really?"

"That's what this town needs. A good murder, you know?"

"Tucker, you're sick." I have these sudden pangs of fear. Suddenly I picture a trial. Testimony about Mr. Carver and Melanie, Mrs. Carver and me. "I gotta go," I say.

"One last thing. Do you realize who you're talking to?"

"Yes."

"I don't think you do, Gilbert. I don't think you have a clue."

"Bye..."

"Wait! You, my friend, are talking to the new assistant manager of Endora's finest new restaurant establishment."

I utter the obligatory, "Congratulations."

"Thank you." He goes on to explain how he's been going to Motley to the "other" Burger Barn for orientation. He says that he secretly hopes Mrs. Carver murdered Mr. Carver, because that would bring tourists and curiosity seekers to Endora. It would mean lots of business. "I expect to see you at the grand opening, Gilbert. July 14. Mark that day on your calendar."

What calendar?

"The fourteenth, you say?"

"Yes. Gilbert, you're the best friend ever."

"I'm making a note of it right now," I say, stretching out my fingers, not writing a thing.

39

Not since Arnie lost his eye or the Byers twins' accident has this town talked so much about any one thing. The funeral was delayed two days pending the autopsy report. The most popular theory is that Mrs. Carver killed him to collect the insurance. Apparently, most people knew about Mr. Carver's affair with Melanie. I keep waiting for an investigator or detective to come ask me questions—but no one has showed up yet. No one seems to know about Betty Carver and me.

Bobby McBurney dropped by the Dairy Dream and while ordering a milk shake, he told Ellen that the county coroner sent Mr. Carver back in pretty bad shape from the autopsy. Apparently Bobby and his dad were up the whole night piecing the body back together. Ellen was so shaken by this she threw up next to the sugar cone box.

It isn't until today, Monday, July 10, four days after Mr. Carver died, that the county coroner has given the okay for his burial. Apparently, while the death was suspicious, no evidence could support that he was murdered. Tucker's dream of a sensational trial has quickly disappeared and Mrs. Betty Carver will be free to walk this great land.

In the past, Mr. Lamson would close down for the whole day when someone so important died, but in an effort to remain competitive, we're open today from 7:00 A.M. to noon. This will give us two hours to clean up and get to the church. Food Land never closes down for holidays let alone the funeral of the town's last remaining insurance man. After all, business is business, and besides, people are usually pretty hungry after a funeral. I guess it's because we all realize that time is running out and we better eat all we can. Please don't mention that to my mother. Everyone must be over at Food Land because our store is empty. It's about eleven-fifteen. I'm unpacking the half-gallon containers of whole milk when someone enters the store. Mr. Lamson is busy in the stockroom so I zip down Aisle One only to find these little hands, four of them, grabbing multiple candy bars and packs of gum and Tootsie Rolls. This soft voice says, "You can have whatever you want."

I come around the aisle. "Hi, Todd. Hi, Doug."

"Say hello to Gilbert Grape, boys."

They make no attempt at words.

The boys are dressed in these identical blue suits and Mrs. Betty Carver wears the sexiest black dress I've ever seen. Were it not a sad day and were her boys not in the store, I would take her by the hand, walk back to our small produce section, hike up her dress, and mount her from the rear.

"I told the boys they could have whatever they wanted. Please don't think of me as a bad mother."

"I never would think that," I say.

The boys look like they've been crying for days. Their arms are full of candy and chocolate bars and bubble gum cards. Mrs. Carver asks for a pack of cigarettes and wonders if menthol is what women should smoke.

"I don't know," I say.

She says she'd like a pack of Salem because it's the girls in those ads that she'd most like to resemble. She says this as if she truly believes smoking will make her more beautiful. "Ken would never let me smoke. It was a health risk. But we know what happened with Ken, don't we?"

I look at her, forgetting for a moment that this is the only woman I've ever seen naked.

"Gilbert, will you ring all this up? We need to get over to the church."

"It'll be no charge."

"Oh, please. I insist."

"No, ma'am."

She had started to open her purse but stopped after hearing me say "ma'am." "You seem to be forgetting something," she says.

I want to say, No way can I forget, no way will I ever forget the way we kissed that first time, the way you taught me how to hold you, the way your hands moved all over me. No way could I forget the gas-station bathroom, our spot at Skunk River, all those times on your kitchen floor. But I don't say anything. I look at her like we've never met. She is the customer and I am the worker. She smiles. She knows that I can't forget. Forgetting, in fact, will be much easier for her.

I begin ringing up the candy bars, the gum—every now and then letting a bar or two go by without registering it. Mrs. Carver pulls out two twenties.

"But your total is only twelve seventy-five."

"Keep the change."

If she wants me to feel like a prostitute, she's succeeding. "I can't accept this."

"Yes, you can. You must. For me."

I press myself up against the checkout counter in an effort to hide my erection. She sends the boys out to a black funeral limousine which I just realized has been waiting all this time. Bobby McBurney sits in the driver's seat. He would wave but he's working.

"They've taken this hard," she says, referring to the boys.

"Huh?"

"My boys have taken this hard."

"I bet."

"Yes, you know about such things, don't you?" She puts her left hand, the one with the wedding ring, on top of mine. "You were how old when your father . . ."

"I was seven."

"Oh, the same age as Todd."

"Yes."

"So you understand what my boys must be feeling."

"Yeah, I guess."

"Of course you do," she says, cutting me off. She starts to tap the pack of cigarettes out on the back of her other hand. "Have you missed me?"

"I haven't seen you much lately."

"I know, but have you missed me?"

I say, "Yes."

Mrs. Betty Carver smiles. She knows when I lie, and starts to smack the pack harder. "I've seen people do this before they open the pack. Is this what people do?"

"Some people," I say.

"Are you one of those some people?"

I want to say that I don't know what I am but that I wish she would leave and I'm sorry that we ever got involved and another part of me wishes we had never stopped but I am twenty-four and you are significantly older, Mrs. Carver, and we probably learned all that we could, so let's get on with it and please take your change.

I've slowly gathered up the dimes, a nickel, two ones, a five, and the extra twenty. I reach out to give it to her but she refuses.

"A little thinking and you might realize that Mr. Carver was in insurance and one of the few fringe benefits, in fact, the only fringe benefit is that they give loads and loads of life insurance to the survivors." Mrs. Carver smiles in a way that suggests she expects me to be impressed. I don't blink even. "Guess what Ken was insured for?"

I don't know and I say nothing.

"Let me say that it's more than enough. A couple of commas, many zeros."

My face doesn't even move.

"You're wondering if it was an accident, aren't you? The people in this town are all wondering, aren't they?" She grows desperate. "Tell me what people are saying!"

"I don't know what people say. I'm not the telephone operator."

"You hear things, though."

"It is suspicious. Drowning in a wading pool. That's not an easy thing to do."

"Mr. Carver didn't know how to swim. Did you know that?"

"No. That subject never came up."

"Well, he couldn't swim. I hope you'll let people know...."

"I'll tell all my friends."

"Don't get smart with me, young man." Her skin is beginning to change color. She explains that Ken drove to Motley and bought a wading pool. "He was filling it with a hose, had a heart attack, and fell in the water. The boys thought their daddy was playing a joke on them and by the time they came and got me and we pulled him out, he was gone." She has opened her pack, awkwardly. That same kind of awkwardness I felt the first time she undid my pants. This time, though, with the smoking, she's the virgin. I take a book of matches from the cash register and light her cigarette. She coughs slightly and says, "You don't believe my story? You think I killed him, don't you?"

I'm silent. I'm more enamored with the way she holds her cigarette. Her fingers are afraid. This is more interesting than whether she's a murderess. To me, the man deserved death but perhaps a more violent, gruesome end would have been more appropriate.

Phyllis Staples, the town's piano teacher and mother of Buck, who works for the Standard station, enters the store. Mrs. Staples goes back to the dog-food section. She has a collie named Lassie. That's the kind of original thinking that just makes this town such an exciting place.

Mrs. Betty Carver continues in a whisper. "Gilbert, the last time Mr. Carver and I made love was the night I got pregnant with Doug. No kidding. To Ken, sex was for making boys. The second boy was a kind of human insurance. Fortunately, for me, there was another little boy. You."

I say, "Oh." This all might be too deep for me. My erection is gone and I look for something to act as an ashtray. I find an empty Coke can and hold it out and she flicks her ashes in the opening. She's standing with the cigarette, not smoking it, and I think an onlooker, peeking through the store window, not hearing the conversation, would probably chuckle. The sight of this woman, dressed in her funeral black, holding a cigarette, talking to Gilbert Grape, while Mrs. Staples struggles up to the counter with a ten-pound bag of Gravy Train—the sight is too much. Mrs. Staples pays for the dog food; I offer to carry it out. She says that she can manage, that she's always been able to manage. She doesn't offer any condolences to Mrs. Carver, which seems rude. But then again, there are many who don't ever acknowledge death.

As she leaves with the dog food, I almost let out a bark.

"Phyllis is angry at me. She plays all the funerals, you know, but I don't want music at Ken's. She thinks I've got something against

211

her. But my problem is not with her at all. It's with my late husband. Doesn't that sound odd? *Late* husband?"

I say, "Maybe you can tell her after this is all over."

"No, I'll be gone after this is over. I'm thinking about taking my
boys to St. Louis. How does St. Louis sound?"

I shrug.

"Ken hated St. Louis. I think it has a nice ring to it."

Mrs. Betty Carver's hair has been unraveling since she walked
in the door, giving her that crazed look that makes her killing him
conceivable. Part of me wonders what took her so long. "You're
thinking I killed him. I can see you thinking it in your eyes. I've
always been able to tell everything from your eyes."

I say, "I guess I've been thinking that it's possible. Your killing
Mr. Carver, that is."

"Gilbert," she says–and she says this like she's asking for
another loaf of bread or checking the price of Rice-A-Roni–"how
can you kill a man who'd already been dead for years?"

"Good point," I say. And she knows it. She completes winning this
round by putting out the cigarette in the can which I still so dutifully
hold. Doug comes back in the store. He's got chocolate on his lips.

"Mommy," he says.

"Mommy's coming, honey."

Smoke starts to billow out of the can.

"Good-bye, Gilbert."

She leaves the store. Bobby McBurney holds open the limousine
door for her and before getting in, she pulls down her widow's veil.

40

A my and I go straight home after the funeral.
    Momma asks, "How was it?"
Amy says, "Good. Not the crowd we had at Daddy's but a lot of

people just the same. There wasn't any music, so the service was short."

"Like life," Momma says.

I'm heading for the stairs, hiding the Coke can behind my back.

"What are you doing with that can?" Momma calls out.

I shrug and laugh because no reasonable answer comes to me and I continue up the stairs. In my room, I dust off a corner on my lowest shelf. I look in the can and see that the cigarette butt has her lipstick on it. I remember the feel of her lips. I've never won a prize or a blue ribbon or a plaque, but as I set the can in its new home, next to the Styrofoam cup filled with Becky's watermelon seeds, I think that maybe, finally, I've won something.

In the bathroom, I look at myself in the mirror. Not bad. I undo the belt to my polyester brown pants, I unclip my tie, I am twenty-four years old and my only tie is a clip-on. I refuse to learn how to tie a real one. The reason is that my father set a precedent for tying knots around the neck and it's an example I choose not to follow. This line of thinking has gotten me out of wearing ties except at the most festive of occasions–funerals. And I've only been to three. The first was my father's, when I was seven. The second was my Grandfather Watts's, when I was ten. He lived across the state in Martinsburg and he died when a tractor fell over on him.

I turn on the shower and step under the water.

It occurs to me as the water pours on me, my funeral clothes scattered all over the bathroom floor–it occurs to me that my brothers, sisters, mom, and me are the last of the Grapes.

Momma was an only child and her mother died when she was a little girl. My other grandpa, Lawrence Grape, drank himself to death; this happened before I was born. Apparently he was mean and bitter. He had two boys–my dad, Albert Lawrence, and Gilbert Palmer Grape. Gilbert Palmer died in World War II. He was shot down in a plane and he's buried with the other Grapes, about four graves from my dad. It seems my other grandmother, Dottie Grape, blasted my mom and dad for not naming Larry after Gilbert Palmer. So when I came along, the family was in ecstasy, because they could appease my Grandma Dottie, who lived alone in Alden, Iowa.

Grandma Dottie has lived, if that's what you'd call it, in a nursing home for the last eight or nine years. She's forgotten everything and everyone. My mother despises her and the only memory any of us has of her is how when she'd blow smoke in our faces, we'd cough, and she'd just blow some more. For all practical purposes, Grandma Dottie is dead. We have no aunts, uncles or cousins.

I turn my shower into a bath by lifting the stopper above the faucet. I pour in Arnie's bubble bath. The pink bottle is still almost full from lack of use. It's been almost a week since his last cleaning.

I sit down slowly in the hot water, the bubbles cover me, only my head sticks out. The ends of my hair get wet. The heat from the late-afternoon sun and the hot water makes my face sweat; breathing in the air burns my throat. It's at times like these when I can perfectly understand why so many need Jesus or drugs or Burger Barns, anything to make the day bearable. I touch myself until I've an erection. I let the water out of the tub and stay there as it drains. When the water gets to the side of me, then below me, I relieve myself. I make a moan sound that hopefully no one heard.

After dinner I put on clean clothes, comb my hair, and slap on some of Larry's aftershave that he left behind. I go down and out to my truck. Ellen is on the porch marking verses from a brand-new white Bible that she now carries with her everywhere. "Where you off to?" she asks. "I can smell you miles away."

I laugh off the smell comment. She's one to talk about smells.

"I'm highlighting the good parts," she says. "The pertinent parts and I hope when you've a minute you'll thumb through this because I think it will give you some compassion for your sinful self...." She continues talking, chalking up points for heaven, she must think, as I get in my truck and drive away.

At the Carver house, I knock on the door. There are relatives still inside, boxes for packing, too, and Neil Diamond plays on a stereo. An older woman who looks like Mr. Carver in drag opens the door. She must have been his mother.

"Could I speak with Bett...Mrs. Carver?"

She turns on the porch light. She looks me up and down: obviously something about me truly disgusts her.

"I can't look any better than this, lady," I want to say. But I smile the I'm-sorry-Mr.-Carver-died smile and this seems to make things better, for the moment.

The woman shuts the door. The wait must be five minutes. When Mrs. Betty Carver opens the door, I expect to see her still dressed for the funeral. She wears jeans, though, and one of Mr. Carver's T-shirts that is baggy. It looks sexy on her.

"Gilbert," she says.

"Hi." I stand there as she waits for me to talk. "I wanted you to know . . . uhm . . . St. Louis sounds like a good . . . opportunity. . . ."

Smiling like a proud parent, she nods.

"Well . . . it could be a great opportunity . . . I've always found St. Louis . . . uhm . . . uh . . . and after Arnie's party . . . I'm . . . uhm avai—"

"Gilbert," she says, "oh, Gilbert."

"I think you know what I'm trying to say."

"We've already said our good-bye."

"Yes, but . . ."

"If we keep on saying it, it won't mean anything, will it?"

The door opens and little Todd says, "Mom. Mom! Uncle Dan is doing magic. Come see, Mom! Come on!" He pulls on her T-shirt.

She says, "In a minute, Mommy's finishing up with Gilbert Grape."

Todd goes inside and the door closes. The porch light goes off, leaving Mrs. Betty Carver and me in the dark.

"Todd must have . . ."

"It's okay. . . ."

"He must have bumped the switch. I can turn it back . . ."

"No."

There is nothing to say, nothing left to do. She sees through me; she sees me wanting to use her for my escape. We stand for a bit, then she swings open the screen door, goes inside, letting the door slowly close.

Uncle Dan must be doing his magic because the music has been turned down and I hear the "ooo's" and "ah's" of the relatives, the laughter of the kids. I stand there listening.

I make sure my headlights are facing the Carver house when I snap them on. I position my truck so they shine bright on the living room window. This way she'll notice as Gilbert Grape drives away.

Tucker's light is on. The TV is on inside. I can hear pro wrestling. I have to knock real loud.

Bobby McBurney opens the door. He has replaced me as Tucker's best friend. "Gilbert."

"Hi, guys."

I'm let into Tucker's garage/apartment in such a way that I feel like an unwelcome visitor to a top secret club.

"I didn't see your hearse, Bobby."

"Yeah, well, my dad doesn't like me to drive it for a few days after a funeral. Seems a bit tasteless to remind people of death at such a tender time. Give it two or three days and I'll be back at the wheel. Of course, if somebody else kicks off, then I'll be stranded a few more days."

On TV, a big, fat guy with a bunch of tattoos beats on a little, more muscular guy who wears a snow mask. Tucker leans forward, intent on the wrestling. I sit and ask myself, "Why, of all places, did I come here?" Finally, after the tattooed guy practically chokes the masked guy on one of the ropes, the masked guy pins the tattooed guy to the screaming delight of the fans. It breaks to a commercial. Tucker lowers the volume and turns to me. "We looked to you for advice. We uh..."

"Entrusted," Bobby says.

"Yes—with the truth of our girl situation. You have offered no advice. No counsel." Tucker goes on to say, "You're lucky we even let you in tonight. I seriously considered leaving you outside, standing alone, so you could uhm..."

"Contemplate."

"Yeah, contemplate your lack of action, your inability to care for your two buddies, Bobby and Tucker."

Am I hearing this?

"You didn't seem to appreciate our ideas but you gave us no other idea, no other alternative."

I think fast. I need these guys right now. I need the comfort of stupid people.

"Friends help friends, Gilbert. Friends call. Friends talk. Friends are . . . uhm . . . uhm . . . friendly."

Bobby nods in agreement.

I go, "You guys think of me as some mastermind with girls."

"No, we don't."

"You're just luckier."

"If that's the case, then why did you turn to me?"

"Because you have experience." Tucker sounds like a commercial for the Army Reserve.

"I did come up with an idea. I've been mulling it over." (Yeah, for about twenty seconds.) "But it sounds like you guys aren't interested in my ideas anymore. . . ."

Tucker says that they are interested, *very* interested but that they don't want to get their hopes up.

Bobby is cooler about it all but he, too, is dying to know my thoughts.

"You guys know Cindy Mansfield?"

"Yeah."

"Well, Cindy has a group of girls that meet Sunday nights at the Church of Christ. They have a Bible study, they hold hands when they pray. They hug a lot. My little sister is the newest to belong to the group but there must be ten, twelve girls of varying ages."

"What are you saying?" Tucker asks.

"I think I'm being clear."

Bobby nods, he's gotten my drift.

Tucker asks several minor questions that do not deserve repeating. I explain that much killing and lovemaking have been done in the name of Christ. Christians "forgive" so easily, they are more apt to sway from "the path" because they can always forgive themselves. They can forgive you.

Tucker goes, "Ohhhh, I get it."

I pop open one of his obscure beers and chug it. I grab another for the road, and as I'm about to leave, my short little friend says, "Gilbert?"

"What, Tucker?"

I look down at him, a smile forms below his watery eyes. "Praise God."

"Keep practicing," I say.

"I love Jesus. Jesus saves."

"Really practice, Tucker. You sound stilted."

Bobby paces the room, rehearsing his lines. His script goes something like this: "I was asleep when it occurred to me. The emptiness of my life. I had a dream. And this group of people, you girls, were in the dream. A voice said go to them. Go to those girls and ask for entry into their midst."

"Midst is good," I shout. "Midst is biblical!"

Tucker starts singing "Jesus loves me," but he has to stop because he doesn't know the words.

Suddenly, I'm the greatest guy and I leave, secure in their esteem. I drive the streets of my town. I'm looking for action.

I pass the old Lally place. I find Becky standing in her front yard, looking up at the night sky. I roll down my passenger window. I'm about to say, "What's up?" when she points up and whispers.

"What?" I say.

She points again but I don't look at where she's pointing. I look at her. "What did you say?"

"The moon, Gilbert. What a thing–the moon."

Oh Christ. Get me out of here.

I hit the gas and drive off.

I head to the cemetery. I walk around the graves and look all over–at the tombstones, the trees, even at the dent in my truck's fender. I look everywhere–everywhere but at the moon.

41

It's late afternoon of the next day–Monday, July 11–five days till the festivities. All morning and afternoon we've been cleaning the downstairs in preparation. Janice called during lunch and will "check in" daily until she arrives on Saturday. Larry sent an extra check to cover "necessary expenses." And Mr. Lamson has given me more time off to help ready the house.

Moments ago the retard hopped like a kangaroo through the kitchen tracking his filthy, muddy feet across the clean floor. Amy looked up and rationalized the situation. "Since Arnie will be eighteen in a matter of days, we've left it up to him to decide when to bathe. He's almost an adult. What with him itching all the time and the dirt getting so thick—surely he'll break down and clean up any moment now." She waits for my response but I have none. "Isn't it a great idea letting him make an adult's decision?" Amy Grape has found it yet again. The bright side.

But she knows damn well that I've tried everything to get the kid in water. And she knows that it's no use.

Momma keeps reviewing the schedule for the big day. We did the planning, but she has to approve everything—the menu, the party colors, the guest list. The retarded kids from a three-county area—of which there are maybe ten, all of whom are assorted shapes and sizes, all of whom speak in those garbly, retarded voices—will be over for a few hours on that afternoon. There will be party games and the opening of presents. Each activity has been carefully planned, food is beginning to be stockpiled and it's all designed to run like clockwork.

So.

I've almost finished remopping the floor when Amy comes into the kitchen and says, "A big truck pulled up out front. See who it is." She sends me outside for understandable reasons. Ever since Muffy, she has had a particular aversion to big trucks and their drivers.

Out the door, I come upon a guy, younger than me, who is balancing on the curb. An older guy sits in the passenger side, holding a pipe but not smoking it. The younger guy says, "I'm looking for a Mr. Arnie Grape."

"He's around here somewhere."

"I have a delivery for him."

"I'll be happy to sign...."

PETER HEDGES

"No, sorry. He has to sign."

"Great, but . . ."

"Buddy, that's the regulation. Only Arnie Grape can sign."

I explain that my brother is special.

"Yeah? So? We're all special. Listen, he signs or there's no delivery."

A muddy, grimy figure comes around the side of the house carrying a big rock. Unable to lift it above his head, he lets it drop on the sidewalk. He growls at the man.

"Come here, Arnie," I say.

The delivery man looks at the dirt boy and quickly hands me the pen. I'm tempted to say "I told you so," but I don't. I sign next to the X. The delivery man hands me a card. "It's for uhm uhm . . ."

"Arnie," I say. I open it and read it out loud slowly.

> "Arnie,
> a little early but Happy Birthday just the same."

Amy and Ellen watch from the porch as the two delivery guys lift the back door of their truck. Amy calls through the screen door to Momma, giving a play-by-play report on what she sees. "It's for Arnie! An early birthday present! Who's it from, Gilbert?"

I tell her.

"Momma! It's from Mrs. Carver! What is it? Tell us what it is!"

I tell Amy what I'm guessing.

"Gilbert thinks it's a trampoline, Momma!"

"Yep, that's what it is," the young guy says, passing the metal legs out of the truck.

The men and I carry it to the backyard and, after Arnie shows us where he wants it, we assemble it. Ellen brings a five-dollar bill as a tip for the men. They flirt with her and she relishes their eager eyes.

As the men drive off, Amy calls out, "Dinner!"

Ellen pleads for "one minute"–Arnie climbs up on the tramp. He tries to jump up and down, but he keeps falling over. Ellen, eager to try, gets up and stands on the edge, and shouts, "My turn! My turn!" As she jumps, her little breasts jiggle. She is the only Christian in town who doesn't wear a bra. Arnie paces on the grass, mumbling, "It's mine, it's *mine*." I wonder if Mr. Carver is watching this from wherever he's gone to.

220

I tell Amy I won't be eating. The gift to Arnie feels more like a stab aimed at me. While the others eat dinner inside, I lie on the trampoline and look at the sky. I hear Ellen telling Arnie to stop spitting his food. Momma asks for thirds. Amy makes a polite plea to Arnie about bathing and the "immense joy" to be found from being clean. Arnie wisely points out that Momma doesn't bathe. Amy explains that Momma's a grown-up and older people don't get as dirty as younger people. Arnie doesn't buy her reasoning. Ellen asks to be excused so she can shower.

The last thing I remember before falling off to sleep is the sound of her shower coming from upstairs. This must have made me dream that it was raining.

I dreamed that it rained and rained and Arnie got clean and that my dad and I went fishing. We didn't catch anything. We didn't say anything. It was fine, just fishing, just sitting in the boat with him, just fishing was fine.

"OH MY GOD!"

I open my eyes to find that the sun hasn't gone down any. It must have been a fast dream, the length of a cartoon.

"OH MY GOD!" Amy screams. "HELP!"

"What is it?" I shout, getting up from the trampoline.

"MOMMA! MOMMA!"

I run to the house.

"No! Nooooo!"

I'm up on the porch steps and inside fast. Amy is reaching across the table, trying to get to Momma, who is all pale and unable to breathe. Momma's shoulders are locked up around her neck. Dinner is clogged in her throat.

"Momma! Momma!"

I try to put my arms around her to do that thing where you make a fist and pull up and back fast to dislodge the food. But I can't get my arms around her stomach. Ellen runs downstairs half dressed. I'm holding Momma's mouth open as Amy reaches in, trying to get her enormous tongue out of the way. Momma is going to be the color blue in moments—we're all making noise, saying things that I don't even hear. It's absolutely quiet and painfully loud at the same time.

Arnie is watching and keeps asking, "Why? Why? Why?" and none of us answers him. The lasagna and the corn on the cob and the blueberry muffins are all a kind of soupy, mushy goop in Momma's mouth.

"Don't die," is what I want to say.

Amy takes hold of Momma's jaw, I make both my hands into fists and press several rapid punches into her midsection, hoping to bust open the air passage.

"Call Dr. Harvey!" one of us shouts.

Dr. Harvey's number is written in red ink on the wall above the phone. He lives all but three blocks away.

Ellen dials and talks.

"Is he coming? Is he coming?"

"Come on, Momma. Come on! Spit it out! GET IT OUT!"

Her eyes close, then open, then close. Arnie is screaming, "Don't yell! Don't yell!"

"Get him out of here!" Amy says.

"Arnie, come here. I got this surprise." Ellen pulls at his arm, begging him to follow her. "Arnie! ARNIE!" Arnie doesn't. Instead, he takes a dinner glass and heaves it against the wall; the glass shatters. Oh, great. He takes Momma's plate and sends it soaring straight up–it breaks into pieces and rains down on top of us. I tackle Arnie and carry him out, drop him on the porch. Momma is making this muted scream sound now. My mother is going to die. Right now. We all know it, we all sense it. And there is nothing we can do.

Ellen is saying, "Please, Momma. Hang on, Momma!"

Amy starts apologizing. "I'm sorry. It's all my fault. I love you, Momma. Don't, don't give up. Dr. Harvey's coming. He's coming."

For some reason I start hitting the back of her head, popping it hard. Suddenly, the chunk or mass or blockage of food erupts out, liquid comes out her nose and the food bullets down on the table.

Momma breathes in deep and fast. Loud and scared.

Dr. Harvey hits the door running. He wears pajama tops and dress slacks. He hurries to Momma. We clear out of the way and wait to do whatever he asks.

*   *   *

It's fifteen minutes or so later, and Dr. Harvey is leaning toward Momma, who whispers that her throat is sore.

"It probably feels like you delivered a baby out your mouth." Dr. Harvey says that to lighten the tension, to keep us loose, but no one laughs. I can tell he regrets saying that by the way he smiles.

I've washed my hands, Amy is cleaning up the broken glass and Momma sits in her chair, still shaken.

Most doctors would have left by now but not Dr. Harvey. He was my father's best friend. He moves next to Arnie and explains for yet a third time that Momma's going to be all right. Arnie keeps repeating "not funny, not funny."

Ellen is getting the vacuum cleaner for Amy when I see the McBurney Funeral Home hearse pull into our driveway. I am out of the house fast.

"You get the fuck out of here, motherfucker! Go! Go!"

I'm pounding on the hood of the hearse. Bobby McBurney is inside and he goes to lock the doors. But I get the passenger side open before he can lock it and I grab him and say, "You got some nerve. She isn't dead. My mother isn't dead! You fuck!"

I'm about to punch him, he's white in the face and smelling like some cologne or something—when Ellen screams from the porch, "Stop it! Stop it!"

I pull back, get out of the hearse, and point firmly, violently for Bobby to drive away. "Get out of here, you motherfucker."

"He's my date."

"Huh?"

"Bobby's my date."

Bobby shifts to reverse and starts to back out.

"Oh, great!" Ellen shouts. "This is the end of my entire life!"

She bursts into tears, Bobby is terrified and as he shifts to drive, I run out in front to block his escape. He drives toward me—I climb up on the hood. "Let me explain," I'm saying. Bobby shakes his head. "Let me explain, Bobby. Our mother . . ."

Ellen is running alongside the hearse, squeezing her Bible. "Gilbert thought you were coming for Momma. Bobby, our mother just about died. He thought that's what . . ."

Bobby stops the hearse. He won't look at me. I ripped a couple of buttons off his shirt, his neck is red where I was squeezing it.

I slide off the hood. "I'm sorry," I say to Ellen. She tells Bobby that she has to cancel the date—what with Momma and all. I tell her to go on. "Have a great time. Amy and me will take care of Momma."

She reluctantly gets in the McBurney Funeral Home hearse, and they drive off. I'm walking back to the house when I find Arnie clinging to a tree. I peel him off and we go up the porch steps.

Inside, Dr. Harvey is making Momma drink water.

"It hurts to swallow," she says.

He refills the glass.

She takes a small sip and says, "It hurts."

42

It must be midnight now. Looking out the kitchen window, I see her lit cigarette. I go to Amy, who is spooning Momma some applesauce. Amy says, "All is calm now, Gilbert. You go out for as long as you need." Momma looks puzzled and Amy says to her, "Gilbert's friend is out back."

I called Becky after Dr. Harvey left half an hour ago. She said she'd be over right away. She asked what this was all about and I said, "Nothing, really." But I'm sure she heard the quiver in my voice.

I walk out the back door. We don't hug or kiss. It's more of a handshake than anything. I explain the day; the trampoline, the little brother who won't bathe, the taste of death.

Soon I'm pacing in my backyard, the dry grass scratching my bare feet. Arnie is in bed, Ellen's still out, and as Amy sits with Momma, watching an old movie, the house glows blue from the TV.

"It's like you're somewhere else."

"Yes," I say. "We almost lost Momma."

"Oh," she says. "But she didn't die. That's good, right?"

I don't say a thing.

"You're not happy about that?"

I shrug.

"You want a drag?"

I shake my head.

Becky exhales. Her air sounds nice.

I sit on the swing out back. She's on the ground in front of me, her legs crossed Indian style. The sky is full of many stars.

"I feel like dancing," she says. "Or running around naked, singing to the moon. Something to remind the living."

"Huh?"

"Remind the living."

"Of what?"

"That we're alive."

"I know I'm alive, thank you very much."

Becky puts the cigarette out on the bottom of her shoe, stands, and does a cartwheel. Then she starts this rhythmic, pulsing kind of movement. "Come on," she says.

I refuse to move.

"Your mistake," she says as her movements get even bigger, her arms whipping everywhere, her head and hair whooshing around.

"I make lots of mistakes," I say.

The last five minutes have felt like five hours. I'm still on the swing and Becky's rain dance has continued nonstop. I've no words. She is giggling and whooping and it's not like she's trying to pretend she's having a good time. She's not a faker. It's the middle of the night, we're in Endora, Iowa, and this girl is very much alive. I want to bury my head in my pillow. I walk over to a small tree of ours which has these orange berries. I yank off a handful and start tossing them at her. The first two miss, the third hits. She suddenly stops. She looks at me. Into my eyes. Piercing me.

I look at her like "What? What's wrong?"

"I don't know about you, Gilbert. You call me late at night . . . and I come over . . . you say nothing."

I throw a fourth berry, a fifth.

"... stop throwing those ... you pretend like nothing ..."

Quickly picking a bunch of them, I wind up like the baseball pitcher I never was and throw about ten berries. They spray Becky.

"... and then you throw things at me ... !" She stops talking. She walks quickly to her bike, which leans against the side of the house. I follow after her. She starts to get on her bike and I say, "Let me walk you."

"No."

"Let me, please."

"Fuck you."

"Sorry about the berries. Sorry."

We walk without words for some time. The only sound is the click from the bike and the crickets. She smokes. My hands tremble.

"You're so cut off from yourself."

"No, I'm not," I say, stuffing my hands in my pockets so she won't see them shake.

"Feelings, Gilbert. They're what people are supposed to have."

"I have feelings."

"Ha."

"I have plenty of ..."

"You stopped having feelings a long time ago. Look at you. You almost lost your mother and you're out walking with me."

"Yes, because ..." I say. "Because uhm I'm trying to live. Don't you see?"

She stares at me some more. Then she takes the handlebars, pulls her bike from me and gets on. Her cigarette drops to the ground.

"I feel! I'm a feeling guy!"

She rides away.

"You're just afraid of me, little girl! You're scared, too!"

She's gone.

I look down. Her cigarette is still smoldering. I bend down, pick it up, walk home down the middle of South Main, attempting to smoke what's left.

"Momma's sleeping," Amy says, meeting me at the front door.

I say, "That's good."

"You know how long it's been since she slept at night?"

"True. All this commotion must have been hard for Momma to swallow."

Amy doesn't get my joke, which is not surprising for a woman who doesn't think our family is funny. "We almost lost her, Gilbert."

"Yep, I know."

Momma snores and snorts, and with each burst of sound, Amy seems to feel better and better.

The TV is on but the sound is down.

"Hey," I say. "Let's turn off the TV. It needs a rest." Our TV plays around the clock.

"Momma likes the light. Helps her sleep."

"Fine, okay, whatever."

"Gilbert?"

I'm on the second stair, heading to bed.

"Huh?"

Amy whispers this with special intensity.

"Let's make Arnie's birthday the best one ever. For Momma." The blue light from the TV casts a shadow on Amy. "Gilbert, did you hear me?"

I stop and look long at her. The flickering light makes my sister of thirty-four look about eighty-two.

"What's the matter?"

I say, "Oh, I was just thinking how we're not so young anymore. I was thinking how I used to like us better."

"I know what you mean. I used to like us better, too. We never do anything. As a family. Like other families. Like real families. That's why Arnie's birthday is so uhm..." Amy's thoughts trail off, partially because she's sleepy, but mainly because a thump, like a muffled drum beat, comes from upstairs. Arnie has begun his music making. The thump becomes a thud.

"I better stop the kid before he crushes his skull. You coming to bed?"

"Can't yet."

"Momma will be fine."

"Ellen, though."

"What? She's not back yet?"

Amy says, "No."

Arnie crouches on his knees and baps his head in his sleep. Instead of waking him, I jam a pillow between him and the headboard and this muffles the sound enough and pads his brain. Clouds of dust and dirt poof out with each thud.

Back downstairs, I offer to go drive around and find the puberty girl. Amy says no need. I'm going back upstairs, when she asks me to wait up with her. So I do. We watch an old movie with the sound down. Amy whispers, "I hope Momma doesn't wake up. Ellen still being out would worry her." This movie craves more commercial breaks.

I say to myself, Bobby McBurney better not touch my little sister or I'll beat his ass.

"Something going on, Gilbert?"

"Huh?"

"Something you're not telling us about. You seem to be drifting."

Me? Never, I say to myself.

"You're not yourself. Your mind and such. Something going on?"

I must have fallen asleep, because I don't remember the answer I gave Amy or the end of the movie, for that matter. I wake up to find Amy opening the door for Ellen. I stand up fast, shake my face as my little sister bounds in with a "Howdy, everybody." Amy sighs and I look out the window and see Bobby and the hearse drive off.

"Good night, everybody," Ellen sings as she skips up the stairs. The kid is so fast and we're so tired that she gets by us with no problem.

Amy looks at me. "Did you smell beer on her?"

I shrug.

"I smelled beer," she says.

It occurs to me that getting drunk is the right idea wasted on the wrong person. "You want me to talk to her?" I ask.

"No."

"She's just a kid."

"I know. Tomorrow I'll lay down the law."

"Good," I say, knowing full well that Amy will turn soft. As I climb the stairs, two steps at a time, Amy goes to check on Momma and grab one last snack. Ellen has gone in the bathroom and as I pass the door, I hear her vomit. "Don't forget to flush," I say, through the door. I listen for an answer. She pukes again.

"Youth," I say to myself as I climb in my bed and put my left hand down my underwear.

Part Five

43

". . . she gets her braces off and she's like a dog without a leash for the first time. One minute she's a beauty queen–next minute she's a Christian–now she's staying out too late."

Amy's face is looking over me in my bed. I roll over on my stomach to hide my erection, the same one I went to sleep with last night.

"You've got to explain to her about guys, Gilbert–make her wise to men's true nature. Now that her teeth are straight, I fear the worst."

"Okay, okay, I'll talk to her."

Amy continues and I drown her sound by sandwiching my head between a pillow and my mattress. I squeeze it tight until she's gone.

First I throw on some shorts and a red-and-yellow Iowa State University T-shirt (Janice's alma mater). While peeing, I hold my breath–the bathroom is filled with Ellen's beer/vomit stench. I walk down the hall and knock on her door.

"It's open."

"Hey, Ellen."

My sister is lying on her pink bed, her face and hair still hung over. She is reading a *National Geographic*. In my nicest voice, I say, "Since when did you start reading that?"

"Since now."

"Reading stuff like that people will begin to think you're smart."

"Just don't tell anyone, then."

"People change. Your reading that proves my theory that people change."

"I'm not reading really. I'm just looking at the pictures." She's been flipping the pages very fast.

"I'm relieved you aren't reading."

She flips her hair back. We both know why I'm in her room and it's a waiting game to see who will speak first.

"Oh God!" Ellen says this, most likely, to avoid what I'm about to say.

"What is it?"

"Look at that."

Ellen shows me two pictures on a lost tribe from Africa or somewhere, some primitive tribe. The first picture I look at is a closeup of a man with a huge yellow hoop through his nose.

"Ouch," I say.

"Look at the other one."

It is five women and many babies. The women have no shirts or tops on, they are on the edge of the water doing laundry by hand, their breasts are hanging out.

"Can you believe that?"

I shrug.

"This magazine is in libraries all over. These women aren't even ashamed, or embarrassed. I'd be so embarrassed."

"Speaking of embarrassment..."

Ellen stops, she looks at me, squinting her eyes as if to burn a hole in my head. "I really can't be bothered, Gilbert."

"You're sixteen. You're underage and you aren't..."

"Yes, Father!"

I look away and speak softly. "I'm not your father. I don't want to be."

"You're trying to be him, though. Don't you scold me! I have one father and if he didn't want to stick around to see me be born, then that's fine! But you can't take his place!" Ellen's face is all red, veins stick out of her throat. "Last night Momma almost died! I found comfort with my *Christian* friends! We drank a little, so what! I hate you. I hate my stupid brother who thinks he's my father! I hate my family!"

I whisper, "Don't for a second think you're alone in that."

"What? What did you say, Daddy!"

"I said, Don't think you're the only one who gets to hate around here!"

This confuses Ellen long enough for me to stand and leave the room.

"Shut my door, please."

I leave it wide open. I pass Arnie, the dirt boy, who waits in the hallway. "Go to it, sport," I say.

Arnie runs into Ellen's room and jumps on her.

"Arnie, stop it! You're getting my bed dirty! Arnie!"

Downstairs, Momma bangs her fists on the table and shouts, "Where are my Cheerios? Where are my Cheerios?!" Amy, in the bathroom, calls back. "In a minute, Momma, in a minute." In the kitchen, I locate the big flowered salad bowl, pour in half a box of her cereal, carry it along with a gallon of milk to the dining room and set it out like a high-class waiter.

"Aw, Gilbert, since when did you start loving your mother?"

"Is that what this is?"

Momma changes the channel, Amy flushes, and Arnie continues terrorizing Ellen upstairs.

I start my truck and see that I need gas. I drive the extra distance to Dave Allen's station because if I had to listen to that bell sound today, I think I'd crack up.

"Hey, Gilbert," he says, a toothpick jutting out of his mouth. Certain people look wise with a toothpick. Dave is one of those people.

"Hey, Dave. Why you so happy?"

"The regional manager was in town yesterday. Checking the books, you know. Assessing the whole operation."

"And what was the assessment?"

"He was pleased."

"Good, Dave, I'm happy for you. I know that regional managers are very important people. Powerful people."

"In their own way, yeah, I guess they are."

My tank is full and I pay the $15.62 in exact change. I start up my truck, he comes up to the window and says, "Gilbert, you haven't let me say what I've got to tell you."

"I'm all ears."

He's about to speak when a car horn honks. It's Melanie's Volkswagen bug. She waves frantically for me to follow.

"Later, Dave," I say, interrupting him.

I set out after Melanie. I follow her out of town, east on Highway 13 and when she turns off at the cemetery, I pull up behind her. I watch from my truck as she puts flowers on Mr. Carver's fresh grave. Melanie's wig seems to have wilted a bit and as her body walks toward my truck, she uses every ounce of energy to keep herself erect. I roll down my window and when she smiles, I see she's been a little sloppy with this morning's lipstick.

"Gilbert. Uhm. I'm not dealing. Well. With this."

I focus on her mirrored sunglasses and try to forget about the streaks of red on her teeth.

"I miss him," she says. Melanie lifts the sunglasses up for a second to wipe the tears. Her eyes are spider-webbed with red and the bags beneath them are swollen and purple. "There is something else you should know. Ken and I were. Lovers."

"No!" I feign surprise.

"Yes, Gilbert. He understood me. He held me. Surely you understand. You must be experiencing your own personal pain. Am I right?"

"I'm doing fine."

"But surely you ache at night, too."

I look puzzled, scrunch my face in that I-don't-know-what-you're-talking-about way.

"I always knew about you and Betty. It somehow made my affair okay. So, now I'm alone. You're alone. Maybe we can be there for each other. You know, during this difficult time. What do you think? Gilbert?"

"What are you saying?"

"Ken is gone. Betty is gone. And I need...and you... maybe...?"

Is she saying what I think she's saying?

I explain to Melanie that she deserves better. "In no way can I be the kind of man Ken Carver was—there is just no way."

"Not true, Gilbert. You're very similar in lots of ways."

Melanie reaches for my hand which I retract from the window. I explain that I'm not ready for a relationship right now. "I need some time."

Melanie nods like she understands, laughs as if she's been there, and then shakes her head like she's remembering 1969. "Of course you need time."

44

Back in Endora, I turn into the Dream without thinking why. Two dirty trucks are parked out front and inside are three real big, greasy construction-worker types. Ellen's working alone. As I saunter up to the take-out window, she turns my way and I can see she's been blushing. Her smile fades as she slides open the window. "How may I help you?"

The men inside talk in whispers to themselves. I recognize them. They are the men who've been working on the Burger Barn. They each hold one of those extra-long beer cans that they sip in unison. These are the kinds of guys who love to have paint and cement and dust on their clothes and in their hair—guys who savor their sandpaper hands. And Ellen is at that age where she's dazzled by anyone who can speak a complete sentence without his voice cracking.

"Sir, how may I help you?" Ellen repeats. She is talking to me like we've never met. "Would you like a chocolate swirl, perhaps? We've got nuts, swirls, sprinkles, banana chips . . ."

I whisper, "I know what you've got."

"Go away," she whispers back.

"No way. You can't trust these guys."

"Do you know them? Don't think so, Gilbert."

"No, nor do I have any desire to."

"Where do you get off?"

The three giants have stopped muttering to each other and look in our direction. Sensing this, Ellen turns and with the sweetest smile ever, she says, "Guys, it'll be just a minute."

They mumble, "Okay, baby," and, "Shit, baby," and, "No hurry, baby, we got all day."

I gulp my throat.

The ugliest of the three, which is an accomplishment, says, "Hey, buddy, you got a hiccup?"

"No, I'm fine, thanks." Then to Ellen, I whisper, "I'm concerned for your safety."

"I got a cure for your customer's hiccup. You send him out back, I'll cure that hiccup right fast."

Ellen says, "I don't think the man has a hiccup." She hands me a Styrofoam cup of water. "Are you ready to order, sir?"

"Hey, Donny," one of them says, "do you get the feeling that these two know each other?"

"Yep, I get that feeling."

"You two know each other?"

Ellen turns and with the sincerest tone says, "No, I've never met this man before."

I've just experienced my first verbal death. The men laugh and wave bye-bye as I walk in a daze to my truck. The heat is great. Endora is a sauna. If I stay in this town, I know I'll melt away.

At home, Amy reiterates, "Friday. Please, Gilbert. Get him clean by Friday."

I'm about to say "Yes" when the phone rings.

"Grape residence, Amy speaking." Amy listens. "Oh my. Oh yes. Of course!" It sounds like Amy has won some telephone jackpot.

When she hangs up, I'm all over her with questions. "What is it? What was that about? What's going on?"

"Lance is anchoring the ten o'clock news tonight."

"No."

"Yes, Gilbert, he is."

So it's dinner and we've received six phone calls since Mrs. Dodge called with the news about her son. I am not eating. I merely sit motionless and massage my stomachache.

As Amy serves the fruit salad, she says, "Phyllis Staples called to say the Church of Christ rented a big-screen TV to watch the news on. I've only seen that kind of TV on game shows. It would be like a movie, watching the news on such a big screen."

Ellen says, "Lance and his mother went to the Church of Christ every Sunday. They're superreligious. They know God and God knows them."

Amy asks, "Arnie, would you enjoy the big picture of a big-screen TV?"

He looks up from his plate, the dirt caked and streaked every-where. He goes, "Jeez, Amy. Jeez."

Amy nods like what he gave was an answer.

Momma, eating in her spot in the living room, chimes in with this thought: "Up until now, Lance has only done 'on the scene' interviews, special reports, and that real interesting feature on the Polk County Crafts Fair. Anchoring, though, is it. It's the Academy Awards of Iowa."

Amy and Ellen stare at each other. Arnie scratches his head with both hands.

Later, as we finish up, Amy reiterates, "It's not every day that we get this opportunity to see a big screen. Anyone interested in joining me?"

Only Arnie looks like he's seriously weighing the options. Certainly Momma won't be going anywhere tonight. And with my aversion to any of the Lord's houses and to Lance, I plan to stay inside. I turn to Ellen and say, "What are your plans, Ellen, dear?"

She sighs and all of a sudden goes, "Life! Nothing is simple, nothing is clear-cut. I've got invitations to Cindy's house, the Hoys', to five different churches, Bobby McBurney's mortuary, and now you're adding the big-screen possibility. I don't know if I can take this anymore. I wish life weren't so complicated, you know. This depresses me to such a point that I can't eat."

"Me, too."

"Shut up, Gilbert."

"No, like you, I've lost my appetite."

"What now—wait—what is going on here, Gilbert? Are you saying that I'm the reason you aren't eating?"

"Yes, something like that."

"Well, I have heard plenty of crap in my day but this—oh my God—this is top-of-the-line crap coming from you. Don't blame me because you hate your life. Don't blame me because you don't have any excitement, all right?"

Ellen continues in this vein until, I guess, she realizes no one is listening. She stops, stabs her fork into her cole slaw, and says something to the effect that no one in our family understands her. I suspect she's right.

I move close to her and laugh in her face.

She goes, "See! See what I mean!"

Amy says, "Enough, you two!"

Momma, who is eating in the living room, calls out the following in garbled tones as her mouth is full of food: "YES! ENOUGH OF THAT! LET'S BE ONE BIG HAPPY FAMILY! IS THAT TOO MUCH TO ASK?" She sputters and spits as she says this.

Ellen looks at Amy and whispers, "Did anyone get what she said? Did anyone get what she just said?"

"Something about being a happy family," I say.

"Oh, sure."

We're polite and civil to each other for the next several minutes. We pass food when asked, say "thank you" and "please" and what keeps me sane is knowing there's only five more days of this.

"Oh," Ellen says, and in an attempt to make up with me, she volunteers to do the dishes.

"What about your rash?" I interject.

"My hands will endure," she says as she starts running the water.

I want to tell her that she's going to have to do dishes for years to make up for all of the cruel pain she's inflicted, but I don't say anything. I smile the it's-okay smile, the kind of smile my family has perfected.

"Sorry about this afternoon, not recognizing you. But, Gilbert, brothers can get in the way with other guys. Having a brother humanizes me. And I didn't want those men to think of me as human."

I almost say "You succeeded." But instead I watch her as her hands get covered with dishwashing suds. She drones on and on, barely scraping the plates, and I pray for the return of her rash. Arnie runs past and he's so embarrassingly dirty now that I almost pick him up and dunk him in the sink. I look around the kitchen and consider my future here. The mess and stench are unbearable. Once upon a time my family had a certain fuzzy charm. Not anymore. Now we're like a boil on the butt of Iowa.

And tonight everyone in town will be rushing to their TV to watch some phoney fool us all–Burger Barn is almost built, the school is burned down–Arnie is soon-to-be eighteen–and I have Lance Dodge to thank for my sudden clarity. My next move is obvious, I will leave this place. I will leave Endora.

"Gilbert, you're smiling all of a sudden," Amy says as she wipes Momma's face with a wet rag.

"Yeah?"

"I haven't seen that smile in soooo long."

"Well..."

Amy wants to know what is going on inside me that would bring forth such a rare expression of joy. She wants to know my thoughts.

I shrug.

"What is it, Gilbert?"

This family is nowhere to be found in my smile, nor the girl from Michigan. My decision to leave, to escape–my new life–is the reason for my toothy grin.

45

I pull out the junk from under my bed. Dirty socks aplenty, old clothes I haven't seen in years, a couple of dusty magazines that specialize in naked women, and my dress shoes, which are brown and need polish. The left shoe somehow got crushed under something down there and it's all bent up, smooshed up. I won't be taking much to wherever I'm going, but it's time to begin to pack.

I hear Amy's tap, and before I say "Come in" I shove the magazines under the bed.

She cracks open my door. "Arnie decided on the big screen."

"But he's so dirty..."

"Still. He wants the big screen."

With the door wide open now, she sees the mess I'm sorting through. She sees the waiting suitcase.

I say, "What about Ellen?"

"I don't know her plans, but I'm pretty certain she'll be somewhere other than home tonight."

"That's good," I say, "because Ellen is . . ."

"I know, Gilbert. I know how you feel."

"Thanks," I say. She shrugs like it's nothing and heads out the room. "Amy?"

She stops.

"There's something you should know."

She turns. "Gilbert, I'm not dumb. I may be a lot of things but I'm not dumb." Before walking away, she looks at the half-filled suitcase and stays fixed on it. "Gilbert," she says. "You'll wait till after the party, won't you? You'll be here for the party."

I look at her. "Yes."

She walks away leaving my door open.

"Amy?"

"Yeah, what?" she calls back.

"Try sprinkling some of Larry's old cologne on Arnie. It'll cover up his smell."

"Yeah, okay."

I resume my sorting and folding. Every time I decide on a shirt or match a pair of socks, the look on Amy's face flashes at me. Part of her died when she saw my suitcase. I want to explain everything to her but I don't know how. I decide to stop packing for the night. I sit for a long while doing nothing. Then I get out my tenth-grade yearbook, which is more like a magazine, and open it to where a torn piece of paper sticks out like a bookmark. I look at my picture. Not bad. Three pictures up is Lance Dodge, before the gym workouts, before the perfect teeth, before the facial hair. I spend a moment amazed that a guy like me could manage to end up on the same page as a man like Lance.

Later I lie on my bed and look at the cracks in the ceiling. Ellen is picked up by some friends. Amy and Arnie get in the Nova and drive off to the Church of Christ.

It's five minutes and something seconds until the news will be on. I'm in my room going through papers, proud that I'm the only one in Endora not watching TV.

Momma calls from downstairs, repeating my name—and, like a dripping faucet, she will persist until I appear.

Now I'm at the TV, adjusting the rabbit ears, twisting the hue and the color, not knowing which button does what, trying to make sure Lance looks green.

Momma goes, "That looks good. That'll be all."

I've been excused. I thank this unknown god of ours by getting myself an Orange Crush from below the kitchen sink and some Highland potato chips. They make Highland potato chips in Des Moines, so I trust them.

From the kitchen, I hear the news start with the announcer saying, "The Ten O'clock Evening News with Lance Dodge!" He lists the others, but I don't hear their names. The news theme music is full of trumpets and typewriter sounds. I sneak a look from the dining room. The camera shows the news desk, which is shaped like a giant 3. Lance sits in the center wearing a blue suit and a red tie with white dots.

The camera cuts up close. His face fills the screen and his hair has that just-got-cut look. He's never looked so confident, so certain of himself before. He spits out the words like he invented them. His eye movements are barely noticeable. You can't even tell he's reading.

I try to imagine the churches filled with people, all the bars and houses, the entire town cheering him on. I feel around my eyes the welling of water, but I cut that concept short. No tears, thank you very much, not even because of Lance Dodge.

At commercial, I get a fresh pack for Momma, unwrap it, offer her a cigarette, and after it settles between her lips, I light it. "I've got a gentleman for a son," Momma says.

Back comes the news and Lance is the entire TV picture.

"Gilbert?" Momma says.

I don't say anything. I sit there, shaking my head probably.

"This isn't such a good time for TV," she says, pushing her

channel changer, turning it off. Sometimes Momma can be merci-ful. "Do you want to talk?"

"Good night, Momma."

"The boy has talent, Gilbert."

"No doubt," I say, climbing the stairs.

"Well, if you ever want to talk . . ."

I go upstairs to my room. I block my door with my red chair and lie on my bed, my clothes still on. The ceiling in my room has these shadows that look like rain clouds.

It takes hours, but finally I fall asleep.

In my sleep I hear this shouting. "Go! Go away!"

Turning on the light to Arnie's room, I find him sitting up, his white sheet wrapped up around his brown, muddy head. His neck and arms are caked with dirt and his face scrunches from the sudden light.

"What, Arnie?"

"Nothin'."

"What is it?"

"Nothin'."

"You having a bad dream?"

"No."

I readjust his pillow, grab a stuffed dinosaur and two bears, and set them near where his head is supposed to be resting. "Sometimes when people sleep little movies happen in their heads."

"Dreams," Arnie says.

"Yes."

"This was a dream. Bad and scary."

"Yep. And you know what, Arnie?" He looks at me, his eye having adjusted to the light. "Don't worry–I won't let anybody hurt you. You know that, right?"

"Yes."

I hug him goodnight.

"Stay. Stay!"

"But . . ."

"Don't leave, Gilbert. Don't leave."

I turn off his light and climb onto the lower bunk, lying on top of the covers. "Arnie?"

"What?"

"Sometimes a person...uhm...a person has got to break loose...get away from..."

"But you stay. Promise? You stay here now. Promise?"

"Okay, Arnie. I'll stay tonight."

"Yep." He giggles.

"Hey, Arnie. What'd you think of Lance Dodge?"

He gets quiet. "Oh boy. What a gee-nus."

"Genius. The word is genius."

"Yep. I know, Gilbert, Jeez, I know."

I wait the twenty minutes or so it takes for Arnie to start banging his head and I slip out of the room. Downstairs, Momma is talking.

"You've got some nerve. That's what I think. What? Arnie is just fine, thank you. Dirty, yes. But he's fine and you got no right...you got no right..."

When I reach the bottom of the stairs, I see that the TV is on casting its blue light, a commercial plays softly, and whoever Momma's talking to must be in the kitchen. I sneak down the hall.

"No...we've done right by Arnie...no agency, no home would have been better...we've hung on...sometimes that's enough...what? I know you're sorry...you should be sorry...."

I look into the kitchen and see Momma at her table, sitting straight, gesturing with her lit cigarette, a bag of chips and a bowl of fruit at her side.

"Momma?" I whisper.

Her head snaps in my direction. Fire is in her eyes.

"You all right?" I say.

She stares into the darkness where I stand.

"Who you talking to?" I ask.

She puts her cigarette in her mouth, closes her eyes in that I'm-about-to-inhale way and says, "Since when do I gotta be talking to someone?"

She's got me there.

"Maybe I was sorting out thoughts, maybe I was thinking out loud."

I move closer, past the mounds of dirty dishes, past the stinking trash under the sink. I hear a fly buzz by in the dark and try to swat it with my hand. "It sounded like you were having a conver-sation," I say, in hopes that this will explain my prying.

"Go to bed."

"But are you all right?"

"Good night."

She hits the volume up high on the TV. I'm at the foot of the stairs when she erupts with, "That Lance Dodge was something else!"

I turn and see her smiling so proud, so in awe of Lance.

"His mother must be so proud! Don't you think, Gilbert? Don't you think?"

I look at her, all fleshy and large. I try to speak, but there are no words.

"Amy said he might be made permanent anchor. There's a good chance! He'd be on every night! What do you think about that? Huh?"

I climb the steps slowly. My mother keeps on talking, and I know that I will go. I will leave here. After Arnie's party. I will get in my truck and drive away.

I wake up early and look around my room. I curl up in my bed, curl up in a ball. It just hit me. I'm leaving Endora with nowhere to go.

46

At breakfast, everyone is bubbling "Lance this" or "Lance that." Arnie tries to use a finger as a butter knife because, in his words, "All the silverware is dirty." This from a boy whose hands look like charcoal. I stand on the porch studying the sky. The dark clouds, the smell of rain.

Amy comes outside and I say, "Look at those clouds."

"You shoulda seen Lance."

"Maybe," I interrupt, "we can lock Arnie out of the house and he'll get washed clean."

"Maybe," she says as I climb in my truck.

"You woulda loved the big screen." Amy stops. She sees the slouch of my body, the blankness in my face. She is about to talk when I turn the key, rev my truck, and shift to reverse. She looks at me as I back away–I see her figure it out.

I drive off.

I drive to ENDora OF THE LINE for a morning six-pack, but when Donna inquires first thing if I saw him and if it wasn't won-derful, I pivot around and walk out without saying a word.

At the store, Mr. Lamson seems in fine spirits and business is brisk, as it looks like rain. The dark clouds have come racing in, but the talk is still all about Lance.

At around noon a big orange-and-blue moving van drives past the store. I stop working and watch as the Carvers' things drive away. Trailing behind is the Carver station wagon, loaded full with sloppily packed boxes. I almost run out to the street and chase her car down.

Mr. Lamson is all smiles, helping the customers the way he always does, as if they were the most important people in the world. He waves to me. "We've got the dairy coming any minute. Straighten the milk up, will you?"

I walk to the blue crates. I start to push the skim milk next to the other skim and separate the whole milk from the low-fat. Something about milk always makes me think of my mother and while that might seem obvious, the thought of my mouth around her nipple, the thought of her feeding me, filling me with her milk is not a comforting thought.

Lance's picture–the one that hangs next to the Wonder Bread clock–stares down at me. I decide that I will steal the picture and leave it, gift-wrapped, in the trash. I've never seen my mother so proud or impressed with anyone as she is with Lance.

The dairy truck arrives. I do my duty and head on out of work back home. The clouds have made the afternoon feel like nightfall; they are black and bruised, soggy.

I'm driving home from work wondering what to do now. My plans don't feel like plans anymore. A quick check of my rear mir-ror and I find Becky waving her arms, pedaling fast, trying to catch up with me. I won't pull over. I put my foot on the gas and speed up. But she is still gaining on me. I realize that she will catch me eventually—she will call when I least expect it—she will materialize at any moment, anywhere. So I pull over. She coasts up to my side of the truck. Rolling down the window, I expect to hear her gasping for air, but she isn't even panting. "You should be..."

"I'm in great shape."

"Oh. It's gonna rain," I say.

"I know. Isn't it great?"

"It's not a good idea to ride your bike in the rain."

"Okay. Whatever you say, Gilbert." She looks at me like she knows something about me that I don't know. She studies my face and says, "You look down."

"Me? No. Never."

"It's Lance. Last night was tough for you, huh?"

"No big deal," I say.

She looks at me. My eyes avoid contact. She giggles. She seems to have enjoyed Lance's spectacle and its effect on me. "You aren't Lance, Gilbert. And thank God you aren't."

I look at my odometer to see how many miles I've driven.

Becky keeps talking. "Anyway, bigger things are in store for you. Things right here. Important and special things right here. Right under your nose."

I'm getting very tired awfully fast of her smugness, of her confident all-knowingness, which I now happen to think is fake.

"Gilbert?"

"Yeah, what?"

"Oooo. Hostile."

"What? What? Please finish, so I can go."

"You can go now."

"Finish."

She moves closer and says softly, "Don't worry—one day you'll leave Endora."

"Who said anything about leaving?"

"Well, it's the natural thing. It's what people do nowadays."

"I'm not people!"

She looks at me, shakes her head, and snaps back, "You are

definitely not people. Trust me. You'll leave when the time is right. But there's something you should know."

I start up my truck. This girl has a new name and it's ass pain.

"Gilbert ... stop ...!"

"What?" I shift to drive but put my foot on the brake. This way I can get away fast. I turn and look at her, my eyes cold. Becky sticks her face through the window, her lips find mine and they are soft and they stay there long.

Kiss.

She sits back on her bike. I squeeze my eyes shut and open. She starts to ride off. I shout "Hey, wait!" She doesn't. I drive after her, honking my horn. Becky is getting away, so I go faster. I get so close that if she were to fall, my truck would run her over. So I slow up a bit. When she rides over the railroad tracks, a drop hits my windshield. Another drop. Many drops. I put on my brakes and watch as she rides away. I touch my lips. She looks back over her shoulder. I sit in my truck, engine running, and let the rain blur my windshield. The drops hit my roof and hood so hard they sound like bullets.

All over the county farmers are dancing and praising God. And somewhere, Lance Dodge is somewhere, and the other Grapes are preparing for their return. Meanwhile, a crazy girl rides away, free, and here on this street, my truck waits on top of the railroad tracks, in the pouring rain, and I sit, the back of my hand pressed against my lips. Oh my.

So I turn on my wipers, they squeak the water away, and I drive home slow, oh so slow, in the rain.

47

The rain pelts me as I make my way from my truck to our front door. I swing it open and find Amy standing there holding a photo. "Hey, Amy."

She extends it and says, "For you."

"What's the occasion?"

She whispers, "It's your going-away present."

I don't know what to say. I look at the picture. It's a man in his early twenties, messy hair, an easy smile. The man wears a red and black flannel shirt and holds a Christmas tree that he's obviously just cut down. The picture is me if I were alive in the fifties. The picture is of my father. "Wow."

"Amazing resemblance. Unbelievable, huh?"

"Yes."

"Gilbert, you're like him in so many ways. Loyal to a fault. Maybe if he had left . . ."

"Amy . . ."

"Maybe if he had got out, he wouldn't have . . . you know. I don't want you to end up like Daddy did."

"But I would never . . ."

"You don't know that. You never know."

There's a silence where I look back at the picture, I study my dad. Finally, I say, "My smile isn't as nice."

"Wanna make a bet?" Then Amy continues, "Hey, Arnie's hiding in the basement. If you could get him out in the rain it would clean him up. Do that for your sister, will you?"

"Arnie?" I call out. "Arnie?" I say his name softly, as if I'm his best friend. "Buddy, I got a surprise for you. Hey, come on out. I'm not gonna make you go outside, okay? Arnie?"

No sign, no sound.

I look in the laundry room, through the mounds of dirty clothes.

"Promise, Gilbert. You promise?"

Turning around, I see Arnie standing among the support boards and beams. His hair is now completely greasy, his face a cloudy gray with dried dirt. This afternoon he's added a kind of brown oil streak across his face that runs below his nostrils and above his top lip. Some jelly clings to his face from yesterday. All this and Arnie still seems happier than ever.

"Where were you hiding?"

He won't tell. "Promise about not going outside?"

"Sure."

He sits down on one of the lower support boards and I say, "I want to show you something."

"Uhm."

I extend the picture. He sees the photo, his mouth opens and he squeals.

"You know who that is, Arnie? Do you know?"

He shakes his head fast.

"Who?"

He points at me. "It's you, Gilbert, jeez."

"No, it's not."

"Yep, sir."

"No. It's your dad."

"Nope."

"It's your dad and he...uhm...if he were here he'd make you get clean. He'd spank you if you didn't get..."

Arnie says, looking at the photo, "You shrunked, you shrunked." I try to take back the picture but Arnie hugs it to his filthy chest and runs out and up the stairs.

In the family room, Amy is setting out the party decorations, party hats, paper plates, and plastic forks and spoons even though the party is three days away.

"Amy," I say. "I tried."

"You've got to get him clean. By Sunday!"

"Okay, okay."

"You have to do it."

"I hope I can. But I don't know if..."

"Tie him down if you have to. You have to get him clean."

"Amy?"

"Yes, what, Gilbert? What, what, what?"

I want to tell her about how I hate being told I'm like my father and how it's not my fault I look like him and that I don't know what will happen but, if I stay here, stay in Endora, I don't know what I might do, even though I've no real idea of where to go and then this afternoon, to top it all off, the Michigan girl kissed me–kissed me–and quite simply I DON'T KNOW WHAT TO DO

WOW

251

and while I'm searching for the best way to express this, she asks,
"What is it?"

"Forget it."

"No, what?"

"Uhm. Uh. I love you."

Amy drops the bag of forks and says, "You don't know how
much I needed to hear that." She hugs me, her flabby arms soft
against my back, her eyes closed while mine look around, look
around at the stacks of party supplies. Amy holds me like a
lover while I pat her shoulder with one hand. The rain pounds
down, the drops bounce off the ground. Maybe later there will
be lightning.

All afternoon we prepared for the party and now we're sitting
around the living room eating frozen pizza. When the six o'clock
news comes on, I stand and go outside to my truck.

I drive in the rain to ENDora OF THE LINE.

"Donna, don't ask questions, okay?"

"Sure, Gilbert," she says, putting out a Marlboro.

"Condoms. I need them. And don't judge me. Don't look at me
all funny."

Donna giggles and rings up a small box of three. The box is blue.
I pay in exact change.

"I want to ask 'Who's the lucky girl?' "

"You can ask but . . ."

"But you won't tell me?"

"That's right. See ya, Donna."

"Everybody knows who it is, Gilbert."

I am gone.

The rain pounds my windshield so I can barely see. I drive up
slow to the old Lally place. Becky is standing in the yard, drenched.
She comes toward me. I check my pants and the condom I took out
of the box is waiting in a front pocket. The other two wait in the
glove compartment.

"Hi," she says.

I roll the window down a crack. "Get in."

"It's great out here."

"You're all wet. Come on, get in."

Becky walks around in front of my truck and opens the passenger door, she climbs in. Her T-shirt is wet and her nipples stick out and it's all I can do to keep my hands on the steering wheel. She sees me look at her chest. Most girls would get embarrassed, most girls would fold their arms. But Becky sits motionless, stares at me and says, "Insides. Count."

We sit and listen to the rain.

Then I say, "I was down, really down, earlier today. Looking for a reason to go on. You ... uhm ... you caught me off guard."

"When?"

"When you ... uhm ... kissed me."

"Oh."

"I'd given up on ..."

"On what?"

"On anything physical."

I giggle and she stares at me. I look at her like "May we pick up where we left off?" but she looks away.

"Let's go somewhere," she says.

Yes. Yes yes yes yes yes.

I'm driving out of town toward the cemetery.

"Gilbert ..."

"Yeah?"

"Don't try anything, okay?"

"What do you mean?"

"The kiss was to give you hope. Nothing more."

My driving slows. "What are you saying?"

"You were looking down, nothing was going your way. You look sweet when you have feelings. I couldn't resist."

"Oh, come on—what are you saying?"

"There'll be no more kissing. Not for the time being."

I look at her like "WHAT?"

"You're too cut off from yourself. Right now you are. When you're vulnerable, you're kissable. But now ..."

"Me? No way. I am many things, but I am not cut off."

"You're out of touch, out of sync. You don't like yourself. You don't even see yourself."

I've got a condom in my pocket, I think to myself. All I need to see is her naked body. "One kiss."

"No."

"A little peck?"

"No. No no no."

"Come on."

"No, if you are so eager to run away from yourself—imagine how quick you'll run away from me."

"Fine. Okay. Yeah, whatever."

I drop her off. She's a tease. Becky is a total tease.

"Maybe one day we'll hold hands, maybe."

She shuts the door and goes in to her grandma. I sit in my truck screaming unrepeatable things. I wipe my mouth on my shirt, rubbing hard, rubbing away the memory of her lips. "BITCH!" I scream.

It's night now and I'm in bed naked. I'm angry and lonely, and if an erection can be profound, mine is. I do the obvious.

Outside the rain has slowed, the ground and streets have been washed clean. I hear Momma downstairs, screaming with Amy about when Arnie will take a bath. Sleep comes quick, as it's the only decent option.

In the morning, Arnie, the human alarm clock, arrives outside my door. He chants, "Burger Barn, Burger Barn."

"Shit," I say to myself, jumping out of bed fast. I overslept.

Outside there must be two hundred people, all shapes and sizes and I know every one of them. Arnie and me watch from my truck. Tucker's dad walks around with a video camera filming the festivities. Tucker is standing among the many new employees, wearing his Burger Barn hat. He's a good head taller than the average worker.

Speeches are made. The air is full of that burger and french-fry smell. Sniffing with his nose, Arnie rubs his tummy and I say, "Arnie, please."

"I want to eat! I want to eat!"

"You're not getting out of this truck."

"But I want . . ."

"You're too dirty."

"Yep!" Arnie couldn't be more proud. "Yum, yum."

He starts to get out of the truck. I grab his arm, holding him inside. "No, Arnie, you stay put."

He pouts.

The crowd applauds and while Mayor Gaps cuts the ribbon, the Motley High Jazz Band plays "We've Only Just Begun."

The ceremony ends and Tucker hugs his parents. A photographer from the *Endora Express* is taking pictures. People crowd inside to get the first taste. Looking out the back of my truck, I can see that there must be forty cars in the Food Land parking lot. Business is booming.

"I want food. I want food!"

I start up the engine, say "Arnie, not today," and begin to pull out when I get a great idea. I turn to him and negotiate a deal. I tell him that if he'll submit to a good scrubbing, if he gets extra-clean, I'll being him back to the Burger Barn for a meal.

"When when when?"

"As soon as you've dried off. I'll bring you here and you can order what you want."

He says, "Okay."

"It's time for that bath."

He nods his head. "Okay."

"Afraid so, buddy."

"Okay! I SAID OKAY!"

I'm so used to him refusing that I haven't heard him agree to my terms. "This won't be a moment too soon, Arnie. You want to get clean, don't you?"

"Yes!"

At home, Momma's guessing the answers of a game show and Amy is taking the cake layers out of the oven. I give her the thumbs up. She looks at me, puzzled, so I mouth "You'll see" and point at Arnie. Then I take him by the hand and we climb the stairs. I pour in the bubble bath, dump in his plastic toys. "Let's go for a swim, buddy."

"You get in too."

"What?"

"Get in too, Gilbert!"

I haven't taken a bath with my brother in years. Not since pubic hair. But I'll do anything at this point, anything to get him clean.

As I'm stripping, the dirt ball is pointing at my privates, screaming his shrill giggle. "Arnie, shhh. Please." He finds this extremely funny. I get in, sitting down slowly in the scalding hot water, and smile at him once I'm comfortable. "Okay, Arnie, dive in. Burger Barn here we..."

He turns and runs out of the bathroom. He thumps down the stairs and the screen door slaps shut.

Still in the tub, bubbles all around, I shout, "I did not make this mess! I did not make this mess!"

48

I get into the water with him..."

"Yes?"

"And he outsmarted me."

"You have two days. The party is in two days."

"I know."

I'm air drying in the kitchen with Amy, who is busy with this year's birthday cake, which will be a three-layered affair. Momma turned the TV to one of those morning talk shows. Today's topic is adoption and she immediately fell asleep. Ellen has gone to Motley with her lip-gloss girlfriends, where she's supposed to be buying Arnie a new birthday outfit.

"I have a list of groceries, Gilbert."

"Okay."

"You get them today?"

"Sure."

"Janice called. She's coming in tomorrow night. She said for me to break this to you gently. She'll be renting a car and won't need you to pick her up. She wondered if you'd be upset."

"What do you think?"

"She's going to drive straight to the beauty parlor."

"Beauty parlor?"

"Momma wants to go to the Endora's Gorgeous, what do you think about that?"

I want to say, "It's going to take several weeks to resurrect Momma's face," but instead I go, in a less than enthusiastic way, "Great." *interesting*

"I think so, too."

"Better make an appointment."

"Gilbert, please. I spoke to Charlie."

Charlie is the owner of Endora's Gorgeous and chief beautician. Charlie has arms the thickness of my fingers. Charlie is a woman.

"Yeah?"

"And get this. She's staying after work tomorrow to accommodate us. Momma's appointment is at six. Charlie said she'll stay as long as it takes."

"I hope she's got all night."

"Gilbert."

"All night and the entire next day."

"Shush."

"Anyway, Momma's going out will be the talk of . . ."

Amy goes on to explain that Charlie is going to put sheets in front of her windows so no one can look in. Amy plans to drive rarely traveled back roads to the parlor, and Momma will enter from the back door. Detail upon detail has been worked out so that Momma won't be seen.

I want to tell Amy that we've got to be realistic about such things, no way is Momma going to benefit by time spent in a beauty parlor, but instead I say, "The cake is huge."

"Yes, it is. Today is layer day. Tomorrow I frost. Gilbert, I think it could be my best ever."

"No doubt."

Amy does many things right, but one thing is not the baking of birthday cakes. Each year they come out uneven. Often they're littered with random hairs and bits of eggshell. The harder she tries, the worse they seem to look and taste. In an effort to improve, she started on Arnie's cake two days early.

I ask, "How many retards are coming to the party?"

"Gilbert."

"Well..."

"Six of Arnie's friends have confirmed. Still need to hear from two others."

Amy speaks as if this is a party at the White House. When she says "friends have confirmed," she means that someone confirmed for these kids, many of whom are not kids at all, and all of whom have no phone dialing capabilities. They range in age from six to thirty-five. Arnie is the third-oldest–the biggest–the sloppiest.

"I want you to supervise the party games on Friday. Will you do that for me? Think up some activities that can revolve around the trampoline."

"Of course," I say. "Whatever you want me to do."

I'm holding the cake pan. Amy takes a knife and loosens the sides, when the screen door swings open.

"You back already? Ellen?" Amy calls out.

There is no answer. The door closes.

"Must be the wind," I say.

Setting each layer out on the counter, Amy is about to stack them, when a shorter, stockier, balder, blander version of me walks into the kitchen. Amy grabs my elbow and we watch as he finds the peanut butter, the jelly, the bread and begins to make a sandwich. We stand there waiting for him to say, "Hello." Say something, anything. He cuts the bread at a diagonal into two triangles. He looks up at us and without blinking, without acknowledging that he's been away a year with no phone call, only his monthly checks, he says, "Oh, hey–you want one, too?"

Amy can barely talk. "You know how I hate peanut butter. You know that."

As he crosses out to the porch, he mumbles, "They say that taste buds change every twenty-one days. It's like we get a whole new set of taste buds."

The screen door crinks shut and Amy doesn't know where to move or what to think. She says, "The nerve."

"Yes," I say.

Momma kicks into a snore from the living room and Amy starts pinching the top cake layer. She wasn't prepared for our other brother.

"Don't you want to frost it first?" I say.

Amy stops. "Yes, of course." At this point, Momma's snore surges to a new decibel.

The screen door opens and he shouts, "Momma! Momma!" The snoring stops. "Momma, you're snoring."

"Am I? Was I?"

"You were, yes."

"I'm sorry."

The screendoor slams as he goes back to the porch and his peanut butter and jelly. Momma says, "It's not that I'm making a choice to snore. The snoring just happens. It's not that I like that I do this, Gilbert."

From the porch, in a loving, dulcet tone, he says, "I'm not Gilbert. I'm Larry."

"No, you're not. You can't fool me. The son of mine who you refer to only comes back on my little boy's day."

"I know. That's why I'm back today."

Momma says, "But Sunday is his birthday and, Amy, what is today?"

"Friday, Momma."

"Yes, so you see, Gilbert? You can't fool your Momma."

There is a silence that seems like forever, but it's probably only been three or four seconds. The screen door opens yet again, Larry's boots smack the floor and move toward Amy and me.

Flustered, his bald spot casting blotches of light on the kitchen ceiling, he asks, "Today isn't his birthday?"

Amy shakes her head no.

Larry looks at me for confirmation. "This is some joke, isn't it?"

You're the joke, I want to say.

"You're early by two days," Amy says.

He smiles but not because he's happy.

"It's real good to see you, Larry," she says. "You look good."

I say nothing to him, proud that I don't say what I don't mean. But when he looks over at me, I smile, even though later my lips will feel guilty.

Larry looks at his feet, laughs like the joke was on us and strolls out of the house. Chasing after him, Amy says "But we could use some help around the house..." but before she can say "...painting the picnic table..." the screen door slams. Larry climbs into his new car and drives off.

The screen door at our house is a kind of living punctuation mark.

Amy whoops up her arms and says, "Same old Larry."

"I'll paint the picnic table."

She utters a firm "no" and tells me not to worry about it. "Put all your energies to getting Arnie clean. Where is he, anyway?"

I shrug.

She pats my shoulder in that everything-will-be-all-right way and says, "You think you might look around for him later?"

I say, "Yes, later. I'll track him down later."

She slowly turns the cake, pushing down any of it that she pulled up. "Makes me feel like I can sit down and rest. What with being ahead of schedule and all."

"Quite a cake."

"Yes, Gilbert. This cake is divine."

We go on as if our brother Larry didn't exist.

Minutes later, the phone rings. Amy answers.

"Yes... uh-huh... I know... we know... we're working on the situation, Larry...."

Larry on the other end? Larry dialed our number?

"...I know it's disgusting...but Arnie is almost an adult"— Amy's face is turning red—"well, if you gave a good goddamn maybe you'd be around here more often, maybe you'd be around here to help!" She slams the phone down.

"You okay?" I say.

"He's driving out of town, right? And he sees Arnie digging for worms. Arnie runs over to him to give him the worms, and he said he couldn't even recognize him under all that dirt. The nerve–the *nerve* of that man." Amy goes out in our backyard. She pounds the picnic table with her fists and screams, "Fuck you! Fuck you!"

I've never been so happy to hear anyone swear.

49

So he was two days early?"

"Yep."

"Well, he's probably been under the gun at work. Pressure, you know."

"Where does he work?"

"How do I know? I'm just Janice."

"You seem to know more about him than anybody."

"Larry keeps those things to himself. I know more about him because I'm trained to understand people."

I don't respond to that. I move the phone to my other ear.

"So why aren't you at work, Gilbert? Huh? Why aren't you at work?"

"This week I'm only putting in half days."

"That's great, Gilbert."

My sister Janice is talking fake. She could care less when I work. She's been calling every day lately. She's already asked me a bunch of inane questions and heard none of my answers. "So how's the weather there?"

"It rained."

"I loathe rain. Rain is so inconvenient."

How can rain be inconvenient when the crops and trees and fields have needed it so?

"It better not rain on Arnie's birthday. We deserve nice weather that day. Don't you think?"

"Sure, whatever."

Janice launches into a verbal essay on the clothes she plans to wear. I set the phone down, walk to the fridge, pour some ice water, drink it, pour some more, return to the phone. "... So what do you think about that?"

"Uhm. Yes."

" 'Yes'? Yes is all you can say?!"

"Well ... yeah ... *yes* is the best word."

"Get me Amy! You're deliberately hurting me!"

"No. I meant 'no.' Really."

She listens. "I can't believe you said 'Yes.' You're so insensitive, little brother. *I'm so looking forward to seeing you.*" Then she's silent. I hear her inhale on a cigarette. "Did you just hear the sarcasm in my voice?"

"Yes."

"Because, Gilbert, you could drive to South Dakota and I'd never know you were gone."

I drop the phone on the floor. I hear her faint voice, yelling, "I WAS ONLY KIDDING." The phone hangs by its cord. The receiver spins itself out.

At four o'clock in the afternoon, I hook up our sprinkler. Wearing Hawaiian shorts, I stand under it and pretend to play in it. Arnie watches from behind the sycamore tree. "Having lots of fun," I say.

Arnie doesn't budge.

"You really must try this, ol' boy."

He shakes his head.

My demonstration of water games reminds me of my time at the Carvers' with the trampoline. Mrs. Carver has only been gone two days. Every time the phone rings, I'm hopeful it's her calling to announce a change of plans, her offer to let me live in St. Louis. But who am I fooling with this fantasy? She won't be calling.

Ellen is dropped off by her friends, who laugh and scoff at the dripping me. She gets out of Cindy Mansfield's mom's blue station wagon. The girls shout "Praise God" to Ellen, who throws her hair back in agreement. They drive off, honking and waving. Ellen looks past me and says, "Arnie, wait till you see what I got you." She marches into the house. The retard follows.

You forget that my paycheck bought those clothes, I almost say, as the sprinkler sends rain down on me.

"Gilbert? I've missed you this week," Mr. Lamson says this as he loads me up with the groceries.

"Yes, sir."

"My days aren't as happy when you're not around."

"I have mutual feelings."

This is the truth. Lamson Grocery, and I didn't know this until this week, is my one escape, my desert oasis.

"Mr. Lamson?"

"Yes, son."

"Working here is like walking on the moon."

He looks at me. He stops, then breathes, then mashes his lips as his eyes mist. "Oh, Gilbert, what a nice thing to say." He lifts up a huge tub of peanut butter. He hands the tub to me. "For Arnie."

"Oh, boss, you shouldn't have."

aww so sweet

I leave work, weighed down by the peanut butter, only to find Becky sitting on the hood of my truck. She smiles, her head tilts like a puppy dog's. I set the grocery sacks in back and say, "Off my truck."

"No."

"Get off. Off."

"No."

"This is my truck. I paid for it. It's mine. Get off the hood."

"No."

"Goddammit–get off my hood–get off my back–get off my hood!"

Becky shakes her head. She slides off and starts home.

"And stay off," I say. "Stay off my hood."

She turns my way but keeps walking. "It's not that I don't want to kiss you. I do. But..."

"But what?"

"If you could see yourself, see the hate in your eyes. If you could see the . . ."

I cover my ears. She is gone. I go, "Aaaaaaahhhhhhhhhhh!"

I drive to the car wash and spray down the hood. Normally I'd wash the whole vehicle, but my family's food is packed in back.

When I get home, Amy and Ellen are in back. Arnie is nowhere to be seen. I unload the groceries with no help from the others. In the house, I find Momma awake, talking to herself, "I just want to see my boy turn eighteen. . . ."

"We know, Momma."

"Was I talking to you?"

"I gathered you were. As I'm the only one here."

"Gilbert?"

"Yes?" I stand in front of her, studying her as if she were an animal in a zoo—her hair in clumps, her skin bleached out. The absence of blood.

"You think when I'm talking that I'm always talking to you? Is that what you think?"

"No. It's just that I'm the only . . ."

"Your father."

"Huh?"

"I was talking to your father. I do that sometimes. I'm still so mad at him. So mad that I want to kill the man. But, as you know . . ."

"Yes, I know."

"He did that for himself." She leans forward, putting her stone elbows on the shaky table. "And you know what your dad says to me when I talk to him? Do you know what . . . ?"

"Sorry," I interrupt. "I'm sorry that . . ."

"Yes. He says he's sorry."

Momma sits for a moment. Her swollen hands cover her face and I say, "Oh, Momma," and she utters all these words that I can't make out because of her crying.

Finally, she gets enough composure to spit out her thoughts, a word at a time. "Sorry. Doesn't. Bring. Albert. Back. It doesn't. Erase. What we've become."

Those words sit in the air for quite a long time before I find the courage to ask, "What do you mean?"

"I mean that my kids all want to kill each other, I mean that my house is caving in. Have you noticed this floor? I'm shoving this house down the drain."

"No, you aren't."

"Look at the floor. Look at the curve."

"Momma, you aren't ..."

"Don't say what I want to hear. Look at me, Gilbert. Tell me the truth. Tell me."

I want to forget all words, I wish I were a two-year-old.

"Say this—'Bonnie Watts Grape'—repeat after me, Gilbert."

I don't.

"You will repeat after me, young man!"

"Okay, okay."

" 'Bonnie Watts Grape ...' "

I say dutifully, " 'Bonnie Watts Grape ...' "

" 'Is my mother ...' "

" 'Is my mother ...' "

" 'And I hate her.' "

I stop the repetition.

"Repeat after me—I hate my mother."

I start out of the house.

"Gilbert? Gilbert!"

"Okay," I say. I look at her, glaring her way. "I hate you. Deeply. Completely. I. Hate. You."

Momma's eyes seem to swell. She looks at me hard and long. She thought she was going to enjoy my hate, but it has broken her. I can't watch, so I barrel out of the house.

It takes three hours of driving on county roads, two cans of beer and a pack of cigarettes for me to try and forget that conversation. I fail.

50

It's the next morning, the day before the big day, and Momma is ignoring me. I won't apologize for last night, though. I gave her what she wanted. She'll have to deal with it on her own for a while.

Yes, Arnie's still a dirt ball.

Amy is touching up the frosting on his cake. It is white with white frosting. The retard likes lots of icing, so she's used up two cans of it. Momma has a game show on and she wants to win, so she calls Amy into the living room.

I study the cake as each guess they make turns out wrong. "Happy 18th birthday, Arnie!" is written in green block capitals. Only the candles wait to be put in their place.

Amy returns to the kitchen, shaking her head. "Some day Momma and me are gonna win something."

"Well," I say, "this cake is a winner."

She looks at it with a critical squint. "You think?"

"It's your best. It is the most complete cake you've ever–what's the word?–sculpted."

"Gilbert..."

"It's almost a crime to eat it, you know. Almost a crime to cut it into slices."

"But..."

"Yes, we must, though. We must serve the cake to whoever wants it. Arnie's retard friends, Janice, even Ellen."

I pat Amy on her sweaty back.

Minutes pass.

The cake is close to perfection. Arnie runs into the house with a jar full of baby grasshoppers. Wanting to keep the cake a secret, Amy gives me that "get rid of Arnie" look. I quickly block the hall and say, "Hey, buddy..."

"What?" he says. "What, what, what?"

"Hide 'n' seek, what do you say?"

"No."

"Come on..."

Sensing the impossibility of the kitchen, Arnie tries to crawl under my legs. I catch his head in between my knees and squeeze, trapping him.

"Gilbert, Gilbert..."

Momma hears the struggle and certain that I'm in the wrong, she starts shouting, "Gilbert, Gilbert," and before I know it, Amy is behind me, her body quivering. She, too, speaks my family's favorite word. "Gilbert."

Arnie is still squirming between my legs when I turn to Amy. He bites into my thigh. I lift him by his ankles. The grasshopper jar falls and rolls toward the front door. I set Arnie loose. He dives for the jar and looks up at me. I point and say, "Outside. Arnie. Outside!" Momma is screaming now, "I JUST WANT TO SEE MY BOY TURN EIGHTEEN! IS THAT TOO MUCH TO ASK?" He runs outside with his grasshoppers, and Momma stops her noise making long enough to light a cigarette. Amy waves me back to the kitchen. I hold up a finger as if to say "one minute" and look out our front door. Arnie stands in the middle of the yard, ramming his head into the trunk of our sycamore tree. Turning, I head to Amy when Momma asks, "How is my boy?"

"I'm fine," I say.

"Arnie. How is ARNIE?"

"He's fine."

"What's he doing?"

"Adjusting, Momma." I check on him once more and see that he's moved to the mailbox. He puts a grasshopper in its place and brings down the metal flag fast, snipping off the head. Arnie's adjusting.

In the kitchen I find Amy on her knees. In front of her, like the baby Jesus, is the cake, splat on the floor. The frosting has squished out on all sides.

"I barely bumped it. It just slid off and fell. In slow motion, it fell. And I couldn't get to it... and... and... what am I gonna do?"

I say things meant to help: "It'll work out." "Everything will be okay," etc. But it makes matters worse. I'm about to suggest making another cake, when Amy says, "I can't do better than this."

She's right. She can't do better.
I ask, "So what do you want to do?"

Let me say this—my big sister dug deep inside herself, gained the needed composure, and dialed Food Land. She spoke steady and clear. I cringed as she ordered. When she hung up, she said, "Be sure to see Jean in the bakery section. It'll be ready for pickup at seven o'clock."
"Me?"
"I'd do it, but we'll be with Momma at the beauty parlor."
"But . . ."
"Thank you, Gilbert."

I've been standing here—in the kitchen—motionless—for the last five minutes. I've watched as Amy took a washcloth and wiped up the last of the frosting on the kitchen floor.
This is not the time to protest, I decide, swallowing the gallon of spit that has filled my mouth.
Amy says, "I know how you feel about Food Land."
I don't think she does.
"It's sweet of you to do this." She kisses me on the cheek, just as Judas did to Jesus. "Really sweet."

51

I'm on my way to Hell.
Driving across town, I see Dave Allen's station in the distance. I could use some gas. As I approach, Dave is shouting something, trying to flag me down. I reach down to turn off the radio when I hear "bing-bing" or "ding-ding" or "ringa-dinga." I slam on my brakes. Dave has his arms almost up in the air, as if to surrender. I back the truck up slowly because this can't be. Bing-bing. Ding-ding.
"Dave! What the hell . . . ?"

"I tried to tell you last time you were here. The regional manager..."

I spin my tires fast, squeal out, covering my ears as the truck shoots over the cord.

The giant letters are glowing their fluorescent bright red. Each letter must be three times the size of me. As my dirty shoes hit the floor mat, the electric doors swing open and I enter. For the first time I feel the power a foot can command at Food Land. I'm inside, and the brightness of the lights and the glare from the shiny floor overwhelm. My eyes move around like a kid's on Christmas Day. For a moment, I forget about my family, my mammoth mother, my life, and I see not two, not six, but twelve cash registers. The workers wear red-white-and-blue uniforms. They flash toothy smiles. Music pours out from a sound system. The people in the store, the countless people, blur into a dream as I walk down Aisle One. I see more than fifteen types of bread, loaves of date-nut and walnut. Aisle Two is the canned items, and everything imaginable is there, in abundance, stocked in sequence, each can clearly marked. I see workers everywhere. People grabbing food, sacking fresh vegetables, weighing peaches on shiny scales.

I remember why I'm here and I go off to find the Bakery section.

"Yeah, I'm here to pick up a cake for Grape," I say, looking around for Jean, the cake lady.

A guy with curly brown hair turns, his face all sweaty, his fingers covered in flour. His name tag reads "Jean." He says, "The Grape cake?"

"Yeah. Grape. Arnie Grape. He's turning eighteen."

Jean the cake baker breathes deep. His eyes veer as he tries to remember.

"Surely there aren't *that many* cakes...."

Jean's eyes dart to mine, his head starts to quiver. "Excuse me?" This Jean speaks with a lisp. He has a girl's name. Go figure. "Don't think for a moment you're the only cake in this county!"

He opens the big silver refrigerator in such a way that it is difficult for me to see inside. But I stretch to my left and see, in a flash, that there is only one box inside and that the rest of the fridge is empty, spit-shine clean.

But Jean takes an eternity checking all the shelves, looking here, looking there. He doesn't know that I know what I know. Finally he brings out the cake, saying, "Oh, here it is." He lifts the box lid for me to inspect.

"Fine," I say, approving the white cake, with white frosting, green lettering, "but you forgot the candles."

"Oh my," Jean says, covering his mouth.

"Eighteen candles, Jean, okay? Like my sister ordered."

"Yes, sir. Right away. Will take just a second."

Rather than watch this sorry baker arrange the candles, I wander up and down Food Land. Aisle Seven has children's toys. Aisle Eight has baby diapers and Tupperware galore. Aisle Nine is juices and Hi-C and frozen TV dinners. Rounding Aisle Ten, I see two eyes, surprised eyes.

"Gilbert."

"Hi."

Mr. Lamson is standing *in Food Land* in front of me.

We say nothing. There is nothing to say. We just stand there for a time, not looking at each other but not knowing where to look.

"Sir, I uhm . . . Arnie's cake uhm . . . you see . . ."

Mr. Lamson holds up his hand for me to be silent. So I stop my talking. He bites his lower lip, then rolls it out like an ocean wave into a beaming smile. "Have you seen the lobsters?"

"No, sir."

"Be sure to see the lobsters. My God, what a sight. And the cereal selection. It's . . . well, I've never seen one quite like it . . . and frozen orange juice for less than a dollar . . . all of their prices . . . all of their prices, Gilbert . . . many good bargains here . . . and . . ."

I try once again to explain about the cake. Mr. Lamson looks around and says, "No need to explain, son. We've been whooped."

He pushes his empty cart down Aisle Ten. I watch him look from side to side, floating along slowly, studying product after product. His simple flannel shirt, his noble brown shoes move away from me, reducing Mr. Lamson in size but not in stature.

"Wonderful surprises" echoes in my head.

I count the green and white candles. Jean turns the cake so I can see it from every angle, but it makes me lose track. "Fine," I say. "Just fine."

"Is that all you can say? Is that all you can muster up?" Jean is starting to huff now; his top lip is beginning to drip sweat. One drop hits the cake box, causing the white paper to puff out.

I gesture for him to close up the box. Jean doesn't. "This cake, if you'll excuse my saying so, *deserves* much more than a *fine*. This cake is *good*."

I pull out the twenty dollars Amy gave me. The cake was quoted at $14.50, and in an effort to exit quick, I say, "Keep the change."

Jean closes the box, tapes it, inserts it into two sacks for safe-keeping, and smiles smiles smiles.

I walk away slowly.

"Have a nice day!"

As I approach the electric doors, the sound system plays a dentistlike version of "Let It Be." And I try. But the image of Mr. Lamson flashes in me. The image of him and me being here at the same time—staring at each other—knowing that we've both bowed down and stuck our tongues up the asshole of America.

I disappear from Food Land.

A note at home leaves dinner instructions for Arnie and me. I put the cake in the space Amy made in the refrigerator. I don't unwrap it. Arnie keeps saying over and over, "What is it? What is it?" and I say, "It's a surprise." I make the grilled-cheese sandwiches and pour the kid his chocolate milk.

As he eats, a ring of yellow-orange cheese forms around his mouth. This is in addition to the oil stains, jellies, chunky peanut butter, bits of potato chips and cheese puffs, various flavors of Kool-Aid, ketchup, and mustard. He has become his own abstract painting.

Arnie and I are watching TV. The ladies loaded Momma into the Nova at about 5:30 P.M. No one saw, because they pulled Amy's car into the garage. They got to Endora's Gorgeous by six. It's about eight-thirty now and they still aren't home. The house is different with Momma out of it. The house seems relieved.

The phone rings. I make my way to the kitchen and answer.

"Gilbert, you get the cake? Did you?"

"Yes, Amy."

"How does it look? Not as good as mine, but it looks . . . ?"

"Great. It looks mighty nice."

"Arnie. How is Arnie?"

"Watching TV, Amy. Arnie is superb. *Arnie* is doing great."

"You won't believe it, what Charlie is doing here. First of all she is giving Momma the works. The whole works. A mud facial, a new hairstyle, easy-to-apply makeup. Janice and Ellen are watching real close. It's like a real lesson in beauty happening here. . . ."

I'm looking around the kitchen at the failed attempt at order. The greasy counters, the yellowing floor. Beauty? Arnie is changing the channels fast in the living room. I could tell Amy about Mr. Lamson at Food Land and Dave Allen, too. I've got to tell her these things. I want her to know about the day I'm having, how hard it is for me to keep hanging in there. But Amy's voice has a rhythm, a spunk to it, and I haven't the heart to interrupt.

Before hanging up, she sings, "If you get Arnie clean, I'll love you forever."

"Jesus, Amy. Don't sing."

"Get him clean."

"Okay. Just don't sing."

I hang up.

"Gilbert, what's the fridge thing? What's that thing?"

"A surprise for Arnie is what it is."

"Oh."

Arnie is sitting in Momma's chair. He has put a cigarette in his mouth backward and he pretends to smoke.

"That's not good for you."

"What?"

"Smoking. Smoking is not good for you."

"You do it."

"Yeah, and look where it's got me, huh?"

"Yeah."

I turn off the TV. There is nothing on worth watching. Since Lance's triumph, the TV and I have not been the same.

"Gilbert."

"What, Arnie?"

"You're shrinking, right?"

"That's right."

Arnie wiggles his toes and says, "Gilbert's shrinking," five times fast.

52

L ater, there's a knock on the door.

"Hello?" I say from behind the screen. "Helloooo?" I turn on the porch light. A soft breeze blows a certain perfumy smell. "You can come out."

She steps out from behind the evergreen bush.

"Yeah," I say. "What is it?" The skeptic, the I'm-over-you quality to my voice is ignored by the Michigan girl. She gestures for me to come outside.

"No way."

"Come here. I've got something for you."

"Bull."

"Come see."

Becky is getting hit with this light from inside our house, which casts shadows that make her look angelic. She waves her soft hand again and I drift out and stand on my porch. "I've got a present for you," she says.

My eyes look around to Arnie's bush, to the sycamore tree, to the evergreens in front. "I don't see anything."

"Wait," she says, disappearing behind the house.

So I stand on the porch, waiting. I'm Gilbert Grape. I'm twenty-four years old. My life is not moving in a respectable direction. This proves it.

"Close your eyes," she calls out.

"No way. No fucking way."

"It'll only take a second. Please, Gilbert."

I shut my eyes for no real reason. "They're closed," I say.

I hear the sound of feet moving, a stick breaks, as if something is moving close to me and I get a chill.

"I'm gonna look," I say.

"Not yet."

I feel this warm rush of energy, this heat around my body. She must be close to me. I whisper, "What are you doing?"

I feel her hand on my forehead. She touches my temples and lightly moves down my arms. I feel this warmth whoosh through me, this warm heat, pulsing.

"What are you doing to me?"

I'm waiting for an answer when Becky says, "Open your eyes now."

At first it's blurry. Then I see a face inches from me. The little whiskers, the early wrinkles. The face looks scared. I half smile nervously, the face half smiles. Looking to the periphery I see that Becky is holding a big, round mirror, and the face I'm looking at is my face.

"See. See what I mean. See the hate."

I'm about to say "No, I don't" when Arnie shouts, "Gilbert, Gilbert!"

I move my head to see him in the mirror. He's standing in the doorway behind me. There's frosting all over his chin, up around his nose.

I punch at the mirror with the palm of my hand. I hit hard. Becky steps back and it drops to the ground. I jump on it but there's no break. Not even a crack. Arnie is giggling and Becky is saying my name over and over. Instead of saying "Shut up" or slapping her silly, I find one of Arnie's big rocks on the side of the house. I struggle to get it above my head—I let it drop, and still the mirror won't break.

"You don't fix things by destroying them."

I look at that girl and murder her with my eyes.

"There's a better way. Find the better way."

Arnie says, "Gilbert's getting weaker, getting weaker and weaker...." I turn to him and point firmly. "Shut up! Go inside!"

Arnie shakes his head no, then licks the palm of his hand where he's been hiding a helping of frosting. "That does it," I say, opening the screen door, then slamming it, locking the metal latch.

Becky says, before I close the front door, "Gilbert. Love Gilbert."

I shut and lock the wood door, grab Arnie by the wrist, and inspect his hand. Traces of frosting remain. I drag him toward the kitchen.

"Owww. Owww."

In the fridge, the cake, which Arnie tried to rewrap but failed, sits with the memory of a retarded boy's fat fingers. He has dug out major portions of the icing. Arnie squirms and squirms, but I won't let him go. "You know what that cake cost, Arnie? You know the cost? You don't understand," I say softly. "You know why you don't understand?"

Arnie is trying hard to get away.

"Hey! You know why you don't understand?"

He bites into my wrist big time and my left hand cracks him on the side of his head. Arnie's teeth let go as he falls to the floor. His head hits the metal trash can.

"Owwwww."

He holds the back of his dirty head. When he starts to sit up, I give him a swift, pointed kick to the chest. He goes flying back, his head smacks hard on the floor. He doesn't make a noise. He's in shock. Then he begins to whimper.

"Go to the tub, you little fuck, get up to the tub."

Arnie doesn't move, though. I step over him and drag him by his arms down the hall, his legs kicking, his shoes scuffing the walls.

At the bottom of the stairs, I am firm. "Upstairs. Upstairs."

Arnie won't move.

I pull his hair and he stands fast.

"Upstairs."

I push him, but he won't budge. I start punching his back. Each punch harder until he takes a step. He stops. I punch him harder. He takes another step. And another.

"Ow, ow," he says.

"Move it, Arnie."

I slide open the shower door and force him in the tub. He stands there, his bottom lip pushed out.

"Strip," I say.

"No."

"You will strip."

"Nooooo!"

I turn on the water anyway, pull up the shower knob and the water sprays on him. Arnie shakes himself, going "Ooooooo!" And I say, "Can it, Arnie!"

"Noooooo."

"Take off your clothes. Take 'em off!"

"I can't with the water..."

I push the shower knob down. The water comes out the faucet. "Strip!"

The water below is already a dark brown.

"Do it now!" I scream.

"Gilbert..." He lifts up his filthy T-shirt. It gets stuck around his head but he gets it off. He pulls down his pants but stops when he realizes his shoes are still on. I reach down to undo his laces when he lets fly with a wad of spit. It hits my neck. I get one shoe off when he spits again. I pull up the shower knob, water pours down. He's about to spit again when I slap him hard. Once. Blood comes from his nose and I can't stop. My right hand, my left, my right, my left. Arnie falls to the base of the tub, the water showers down. He tries to block my hands but I'm too fast and strong. His head is getting smacked back and forth, his struggle stops and he's saying something and it isn't until my slaps slow and I turn off the water that I hear what he's been saying.

"My eye. My eye. My eye."

Arnie covers his good eye with both hands. The blood continues to flow. He is past crying, past pain. He lies there, in his wet underwear, his pants still at his knees, his muddy fingers clinging to his head. I run for ice and towels.

The ice cubes won't come out so I slam the tray hard on the counter, several cubes scatter. I grab four and some towels and am up the stairs fast.

"Here, Arnie."

He pulls back, shouts, "No!"

The blood from his nose has mixed with the dirt on his face.

"Shit. Shit," I say. "Take the ice, at least. Uncover your eye,

Arnie, and take the ice. You can see, right? You can see out of your eye, right?"

He removes his hands, looks at me, and blinks.

"You can see, right?"

He nods.

It takes twenty minutes to get him calmed down, the ice pressing to his face. Arnie goes quietly to bed, half clean. I'm standing quietly outside his door, listening as he whimpers softly.

All my life it's been: "You don't hit Arnie. Nobody hurts Arnie." And in one night, all of that is burned away, and it was easy and quick.

I am beyond hate for myself.

He's asleep now. I clean up the mess in the bathroom first. I wash the towels and dry up the spilled water. Downstairs I clean the kitchen. I take the cake out of the refrigerator. I find what's left of an old can of frosting, remove the cellophane, and begin to patch and repair the cake.

53

It's after midnight when the headlights of two cars move through our darkened house. The women are giggling and I hold the front door as Momma waddles in. They all smell of different perfumes. Amy and Momma both have new hair, Momma's is in curls and Amy's is feathered and bushier.

"Look at your momma," Momma says. "Only for that boy and this day. Remember that. Only for that boy and this day. . . ." She sees me and she turns silent. "You probably hate my new hair, don't you, Gilbert?"

"No," I try to say.

Janice and Ellen come in from outside. They're talking at the same time about how wonderful "the girls" look. Janice suggests a haircut for me. "I've got the proper kind of scissors." She cuts all her boyfriends' hair, she says. Ellen talks about how maybe one day she'd like to open a beauty parlor. Janice looks concerned and Ellen assures her that she'd prefer to be a stewardess, but she does add, "Imagine the satisfaction."

"Of what?" asks Janice.

"Of making the ugly beautiful."

Everything stops for a second, awkward. Momma says, "And what do you mean by that?"

Ellen looks around. Even she realizes what she just implied.

Amy intercedes with, "She didn't mean anything by that, Momma. Nothing at all, right?"

Ellen says, "I didn't mean a thing."

Momma goes, "Hey, you think I don't know? This new hair is the biggest collective waste of time. I look like a ball of yarn!"

The girls protest, "No, Momma, you don't."

Momma screams, "I LOOK WORSE AND WHO WOULD HAVE THOUGHT THAT WAS POSSIBLE?"

I watch them, hear every word, but all my thoughts are of Arnie.

Momma gets situated in her blue chair. Janice suggests that she sleep upstairs and Momma mumbles something about this being her house and she sleeps where she wants and that even ugly people should get to pick where they sleep.

Janice goes, "You're not ugly."

"Yes, I am. I am most ugly. And nobody's gonna see me. Nobody."

Ellen and Janice say, "Oh, Momma," at the same time.

She says simply, almost with pride, "Nobody's gonna see me."

I escape into the kitchen where I find the new-and-improved Amy looking disappointed at the Food Land cake.

"Arnie got into it," I say, looking guilty.

"Wouldn't you know it?"

I want to tell Amy about what I did to him. I lost control, I beat up Arnie—what will I do next? I'm about to confess, when she says, "Do you like this new look on me?"

She doesn't look like the Amy I know. Her hair is feathered and frosted. Her upper eyelids are painted blue. She holds up a white bag. "Charlie sold us all these makeups and eyeliners and crud. Janice says they're all things we *must* have, so of course we bought them."

Amy keeps on talking. I'm looking at the cake, only thinking about Arnie. "Gilbert, come back. You've drifted off."

"Oh, sorry."

"Something wrong?"

"No."

"Thanks for picking up the cake. Hey, you get Arnie clean?" she calls out.

I say nothing as I start up the stairs.

Ellen and Janice are on the porch, giggling. Momma sits in her chair, pulling at her hair.

"Shhh," I say to the girls, "he's asleep."

"Who is?"

"Arnie," I say.

Janice calls back, one of her brown cigarettes in her mouth, "Since when did you care so much about Arnie's well-being?" Ellen takes a drag from Janice's cigarette and coughs.

Normally, I'd say something smart in return, I'd fight back. But tonight—and for the first time in a long time—I think Janice might be right.

"I was only joking," she calls out. And then to Ellen, I hear her ask, "What's up his ass tonight?"

I sit in my room and wait for them all to go to sleep.

It's the middle of the night and my stomach is wrenched. I can't take it anymore. I had planned to prepare a breakfast treat and have it waiting for him in the morning. But there won't be any sleep until I apologize, until I beg his forgiveness. So I approach his room. I look at the sign on the door, "Arnie's place." I crack open the door. I step around his toys, his room is dark, my hand reaches for his mattress when I see his window open, wide open. He isn't in the top bunk or the bottom. He's not hiding in his closet. I look out the window. He's climbed out and down or else he fell.

Jesus. Arnie is gone.

I move to my room fast and get my shoes. Downstairs, Momma sits with the TV on. She is mumbling about something, talking in her sleep.

I move around our yard, whispering, "Arnie? Arnie?" I check the trampoline, the swing hanging off the willow tree.

I drive up and down the streets, checking the water tower. No Arnie. The Civil War cannon on the square. Back to the water tower. I call his name, but there is no answer except for a soft wind. My hands are trembling and I drive along the highway to see if he's trying to hitch a ride to the cemetery. One time we found him there—he was jumping up and down on our father's grave. He told us it was to "wake him up." There is no trace of him. I drive to the railroad tracks and the abandoned bridge.

I'm at a loss as to where to check. I picture all the things that could have happened. Hit by a car or maybe he fell off the water tower or maybe he's lost in a corn field.

At the south stoplight, I hear water sloshing. I get out of my truck and run across the road, leaving the engine running and my headlights on. I'm fifty yards from the Endora town pool when I hear splashing and Arnie going, "No. No!"

There's a blue light that shines on the water. From the fence, I can make out Becky swimming in her undies and her bra. Arnie sits in the lifeguard chair. He's still in his Superman pajamas, but without his cape. Becky is splashing and treading water, her hair in a ponytail. They don't see me. I put my fingers in the chain-link fence and watch as Becky stretches out her arms. She says, "You can do it, Arnie. You can."

"No. Noooo."

"Remember what I told you?"

He nods.

"And we don't want that? Right?"

Arnie slowly stands, lets out a yelp. He tries to jump, but it's more like a fall. He makes a big splash when he hits.

He flails about and Becky applauds.

And as the remaining dirt on Arnie starts washing away, it begins. My eyes burn at first from the sensation. It feels like chunks of ice moving down my face. They roll and roll. I need windshield wipers, I say to myself.

I walk back to my truck, turn off the lights and the engine, and sit with the window down. I bite my lip and feel them streaming down, without effort, these tears. I listen to the splashing laughter and Arnie screaming, "I'm a fish. I'm a fish."

I stay in my truck and watch as Becky and Arnie climb back over the fence. She puts a towel on his head. He looks like a boxer after a fight. I drive my truck up, my eyes must look red and puffy, and say, "Need a lift?"

Becky looks surprised. It's maybe the first time I've caught her off guard. Arnie, his face and body cleaner than ever before, covers his mouth to hide his smile.

I open the passenger door, he leaps toward me, wrapping his arms around my back and kisses my neck.

"Gilbert. Gilbert."

We hold each other–there's a battle to see who can squeeze the hardest. Either Arnie forgot or he forgives too easily.

He rides in the bed of the truck and Becky rides in the front with me.

"How'd you . . . how'd you . . . ?"

"He was running down Main Street. I was out walking."

"But . . . ?"

"But what?"

"How'd you get him . . ."

"That was easy. I told him you'd leave Endora if he didn't . . ."

"Oh."

"He loves you, Gilbert."

"Yep." I know this. Doesn't she know that I know this?

"And you love him."

I press my foot on the brake and come to a stop. Arnie taps on the rear window. "Yep," I say. She rests her hand on mine.

"Thirsty!" Arnie shouts from the truck bed.

I stop off at ENDora OF THE LINE and get Arnie a root beer. He drinks it on the porch and falls asleep without finishing it.

"I'll be back," I say. I carry him upstairs to his bed, the way my father used to carry me.

Becky and I sit on the porch and she says that she's not sleepy. I say, "The sun will be coming up soon." She has one cigarette left in her pack. I go inside and borrow Momma's matches and we smoke it. We sit on my porch, everyone inside asleep, and it suddenly occurs to me. "It's Arnie's birthday."

"Yes," Becky says. "It's his birthday."

Part Six

54

We talk for a while, Becky and me. I drive her home, and as the sun is rising, I sit on our porch.

I must have nodded off for a bit because I'm woken up by a rapid succession of pokes landing on my forehead. "Okay, I'm awake!"

I open my eyes and see him half smiling, smelling of aftershave, his hair still wet from a shower he must have taken at a nearby motel. He goes inside the house, calling out, "What's for breakfast?"

"I don't know, Larry."

"Where is everybody?"

"Still asleep," I say, following him.

"Smells the same."

I can't tell if Larry means that to be a good thing or not. Surely the smell of our house, even though it might evoke some perverted nostalgia, is not a pleasant one.

It's early morning. Larry cases the downstairs, studies Momma, puffs his cheeks full of air to indicate how big she's gotten. Then he says, "Help me unload the car." So we go out to his car and it is packed full of presents, different-shaped boxes, all nicely wrapped, expensively wrapped.

There must be sixteen, eighteen boxes now sitting in the family room.

I say, "You outdid yourself this year. Arnie is gonna die."

"Not funny."

"It's a figure of speech."

Larry squats. He wears brown polyester pants and brown shoes, a yellow shirt with a brown tie, a belt, brown. He cracks a smile looking at all the gifts. He must be picturing the look Arnie's face will make.

"The kid will squeal," I say.

Larry keeps looking around, as if I don't exist, as if he's alone in the house. I'm about to say "Yoo-hoo," when he stands, brushes down his pants, and heads out the house to his car. He drives away without so much as a good-bye or "Be back in a few."

I got out back and sit on the swing. Larry's swing. The one he built. I remember how he used to push me.

It's an hour later, at least, when Amy taps on the kitchen window. She waves me in.

"I checked on Arnie. He looks so clean. I barely recognized him. Thank you, thank you, thank you!"

I take Amy into the family room and show her the stacks of presents. "Larry was here."

"Christ. Go wake Arnie up."

"Let him sleep."

"Wake him up. This is his day."

"Let him sleep."

I am firm and Amy gestures a surrender. "You win."

Later, Ellen and Janice are on the porch. Momma is up. No TV today—she is supervising Arnie's restacking of the presents, Larry's presents, with which he will try to make up for a year's absence.

I'm decorating out back, when Larry's car returns. He stands in front of his car, his arms extended, expectant, and calls out, "Arnie, Arnie! It's your brother. Your favorite brother."

Arnie bounds out the porch and leaps into his arms. Arnie has been bought.

I hear Janice and Ellen oooing and ahhhing over Arnie and how clean and nice he looks. Momma, too. Momma is shrieking she's so happy.

I keep decorating, tying balloons to the edge of the trampoline. I pop a balloon and look around to see if anyone heard, if anyone noticed. No dice.

He wants to be seen

For the party, activities have been planned from one to three. At three, there will be cake and ice cream. At three-thirty, there was to have been a dance to early Elvis songs, Amy's idea, but I suggested that a bunch of retards dancing in public would be quite a scene. One retard is fine. But a party load of them could cause quite the uproar.

Tucker calls to say he had hoped to stop over. "But with this being the Grand Opening week and my extra duties as assistant manager, I'm going to have to RSVP."

Momma went into the bathroom at about noon and she's still not emerged.

I knock on the bathroom door. "All the retards are here. The parents, the neighbors. There are fifty people in our backyard, Momma. Amy says you want to watch from the house. Well, okay, whatever. The party has been a success, a real gem of an Endora event. Maggie Wilson took some pictures for the *Endora Express*. But the cake is beginning to droop in the sun. You've got to come out, Momma. Momma?"

She slides open the door, her eyes all red. I say, "Hey, you okay?"

"Gilbert, every day I prayed to God who I hate. I prayed for one thing. Keep my Arnie alive long enough for me to see this day . . ."

"I know."

"Let me finish. I prayed to that bitter bastard of a God, I said 'Let me see my boy turn eighteen and I'll forgive you.' Now, I've done my forgiving. And now, I'm ready for some cake." She pushes through the door and I move out of her way so as not to get squashed. She is breathing heavily, the back of her tentlike dress dripping in sweat, her feet in a pair of Larry's slippers. She shuffles to the back door and looks out at the party, which is in full swing. Momma won't go out in public but the people sense her watching. They know she's here. Even though they can't see her, they know Bonnie Grape approves.

I watch as she sees the kids bouncing on the trampoline, the parents chatting among themselves, and neighbor kids straddling their bikes. "Mr. Lamson just dropped by a gift. He's waving at you, Momma." She steps back farther into the house. I open the door and call out, "Thank you, Mr. Lamson. My mother sends her regards!" He nods and smiles and gives Arnie a pat on the back. Mr. Lamson walks to his wife and their Dodge Dart.

I shout, "Cake! Cake!" and the kids come running. Hardly kids, I say to myself, seeing that some of them are older than me. One of them, Sonny, is thirty-five, and he's lost most of his teeth. He walks with a limp, and he has a facial twitch. His mother must be seventy—she yells at him to get over to the cake. "You love cake, Sonny," she says. "Cake is your favorite."

Sonny's mother is the only person other than family allowed into the house to see Momma. They are old friends from way back.

The kids gather and Amy brings out the cake with the candles flaming. It takes Arnie five tries to blow them all out, but he does, and the kids jump up and down. I look at the back door and see Momma in the shadows, smiling, watching quietly. She has nothing to say, and it isn't until Ellen tries to take Momma's picture through the window that she speaks. She waves at Ellen and yells, "NO PICTURES! NO!"

Ellen laughs, thinking Momma is joking. "Come on, everybody loves to have their picture taken."

Janice says, "Say cheese, Momma."

Momma signals for me to stop Ellen. So when Ellen opens the door to take a picture, I lunge for the camera and end up tackling her. I'm able to wrestle it from her. The retards all stop their screaming and bouncing about and look at me as I pin my little sister.

Ellen whispers, "This the only way you can get it, huh, Gilbert?"

Larry watches all of this, like it's a movie, as if nothing he could say or do might affect the outcome. He looks like he's enjoying the show. I've a good mind to sell him popcorn. This isn't a movie, I want to shout.

Momma taps the kitchen window, her signal for cake, and Amy cuts off a huge piece and takes it to her.

Arnie eats only the frosting. Then he tries to steal Rica's cake. Rica is a nine-year-old retard with a giant, bumpy head. Her mom tries to keep Arnie away. This happens right in front of Larry's eyes, next to the trampoline. He does nothing to intercede, so I push through the noisy kids to where Arnie and Rica are at war. I pull him away and say, "No, Arnie. No."

"The frosting. The frosting!"

"No," I say. "That's for Rica."

Arnie runs to Larry, who offers a sympathetic hug. I look at my older brother, the "man" in my family, and think, "Some man."

Amy brings out a sack of party gifts and Arnie thinks they're all presents for him. She tells him that he already opened his presents and these are for his guests of honor.

We wrapped candy bars and lollipops and plastic toys for the other kids several nights ago. Amy says this is what polite people do, courteous people. This way the other kids don't feel left out.

Arnie protests more, and Amy recounts all of his gifts and he begins to remember. This seems to calm him for the time being.

Arnie opened his presents from the family earlier this morning. Of course, he opened Larry's gift first. It totaled seventeen boxes. It was a giant train and each box had a different piece of track or a car or whatever. They assembled it in the basement and Arnie was bored with it by the time the guests arrived for the party. Janice gave him a certificate for a plane flight anywhere in North America with a friend. Ellen has already begun campaigning to be the chosen one. Amy made him a new set of pajamas and I gave him a piggy bank and eighteen silver dollars. Momma gave him his life, or so she says, and told Amy if that wasn't enough, she didn't know what was. She also gave him a hug and a kiss.

The kids have unwrapped their party favors, eaten the choco-late, and they're getting restless. "I'm all out of ideas," I say to Amy. Suddenly Janice raises her hands and jumps up and down. "Who wants to go on a plane flight?"

The guests go "Yes" and "Yeah" and "Me me me!"

Amy and I are asked to set out the benches and chairs. Ellen and Janice line people up in rows. Arnie is to be the pilot. The others sit in their seats, waving to their families, as Janice goes over flight instructions and Ellen demonstrates.

Amy says to me, "Isn't this great?"

I look over our backyard, the people watching, cake plates and wrapping paper everywhere, rows of retards pretending they're flying, my mother watching from inside, her face pressed against the window and I've no words.

"Isn't this great?" Amy repeats.

"Uhm. It's great."

55

It's four-fifteen and only three of the retards are left. Amy is in the kitchen. Larry and Janice are on the front porch. Ellen is still running around documenting the party. All day long she's shot pictures of people to the left of me and then to the right of me. But never me. I say nothing and pretend not to care.

I'm in the downstairs bathroom digging around for a Band-Aid. I find the box and pick the appropriate size. Sonny, the oldest retard, scraped a knuckle on the sidewalk and I'm performing first aid.

I've finished putting the Band-Aid on Sonny when Amy says, "Boy, those kids sure scuttled out of here fast."

"Yeah," I say.

"The party wasn't that bad, was it?"

So I launch into a lengthy tirade or whatever about how the party was a tremendous success, the kids had a good time, a grand time. And the fact that they've left an hour before the party was scheduled to end is not due to their lack of enjoyment. "Amy," I say, "these kids were having too much fun. They were about to burst. No, they had to hurry home to their mediocre lives. Too much pleasure and it begins to hurt." Not that I would know about too much pleasure.

The remaining kids scream, "Gilbert, Gilbert," so I go out back. I have developed a brilliant system where each of them gets their turn. Each turn is fifteen jumps, then they rotate. I've earned their respect as I'm the only one who can count.

"Gilbert, Amy would like to see you in the kitchen." Ellen delivers this message, her camera clutched in her hands.

Take my picture, I almost say. Instead, I tell the kids to take a break from the jumping.

I sprint to the back door and into the kitchen because the retards have started a chorus of "Hurry up, hurry up."

"The tramp is quite a success," I say to Amy, my body out of breath, my nose and neck beginning to burn from the sun.

"I'm glad." Amy has been bagging up the plastic plates and party dishes. She always seems to be cleaning up somebody's mess. "Gilbert. Brace yourself."

"Sure, okay." I jokingly grab the orange counter top with the backs of my hands.

"I'm serious. I've got some news."

"Yeah?"

"Okay." Amy looks stern.

"Did somebody die?"

"No. Gilbert?" This eerie silence from Amy is beginning to worry me. I squeeze the counter, my fingers turn white.

"It's what Arnie wants and it's his day and if that's what he wants, we'll give him that, and so, for dinner, we're going...all of us...and your presence is expected, requested, and so thanks, favorite brother."

She moves to kiss my cheek.

"No," I say. "Never."

Momma calls from the living room where she's been talking with Sonny's mom about whatever the mothers of retards talk about. She says, "Listen to Sonny's mom."

Sonny's mom pops her head into the kitchen, her dentures a little loose, she struggles to say the simplest things. "Sonny and me went to the Barn for the first time. Yesterday. For brunch."

Brunch? Surely she's kidding.

Sonny's mom licks her lips; her brittle hands fluff her blue hair.

"Let me say this, Gilbert." She says my name with relish. "Best burger I ever had. Ever."

"Hear that?" Momma screams out. "Best burger ever."

"And," Sonny's mom continues, "don't assume because of my petite size that I don't know a good burger when I taste one. These burgers–I give you my word–are the best."

Amy looks at me as if I have no choice.

The retards' chant of "Hurry, hurry" has built to a scream. Ellen takes a surprise picture of Amy standing there and the back of my head. The flash blinds Amy, and I push Ellen out of my way and go outside.

When the retards see me, they let out a cheer and start begging for who gets to go next.

Pulling Ricky and Rica with the bumpy head out of the way, I say, "It's my turn."

I start my jump.

I go up so high that the kids all stop their complaining. They admire the height Gilbert Grape can achieve. Their jaws drop in awe.

Amy stands by the picnic table, drying her hands on her jeans. She shakes her head and mouths some words. My jumping slows, I fall to my knees, dribble a few times and then call out a "What?" to Amy.

She mouths two words. Burger. Barn. Then she points a finger at me. She nods—certain that she's won.

Amy drives her Nova. Arnie stretches out in back, bouncing on his seat the whole way. Larry drives his car. Ellen rides in the middle. Janice is to the right. She holds her brown cigarette out the window. Momma gave her order to Amy. She'll be waiting at home, and we're to bring her the food she requested.

I follow in my truck slowly.

They hit all three green lights on the way. I slow down enough to be stopped by the light in front of Dave Allen's. Dave is checking the oil on a Plymouth. He sees me, half waves. I look out the other side and wait for the light to turn green.

At the Burger Barn, it takes a minute to find a parking space. They are already inside. The place is packed, and my hope is that maybe there isn't enough room for us Grapes and that we'll have to go elsewhere, preferably home.

I open the door, which is designed to look like the wooden kind on "Gunsmoke" and other westerns, the kind you push through and they slap back on their own. But there is no push-through or slap-back, so I don't know who those Burger Barn people think they are fooling.

Looking through all the clusters of families and kids, I don't see my people. Far across the restaurant, though, in his polyester blue pants, in his orange and blue shirt, stands Tucker Van Dyke. I notice his name tag, with the words Assistant Manager spelled out in capital letters. He gives me the thumbs up and points with his head to his right. I move toward him. The noise of the people ordering and eating is intense and the closer I get, the bigger his grin grows.

"Tucker, enough" is what I almost say, but instead I say nothing and smile back. Even he can obligate my lips.

"Look," he says, pointing to the corner of the room. A sign hanging proclaims, "Reserved for Arnie Grape and friends."

I walk to where my family sits. They all look up. Larry and Janice and Ellen are seated on one side. Amy and Arnie sit on the other side. I'm to squeeze in between.

Tucker approaches and speaks to all of us. "Normally, you'd stand in line to place your orders. But, seeing as this day is Arnie's day, the management has provided you the exclusive use of one of Burger Barn's finest. This is Maggie," he announces. Maggie, a fourteen-year-old sixth-grader, who Ellen claims has been held back twice, appears with her pad ready to take everybody's order.

Amy starts reading Momma's order. Maggie writes quickly and when Amy is done talking, Maggie turns and walks toward the kitchen.

"Maggie," I have to call.

She stops.

"You got to get everybody else's order. That was for our mother. We'll need that to go when we're ready to leave."

Maggie looks confused momentarily, but then she puts it together. Whew. She takes everybody else's order. When she gets to me, I shake my head.

Ellen snaps, "Gilbert, order."

Larry says, "It's on me."

Amy says, "You've got to try the Silo fries. Or have a milk shake."

I order "water" and everybody is beyond mad. Ellen whispers into Janice's ear, Janice looks at my shirt, then my face and giggles. Larry lights Janice's cigarette and she blows her smoke in my direction. "I won't be eating a thing," I say.

*   *   *

The food comes and everybody is eating and they all seem to be oooing and ahhhing over each bite. "Yum-yum" is what I keep hearing, and it's all designed to make me regret my decision not to eat, I know it.

I remember how Becky said regret is the ugliest word.

Followed by family. Family is a terrible word.

"I have no regrets," I say, wishing I hadn't.

Janice spits up some of her vanilla milk shake, Ellen chokes on a fry. Larry looks at me like the word "regret" is a word he's never heard before. Arnie is under the table because he dropped a slice of pickle. Amy is on her third burger. She's the only one smiling. She's determined to believe this is the most beautiful day ever.

Over the microphone sound system, a voice can be heard. "Farmers and friends, the Burger Barn is proud to announce that in our birthday room—at this very moment, Endora's own Grape family is celebrating the eighteenth birthday of Arnie Grape. So all you Burger Barn animals, join us in singing 'Happy Birthday.' "

Tucker rounds the corner holding a cake shaped like a cow. Many Burger Barn employees and a crowd of customers follow. They stand and sing an off-key but sincere version of "Happy Birthday." Arnie has cupped his hands over his mouth to cover his smile.

Amy's face is dripping and the others, Janice and Ellen, sing along. Larry watches, detached.

I must say that this catches me off guard. There must be fifty people singing and Arnie is squealing now and he sticks his fingers in the cake and nobody minds and Momma would be loving this if she were here.

The singing echoes while Arnie takes three tries to blow out the candles.

The second cake of the day is cut up by Amy and eaten by everyone. She offers me a piece. I take it and eat two bites.

But I have to excuse myself. I move to where people place their orders and flag Tucker down. "Thanks," I say.

"Don't thank me," he says. "Thank Burger Barn. I am merely a conduit for their vision. It's the Burger Barn way."

Tucker would keep talking but he sees that my eyes are full. He says, "What is it? What's wrong?"

He pulls me through an employee door and I stand where they make the french fries. The other employees walk carefully around me as my back shakes and my face remains covered by my hands.

Tucker has no words. He lets me stand there, out of the public eye.

"This started last night and I uhm I can't seem to stop. I feel so stupid," I say. "So stupid."

Later, I thank him.

He says, "It's my job."

I ask for Kleenex. He hands me a stack of Burger Barn napkins. I use them to dry around my eyes.

56

After the Burger Barn, we drive home. Larry, Janice, and Ellen in the lead, then Amy's Nova, with Arnie in back, follows.

At the top of our street, Amy puts her left arm out the window and sticks a thumb up in the air.

At home, the women go inside to give Momma her food. Arnie gets an old croquet mallet out of our garage. He runs around slamming it down on whatever anthills he can find in the dirt or in the cement cracks.

Larry and I are out back of the house, considering the trampoline. I sit on it. He goes to the swing. He pulls on the rope to check its strength. "Hmmmm," he says.

"How's the swing?" I ask.

Larry looks at it for a time longer than the swing probably deserves. He looks at me, scratches his head, laughs to himself, and looks the forty, fifty feet up to where the rope is tied to the branch.

"Larry?"

"Hmmmm."

"How. Is. The swing?"

He takes in a deep breath and says, "Still sturdy." He sits on it and looks up.

"I remember the day you climbed up there—I was a fourth-grader and you were a big-time senior. Momma said for you not to and Amy was sure you'd get hurt, but you did it anyway. You remember how no one said it could be done? But you did it. Do you remember that?"

"No."

"Come on—and how at night, you'd stay up with a flashlight, guarding it so the neighbors' kids wouldn't sneak over and take a free swing. . . ."

"No."

"You don't remember?"

Larry shakes his head and gestures for me to get off the trampoline. He steps out of his brown shoes and crawls out to the center.

"Don't you want to change out of your clothes? A person does not jump on a trampoline in a dress shirt and a tie. Larry, I've got some cutoffs, some gym shorts."

Again Larry has no answer for me. Standing now, he rises up on his toes and back down. He does this many times, never leaving the ground. "Stupid."

"Huh?" I say.

"Trampolines are stupid."

"You've got to jump, though. You've got to get up in the air."

"I am."

"No, you're not."

Larry continues this timid move of toes up, toes down.

"JUMP!" I scream.

Larry does, out of fear; he almost falls over; his arms shoot out to regain balance. Larry is pissed. I laugh and this might be the first laughing *at* my brother that I've done in a long, long time.

"I can still kick your ass, Gilbert."

"Yeah, I know."

"So shut up."

"JUMP!"

This time Larry stops moving and Arnie comes squealing around the house from the front, hopping kangaroo style. He comes jumping our way, ketchup smeared on his chin and a chunk of pickle still stuck in his teeth.

"Jesus, get that kid a napkin," Larry says.

"Hey, Arnie, do you know the words 'dental floss'?"

Arnie stops his hopping and goes, "Jeez, you guys. Jeez."

Larry sits down on the trampoline. The idea of jumping is too much for him. He's as scared as I am, as scared as everybody, even though he'll never admit it.

The sun is back behind trees now, the sky is growing dark and this day, the big day, is almost over.

Ellen stands on the porch, waving us her way.

"What?" I yell.

She waves more frantically.

"Something's up," Larry says, putting on his shoes and heading toward the house. Arnie tags along. I lean on the trampoline until they hit the porch steps, then I follow reluctantly.

In the house, I hear through the screen door "Oh, Momma, you can do it. Yes, Momma."

Momma is on her third stair step. She's looking down, careful that each move she makes is on target. Janice is above her, walking backward, coaxing her on. "Yes, yes." Larry and Amy have moved behind her and have their arms stretched out to catch her, as if such a catch were possible. Surely they would be killed if she fell. I don't do a thing to help, really. I say a few "Hooray for Momma"s and a few "You can do it"s, but my mouth, for the most part, hangs open; my head shakes itself.

This is supposed to be a natural thing, climbing the stairs. Not in the Grape family–here, the simple becomes the extraordinary.

"Gilbert should be helping," Momma huffs out.

The others call for me to get involved. I put my arms up but study an escape route in case Momma tips over. I'm behind Larry and Amy, and my chance of survival seems best. Arnie disappears into the living room and drums on top of the TV.

* * *

Momma is halfway when she says, "I can't go on."

"You're halfway," Larry says.

"Who said that?" Momma is in shock.

"Larry did," Janice says.

"No," Momma says. "Larry? Larry spoke?"

"Yes," Amy says.

"Larry, my son, Lawrence Albert Grape *spoke* to his mother?"

"What's the big deal about that?" Larry asks.

Momma makes a sound that would be a laugh were she not out of breath.

"I have..." Momma can barely speak she is so out of breath. "I have renewed..." She breathes in deep, determined to speak. "I have renewed *strength*."

Larry, Amy, and I push Momma while Janice and Ellen pull from above. She completes the final steps. She makes it to the top and into her room which she hasn't seen in months, if not years. Momma lies down on the bed and before we can get her cigarette lit, she falls asleep.

We turn on the two window fans and leave her to rest. Amy gets the hand bell from her room. This is the bell she uses during the school year to signal the end of recess. She sets the bell on Momma's night table. If Momma wants any of us for anything, she'll ring it and Amy or me or whoever will come running.

57

Larry is in the kitchen listening to Amy, and he's got his checkbook out. A good sign. Upstairs, I press my ear to Ellen's door and make out vaguely that Janice is recounting her sexual adventures. The girls giggle in that girl way. I check on Momma and find her sleeping soundly, a soft snore, her beauty parlor curls crunched on a feather pillow.

Back downstairs, I see that Amy's looking sad. I say, "Why so down, huh?"

She says, "Look at my hair. One night of sleep and it looks awful—it will only look good when Charlie styles it. It will never..."

She continues on. Larry is signing a check and smiling.

I look out the back window and see Arnie sticking old sheets up through the trampoline springs. I go out back and call to him. "Arnie, what you doing? Building a fort?" He pokes his head through one of the sheets and shakes his head. I say, "What then, what you doing then?"

"Jeez, Gilbert, jeez. You're dumb."

I walk over toward him, saying, "Yes, I know. I'm very slow at these things. What are you making?"

"A rocket ship."

"Oh. So uhm where you going to?"

"Not telling."

"Okay."

"To find..."

"To find what?"

"Find Albert."

This stops me. I crawl under the sheets and watch Arnie as he builds his rocket ship. I say to Arnie that Dad really missed out, not being here today. "He would have been proud of you. He would've liked all your friends and all the people from town. He really missed something."

"Yeah," Arnie says.

"And he really missed getting to know Arnie Grape."

"Yeah, he really missed out, yeah."

Later Amy and I clean the downstairs, while Janice carefully takes down the streamers and the birthday signs. "We can use them again next year."

Already we're talking about next year. I want to say, "Can't we just take this year, take this day?" But that wouldn't sound like me at all. It sounds like something Becky would say, so I just go, "Good idea, Janice," and leave it at that.

"What did you just say?"

"I said 'Good idea.' " Janice is holding a stack of party hats, looking confused. "Good idea about the saving the decorations, Janice. That's all."

"Amy?"

"Yes?"

"Gilbert, our brother, you know, Gilbert?"

"Yes, I know him."

"He just gave me a compliment. Can you believe it?"

"Well, I'll be."

"GILBERT GAVE ME A COMPLIMENT. I CAN DIE NOW! I CAN DIE!"

"Shhhhh," I say. "People are sleeping."

Janice starts for the porch. She stops off at her purse and takes out her pack of brown cigarettes and a lighter.

"There's some cake left," Amy calls out.

"No, thanks."

"Oh, come on, you guys. Help me eat this. Let's get it all eaten before Momma wakes up." Amy hands me two plates full and says, "The smaller piece is for Janice." Amy cuts a piece for Arnie and Larry, and goes out to make cake deliveries.

Janice takes a bite and then a drag from her cigarette, then another bite and so on. She has a smoking and eating system.

Suddenly it's feeling like those lazy hours after a Thanksgiving meal or late on Christmas afternoon. Amy comes down the stairs still carrying three plates of cake. I've only been poking at mine. She goes, "You should see upstairs. Arnie's fallen asleep in Momma's room, curled up at her feet. And Larry is out back resting on the trampoline, face down even. Ellen wants to nap but she's got her Bible meeting."

"How nice," Janice says.

Amy sets down the extra plates of cake. "So eat up, you two, let's finish it off."

"I'm full," I say.

"Gilbert, help us eat this."

"You're skin and bones," Janice says. "Yes, Amy, we'll be glad to eat the cake."

*   *   *

It takes about twenty minutes of chewing for the three of us to eat what's left.

Amy leans back and says, "The day was a success. I'd say. Even your older brother had a nice time. Even Momma. All the people. And the Burger Barn was a good idea, don't you think? Thanks for all your help, you two. It means so much. . . ."

Amy is about to get mushy, so I stand, put out my after-cake cigarette on the cement step, and am about to go inside when Larry comes around the side of the house.

Janice says, "It's getting close to dark, Lar', you heading on?"

Larry looks at her like "Whatever are you talking about?"

Janice says, "The day is gonna end. You'll be heading on, right?"

"Yeah, soon. Yeah."

Amy goes, "Well, all in all . . . it's been unbelievable . . . this day."

It's true. Today's headlines seem unbelievable. Larry Grape speaks. Arnie Grape makes eighteen. Bonnie Grape sleeps in her very own bed. Gilbert lets Janice and Ellen live.

Still, though, things could be better. In an effort to improve the quality of my little life, I go into the deserted kitchen and put the cake plates in the trash. The other Grapes are outside or upstairs and I'm alone. So I lift the phone up off the receiver and dial seven digits, quickly planning what I want to say.

"Gilbert," Amy calls from the porch.

I hang up before the phone is answered. I walk to the door and say, "What is it?" when I see a bike come coasting up.

It's Becky.

Her hair is pulled back in a ponytail and she wears tan shorts and sandals. No makeup. Nothing but the truth.

"Hi!" I say, pushing through the door, suddenly the happiest man. Janice's mouth is stuck open. She's never seen this kind of art. Ellen, who just came down from her room, falls back against the house. Larry's staring, unable to move. Only Amy stands and walks down to her. She extends her hand. "You must be Becky."

"Yes."

"This is Amy," I say. I bounce down the porch steps toward the beautiful girl. I was just calling you, I almost say.

Arnie comes around the house. He runs to her, his arms extended and touches her face.

I say, "Let's go for a walk."

She says, "When Arnie's finished."

As he continues his exploration, I look up at the porch. Janice is smoking her cigarette double time and Ellen is leaning back on the door, her painted fingers kneading her shirt sleeve.

"These are my other sisters. Janice."

Janice exhales smoke, raises her eyebrows and nods.

"And Ellen, whom I believe you've met."

"Yes, we've met."

Ellen says a faint, "Hi."

"And Larry."

Larry wavers slightly and brushes back his remaining hair, failing to cover his bald spot.

Amy encourages Arnie to finish up and we go on our way. "See you two later," Amy says with what I swear was a wink.

There will be another hour of sun. I guide Becky's bike and we walk down the middle of the trafficless street. We're not alone—the jealous eyes of the other Grapes are with us.

When we get out of range, I try to speak. But my breathing has stopped. "I uhm wanted to uhm..." I try to continue.

"Yes?" she says.

"What is it with you? You an angel or something? Is that it? Is that what you are?"

"No."

"You are. I know it. All you've done for me—and all of the mind reading. You're an angel!" I feel proud, finally coming up with some sort of logical explanation for this girl, if there ever could be such a thing.

"No."

"Come on!"

"No..."

"But..."

"No 'buts,' Gilbert. You just make sense to me. It's nothing more special than that."

"I uhm owe you..."

"No, you don't."

"Oh yes I do. I owe you and I thank you."

"You're talking like it's the last day of school."

"Well, it's what it feels like. The party is over and it was a success and Momma's in her room and Arnie is clean and Larry is
talking and it's all better here, all better."

"Gilbert, fine. Whatever."

"It's over, all the trauma, all the emotions. Tell me it's over."

She's silent.

"It's slowing down here, it is. A new beginning. I'm not looking
for quick and cheap here, just some confirmation. Becky? You listening?"

"Sure, we can kiss."

"So here's the . . . what?"

"We can kiss. It will be nice to kiss."

I laugh out of embarrassment, she says, "Go back to your family.
Tomorrow we can kiss."

I walk her home, no kiss, not even a hug. But tomorrow. The
words were enough, though, and I sprint home, repeating "tomorrow," skipping part of the way, certain that I look about six.

Back at home, Ellen is going off with Cindy Mansfield to her
Bible meeting. The porch has cleared out. Only Larry remains, sitting
with his eyes closed.

I say, "Larry, what's up?"

He goes, "Listening to Iowa."

Oh. Okay. Whatever.

Inside the house, the phone rings. I'm closest.

"Gilbert Grape here."

"Sunrise tomorrow. Want to watch?"

"Yes!" Don't sound so excited, Gilbert, be cool. "Uhm. Okay, I
guess."

"Meet me in the square. Bring your truck and a blanket."

"Bye, Becky."

Click.

I'm left holding the receiver. Inordinate amounts of activity happen in my stomach and groin regions. Oh my. I hang up the phone, and Amy comes around the corner, smiling.

"What's that look for?"

Amy says, "What look?"

"You're such a snoop."

"Gilbert's got a girlfriend, Gilbert's got a girlfriend."

"Jesus, Amy, you sound like you're five."

She laughs and washes her hands in the sink. I'm thinking about spraying her with water or doing something mean when Janice comes into the kitchen carrying her cake plate. "Larry's taking me to get us all some beer. Anybody need anything?"

"Not me," I say.

"Momma's almost out of cigarettes."

Janice says, "Okay. Anything else?"

I shake my head. Amy says, "That's it," and off go Janice and Larry. I open the freezer part of the fridge and break out some ice. Amy is drying off her hands, when I slip three or four cubes down the back of her shirt. She shrieks and tries to put me in a headlock. I take some of Janice's leftover frosting and smear it on her face.

"Ooooo, Gilbert—stop it." She pulls my hair.

"Ow. Okay, Amy. Okay!"

And to make it up to her, I wet a rag and wipe the frosting off her nose and mouth. Amy picks up the cubes that are melting on the floor when binga-binga or dinga-dinga comes from upstairs.

"That's Momma."

While Amy is dropping the cubes in the sink, I push myself around her and take off for the stairs. "Coming, Momma!"

Amy gets hold of my T-shirt. It starts to rip.

"Stop it!"

"I'm going to win, Gilbert, I'm going to ..."

"No way."

She holds my arm and I pull her along.

Binga-binga. Dinga-dinga.

Part Seven

58

We race up the stairs. I win.

"Amy and Gilbert at your service, Momma."

Momma's on her back in her bed and she's looking for us. One of her big hands stretches our way, the other shakes the school bell above her. Binga-binga. Dinga-dinga.

"What is it, Momma?"

She tries to make a sound. The window fans are making this humming noise so I turn them off.

"What, Momma, what?"

Binga-binga. Dinga-dinga. The bell falls from her hand. This raspy sound is coming out her, a rattle. Momma's eyes are having a time of it, she's trying to whisper something, when her eyes start fluttering.

"What is it?" Amy asks.

Momma's eyes close and her head rolls to the side.

I shake her by her shoulders.

"No. No!" Amy shouts. "Come on, Momma, come on!"

I push on her chest, slamming on it. Amy gives her mouth to mouth. She does her best.

But there's no pulse. There is nothing there, nothing left. One second her stomach is rising up and down, her lips smacking together. Next second, it stops. Momma stops.

"No. No, Gilbert, tell me this isn't happening."

"It isn't happening."

But it is.

"Aaaaaaahhhhhhh!" goes Amy, and I put my arms around and hold her as tight as I can. She is convulsing.

"Amy. Amy Amy Amy."

Arnie continues sleeping on the floor. He doesn't hear her scream and pound the bed.

Momma lies there, her mouth half open, her eyes closed, her hair still nice from the beauty parlor, her body covering her bed. I take hold of her hand. It won't be warm much longer. What are these pictures that flash in me? Images of her giving birth to me, sweat all over her face, and imagining the look on her face the first time she held me.

Amy goes, "Aaaaaahhhhhh!" again. Arnie stirs but doesn't wake.

I'm told women scream when they give birth because of the intense pain. And I think about how easily life can just slide away, like thawing ice. And how it's only the living that scream.

We stand there (I don't know how long) not knowing what to do. Finally, Amy touches Arnie's hair and says, "Better wake him up."

"Little buddy, it's your brother. Gilbert here. Arnie . . . ?"

He opens his eyes and smiles. "I know it's you, Gilbert. Jeez."

"I need to show you . . ."

"Gilbert, I was dreaming. I was dreaming about these big gold-fish. They were so big. So big. You shoulda seen 'em. You too, Amy. You shoulda seen 'em too."

When he sees that Amy's face is all red, he stops his talking.

"Arnie," I say. "It's Momma."

He sits up, looks at her. He crouches on the bed and touches her lips. He looks puzzled.

"Momma's gone."

Arnie hits her shoulder. He pinches her and giggles. I guess he thinks it's a joke. It takes a while but eventually it sinks in. He sits quietly by Momma's feet.

Larry's car drives up. He and Janice come in the house with two six-packs of beer. I stand at the top of the stairs and wave them up. "Leave the beer down there," I say.

They do. Janice with a cigarette comes up the stairs first, Larry follows. I point to Momma's room and they go in. Amy is combing Momma's hair and Arnie is holding one of Momma's feet. Janice sees the situation first. They both stand there quiet.

Larry leaves the room to punch a hole through the bathroom door. Janice doesn't scream or cry, her face just stares blank-like. The ashes grow on her cigarette.

It gets blurry for a while.

Then Amy takes charge. She decides that we better call Dr. Harvey or the hospital in Motley.

Janice says to call now. "Let's get Momma out of here."

Amy says, "Not until after Ellen sees her."

Janice starts to object.

Amy goes, "No, Janice. She needs to see Momma first. So, Gilbert?"

"Okay..."

"Go find..."

"Of course."

I pull up to the intercom/drive through part of the Burger Barn. "Good evening. May I take your order?"

"Tucker."

"May I take your order, please?"

"Tucker, it's me."

"Your order, sir?"

"IT'S GILBERT!"

"I know it's you. Are you ready to order?"

"I'm looking for..."

"Gilbert, the district manager is here tonight. He's over by the french fries, but pretend that we don't know each other. It's uhm important for me to make a good impression... so *yessir*—that will be one Burger Barn special, a large order of Silo fries and a Strawberry Moo Malt. That will be two ninety-three."

"Have you seen...?"

"Yessir, your total is two ninety-three. Please drive forward."

I drive up.

He slips a five out of his pocket and hands it to me. I hand it back, and he says, "Two ninety-three out of five. Here is your change. Would you like ketchup with your order, sir?"

"Have you seen Ellen?"

Tucker gets a glimpse of my eyes and stops what he's doing. He mouths, "You okay?"

I shake my head.

He mouths, "What's...?"

"It's Momma."

"Yeah?"

"She's gone."

"Where'd she go?" He says this as he puts about fifteen plastic packages of ketchup in my bag. "Where'd she go?"

"Wherever you go when you're gone."

He hands me the bag of food and whispers, "You mean... no... no..."

"If you see Ellen, send her home, okay?" I hit the gas and squeal out, leaving a tire mark, surely.

I drive fast. The speedometer breaks ninety. My truck stinks from the Burger Barn food. I roll down the window and toss the bag out. I can hear Momma saying, "What's for dinner? What's there to eat?" I wish I'd thrown food out earlier. Maybe if we'd thrown it out earlier, maybe if I had quit the grocery store. Maybe.

I keep repeating "Momma's gone" in my head, hoping that it will sink in.

Parked under the old railroad bridge are many cars and pickup trucks. I pull in and blink my headlights on and off fast. One of the cars honks, annoyed at my light. Some guy yells out, "Hey, buddy, cut that out." I see the McBurney Funeral Home hearse.

I knock on the passenger window. The glass is steamed over and the doors are locked. Bobby McBurney climbs out the driver's side and says, "You had to come and spoil this, didn't you?"

I don't say anything to Bobby. "Ellen, get dressed. You gotta come home. Ellen!"

"Your sister is a big girl."

"Now, I say."

Ellen gets out of the hearse, tying the string to her halter top. "I hate my brother. I HATE MY BROTHER!"

Bobby threatens me. "One day we'll be alone, Gilbert, and I'll kick your ass."

"MY BROTHER RUINS LIVES! HE EATS HIS OWN SPERM!"

The other cars start flashing their headlights, honking their horns.

I drive away slowly, with as much dignity as I can manage.

Tomorrow they'll hear about what happened to Momma. Tomorrow they'll feel bad.

The whole way home she says, "What is it? What is it? Something happened? Did I do something wrong? It's Arnie? Oh, God–it's Arnie."

"It's not Arnie."

I smoke a cigarette. Ellen rolls down the window and forces cough after cough. I drive as fast as I can. She looks for a seat belt.

"There'd better be a good reason, Gilbert, because you've ruined my life. You've destroyed my entire existence."

We're home.

Dr. Harvey is on the porch talking with Amy and Larry. Ellen goes to them. "What is it? What happened?" Janice appears and takes Ellen upstairs.

I get to the porch and Dr. Harvey is finishing saying something. He hugs Amy, shakes Larry's hand, and extends his out to mine. "Your mother was a good woman, Gilbert." I say nothing. Since he's holding the death certificate in his right hand, we shake with the left. "Let me know if I can be of help."

Ellen cries, out of control like. It isn't until after we get her calmed down that she can speak coherently.

She meets me as I'm coming out of the bathroom. "Gilbert..." she says, barely getting out the words. "You know what Bobby and I were doing, don't you? Don't you? In the uhm hearse?"

"Not really."

"We were...you know...doing it...while Momma was... was..."

I look at her puffy eyes and quivering lips. "You didn't know," I say softly. "How were you supposed to know?"

"But..."

"Shhhh. Shhhhh."

"But..."

"It's okay, Ellen. It's okay."

I try to hug her. My arms wrap around her awkward-like, but I try.

We go back to Momma's room. Ellen asks a bunch of questions. "Was she in pain?"

"Didn't seem to be."

"Was she scared?"

"I think so."

"Was she ... was she ... was she ... ?"

I answer whatever Ellen asks. Amy gets a bottle of perfume and starts to spray it on Momma. Janice says, "Enough is enough," and starts to dial for an ambulance.

"Hang up, Janice. Hang up!" I shout.

She stops for a moment, looks at me like I'm joking, and then continues dialing.

"Hang up the phone!" I shout. "I'm not ready for her to be uhm taken away."

Janice says softly, "Gilbert, it's time."

"I'm not ready for them to touch her, to take her away, okay?"

"But ..."

"What are they gonna do with her now anyway? They'll leave her naked under some sheet in some cold room till morning. Dr. Harvey has signed the certificate. I want to wait till morning."

Janice puts down the phone. "Can Amy stop with the perfume, though? At least stop with the perfume."

Amy puts the bottle down.

Janice says, "Let's call before sunrise. I don't want a crowd outside."

"Yes," Ellen says. "Momma wouldn't want the crowd."

Amy decides that we'll call in an hour or two.

"I just need more time to get used to the idea of Momma gone," I say. "It doesn't sink in. It just doesn't sink in, does it?"

We sit quietly, the girls and me. We look at Momma. After a long time of sitting there, Amy asks me to go get Larry and Arnie. "Don't call," I say, as I leave the room.

I find Arnie sitting in Momma's chair downstairs and I say, "Hey, buddy," and he says, "Yeah," and I say, "Amy wants you upstairs, okay?"

"Okay." He walks past me and stomps up the stairs.

I find Larry in the basement pulling apart the support beams. "Larry, stop it."

"What is this? What's this wood? What is this?"

"She was falling through the floor. We didn't know what else to do."

"But this is where . . . this is where . . ."

"I know."

Larry kicks the beams, hitting the higher boards with his fists. "I hate this house. I hate it."

"You have every right to," I say.

"I'm going. Okay? I'm getting in my car and going. I can't stay here. I can't be here."

"I know how you feel . . . but . . ."

Larry has crouched in the corner, like a baby in a womb. "But what?"

"You can't leave just yet. You just can't."

"But . . ." He wraps his arms around his knees tighter.

"It's not a good time to be leaving. Hey, come on. Amy wants us upstairs. All of us. Come on, Larry."

He sits, not budging an inch.

"Come on, buddy." I pull him up. We duck under and around the support beams and walk slowly upstairs.

Amy goes, "You think we could all just sit in here for a while? Just sit together?"

No one objects. Arnie sits at Momma's feet. Amy is at her side. I stand behind Larry in the doorway, blocking him in case he tries to get out. Ellen and Janice stand by the window, smoking. Ellen holds a cigarette of her own.

Amy has brought in a cassette player and she turns on first a tape of Frank Sinatra. Momma loved Frank. When that ends, she puts on Elvis. And while one of us is crying, another stares out the window and somebody else pipes up with some story about Momma.

Janice says that Momma was once the prettiest girl in Endora, and that Ellen looks just like how Momma did as a girl. Larry mentions how Momma was always happiest when she was pregnant. And Amy says she always knew that this was going to happen—Momma dying—but that in no way did she think it would happen now. "I'm glad we're all here," she says. Ellen says that she still can't believe that she's Momma's spitting image, so Amy and Janice get the trunk out. We look at pictures of Momma as a little girl and as a young woman. One is of Momma at about age five, holding a teddy bear. Her face looks so sad and forlorn. And she's wearing a winter hat and mittens.

I'm not saying we all of a sudden decided that our mother was Saint Mary. But even though she was angry, even though she was soooo fat, she was our mother. And we could see in each of us a trace of her. And we knew in some weird way that she wasn't gone, she had just moved into us and now it was time for us to move on.

One of the Elvis songs gets Amy dancing. And Larry, too. Arnie jiggles around with Janice. Ellen is taking pictures with her Kodak, but the flash has stopped working so I don't know if the pictures will come out. I sit on the bed and look at Momma lying there, still. Everybody is moving around her, spinning and laughing. Momma is still and Elvis sings.

I look at Momma and say under my breath, "It's going to take a crane to get you out. You know that? They're going to have to cut a hole in the ceiling. A helicopter, maybe..."

Amy sticks her sweaty face in front of mine and says, "Gilbert, who you talking to?"

"Nobody," I say.

"Then dance," she says. "Dance."

And I do.

59

We're all danced out and Larry has brought up the beer and some of us have opened up cans.

Amy says, "I haven't danced this way in years."

Janice says, "I know some great places in Des Moines where..."

Ellen says, "You're a good dancer, Amy."

Larry belches. Arnie puts his hand up to Larry's mouth and says, "Stop that, stop it!"

We sit in our sweat.

Amy says, "Okay. It's time."

"For what?" I say, feeling this rush of blood around my face.

"Time to call. The sun will be up in a few hours. We want to do this before the sun, right?"

"Uhm."

"Yes," Janice says.

I go, "It's gonna take a crane to get her out, you know that. Have you thought about that?"

"No, it won't."

"They'll have to cut a hole in the roof. She's too big to carry down. It'll take a crane of some kind."

Larry says that there are hydraulic stretchers for people like Momma. He tells Janice to call. Janice stands and walks over to the phone.

"No!" I shout. "Don't!"

"You need more time, Gilbert, is that it?" Amy says.

"Uhm."

"We can wait a little longer."

Janice sighs. "Let's do it. Let's just call, okay?" She picks up the phone.

"Noooooo!"

Arnie covers his ears and the others stop moving and look at me.

"Don't call. Do not call. By the time they get her out, it'll be morning. And there'll be a crowd. And the McBurney hearse will show up. They'll put her in the hearse, Ellen. And the people will talk and talk. Whisper. They'll look at her and feel superior. And they will joke. They will make her a joke."

Ellen has turned away. Janice starts to dial.

"SHE IS NO JOKE! THEY'LL LAUGH AT HER AND POKE AT HER AND JUDGE HER! DO NOT LET THEM DO THAT!"

"Okay, Gilbert, shhhh. Shhhhh."

"SHE DESERVES BETTER! SHE DESERVES..." I try to

breathe. Amy tries to hug me, but I flinch. "MOMMA IS BEAU-TIFUL AND NOBODY IS GOING TO LAUGH!...NO LAUGH!..."

There is no dialing sound, no words of protest—only the sound of me sobbing.

Ellen says, "She's beautiful. No matter what anybody says or thinks, Momma is beautiful."

"So can I dial now?" Janice asks.

I shake my head.

"Well, then, little brother, what do you suggest we do?"

I lunge through the air, ripping the phone away from her, cradling it like a football.

"Well," Janice says.

I unplug it and carry it to my room. I pull out two dresser draw-ers stuffed with clothes, set the phone in the top drawer, and walk back down the hall.

"What are you doing?" Janice asks. The others are watching.

I go down the stairs and set the drawers in our front yard. I find a box. In the upstairs hall, I empty Amy's Nancy Drew collection into the box.

Janice asks, "What is Gilbert doing? Is anyone else interested?"

I walk past her and go down and out. I find some garbage bags in the kitchen. I'm at the top of the stairs when I hear Amy ask, "What time is it?"

Larry says, "Two-fifteen."

Without saying a word, Amy walks past me to her room. She even-tually emerges with a box of Elvis records, Elvis posters, and a stuffed bear that Larry won once for her at the carnival years back. She has grabbed some clothes, too. She stops at the end of the hall, pokes her head in Momma's room, and says to the others, who are standing around, confused, "Gilbert's right. It's gonna take a crane to get her out."

Janice goes, "What the ...?"

Amy says, "Gilbert's also right—they will laugh and judge. And, yes, Momma deserves better." She takes her stuff down the stairs and out onto the front lawn.

I carry down books. I empty the coats from the coat closet and carry them out beyond the sidewalk. It's only Amy and me doing this though. Then Ellen appears on the porch. She holds a few of our photo albums. "Where should I put these?" she asks.

Soon the others are carrying, too. Janice helps Arnie gather up his toys. Ellen gets her makeup, Larry gets the dart board from the attic and the set of encyclopedias and the tools from the garage. We gather papers and pictures and dishes from the kitchen.

No one is saying anything, but it is clear that we all understand.

Amy picks selected furniture and it's carried out and set in the yard. The dining-room table, the family-room sofa. No one is running, no one frantic—but we work quickly. I make sure to get Becky's watermelon seeds and Mrs. Carver's Coke can.

It takes many trips for the yard to be filled with our things. Amy and I look at it all from the porch. Bags of clothes and furniture and old dishes everywhere. The yard is littered with our belongings.

"Amy," I say.

"Yeah?"

"Did you know we had this much stuff?"

"Nope. We sure got a lot." She looks at her watch. "It's a little after five." I hand her the last sofa cushion. "Is that everything?" she asks.

"Yep."

60

It took us three or so hours to empty all we want. Janice is collapsed in the grass and Ellen looks at the sweat on her arms in the light from the street lamp. Larry goes to his car and calls out, "Be right back."

The girls, Arnie, and me all go upstairs and give Momma a hug or a kiss. Ellen tries to take one last picture, but she runs out of film. We all walk around the house with blank faces, sometimes smiling, an occasional giggle or sob—but mainly we walk around with blank faces just soaking it all in. Arnie sits in his room saying, "Bye-bye." He waves to the doors and closet shelves.

When I see the headlights from a car, I go, "Larry's back." We all go downstairs and out into the yard. Larry runs in the house and up the stairs and you can see him, through the window, looking at Momma. He leans forward to kiss her—his head dips out of view.

Back outside, he opens the trunk of his car and takes out the gas can he just had filled. I walk with him to the porch, he opens the door, and we walk into the living room. The only furniture left in that room is Momma's chair. He pours the gasoline all over it. I turn off all the lights. He lights a match and we hear the sound of fire being born. He gets out of the house fast. I take my time.

Outside, the girls have turned the sofa around so it faces the house. Sitting on it are Arnie and Amy. Ellen stands behind them. Janice is sitting on one of our kitchen chairs. Larry runs to the others. From the porch, where I'm standing, I can hear Amy whispering to Arnie, trying to explain why we're doing this and although it makes perfect sense, even Arnie can't understand.

With my back to the house, I watch my brothers and sisters watch the fire grow. The light brightens their faces. I feel the heat on my neck. The downstairs must be in flames.

"Gilbert, get over here."

I turn and look at the fire.

"Gilbert!"

I go and join the others who are watching.

The fire grows and grows. It moves quick and it seems to go right to Momma's room. Arnie says, "Scary, scary."

It won't be long before the sun is up and the police and newspaper people arrive. I look around to see if any of the neighbors' lights have snapped on, and a couple have, but no one is outside yet.

The fire is beautiful.

I remember my date with Becky to watch the sunrise. It will have to wait until another day.

As the fire shoots higher and higher, I look around at my family. I see that Larry's eyes are full and about to drip, and that Janice is staring like she's seen her first rainbow, and Ellen's got her eyes closed—she's listening to the fire. Amy and Arnie sit together on the sofa and he's asking questions. The police lights come flashing through the trees. I take my hands out of my pockets. I put one on Larry's shoulder and the other squeezes Ellen's arm.

Arnie says to Amy, "Look at the lights—look at the lights."

The sirens fill the air, the walls in Momma's room fall down in flames, and Amy says, "Yes, Arnie, look at the lights."

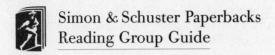

Simon & Schuster Paperbacks
Reading Group Guide

What's Eating Gilbert Grape?

Questions for Discussion

1. In the first chapter, Arnie Grape tells Gilbert, "You're getting littler and littler. You're shrinking." "Stupid people sometimes say the smartest things," Gilbert reflects. With this exchange, what themes does Peter Hedges begin to develop in his novel? How is Gilbert shrinking?

2. Consider the nature of Gilbert's relationship with Becky alongside his relationship with Mrs. Carver. What do these characters mean to Gilbert? Do they present him with the same possibilities for escape, love, and healing? Explain.

3. Remembered chiefly for his relentless "optimism," Albert Grape nevertheless hung himself in his basement. How might this irony persist in Gilbert's own life, particularly in his relationship with his boss, Mr. Lamson? Throughout the novel, what does Gilbert reveal to us about his father? What sort of legacy has Albert left his son?

4. Unlike Amy and Gilbert, who have stayed behind to take care of Momma and Arnie, Larry and Janice have managed to escape, at least physically and geographically. What significance lies in Hedges' decision to make Janice a flight attendant, a job that requires perpetual flight? Why has Larry all but cut himself off from his family?

5. Who is Lance Dodge? What does his success represent to each of the novel's characters?

6. What kind of person is Gilbert's younger sister Ellen? Discuss Hedges' use of dialogue to develop her character. What is the source of Ellen's hostility toward Gilbert? Why might the fact that Gilbert has done nothing since high school bother Ellen, and even frighten her?

7. Critics have compared the narrative voice of Gilbert Grape to that of J. D. Salinger's Holden Caulfield. What similarities and differences exist between the two? Discuss other works of literature or film that echo the themes, characters, or tone of *What's Eating Gilbert Grape* (e.g.: Larry McMurtry's *The Last Picture Show*, Tennessee Williams' *The Glass Menagerie*, Don DeLillo's *End Zone*).

8. On a final tour of the condemned elementary school, Becky hopes to help Gilbert "say goodbye." What comes of Gilbert's recollection of his second-grade trauma? And why do you suppose Hedges places this scene just after the one in which Gilbert witnesses Mr. Carver's adultery with a bewigged Melanie? How does this pair of scenes affect Gilbert? How does the novel unfold in the aftermath of these episodes?

9. About Momma, Gilbert says, "She thought she was going to enjoy my hate. But it has broken her." Discuss the nature of Gilbert's relationship with his mother, who can't seem to look at Gilbert without seeing her dead husband's face.

10. Over many bottles of beer—and accompanied by the songs of Sinatra and Elvis—the Grape children gather around Momma's body to perform a makeshift memorial service. What is happening here? Discuss the characters' tacit decision to burn the house down. In addition to their wish to avoid the embarrassment and humiliation of having all of Endora gather to watch Momma's body removed from the house by a crane, what might the destruction of the house represent to the Grapes?

11. Faced with Momma's steady growth, dwarfed by Endora's barren landscape, and resentful of the invasion of corporate America in the form of the hulking Food Land and the prefab Burger Barn, Gilbert has long felt trapped and dissatisfied with his life. But as "the walls in Momma's room fall down in flames," *What's Eating Gilbert Grape* ends with an unexpected sense of contentment, offering an almost idyllic image of family togetherness: the Grape children huddled before the house as silent spectators. What might Hedges be suggesting here? Are the children liberated? What do you imagine happens to each character after the novel ends? With the house, the school building, and his mother all gone, can Gilbert finally stop "shrinking"? Will he see Becky again? Will he escape? Has he already escaped? Explain.

12. Watch the Lasse Hallström film adaptation of Hedges' novel and compare the two. How does the movie echo the book's themes? How does your reading group feel about the movie's ending?

A Conversation with Peter Hedges

Q. You dedicate the novel to your mother, "who is not fat," and your father, "who is not dead." How did you come to write *What's Eating Gilbert Grape*? Did any particular person, scene, or idea serve as inspiration?

A. In 1986, I was teaching for the first time at the National High School Institute at Northwestern University. My playwriting class needed an example, a model of possibility. So during the first class, I announced, with a false confidence, that I would write a monologue that very night and perform it that weekend at the Faculty Recital, as evidence that theater could be made quickly. Later that night, in a panic, I wrote a short piece called *Going Places with Gilbert Grape* which was about a young man giving a bicycle tour of his hometown. To my surprise, the monologue worked well. Back home in New York City that fall, I attempted to turn the monologue into a play for my friends to act in, but it didn't work as a play. It was to be a novel. And for four years I wrote and wrote and finally, a book emerged.

Q. You make wonderful use of small-town America as a backdrop in both *What's Eating Gilbert Grape* as well as in your latest novel, *An Ocean in Iowa*. Where did you grow up? To what degree did you draw upon your own childhood and adolescent experiences?

A. I grew up in West Des Moines, Iowa, which is a lovely but typical suburb of a large Midwestern city. However, my early years included numerous trips to visit my grandparents and cousins in small Iowa towns. These trips and the particular landscapes, the open sky and acres of corn, the abandoned farmhouses and the small schoolhouses, along with the always-different-but-always-the-same water tower of each town along the way, made a lasting impression.

What's Eating Gilbert Grape is primarily a work of fiction. Invariably, though, little bits of real life entered during the writing process. In an effort to prepare my family, I explained that it was a made-up story, but they may find parts of themselves sprinkled throughout the book. My little brother was particularly sweet about it, especially since he's nothing like Arnie Grape. He did then go on to say, "There's only one thing that I wouldn't want you to ever write about, Pete." I asked him to tell me what that might be. "Well, remember how I used to take grasshoppers and stick them in the mail box and chop off their heads . . ." I covered my mouth, and then said, "Oh, Philip, it's on the first page."

Q. *What's Eating Gilbert Grape* has become a huge cult classic. Share some of the reactions and feedback you've received about it over the years.

A. My favorite fan letter I've received happens to also have been the first letter I received. It came from a bookstore in Eugene, Oregon, and it was written by five or six of the workers, all college aged. They wrote that they enjoyed the book, and then they proceeded to list their favorite lines, of which, happily, there were many.

On my recent book tour, I met many people who drove at times a great distance to say hello. One person in Boston said, "I'm in med school, I'm going to be a neurosurgeon, I read *What's Eating Gilbert Grape* when I was seventeen and lonely, thanks. It helped me." I'm not suggesting my little book turned the life of that young man around. But it helps, as does any book that speaks deeply to a reader. I simply wanted to write a story that I'd like to read. The fact that it speaks to others is, in the words of Raymond Carver, "gravy."

In Anna Quindlen's wonderful essay "How Reading Changed My Life" (Library of Contemporary Thought) she gives several reading lists. One, with the heading "10 Books to Help Make a Teenager Feel More Human" listed *What's Eating Gilbert Grape* along with *Catcher in the Rye*, *A Separate Peace*, and *A Member of the Wedding*. Well, for a writer like Anna Quindlen to place my book with those other books, that's high praise, and a particular source of pride for me.

Q. You wrote the screenplay for Lasse Hallström's film adaptation. How do you feel about the movie version?

A. I adore the movie. It's different in tone. The movie is sweeter, not as funny, more human, has less of an edge. They're different in many respects, but the spirit of the story, the original intent, exists in both. When we made the movie I had two goals; I wanted them to film the scene where Momma leaves the house to get Arnie out of jail, and I wanted them to film the final scene where they burn the house. Those two scenes were, I felt, the most important and special scenes, and happily, we ended up with both of them, and much, much more.